Gripping Novels of Crime and Detection

SIGNET DOUBLE MYSTERIES:

THE KILLER TOUCH

and

THE DEVIL'S COOK

SIGNET Mysteries You'll Enjoy

THE
KILLER TOUCH

AND

THE
DEVIL'S COOK

By
Ellery Queen

A SIGNET BOOK
NEW AMERICAN LIBRARY
TIMES MIRROR

Publisher's Note

NAL BOOKS ARE AVAILABLE AT QUANTITY DISCOUNTS WHEN USED TO PROMOTE PRODUCTS OR SERVICES. FOR INFORMATION PLEASE WRITE TO PREMIUM MARKETING DIVISION, THE NEW AMERICAN LIBRARY, INC., 1633 BROADWAY, NEW YORK, NEW YORK 10019.

Published by arrangement with Frederic Dannay and the late Manfred B. Lee. *The Killer Touch* and *The Devil's Cook* also appeared in paperback as separate volumes published by The New American Library.

 SIGNET TRADEMARK REG. U.S. PAT. OFF. AND FOREIGN COUNTRIES REGISTERED TRADEMARK—MARCA REGISTRADA HECHO EN CHICAGO, U.S.A.

SIGNET, SIGNET CLASSICS, MENTOR, PLUME, MERIDIAN and NAL BOOKS are published by The New American Library, Inc., 1633 Broadway, New York, New York 10019

First Printing (Double Ellery Queen Edition), February, 1982

1 2 3 4 5 6 7 8 9

PRINTED IN THE UNITED STATES OF AMERICA

THE
KILLER TOUCH

Cast of Characters

PROLOGUE

She sat alone on the bed, and the kerosene lamp played its flickering shadow-light on her drawn face. Outside, the surf pounded the minutes to shreds, reducing time to a soft pulp without substance or division. She raised her hands from the writing pad on her lap and ran her fingers through her black hair. Her hands moved jerkily as though in answer to someone else's command. She felt her hair lying warm and heavy on the backs of her hands; the hair too seemed not to be a part of her. She sniffed and felt the swollen congestion inside the bridge of her nose. Moisture filmed her eyes as she looked back down at the paper, giving the dark blue lines an outline of light.

. . . so there seems no point in going on, dreading every tomorrow and regretting each yesterday . . .

It sounded melodramatic, the kind of farewell a B actress would write in the hope that it would appear in the newspapers. She tore out the sheet and started another:

Dear Rolf,
Three nights on this island and a week away from you have given me a chance to think about all that has happened and I have decided

She drew a line through the last phrase, and added: *since I married you.* Still the letter seemed a sticky, sentimental coating on the purity of the act she was about to commit. The act wouldn't hurt Rolf. Inconvenience him, yes. Anger him even. But she could never

7

hurt him, any more than she had ever been able to please him.

Tracy gasped as pain gouged her stomach. She pressed her palms flat against it and felt the pain-taut muscle trembling beneath the skin. She touched a finger between her breasts and felt the perspiration, slick, greasy cold. I'm getting sick, and it's too soon. I wanted to get everything done before. . . .

She rose abruptly from the coconut-fiber mattress, belting her white terrycloth robe around her waist. She felt nervous, edgy. There were flashes at the edge of her vision. The stone wall of the room had an unpleasant glow; the furniture was haloed. Overhead, the thatched roof crawled with shadow-life. She heard rasping noises, creaks, murmuring voices in a distant room.

But there is only one room and the other cabins are empty . . .

She carried the lamp onto the lean-to veranda, her rubber sandals grating on the sand-strewn concrete floor. A breeze struck the lamp, causing it to dip low and send up a gray spiral of smoke. She adjusted the wick and set the lamp on a hand-hewn table beside a stack of mold-smelling magazines. *Fate, Astrology, Your Future.* . . . The nearsighted woman who owned the island supplied her guests with the kind of reading she herself liked. Joss at least believed in something.

A soldier crab tried to scuttle beneath her feet, clattered against the table, then folded its claws and lay still. Tracy toed the unresisting object across the floor, opened the screen door, and kicked it out onto the sand. She watched the crab stick out an exploratory claw, turn itself upright, then scuttle away into the night. She stepped out onto the sand and glanced right, then left. The adjacent cabins were dark and silent. Palms rustled overhead, and a tinny cha-cha beat came from the direction of the beach club. The boys had turned in Radio Trinidad on their battery set. No doubt the cleaning women had already locked themselves in their shack, and Joss would be drunk. Nobody would know, nobody would care . . .

Salt-crusted grass crunched beneath her feet as she walked toward the sea. She thought of frost on the churchyard on Sunday morning, walking in patent-leather shoes with her mother and father on either side, smelling respectively of perfume and shaving lotion. Then the odor of ancient varnish biting her nostrils, and the woody-musty smell of the song book in her hands. She had loved to sing hymns, sending her voice out among the others and having it return ... a hundredfold. She'd liked that, and the part about casting your bread upon the waters. ...

Her mind returned to the aching stiffness in her joints. Railroad vines snatched at her bare ankles as she walked toward the phosphorescent surf. When she reached the sand she kicked off her sandals and walked barefoot. Once she'd loved to feel warm sand against her feet; now it was only an irritation, and even the air felt unpleasant on her face, like spiders crawling. Her nose ran and her eyes watered. She had a terrible awareness of the flesh clinging to her bones, of each joining of cartilage, muscle, and tissue; of her brain lying overhead, each movement causing pain to flare up behind her eyes.

Hate my body, hate it hate it hate it.

The sea lay like a pall of smoke, inviting.

The prickly weight of the bathrobe was gone. She left the clothing lying on the sand like dead skin, diseased and discarded. The water was exactly the temperature of the air; it was a pressure on her legs and no more. She stumbled over a rock and barnacles gouged her knees like cinders. She climbed over the reef, felt the coral cut into her feet, and told herself it didn't matter.

The sea was high. A wave swelled up, towered overhead, then collapsed and buried her in greenness. It wasn't water, it was raw force tearing her apart, lifting her body high and slamming it down, dragging her across an object which raked her body with long sharp claws, then leaving her to gasp on the reef. It lifted her again, higher and higher, swinging her in a silken hammock. She relaxed, feeling relief from the pull of muscle in her shoulders, stomach and chest; she drew in a deep breath and waited for her lungs to fill with water—

Air came in.

She opened her eyes and found herself on the sand. A bubbling carpet of surf came forward, buried her, and left her again. Oh, I didn't know it was so hard to drown. If only I could swim, I could go far out . . .

She was tired. She lay there and let the air dry her body. After a time she rose and dressed. The surf teased, bubbling forward, hissing back.

Back at the cabin, she carried the lamp into the bathroom. She smelled the salty-musty odor of old swim suits, and heard the drip-drip-drip of the shower-head which hung like a drooping rusty blossom. She set the lamp on the low stand beside the washbasin and peered at the warped and mottled image in the mirror. She felt a curious, cold detachment toward herself. The upward glow of the lamp shadowed her forehead with the arch of her brows, unplucked and heavy in the center. Her nose seemed long and thin, and the white crescent scar on its tip looked more prominent than ever. Her wet hair lay flat on her skull and framed her narrow face like a cowl. High cheekbones shaded her eyes, and the line of her jaw lent her cheeks a hollow aspect.

You're dying, Tracy.

"I've been dying ever since I married him."

She said it aloud, and felt dismay at the thin sound of her voice. She filled her lungs to produce a deeper resonance; her breasts rose and brushed against the cloth, causing a shiver to spread throughout her body. She gave a shudder which rejected all clothing; her skin seemed raw all over; the robe was an unbearable weight on her shoulders, and the band of her shorts was a hand squeezing her in two.

She closed her eyes, and the lids grated like fine sand. She pressed her fingertips against her eyes, felt the eyeballs rolling beneath the lids like grapes. Got to hurry, she thought, before I get too sick—

She got her safety razor from her toilet case, grasped the rust-rimmed blade between her thumb and forefinger. Her hands began to shake. The third try produced a cut which barely broke the skin. She sat down on the stool, breathing heavily.

If I only had a cap, just enough to get straight. . . .

Stupid. You left your purse on the boat and it's not due back until tomorrow.

Tomorrow! What about *now?*

Maybe you can find some. You had stuff squirreled everywhere.

Again she searched the lining of her clothes. Her lipstick tube. Compact. Fingers of her gloves. Face powder—

Her fingers touched something round, oblong. Joy dissolved her strength, and a small sob escaped her lips. She picked out the gelatin capsule and blew the face powder from its surface. A full one, sure. Rolf always got full measure. The pushers knew better than to hand him fogged caps. Not that Rolf would mind being cheated. He treated everybody with a studied carelessness, half-hoping someone would cheat and give him an excuse.

She separated the two halves of the capsule and dumped the contents onto a sheet of paper. Her body shivered, and she could feel moisture from her nose poised on her upper lip. Her fingers seemed gnarled, blunt and clumsy, but they were steady as she used the razor blade to scrape the powder into a tiny windrow at the edge of the paper. She dumped the powder into a spoon, then held the spoon above the chimney of the lamp until there was only a clear liquid. She took the needle from her suitcase, filled it, and watched the liquid climb the spike. While it cooled she took off the belt of her bathrobe and wrapped it around her leg just above the knee. It was easier in the arm but there was already a string of purple dots like a fading tattoo. . . .

Now the vein throbbed, swollen purple. With flawless rhythm the glass bird swooped down and thrust its glittering steel beak into the knotted worm of the vein. Its glass intestine filled with thick red blood, blended with the fluid inside and became pink. Her thumb pressed down and the fluid disappeared. . . .

Ah . . .

Warmth in her chest, like an explosion of pleasure. It rippled along her skin; her lips spread in a loose smile and a faint breathy giggle escaped them. Finally she withdrew the needle and laid it on the stand. A fly came to drink of the glistening red droplet which hung from its tip. She regarded it with a benevolent smile. Get high, little fly. After a long time she carried the lamp into the bedroom and sat down on the bed. The room seemed to flatten out and relax like a cat stretching itself before a fire. Before it had been a jangling, jarring chaos of corners and angles; now it was exactly right, and there was beauty in each joining of stone. The air was filled with streamers of light, rose, purple, green and blue; they wove themselves into a net and enveloped her, swinging her gently. Smoke curled from the lamp like a satin ribbon edged with purple and orange. She felt a gratitude for the lamp and then no gratitude; she was the lamp, the house, the sea and the universe, all joined in one.

But . . .

Someone was standing in the door behind her. She fought to ignore it, knowing that if she came down she could never go as high again.

"Tracy."

Rolf's voice. How had he got here? What does he want? I'll push him out of my mind, not even think about him . . .

But the effort of holding herself high caused her to lose it. She felt herself coming down, down.

"Please, Rolf," she spoke without turning. "Later we can talk."

"Just struck yourself, did you, baby? All squared now, eh?"

"Mmmm."

"What are you writing?"

A hand appeared from behind her shoulder. It seemed almost to be hers, except for the long spatulate fingers. The square-cut diamond on his little finger caught the lamplight and sent yellow shards flashing around the room. She would have enjoyed the diamond universe, but Rolf was reading her letter. Why did he read aloud?

"You've decided what, Tracy? What have you decided? Suicide? You've mentioned it enough."

Round rolling words like lumps of cold gravy dripping on her head. She knew the answers but there were more important questions, and each question had its own answer.

His hand grasped hers and held it under the lamp. She heard him laughing. "You couldn't do it, could you? Not while you had your needle. I counted on that." He released her hand. "How do you know death isn't the same thing, Tracy, only better? How do you know death isn't the biggest fix of all?"

He turned her to face him; he must have done it roughly because she felt pain somewhere behind the soft pillowing pleasure. She lowered her head, but he lifted her chin and met her eyes.

"Look at me, Tracy. You know something funny?"

She wondered if it was the lamplight which made his face seem molded in wax. Even the blond mustache looked like the ones they put on department store dummies. But the pale blue eyes were real; they held a look of amused pity as though he had somehow learned the hour of her death.

The eyes didn't change when he slapped her.

"Answer me, Tracy. You know what's funny about your trying to kill yourself?"

She looked out of a long dark tunnel; she was hidden up high behind her eyes, protected by the hard helmet of her skull. She would stay here quietly, warm and cozy, where he couldn't hurt her.

He slapped her again, then again. The waxy mask

seemed to crack and fall away, leaving a wizened old man's face. His hands encircled her throat, and she realized abruptly there was no use hiding inside her skull. There was no air. She clawed at his hands, and up inside her brain the cells began blinking off like lights at bedtime.

ONE

Burt March sat on a coil of rope and watched the green-yellow islands of the Grenadines sail past. The schooner wallowed through a heavy sea, but there was no wind and the sails were furled. From below came the intermittent growl of the diesel engine; an occasional vile whiff of exhaust fumes reminded Burt of the city he'd left the day before.

He gazed around the open deck, crowded with islanders returning from St. Vincent after selling their vegetables, pigs and chickens. A rum bottled passed from one black hand to another; a Negro girl flashed him an over-the-shoulder look, then reached into her basket and tossed him a ripe mango. He caught it and smiled at her; she turned quickly to whisper to a girl who sat beside her. Their burst of tinkling laughter pleased him; he was glad to leave the grit and sticky July heat of Florida, to forget the pinch of a shoulder holster, and to be among people who didn't know him as Dective Sergeant Burton March of the Crystal City Police Department. He hated the puffed, indignant faces of solid citizens, the uneasy look from those who had nothing to fear from him, and the pinched, scared faces of those who did. He hated the scared faces most, maybe because he knew others in the department who liked them scared.

A boy picked his way across the deck, collecting fares. Burt drew out his wallet and removed a British West Indian dollar. "I get off at Isle de Trois."

"I think we don't stop there, sir."

Burt looked up. The boy was shirtless and barefoot, with trousers cut off at the knees. "Why not?"

15

"Too much sea. The water very swift there, no good bottom to hold anchor."

"Well, can you get me in close? Joss could send out a boat to pick me up."

The boy nodded. "I ask the captain."

As the boy started away, Burt called, "How old are you?"

"Fourteen year." The boy squinted at Burt for a moment, then shrugged and started up the gangway.

Burt sighed and pulled a paperback book from the pocket of his white canvas trousers. *The same age.* Funny. And the kid that got sick on the plane looked around fourteen, too. Burt remembered the smell of fear in the darkened store, the roar of the other's gun and the ripping pain in his thigh, then his own reflexive shot at the muzzle flash. He saw again the beardless face, curiously feminine in death, and the ugly redness where Burt's slug had torn through his throat. . . .

Burt closed the book and returned it to his pocket. There would be time to read on the island, time to dive in the air-clear water, fish, and walk on the salt-white sand and put strength in his leg, or just to sit at the top of the island's lone hill and think. What about? Well, think about reaching the age of twenty-eight and deciding you've picked the wrong career. That would keep him busy for his entire month of sick leave. He wondered if he should've sent Joss a wire . . . but then she'd told him once that nobody came during the summer. He'd probably have the whole square mile of the island to himself.

The boy returned and said the captain wanted to see him. Burt planted his bamboo cane and rose. He was slightly less than six feet tall, heavy-set in a hard-muscled way which made him look average. He used the cane no more than necessary to steady himself on the rolling deck.

The wheelhouse swarmed with girls in bright-colored dresses. It was a mark of status for a girl to ride with the skipper, and Captain O'Ryan was notoriously free with his favor. He was a blue-black Negro who walked softly, talked slowly, and had a barrel-chested build.

He grinned as Burt entered. "Mister March. I din' recognize you when you board. Man, you pale, lose weight." He gripped his jaw to indicate hollow cheeks.

Burt held up his cane. "Had a little accident, so they handed me an extra vacation."

"So you rest with Miss Joss, eh? If she leave you be. Maybe I stop off one day when the sea calm down, bring some rum." O'Ryan looked at the deck, dipping and swaying below, then raised his eyes to the southeastern horizon. "I think a hurricane trying to work up." He looked sideways at Burt. "You never been in one of our hurricanes?"

"No."

"Ah, man, they come rare and small, but hard, hard." He grinned as though looking forward to it. "Well, we get you close and see if Miss Joss will pick you up. You give her something for me?"

"Sure," said Burt, then frowned as O'Ryan drew a smart, olive-green leather purse from beneath the binnacle. "That doesn't belong to Joss."

"No, a lady left it on my ship three days ago. She staying now with Joss."

A twinkle in O'Ryan's eye gave new significance to the expensive look of the purse and the seductive scent which rose from it. Burt suspected that if O'Ryan fulfilled his promise to stop on the island, it wouldn't be to visit Burt.

"Pretty lady, huh?"

"Pretty, yes, but—" O'Ryan frowned. "Her eyes move about like butterflies, never still." He shrugged and turned back to the wheel as the schooner approached a cluster of islands. "But you all that way, man, you live too fast up there."

Back on deck, Burt sat on his coil of rope and dangled the purse thoughtfully between his knees. He felt an irritating urge to peer inside and learn something more about the girl. If he dropped it, perhaps it would spring open . . .

Put it away, March. You're off-duty. Forget it.

He set it on the deck between his feet, then braced himself as the schooner heeled over abruptly. They were negotiating the swift frothy channel between two islands. Ten yards away a black jagged rock thrust up from the sea, bird droppings melting down its side like cake frosting. The schooner dipped, then soared sickeningly. It poised for a second, tilted, slid into the trough. There was a shuddering thump against the hull. A wall of white water plumed up and arched overhead. Burt put his head between his knees and felt the water drum against his back. Another swoop, a dip, and another shower, smaller than the first, the schooner righted itself and entered smooth water. Burt settled back and looked at the people sprawled on the streaming deck. A few of the girls were rising to their knees, throwing their dripping hair off their foreheads and, with a total lack of self-consciousness, raising their dresses and wringing out the water. Burt felt his feet squishing inside his white crepe-soled sneakers and decided that getting soaked was a part of inter-island travel, not at all unpleasant.

"Oh-oh, the purse. He looked down, felt a twinge of alarm, then saw it caught in a loop of rope, half-submerged in the runoff water. He picked it up and shook off the water. Better see if any got inside . . .

He paused with his hand on the catch, then shrugged.

The smell struck him again as he opened the purse; an exciting smell of perfume. Ladies' soft leather wallet. . . . Once started, he fell into an unconscious search pattern. The wallet's plastic windows contained a social security card issued to Miss Tracy Dunn, and a Florida driver's license for Mrs. Tracy Keener. Must have quit work after she got married, otherwise she'd have had her card changed. Age, twenty-eight. Well, well, she's a Gemini too, and the same age. Address in North Miami. Evidence was stacking up. Her married status didn't seem very important, since she'd come to the island alone. Where was Mr. Keener? Dead, divorced, separated, working . . . having a ball elsewhere. Weight one-oh-five, height five-four. A good build, provided the weight was arranged properly. Hair black, eyes brown. Folder of traveler's checks, all fresh and new. Whee! Hundreds, tens of 'em. Poor little working girl struck it rich. Probably married the boss's son, or the boss . . . Funny no pictures, probably meant she had no kids. Lipstick, bright red, a little garish for Burt's taste. Well, nobody's perfect, Can of talcum power, funny thing to carry in a purse. Or was it? He took it out and shook it, felt a soft rattle against his hand. Maybe the powder had gotten wet and lumpy . . .

The lid came off with a hard twist of his fingers. He shook out some powder and a capsule dropped into his palm. He felt a coldness at the back of his neck. He looked up quickly. The passengers were busy drying themselves. He cleaned off the capsule and saw the white powder inside. He didn't bother taking it apart. What else comes in capsules which you have to hide inside a talcum powder can? There were fourteen in all. The girl had a heavy, heavy habit. . . .

He put everything back in the can, replaced the lid, returned the can to the purse and closed it. She'd been nervous as a cat, and why not? Carrying a couple hundred bucks worth of heroin. But then, to walk off the boat and leave it . . .

Isle de Trois jutted abruptly from the sea to the south, humped up to a five-hundred foot prominence, then sloped gently to the north. As the schooner neared, Burt could make out the three black crags which gave the island its name. The upper slope was clothed in cedar, frangipani and shoulder-high citronella grass. At the water's edge a line of palm trees overhung the thatched roof of the beach club. In front of the club curved a silver-white beach strewn with conch shells and bleached coral. A gentle swell disturbed the lagoon and caressed the beach.

Burt had first seen the island from the deck of a cruise ship five years ago. He had recognized a scene he'd dreamed of years before, while his breath froze on

the fringe of a parka, his finger stuck to an icy trigger
and his eyes squinted across a frozen Korean landscape. He'd spent his last five vacations on the island,
and while Caribbean prices had ballooned, Burt still
paid the same as he had on his first visit: thirty dollars
a week.

The schooner stopped fifty yards outside the semicir-
cle of black rocks which enclosed the lagoon like the
jaws of a giant beartrap. Burt stood at the rail listening
to the grinding complaint of the engines as they fought
the current which hissed and gurgled around the ship.
A black figure clad in shorts moved languidly across
the beach, dragged a tiny blue rowboat into the water,
and started rowing across the lagoon. Burt recognized
Joss's boatman, Coco. He was a skilled fisherman who
knew every submerged rock within five miles of the island. Muscles corded in his powerful arms as he left
the lagoon and entered the current. Five minutes later
the boat thumped against the hull.

"Mist' March," he said, holding the boat steady as
Burt clambered down. "I din' expect you this time."

There was no time for conversation; Burt took his
bulky canvas suitcase from the cabin boy, settled into
the forward thwart, and helped push off. When they
reached the peace of the lagoon, Burt saw that Coco
wore a blue straw hat. The boatman had two other
hats, one painted red, the other white. He changed
them according to his mood: white when he felt good,
blue when he was sad, and red when he was angry.

"Why the blue hat?" asked Burt.

The boy spoke abruptly between strokes. "No guest.
No fish. No tip."

"The woman who's staying here doesn't fish?"

"Woman?" Coco's expression of disgust encompassed the entire sex. "I never take woman to fish. Too
much play, too much talk."

"She talks a lot, eh?"

"She? Man, I never see her. She remain in her cabin
all day, walk the beach at night."

Frowning, Burt opened the side pocket of his bag

and took out two rolls of film. "Here's some new high-speed film. I guess you've still got that Brownie I gave you."

"Yes." Coco grinned. "Now I maybe change my hat, take you to catch big fish."

Coco tied up at a rickety jetty of poles and wood planks. It was attached to an unfinished concrete jetty begun by Joss's fourth or fifth husband—who had also inaugurated a yacht basin, a hotel, and a new clubhouse, only to abandon the island and depart with a female guest from Barbados. He'd never come back, and Joss had never continued any of his projects.

Burt stepped off the jetty and looked around. Nothing ever changed here; it could have been five years ago. He saw a figure floating at the south end of the lagoon, where the palms arched down and dipped their fronds in the surf. It could have been a corpse, it floated so still, so bonelessly complaisant to each ripple of water. But Burt recognized the mistress of the island, Jocelyn Leeds.

"Joss!"

No response. After fourteen years on the island, Joss was capable of falling asleep in the water. Her boys had to watch that she didn't drift out to sea.

Burt started down the beach. He saw smoke trailing up from a cigarette between her lips. A glass rested on the gentle mound of her stomach.

"Hey!" he called. "Hey, Joss!"

"I'm full up," she called without removing the cigarette. "You should've had O'Ryan wait."

"Don't hand me that. Come and see what I brought you."

"Now who in the world—!" She twisted to look, but a wave broke over her face. She spat out her soggy cigarette, rolled over, and started stroking toward shore. Burt opened his suitcase, took out the green beach coat he'd brought her, and walked down to the edge of the surf. Joss rose in thigh-deep water and waded ashore. Her homemade bathing costume (it was too individualistic to be called anything else, a loose-fitting playsuit

made of a cotton print) wetly outlined a figure which
had once been, obviously, arrestingly full. Now, though
resigning itself here and there to the pull of gravity, her
shape was still good enough to draw whistles at a distance. Once she'd shown Burt an old picture of herself
in a net bra and panties, both of which concealed no
more than the absolute legal minimum. She'd refused to
say whether she'd been a runway queen, a nightclub
stripper, or a freelance exhibitionist; she drew a curtain
of phony coyness over her entire past and was even
vague about the number of her husbands. Burt wasn't
sure whether the Englishman from whom she'd inher-
ited the island had been her third or fourth. Her hair
was the color of bleached straw except at the back of
her neck and behind her ears, where traces of gray
were visible among the auburn. Burt placed her age at
forty-five, but wouldn't have been surprised if she
turned out to be five years on either side.

She walked out of the water, squinting in his direction. She was hopelessly nearsighted but scorned glasses, saying she'd seen too much already. Burt side-
stepped and slid the beach coat around her shoulders.
"Now you can greet your guests decently."

"Burt March!" She gave him an impulsive hug which
dampened his clothes for the second time. Then she
backed off a step. "Burt, you look like hell!"

"Thanks," said Burt dryly. "You haven't changed either."

"But really. You're thin and pale, and carrying a
cane . . ." Her mouth flew open. "You stopped a bullet!"

"Shhh. I'm supposed to be an insurance salesman."

"Tell me, really. Did you shoot it out with a gang?"

"Crystal City's too small to support a gang. It was
just a little jewelry store robbery—"

"And you went in after them?"

"Look—" He sighed. There'd be no business trans-
acted until Joss had the entire story. "Joss, there was
only one. A kid tried to heist a ring for his sweetheart.
He stole his old man's gun and broke a window. He

must've panicked when I came in, I don't know. He didn't live to talk about it. He was fourteen."

"Oh—" Her eyes clouded with sympathy. "Poor Burt. Let's go up to the club and get you a drink."

She slid her arm around his waist, half-helping him through the loose sand. Burt drew no personal conclusion from this intimacy; Joss had a way of making guests feel that she'd been wistfully scanning the sea for their arrival. He suspected it was only half a pose.

When they reached his luggage, she swooped down and held up the purse. "Burt March! You've changed sides!"

"If you weren't like a grandmother to me, I'd whop you. That belongs to your guest, Mrs. Keener. She left it on the schooner."

"Oh?" Her expression froze into neutrality. "I'll have Boris take it to her."

"I'd rather take it myself."

Joss frowned, then gave a shrug of indifference which somehow failed to come off. As they stepped beneath the thatched roof of the club, she gave him a sidelong look. "Whatever happened to Caroline, the girl you brought down here last year? She told me she was trying to get you to propose."

"I almost did." Burt sat down at a rough, hand-hewn table. He kept his eyes carefully on a grackle which was strutting along the railing. "We broke it off a couple of weeks ago. She wouldn't have wanted to marry a cop."

"Now Burt, she told me—" She stopped abruptly. "Oh, I get it now. Okay, we'll forget it. Boris! Two rum punches."

Boris, whose real name was Howard Charles William, was one of the few men Burt knew who could wear a wispy goatee, a purple beret, stride on black bare feet across the plank floor of an open, thatched clubhouse, then bow from the waist with all the massive dignity of a headwaiter at the Waldorf. Burt offered him the bright Hawaiian shirt he'd brought; Boris thanked him gravely and strode behind the bar to mix the drinks.

An Isle de Trois rum punch bore no resemblance to the effete cocktails served in Barbados and Jamaica. It was a potent jolt of black rum, nutmeg, brown sugar and lime. Water had to be requested, and ice was unknown on the island. Burt forced himself to sip the heavy mixture slowly; he was anxious to get to Mrs. Keener, but irritated at his own impatience.

"What's this about being full up, Joss?"

"Oh . . ." She waved her hand vaguely. "I just meant the cabins are all rented."

"But . . . I thought Mrs. Keener was the only guest."

"Her husband's due in a few days. He reserved cabin one, and she's in number two."

"Separate cabins? Why?"

"Maybe it's that kind of marriage, or maybe one of them snores. He didn't say in his letter, and I haven't been able to get ten words out of her."

Burt frowned to himself; he wanted more information, but was reluctant to tell Joss what he already knew. "Okay, that still leaves cabins three and four."

Joss sighed and spread her hands. "A week ago I got a letter from a man named Smith. He enclosed a money order. Wanted two cabins for himself and three associates—"

"*Associates?* A man named Smith?"

She looked at him. "I know what you're thinking and you can stop worrying. If they're gay, they don't stay. But I couldn't tell that from a letter, could I? And there *are* people named Smith." She looked down at her hands. "Hell, I know it sounds fishy. But I needed the money, Burt. It's been a long summer."

"You want me to leave?"

She looked up quickly. "No! Lord no, stay in number one until Keener gets here. After that . . . well, there's my house . . ."

"I wouldn't put you out."

"I wasn't thinking of—" She stopped suddenly and stood up. "Go on, deliver your purse and then we'll have another drink. Lobster okay for supper?"

"Great," he said. He watched her walk behind the

bar, through the door which led to the kitchen. Joss seemed unusually nervous, and uncharacteristically hostile to her female guest.

Godfrey, the mulatto youth who served as dishwasher, beachboy and bellhop, was waiting beside Burt's leg. The boy was painfully bandy-legged, and as Burt followed him along the sandy path, he could see at least a foot of clearance between the knobby knees. They passed cabins four and three, in that order, and beyond them Burt could see the rollers marching in like ranks of plumed soldiers, then crashing down on the sand. It was a good day for body surfing.

Ahead, Godfrey walked beneath tall, somber manchineel trees, setting his bare feet carefully down among the sharp-husked fruits. Both the sap and the fruit were poisonous, and Joss had been advised to cut down the trees. But she had a theory that any change in nature is bound to be bad. Having seen the manicured, geometric ugliness which man had produced in his own state, Burt was inclined to agree.

Ah, here was cabin two. Now he could dispose of this purse, which was turning into a millstone around his neck.

"Godfrey." His voice was lost in the booming surf. He called louder. The boy stopped and turned. "Take the bag on to the cabin. I'm stopping here—wait, here's something." He drew out a flat packet and tossed it through the air. "Strings for your guitar. See you later."

He waited until Godfrey had gone behind the ancient gnarled banyan which separated cabins one and two, then knocked on the door. The silence stretched into a full minute before a low husky voice came from the other side.

"Who is it?"

"Burt March. I just came in on the schooner."

There was another long pause. "Really? I hope you had a pleasant voyage."

Burt frowned. There was no interest in the voice, not even idle curiosity. "Are you Tracy Keener?"

"I—what if I am?"

Her voice had taken on a tense belligerence, almost as puzzling as her lack of interest.

"Did you leave something on the ship?"

"Oh." Was that a sigh of relief? Had she expected something worse?

The door opened slowly to a width of four inches. Burt glimpsed a huge, floppy beach hat which hung down to her eyebrows. A pair of oversized sunglasses covered her face to the cheekbones, and from there to the collar of her robe was a pale leprous expanse of skin which glistened wetly. Some kind of lotion . . .

"Oh, my purse." Her white hand snaked out, clutched the purse, and pulled it inside. As the door was closing, she spoke with the stilted formality of a child suddenly remembering its manners: "Thank you. I've been terribly worried."

And that was all. The door clicked shut, and Burt felt like kicking it in. What kind of reward was that? Hell, for all he'd seen of her she could have been a Martian. Maybe she didn't know about the heroin; maybe the stuff had been a plant.

He walked quietly around the cabin and leaned against the screen door of the veranda. If she were a hypo, she'd be fixing now.

Five minutes later he heard her sandals scrape on the concrete. "Oh! You . . . what do you want now?"

He turned and saw that she still wore her all-concealing costume. The robe ended at mid-thigh and he saw that her legs were heavier than he'd expected from her description. They were thick and muscled, like those of a dancer.

He realized he had no real plan of action, no desire to do more than have a good look at her. "If you'll come to the club, I'll buy you a drink."

"No."

"You don't drink?"

"I—" She made an impatient gesture with her hand. "Look, you brought me my purse. Okay, what do you want, a reward? I'll have to get some change—"

Her voice was rising. It could have been anger, but

Burt heard an undercurrent of alarm. "I don't want a reward," he said softly. "I just thought since we're the only guests, we should get acquainted."

"Oh, well . . . later. I've got a terrible sunburn and I don't feel like—"

"Are you sick?"

She faced him a moment, her chin thrust out in what was unmistakably anger. Then she whirled and went inside, slamming the door behind her.

Jata was scrubbing out the patio when Burt reached his cabin. She was a tall, thin, blue-black woman from Petit Martinique who lived in a world of death, blood and black magic. She wore a skin bag around her neck which might have contained obeah charms, but which really held tobacco. She took the two packs of Granger pipe mixture he gave her and said morosely she hoped he would enjoy his stay.

"Las' night, moon he come up all bloody. Trouble comin', *sieur,* truly."

Burt smiled. "Where's Maudie? I brought her something."

"Look behind you, *sieur*. She follow as always."

Burt turned as Jata's daughter came through the screen door. The girl he'd first seen as a gangly, tongue-tied eleven-year-old with round violet eyes and a braid like the tail of a rat, had now acquired a brazenly buxom brown body which rolled and bounced beneath a threadbare T-shirt. In past years she'd shadowed him around the island so closely that her mother had sometimes locked her in their shack.

"Remember what you asked me to bring you?" Burt asked. "You showed me the picture in the magazine."

Maudie nodded, her round violet eyes fixed on his.

Burt opened his bag and took out the brassiere he'd brought from the States. He frowned as Maudie held it speculatively to her bosom; he'd made the purchase from last year's measurements, forgetting that Maudie was a growing girl.

After the women left, Burt changed to swim trunks and walked onto the windward side of the island. Slimy

gray rock crabs skittered away from his feet. Wet rock
trembled beneath him as a wave crashed against the
ten-foot cliff. Geysers of spray erupted from holes in
the rock and drenched him. He heard the hissing moan
as the retreating waves sucked air into underground
caverns. At night the fumaroles sounded like approaching trains, men groaning in agony or women
shrieking; you soon lost the habit of trusting your ears.

He walked back to the beach and dove into the surf.
He swam past the breakers, rolled over and floated on
his back. Gannets dive-bombed the water around him;
pelicans swooped along the rollers, dragging their feet
only inches above the water. Burt felt a curious mixture
of dread and euphoria; such peace was too delicious to
last.

He left the water, showered, shaved, walked to the
club and downed three rum punches while waiting for
Joss to wake up from her afternoon nap and start her
customary evening drinking. The sun sank into a rosy
haze, and darkness came down like a purple curtain.
Godfrey set a table for two and suspended a Coleman
lantern from a beam. Joss appeared at last, and Burt
saw why she'd been delayed. She'd put on a dress,
something she usually wore only for trips to St. Vincent
or further. Rarer still, she wore a necklace and earrings, and a scent of violets had replaced her usual aura
of saltwater, fish and rum.

They ate langouste tail by candlelight and washed it
down with French wine. Joss talked with sparkling gai-
ety, and for a time Burt was in love with her. The
white light of the Coleman lantern glowed on her bare
shoulders and descended into the valley of her bosom;
the surf thumped and rumbled; the breeze carried the
smell of the sea into the club. Burt felt primitive and
extremely male. It occurred to him that Joss had been
without a husband for nearly a year, and that he himself was now free of ties. The pounding sea ringed the
island and made it a private world.

He looked up as Godfrey shuffled out of the night
carrying an empty tray. "Mrs. Keener's?"

Joss answered with a trace of sarcasm, "Your lady friend is too delicate to eat in the presence of others."

Burt smiled. "You'd rather she joined us?"

"Hell, I don't care." She waved her hand impatiently. "No, that's wrong. I'd just as soon leave her alone. Her husband's letter mentioned a nervous breakdown, said his wife needed rest and quiet and no disturbance." She frowned. "He said he'd been here before, but I can't remember." She leaned forward confidentially. "I'll tell you a secret, Burt. I don't remember people. A week after they leave they get lost in a sea of faces. People think it's my poor eyesight when I don't recognize them again. I let 'em think it. One of the tricks of the trade."

Joss started on rum, and soon her cheeks were flushed and her voice low and husky. Burt drank with her, more than he should, in an attempt to recapture his earlier romantic glow. But it only saddened him. Finally, Joss put her warm hand on his knee.

"Burt, there's something you learn on an island, to accept your own nature. Don't worry about the boy you shot."

Burt felt himself tense. "What's that got to do with my nature?"

"You're a cop, you did your job—"

"Maybe that's the problem."

"Burt, if you weren't a cop you'd be on the other side. You've got a violent nature. It shows in your eyes, like smoke behind a window. You're a rough, hard man—"

"A killer, the newspapers said."

She pushed away her glass. "Oh, hell, I goofed. I wanted to cheer you up, but I got you mad."

"I'm not mad."

"Don't kid me, Burt. You talk soft and you move slow, but it shows. Your body changes. You turn into sharp edges and brutal bone. I had a boy friend once—" She stopped and drew a deep breath. She got up suddenly, and stood swaying, her eyes bright. She spoke in a husky voice: "I'm stoned, Burt. Take me up to bed."

He helped her up the crumbling stone steps behind the beach club and into her one-room cabin. She sat heavily on the bed. "Don't light the lamp, Burt."

"No."

He walked silently to the door. Behind him came the faint rustle and snap of clothing.

"Come here, Burt, and help me with this damn hook."

"No, Joss," he said, opening the door. "I don't think we will."

He was groping his way down the steps when he heard her voice behind him. "Burt, where are you going?"

"Good night, Joss."

The door slammed, hard, and Burt smiled to himself. Joss would have only a vague recollection tomorrow, just enough to look at him uneasily and wonder exactly what she'd said and done. Maybe she'd eliminate him as a candidate for husband number seven or eight, whichever it was.

His head felt light. Not so straight yourself, March. Better take a walk, sober up, avoid tomorrow's hangover. He left the path and walked between cabins three and four to the beach. He walked on the sand and let the spray blow in his face. The surf thundered; the fumaroles moaned. He decided to put on his trunks and take a swim. As he passed cabin two, he saw the yellow glow of lamplight in the window. Strange woman, up late and alone . . .

There was a warning as he opened his cabin door—perhaps a pressure in the air, a smell, or a mental message. Someone else was in the room. He whirled, wasting a precious second in reaching for his absent shoulder holster. Something struck his right shoulder so hard it numbed his arm and sent pain shooting to his fingertips. Burt had no idea who his attacker might be; he didn't even think about it. Here was hostility, and questions would have to wait. He swung his fist at a shadowy bulk and struck a glancing blow somewhere high on the face. There was a sound strangely like a laugh. Could it be? Burt saw the pale blob of a face, and a vivid whiteness where the mouth should be. Lord, he *was* smiling, white teeth flashing. Burt swung again, discovered too late that he'd put his weight on his bad leg. *Fool . . . too much booze.* He missed, staggered forward, and clutched at the other man. The man moved back, quick as a cat, and Burt realized he was going to fall. He didn't feel himself hit the floor; something struck the back of his neck and all the light went out of his mind.

TWO

Joss's voice sliced through a shrieking whistle in his brain.

"You've made a mistake, Mr. Keener, this is a guest, Burt March."

"Yes?" said a calm, cultured male voice. "What was he doing in my cabin?"

"He . . . I said he could use it. Until you came."

Her voice seemed to come from a great distance, but Burt could tell she was still muddled from drink. Slowly he extended his senses; he smelled Joss's perfume, felt a soft fabric beneath his neck. Under that was firm flesh. He opened one eye a slit and saw that he lay on the floor with his head across Joss's thighs. Looking up beyond the curving shelf of her bosom (she wore the robe he'd given her; beneath that there seemed to be only Joss) Burt saw the faintly pouched underside of her chin. Without moving his head he traced her gaze to a man seated on the bed. His legs were crossed negligently, and he was cleaning his nails with a penknife. In the glow of the kerosene lamp, the man looked very tall, with wax-blond hair, blue eyes, and a neat blond mustache. He could have been made up for a part in a Hollywood yachting movie; blue jacket, white linen scarf, white trousers, and white canvas shoes. Burt saw a reddened swelling high on his cheek; it looked incongruous on the porcelain serenity of the face, like a wart on a Dresden doll.

Burt groaned and sat up, blinking his eyes. "What happened?"

"Burt! I was telling Mr. Keener—"

"I'll explain," said the man, and without halting his nail-cleaning operation, regarding his hands from time to time in the lamplight, he introduced himself as Rolf Keener. He'd rented a power-launch in St. Vincent and piloted himself to the island. The surf must have covered the sound of his arrival, since nobody had met him at the jetty. However, since he remembered the island from his last visit, he'd gone directly to his own cabin. He'd just arrived when he heard a prowler outside. Nervous in a strange land, he'd waited behind the door. When the prowler attacked, he'd simply defended himself.

"You swung first," said Burt, aware of a throbbing pain in the back of his neck.

"That may be true." Keener smiled. "I was frightened, you understand."

Yeah, thought Burt, you looked scared with that smile on your face. Keener told a logical story—within the limits of his own logic. If Keener hadn't stopped to see his wife, then she couldn't have told him about the man in cabin one. But why hadn't he stopped to see her? And it was possible that he'd failed to see Burt's suitcase under the bed, or his wet swim trunks on the porch railing, since he hadn't lit a lamp. But if a man is so scared that he attacks the first man who enters, why would he himself enter a strange cabin without a light? There was something wrong here. . . .

Keener rose from the bed and walked to the door. "I'll sleep in my wife's cabin tonight; tomorrow we can make other arrangements." He turned on a smile which did nothing but display perfect white teeth. "You were rather lucky, March. Trespassers are often shot."

Burt stood up and walked toward Keener. He felt tight, ready. "That has a sound I don't like, Keener. If there's anything left to settle, let's do it now."

For a second their eyes locked. Burt glimpsed something hooded and watchful in the other's eyes; maybe it was only his imagination, but there seemed to be a small wizened creature with gray leathery wings, folded and waiting, behind the smooth face. Then Rolf Keener smiled.

"Let's forget it, March." Half-ruefully, he touched

the bump on his cheek. "We've drawn each other's blood. That means we can dispense with a lot of needless formality. Why not step next door for a drink?"

"No, thanks," said Burt. "I seem to have acquired a headache."

Rolf Keener chuckled and walked away. Burt walked through the door and watched him disappear around the banyan; he moved quickly and surely, like a night-hunting animal.

As Burt started back to his cabin, he saw the half-moon sinking down through a pale mist in the west. With a shock he realized that it must be nearly three A.M. It couldn't have been past eleven when he'd left Joss—

The screen door opened softly behind him. Burt jumped, then saw it was Joss, clutching her robe together at the neck.

"Joss, what time did Keener come up and get you?"

"He . . . didn't." She bit her lip. "I came down to see you."

"Why?"

"I don't know. I guess, to finish the mess I started, really botch it up good." She shrugged. "I was still drunk. I'm sober now. When I came in and saw you lying on the floor—"

"Where was Rolf?"

"Sitting on the bed. Said he was waiting for you to wake up so he could ask why you'd broken in."

"Four hours, just sitting there?"

"I guess." She frowned up at him. "You sound suspicious."

"Suspicion is an occupational hazard, Joss. But there's something damn strange about both those people. You may have drawn a couple of nuts."

"Oh, well, aren't we all? I was lying on my hammock a week ago and my first husband came walking up. Wearing hip boots and carrying a fishpole. He asked me if it was a good day for surf-casting and I said sure. He started walking to the beach and disappeared. Next day I decided I was going nuts."

"Not that way, Joss. This guy ... if the way he jumped me is any sign, has a more dangerous problem. It's called paranoia."

"I've never tried it."

"Don't, Joss. You can't enjoy it like you enjoy your everyday run-of-the-mill hallucinations. And it's so logical it's hard to see through it. If a man's trying to kill you, and you're sure of it, you'd probably try to get him first. Right? Sure, that's logical. Or call the cops. Well, a paranoiac works the same way. The only thing is, nobody's trying to kill him. It's all delusion. He tells the cops and they say sure and do nothing. So the nut decides everybody's against him, the cops, the whole world. A guy reaches in his pocket for a cigarette, blam! The nut shoots, figuring he was going for a gun. I remember a case, a man was cutting a roast at Sunday dinner, then suddenly he turned and stabbed his wife in the stomach. She'd poisoned the meat, he said. Another guy shot a man because he bumped into his car. Later he told the cops the other guy had done it in order to hold him there until help arrived. They were all plotting to kill him—"

"Oh, Burt. Mr. Keener was so calm, relaxed—"

"Yes. And wasn't that strange, under the circumstances?"

"Maybe. I'm not sure what you mean."

"Well, I didn't think he was really relaxed. He could have been wound up so tight that he didn't dare allow a single emotion to disturb the surface. That's another mark of the psychopath, Joss; he's so torn up inside that he can't let his mask slip for fear the whole thing will collapse."

"Burt ..." She shivered and drew her robe tighter. "You're giving me the creeps. I'll give back their money and tell 'em to leave."

"No, I'm only guessing. I think I'll have another look at him, right now. He did invite me for a drink."

"What'll I do?"

"Go to bed. I'll see you tomorrow."

The lamp was lit on the veranda of cabin two, and

Rolf Keener was seated at the hand-hewn wooden table with a glass before him. When Burt tapped on the door, Rolf waved at a glass on the other side of the table. "Come in. There's yours."

Dazed, Burt walked in and sat down. "I said I wasn't coming. Why did you expect me?"

"Because you are what you are, Sergeant."

A physical shock tingled along Burt's nerves. His mind whirled for an instant, then he remembered he'd been out four hours. "You went through my things."

Rolf shrugged. "I checked your identification. Wouldn't you have done the same to me?"

Thoughtfully, Burt had to admit to himself that it was true. "It isn't the same thing—"

"Why not? Are you on duty now? Do you carry any warrants?"

Burt frowned at Keener. The subject of his status had been dragged into the conversation by the scruff of the neck; Burt wondered why the man had been so eager for that piece of information.

"I'm not on duty, Keener. But if you found out I was a cop, why the big act with Joss?"

Rolf nodded. "You're good. Very sharp. I put on that act because . . ." He shrugged. "I like to keep as many people as ignorant as possible."

"But you let me know. You didn't have to."

Rolf closed his eyes a minute, then opened them. "That confuses things even more, doesn't it?"

He gave a hollow laugh which sent a prickle of dread up Burt's spine. Here was a man not entirely in control of himself; a man who could work himself into a corner where he'd have to shoot his way out. You never knew what would seem a reason for killing, to a man like that, and Burt began to feel jumpy. He couldn't remember ever having been afraid of a man before, but Rolf came close to filling the bill.

Something else. The silence between their words was filled with the rustle of a mattress, the scrape of sandals on concrete, the crackle of a match. Burt smelled cigarette smoke through the closed door. Mrs. Keener was awake and attentive, but apparently he still wasn't to see the woman of mystery.

"Tell me about the detective business," said Rolf abruptly.

"Tell me about your business."

Rolf smiled. "I'm an importer. Very interesting the way I got into it. I don't suppose you were in World War II ..."

"I was a kid," said Burt. "I sold war stamps and collected paper."

"Yes," the man smiled benignly. "Well, I was in the Office of Strategic Services, the OSS. I happen to be of European extraction, I suppose you detect the accent."

"No."

"No? Well, it's been a long time. In the OSS I commanded a group which went into occupied countries to organize partisan groups. We sometimes used the local currency, but usually we carried a more negotiable commodity, gold, jewels, that sort of thing. To buy guns, food, and allies. It was often necessary to kill men, you understand—"

"It goes without saying in wartime," said Burt. "Why say it?"

"Because ... I have a point to make." He leaned forward, his eyes bright. "Every man has a killer inside him, March. With some people it's weak and easy to hold down. With others it's strong; you try to hold it down and you can feel it snarling and growling inside you." He leaned back and smiled. "I call it the beast."

"I see," said Burt.

"I'm sure you do."

The words came as a shock, and Burt wondered if the other had read his thoughts. For the talk of war spun Burt back to Korea, to those long nights on the parallel when one patrol had followed another, night after night, until death and danger had become a part of life like eating and sleeping, and almost as necessary. One night he'd gone out alone and come back with his knife bloody, and all he would remember afterwards was that a Chinese loudspeaker had played *Sentimental Journey*.

"Go on, Rolf," said Burt in a tight voice. "You were telling about World War II."

"Yes. I let my beast out in those days. I let him rage and snarl and gorge himself; I was a hero, a patriot, but I was never foolish enough to think that society would let the beast run loose when there was no longer any need for him. So after the war I threw the chains on him."

"Did you?"

"Ah, you're thinking about our fight." Rolf reached for the bottle and poured a drink, thoughtfully watching the liquor rise in the glass. He proffered the bottle to Burt, but Burt shook his head, waiting. Rolf capped the bottle, then raised his glass and smiled. "Well, March, you have to feed the beast from time to time. Someday you may need him to save your life."

He leaned back and drank, closing his eyes as though the liquor were a delicious elixir. "Ah well, so I chained up the beast and searched for a socially acceptable occupation. I'd seen millions of dollars' worth of war materials all over the world; now it would never be used. Mile-long rows of airplanes, tanks, jeeps, command cars, rusting on islands, in deserts, mountains. Why not remove the smaller units, radios, optical instruments, electronic gear, ship it home and sell it? You may know how that turned out; the men with government contacts and money covered the deal like a blanket. I made a few thousand, the others made millions before the stink reached the public. Then I thought of Europe, fugitive Nazis with their little caches of jewelry, gold, and art objects. I had the cash, and contacts who could provide them with new identities, and a safe hiding place—"

"You helped Nazis?"

"I'm a businessman, not a patriot. Others took their money and denounced them to the authorities, but I fulfilled my contracts. Is that unethical?"

Burt shrugged; he couldn't get rid of his distaste for

Rolf. The man was likable enough; handsome, worldly and friendly. That was it. He was a good deal more friendly than the situation warranted.

But Rolf was telling how fugitive Nazis had led him to South America. There he'd seen an untapped reservoir of wealth in Indian artifacts; gold, silver, jewelry, pottery, and objects of art. For several years he'd moved the stuff out by bribery and smuggling, selling it to private collectors and museums in the States. But there'd been no limit to the money-hunger of South American *politicos;* the overhead had risen and finally wiped out his profit margin. So he'd liquidated the business and was now at liberty, so to speak, looking for new opportunities.

And he needs a cop, thought Burt. Here it comes.

Instead Rolf said, "Your turn now, March."

Burt realized that the effort of trying to stay ahead of Rolf Keener had amplified his headache into a throbbing agony.

"I'll have to save my story. This headache—"

"My wife can cure that. Ah . . . Tracy?"

Burt turned, half-expecting to see Mrs. Keener in her usual all-concealing attire. But she came out the door bareheaded, and in the pale yellow light of the kerosene lamp her face shone faintly with skin-cream. Her nose was short and faintly tilted on the end. Black hair billowed around her shoulders. He tried to see her eyes, but they were squinted as though she'd come out of total darkness. Her beach coat reached only to mid-thigh and somehow suggested that there was nothing beneath it. That was an unwarranted conclusion, Burt decided; something about the island kept a man on the edge of criminal assault.

"Tracy, can you give Burt March one of your headache treatments?"

"Of course." She smiled a polite smile that held no warmth. There was a poised smoothness about the way she walked toward him; the studied glide of a model in a high fashion show. He tightened up as she walked behind him, then he was enclosed in the aura of her perfume, and her cool fingers began drawing the pain from the back of his neck.

Rolf looked on with the benevolent manner of a father. "She told me how she cooled you this afternoon after you returned her purse. Then I gave you the business in your cabin. You've been treated badly by the Keener family, and we'd like to make it up."

The words made Burt feel prickly, uncomfortable. He leaned forward, away from the woman. "This isn't necessary. I've got aspirin."

"Let her," said Rolf. "She doesn't mind, do you, Tracy?"

"Of course not," said the voice behind him. Her warm breath caressed his neck.

How do you deal with this friendliness, wondered Burt, particularly when you don't think it's real? The whole scene had the unreality of a poorly acted but carefully rehearsed play. The lines were perfect, but there were those very small split-second errors in timing. Rolf, particularly, had the manner of a man reading a script; sometimes he forgot to smile, sometimes he remembered at the wrong time . . .

All right, Burt decided. Play along. You don't learn if you don't listen. He leaned back and let the fingers continue their work. She had achieved an even rhythm which Burt found vaguely sexual. It was difficult to keep from sighing with pleasure. How could a man sit there and let his wife do that to another man?

Wind ripped through the palm trees. The surf thundered; the house trembled. The fumaroles moaned.

"Tide going out," said Burt.

Rolf stood up. "I'll see to the launch. Don't leave."

And Burt sat, aware that there must be method in Rolf's madness of leaving him alone with his wife. Better relax and see what kind of approach she used.

She didn't keep him waiting long. The screen door had scarcely closed when her treatment ceased to be therapy and became a caress. Her fingertips tingled along his jaw, up behind his ears. She blew softly on his neck.

Burt jumped, and she laughed. "Are you one of those men who let a woman do it all?"

The fact that he'd half-expected it didn't dull the surprise of hearing it spoken. She was, if not making a proposition, unmistakably inviting one. What the hell did this island do to women, anyway?

"I was wondering," said Burt, "if you found everything intact in your purse."

"Certainly," she said in a disinterested voice. Then, curiously: "What has that to do with it?"

Burt shrugged. Of course she wouldn't mention the heroin, and he'd better drop the subject before she suspected that he knew. Strange that the woman showed none of the drug's stigmata; still, it was hard to pick a well-fed hypo out of a crowd, unless she happened to be on the nod or badly strung out . . .

"You understand about this afternoon," she said, leaning forward in a way that brought a soft double-pressure against his back. "I wanted to invite you in for a drink, but I knew he was coming. I didn't want him to find—"

Burt laughed.

"What's funny?"

"I've seen women who come on strong when their husbands are near, then turn cold when it's safe."

"Oh?" Idly, her fingers stirred the hair at the back of his head. "You think I'm one of those?"

"I think you enjoy the game, yes. I could die of old age waiting for the pay-off."

"Tell you what you do, Sergeant March. You know the island. You name it. Time, place, everything. I'll meet you."

Burt stopped laughing. "I think you're trying to set me up, Mrs. Keener. Don't."

She was leaning on him, her chin gently gouging his shoulder. Her breath was warm in his ear. "What are you afraid of, Sergeant March? I thought cops weren't afraid of anyone."

"That's enough. I'm leaving." Burt started to get up, but her arms slid around his neck and pulled him back.

The soft breath against his ear became wetness, then sharp, biting pain. He twisted and overturned the chair. He fell and felt her soft form rolling beneath him. He struggled to his feet and put his hand to his ear. Warm blood trickled down his neck. He felt foolish and resentful, as though he'd been tricked into performing in a slapstick comedy.

"Damn!" Burt looked down at the woman. Her beach robe was in drastic disarray, but she didn't seem to notice. She was laughing, and there was a bright red wetness on her lower lip.

"You need a good beating," he told her.

"Really?" She sat up with her arms braced behind her, stretching her long muscular legs out on the concrete floor. "Go ahead, Sergeant. Do your duty."

"Oh hell—!" He whirled and tore open the screen door. Behind him her laughter trilled high above the sound of the surf. As he walked back to his cabin, he realized this was almost the same scene he'd walked out on earlier. Except that Joss had no ulterior motives; or if she had, they were hidden even from Joss herself. Mrs. Keener had a sick thing going, and Burt had a feeling her husband was a part of it.

He took a shower before going to bed. It helped a little.

THREE

Next morning Burt found a shining new padlock on the door of cabin two. He shoved his hands into his pockets and regarded it with a feeling of frustration; he had merely glanced toward the cabin as he walked along the beach, feeling normal curiosity, and now ... now he felt an aching desire to go in. The detective syndrome, he thought; you see a locked door and you want to look behind it. Or is that a burglar syndrome? Maybe there wasn't much difference.

He walked toward the club. It was a gray day, and a steady east wind carried moisture in such fine particles that he didn't know it was raining until he found his hair damp. The lagoon was like a blanket being shaken; the surf washed over the jetty and made tentative passes at the pilings which held up the beach club. Rolf's launch was gone, and Burt could hear Joss's voice raised in shrill anger behind the kitchen.

He found her standing over Coco, who was squatting on the ground, sullenly picking a scab on his instep.

"What's wrong?" asked Burt.

Joss turned, looking sheepish. "This ignorant ass let the rowboat drift away last night."

Coco looked up. "Mist' March, I leave it on the beach where the surf do not reach."

"Let's go see."

In front, Coco showed him the boat's keel mark in the sand. It extended three feet above the line of coral, driftwood and coconut husks which marked the high-water point.

"She lie here when I go to sleep," said Coco. "Not here this morning."

"You must have moved it," said Joss.

"No, mistress. I am sure."

They all stood looking at the marks in the sand as though, if they looked long enough, the boat would materialize. Finally Coco shuffled off, mumbling. Joss shrugged. "Weather like this bugs these people. They don't know it, but it does."

Burt walked with her to the club. "What bugs me is losing the boat."

Joss waved her hand airily and sat down at a table. "Hell, it wasn't worth much. It's just that one by one all my rowboats disappear. That boy gets out there day-dreaming and a boat gets carried onto the rocks; he forgets to put in a drainplug and a boat swamps; he goes skin-diving alone and his boat drifts away." She sighed and signaled Godfrey to bring coffee. "I'll get another one made on Bequia. Meanwhile there's no problem. I just bought a pile of supplies, food and liquor, with the money I got from Keener and Smith. And O'Ryan will be through again in two or three days."

"Suppose somebody gets sick?"

"You feeling bad?" She eyed him quizzically, then shrugged. "I'm sure, if there was an emergency, Rolf Keener would lend his launch."

At that point Burt realized what really bothered him about losing the rowboat. Rolf Keener now had the only means of transportation on the island—and Rolf Keener had gone out early this morning to check his launch.

"Where'd the Keeners go?" he asked.

"For a cruise," said Joss.

Burt frowned at the frothing sea. Fifteen-foot rollers broke against the rocks around the lagoon and sent up explosions of spray. Black-toothed rocks bit through the surface each time a wave receded.

"He's in no danger, Burt," said Joss. "He's got twin outboards, besides his inboard engine, and he seemed to know what he was doing."

"Yes," said Burt. "He gives that impression."

Godfrey brought two mugs of French coffee, hot and

strong and heavy with chicory. Burt sipped it slowly, squinting out beyond the dripping thatch. He thought about Rolf, not because he feared for his safety, but because he wondered what could lure a man out to sea in this weather.

"You made a good impression on him," said Joss after a long silence. "He said you could keep cabin one. He wants you for a neighbor."

Burt gave a wry smile. "I wonder what else he wants."

"Why?"

"He told me his life story last night. Some men do it because they like to talk. Rolf isn't a compulsive talker. I think he wanted to exchange confidences."

"Did you?"

"Wasn't much more I could tell. He knew I was with the police, searched my wallet while I was out cold."

Her mouth dropped open. "No! But that doesn't sound like—"

She broke off as Jata appeared at the railing and morosely held up a mop and a bucket. "Miss Joss, how I'm cleaning cabin two?"

"You'll have to wait, Jata. Mr. Keener wants to be there when you clean."

The old woman's blue-black, wrinkled face settled slowly into a mask of fury. She turned and strode off, somehow managing to convey injured dignity in the way she planted her large bare feet on the sand. Burt regarded Joss with a question in his eyes, and Joss looked down into her coffee. She spoke defensively:

"It sounded perfectly reasonable when he explained it this morning. I ... didn't realize how it would sound."

"Yes. He's very logical ... in his own way." Burt frowned. "I wonder what valuables he had that he couldn't take with him."

Joss wasn't listening. She gulped down her coffee and stood up. "I'd better go soothe Jata's pride. See you at lunch."

Burt breakfasted on soursop juice, fried breadfruit

and red snapper. Boris was sorry, but the rats had stolen the eggs and the mongooses had eaten all the chickens and there was no way to get off the island until
Mister Keener returned.

Burt felt a new twist of unease. "If he weren't here
how would you get off?"

"We would cut the glass, sir."

"Cut the glass?"

"Take the mirror, go up to the *piton,* catch the sun
and flash it to the fishing boats."

"And if there's no sun?"

"If there is no sun, then you wait. The sun always
return."

After breakfast, Burt climbed the steep stony path
which had been hacked through the shoulder-high
grass. By the time he reached the base of the three
black crags, he had to stop and massage his aching leg.
Maybe I'm pushing too hard, he thought, can't afford
to get crippled up at this point.

At what point? Well, before it happens, whatever
Rolf is going to make happen. . . .

A six-foot watchtower had been built on the highest
crag, dating from the days when the French and English had been killing each other to plant their flags
around the world. The eminence was a paved area no
larger than a shot-put ring, with a waist-high parapet
halfway around it. The rest of the parapet had fallen a
breath-taking five hundred feet to the rocks below. Burt
leaned his elbows on the parapet, breathing heavily as
he scanned the horizon. The mist-laden wind cooled his
flushed face. Clots of low gray clouds floated over the
white-capped sea below, seemingly anchored by silver
streamers of rain. To the north, the populus island of
Bequia formed an irregular crescent, pointing a gnarled
finger at the southern tip of St. Vincent. To the south,
a score of smaller islands thrust up from the sea, some
so close together that it was hard to see where one began and another ended. He had visited all of them in
the past; he recognized the jutting red peak of Bat-
towia, inhabited by a few native farmers; he saw the

wooded, rolling hills of Cannouan, the twisting spine of Baliceaux, the yellow-green pastures of Mustique, and the jagged thousand-foot spires of Union. Most of the smaller islands were waterless and uninhabited except for semiwild sheep and cattle, and voracious sandflies. There were none of the usual fishing boats bobbing between the islands, and no sign of Rolf's power cruiser.

He left the tower and strolled aimlessly around the island. At least, he thought he was strolling aimlessly; he realized his subconscious had taken charge when he found himself regarding once again the padlock on cabin two. There was nobody in sight. He walked around the cabin looking for a means of ingress. The windows were small and hooked on the inside. The padlock hung on a rusty hasp screwed into rotting wood; he could have ripped it loose but he wanted to leave no sign.

He stumbled over an accumulation of litter from the cabin: broken bottles, rusty cans, and charred newspapers, all damp and glistening. One small pile had not yet been burned; he supposed it included Mrs. Keener's sweepings. He got a stick and poked through it. Several wads of lipsticked tissue. Funny, there were two different shades, one the dark red he'd seen in the purse, the other a pale orange. Mmm. Maybe women changed their lipstick according to mood. Here was a mass of tangled, knotted hair, filled with lint as though it had been cleaned from a comb. He pulled an end loose and examined it. A pale wavy hair, ash blonde. Not Rolf Keener's, too long for that. Possibly from a woman guest who predated Mrs. Keener, fallen in a corner and swept out only recently. Have to ask Joss. He looked for something to keep the hair in. All the paper was charred and soggy; ah, here was one, wadded up into a tight little ball like a piece of popcorn. He smoothed it and found that there were two sheets of thin airmail stationery. It had been burned carelessly, and much of the writing remained legible. The salutation caught his eye:

r Rolf,
                    Three nights on this island
         away from you have given me a
                         nk about all that has
                       ce I married you and

So, it was written by Mrs. Keener in a blunt vertical
script totally without flourishes. He had not expected
her to write in such a near-masculine hand. He spread
out the second sheet and found only one and a half
sentences intact:

                    no point in going on
         dreading every tomorrow and regretting each

A coldness grew at the back of his neck. He'd read
many suicide notes, and this had the ring of authentic-
ity. Funny, he thought, folding the letter and shoving it
into the pocket of his shorts; this was written by a quietly desperate woman who had decided to end her marriage, perhaps even her life. He couldn't picture Mrs.
Keener in that part at all.

Well, that settled one thing. He had to get inside. He
circled the cabin again and saw that the bathroom was
roofed with corrugated tin. Probably it had once been
thatched, but moisture had rotted the grass. A ladder
led up to a platform which held a barrel of water for
the shower. Burt climbed up and found that the roofing
had merely been laid in place and covered with heavy
stones to keep it from blowing away. He moved the
stones, propped the sheeting open with a stick, and
crawled inside. Standing on the low stand which held
the basin, he pulled out the stick and lowered the roof
back in place.

Inside, he noticed that Mrs. Keener had the same
habit of untidiness he'd found in many otherwise attractive women. Her robe hung on the bathroom door
and a pair of black panties were draped over the
shower head. He touched his fingers to the transparent,
chiffon-like fabric. Little red lips were embroidered

around the bottom. It was the kind of lingerie teen-agers order from the little ads at the backs of true confession magazines.

And what did that prove about Mrs. Keener? Simply that she took pride in her sexuality and liked to adorn it as well as possible. All of which fit the woman he had—met was too weak a word: encountered, maybe, or engaged. Such a woman would hardly consider suicide; if she did, she would write a fiery renunciation of the world, then reconsider and seek renewed life in an affair with a new man.

He froze at the entrance to the bedroom. Had a window blown open or ... what was that breath of coldness? All the windows were closed. Burt didn't have Joss's blind faith in the supernatural, but he'd run into things which couldn't be explained any other way. There was a feeling which often came to him in a scent of past violence; it had been present in the jewelry store, it was here now. A residue of fear or pain, like an invisible mist weighting the air.

He shook off the feeling and made a quick, thorough search of the room. More feminine clothing and inexpensive jewelry—in rather garish taste, he thought—but only one overnight case which held male clothing. Inside the case was a box of thirty-eight caliber ammunition. He catalogued the fact without emotion; Rolf had a gun, no doubt he kept it on the boat. A paranoiac with a gun was a combination devoutly to be avoided under any circumstances, but he had no time to consider it now.

He found the olive-green purse, but the talcum powder and the wallet were gone. Curious; it was as though Rolf had known his cabin would be searched. After removing all traces of incriminating evidence, why had he padlocked the door? Because he knew that would titillate Burt's curiosity? Damn, he didn't like the feeling of being always one step behind the man. ...

He jumped at the sound of tapping on glass. "Sir! Sir!" He saw Maudie's round face pressed against the window. "They comin back, sir."

He hurriedly glanced around the room, satisfied himself that he'd left no signs of his search, and departed the way he had come. Maudie was waiting as he dropped to the ground. He saw no point in asking how she'd known he was in the cabin; she'd been following him, of course. Didn't she always?

He walked away from the cabin and stopped beneath the palm trees. "You know what I was doing in there?"

"No, sir. I think, yes."

He frowned, trying to decipher her patois. "You don't know, but you have an idea?"

She nodded. "I think you place charm to kill him. Because he bash you."

He looked at her and smiled slowly. "You've lived with your mother too long."

"Yes, sir."

She seemed to be waiting for something more, and Burt reddened at the realization that his words could be taken as some sort of proposal. Maudie wore his gift beneath her T-shirt, and it was, as he'd expected, far too small. He failed to see how she breathed. He thought of telling her she didn't have to wear it to please him, then realized it would merely drag him into more semantic confusion. He shrugged and started toward the club. Maudie followed. Burt called over his shoulder:

"Keep following me around, Maudie, and you'll see things you shouldn't."

"Yes, sir," she said gravely.

He walked on, and heard her bare feet slapping the path behind him.

He reached the club in time to watch Rolf negotiate the entrance to the lagoon. A split-second's error in timing would have ripped the bottom out of the sleek, lap-hulled Swedish cruiser, but whatever else Rolf was, he was a skilled boatman. He waited for the swell, then gunned the engine and rose up with it. A wall of spray hid the boat for a moment, then it sailed into the comparatively calm lagoon. Burt was waiting as Rolf tied up at the jetty.

"We've lost our rowboat," said Burt. "You didn't happen to see it drifting?"

Rolf stood up, three inches taller than Burt. He looked strikingly virile and Nordic with his yellow hair blowing and his windbreaker jacket sparkling with water droplets. Burt noted the bulge beneath his left armpit and was half-relieved to know where the gun was.

The woman stood behind him, her eyes hidden by dark glasses. Her nose and forehead were sunburned, and there was pinkness on the long legs which extended below her white shorts. He wondered at her folly in submitting herself to the sun after being burned yesterday. Perhaps she'd been deceived by the haze; many northerners didn't realize the tropic sun could burn through a layer of clouds.

"There was nothing out there," said Rolf. "Everybody seems to be staying in port." He frowned. "Lost the rowboat, eh?" His eyelids drooped slightly. "Then it seems I'm in possession of the only means of leaving the island." He smiled blandly at Burt. "Let me know if I can be of any help."

He walked away, and the woman followed without having spoken, or even nodded to Burt. He noticed that the shorts molded her so snugly that the cloth was shiny tight. It seemed wrong for her to be so blatantly sexual in public; she was the type who waited until it could produce immediate results. Furthermore, she wasn't handling herself in a seductive manner. She walked as though she were self-conscious and uncomfortable, as though she'd been caught unprepared and had to wear a smaller woman's clothing—

"All right, March. Shove your eyes back in your head."

He turned to Joss beside him. "You notice anything strange about Mrs. Keener?"

"It isn't strange. Everybody's got one. Not everybody throws it around."

He had to smile at Joss's criticism of another woman's apparel, considering her own home-made bathing costume. He walked with her to the club and sat down at a table.

"Tell me, did a blonde happen to occupy cabin two before she came?"

Joss frowned. "No. The last ones were two Frenchmen from Martinique. Rum-heads. Threw up all over the joint. Had to scrub it with soap and water to get the smell out. Why?"

"When did Jata clean it last?"

"Yesterday. She couldn't today because—"

"I know. Then it had to be night before last."

"What?"

He hesitated, then pulled out the two sheets of paper and handed them to her. She squinted, then shook her head and handed them back. "Light's bad here. You read."

"The light's perfect and you know it." Burt read the two notes and explained where he'd found them. He didn't mention that he'd gone inside.

"Okay, Burt," said Joss without interest. "She was alone and bugged by the fact."

"Bugged enough to consider suicide?"

"Enough to write a note about it, and enjoy the thought of her husband being sorry she was dead. It's like a crying drunk; you feel way down, you can't figure why you're down, so you invent trouble."

"Maybe." Burt folded the sheets and returned them to his pocket. "But you've got to admit, she doesn't seem to be feeling sorry for herself now."

"So her husband came and she's happy." Joss raised her glass, obviously ready to forget Mrs. Keener.

"One more thing," said Burt. "Have you noticed any changes in her since I came? Has she dyed her hair . . . or anything?"

She set down her glass. "Burt, she had only one head, she wore clothes, she didn't wear a beard. That's all I can tell you. You know my eyesight."

"Maybe the boys—"

"They won't tell you anything."

Her positive tone made Burt look at her sharply. "Why not?"

"Well . . . they're not supposed to look." Joss looked uncomfortable. "We've had some trouble in the past. The boys are typical islanders, you know, pretty direct types. Uninhibited. When they see a pretty woman they . . . look her over. But good. Stateside women aren't used to that, and most of them have this color thing. I finally had to give strict orders to the boys, don't look at the women."

"Hell, Joss. That won't stop it."

"No, but they still won't tell you anything. That would mean admitting they've disobeyed."

Burt had to agree, and reflected that here was the drawback in throwing your authority around; you cut yourself off from sources of information. He decided not to tell Joss about the heroin, nor about the suspicion which was taking shape in his mind. Joss couldn't help him until he knew which way it was going, and there was no point in spreading the burden of silence. With Joss, it would be a tremendous burden. He supposed it was her stage background that made her accept people for what they said they were. It was part of her charm.

Joss broke into his thoughts with somber sincerity:

"Listen, Burt, I don't know what that bump on the head did to you, but you're going to louse up your holiday. Not only that, you'll depress me, and then I'll drink too much and go on a bawling jag—"

"I'm sorry, Joss, but—"

"But, nothing. The weather's bad enough without you catfooting around the island. What we need is a party."

It occurred to Burt that a party might be exactly what he needed to shake out more information. "You're right, Joss. Get the boys in with their instruments—"

"And I'll broil pigeons, and get some more wine—"
She paused. "The Keeners?"

"Invite them, by all means. It won't be a party if
they don't come."

FOUR

Joss managed to produce excellent wine for the dinner, and pigeons braised over the charcoals. She also
arranged that Burt set opposite Mrs. Keener, with Rolf
opposite Joss. Burt could see her visibly melting under
the man's attention, hypnotically reaching for her glass
when Keener filled it.

Burt devoted his attention to Mrs. Keener, and in
the process grew increasingly puzzled. She seemed miserably ill at ease in a dress too small for her. Its décol-
letage might have been breathtaking had her cleavage
not been so grotesquely distorted. Burt half-expected to
hear a pop like a champagne cork coming out of a bottle, and to see Mrs. Keener shoot up to the roof. She
kept squirming in her chair, plucking at her waist, and
plunging a hand inside her dress to make certain ad-
justments when she thought Burt wasn't watching.
Though she ate only one pigeon, she seldom raised her
eyes from her plate. When she did, Burt saw the spar-
kle of moisture inside her lids. He felt a rising excitement; watery eyes, loss of appetite, itching, all were
signs of drug withdrawal. But if she really were an addict, that blew his whole theory to hell. Then he
remembered something which restored it; he had delivered fourteen caps to her, and there would have been
no reason for her to be deprived.

When he tried to engage her in conversation, she answered in monosyllables without looking up. Each time
she spoke, Rolf would pause in his talk with Joss,
stiffen, and relax only when she finished. Finally Burt
asked:

"Where did you work, Mrs. Keener, before you were
married?"

Nobody moved, but Burt could feel the air stretch taut like a balloon about to burst. Rolf pushed back his plate and asked with a half-smile:

"Tell me something, Burt. How does it feel to arrest a man?"

Joss looked annoyed at this abrupt diversion of Rolf's attention. No doubt, to her it was normal dinner conversation, everybody friendly and on a first-name basis.

"That depends, Rolf. Thieves, embezzlers, forgers, I just feel relieved. Here's another man put out of the way before he gets dangerous, one more man stopped short of murder."

"Murder? You think all crime leads to murder?"

Burt put his knife on his plate and weighed his words carefully. "Put it this way, Rolf. Murder is insanity. Crime of any kind is a small dose of the same thing."

"Oh, I don't agree. The profit motive—"

"—is an excuse they give themselves. Show me a financially successful crook, and I'll show you a man who could have made just as much money in, say, the used-car business. Why did he turn to crime? Social protest. The hell with everybody, he says, I won't play their stinking game. So he commits a crime and gets away with it. Why don't they catch me? he wonders. He commits another, then another, getting bolder and bolder until he's finally caught and tossed in the pen. Then he's relieved as hell. See, he says to himself, I was right. Everybody's out to get me."

Rolf was smiling. "And if he isn't caught, I suppose he finally commits murder."

Burt shrugged. "That's the biggest social protest of all."

"Yes." Rolf pursed his lips thoughtfully. "Interesting to meet a philosophical cop. How do you feel when you get a murderer?"

"I feel good, Rolf. Damn good. I feel I'm saving a life, maybe several. Because they don't generally stop at one. It's like getting an olive out of a bottle, the first

one's the hardest. After that it becomes a simple and final solution to everything. Even the simplest irritation,
a waitress spills a drink on your lap and your first
thought is, kill her."

"Burt," said Joss. "That's insane."

"That's my point. A sane man might, under very
pressing circumstances, commit one murder. But he
wouldn't stay sane long. Murder's too big a load to
carry. Even your Nazi friends, Rolf, had to keep telling
themselves they were just following orders."

"And when a cop kills?" asked Rolf softly.

Burt felt the hair rise on the back of his neck. "What
do you mean?"

"I mean, what kind of fiction does a cop provide
himself with when he kills—"

Joss cut in quickly. "Rolf, I want to show you something."

Rolf ignored her. He leaned forward and fixed his
eyes on Burt. "*I* know what they tell themselves. They
say it was an unavoidable accident. I aimed for his legs
but somebody jostled my gun. I fired over his head but
he jumped up and caught the bullet. He was trying to
kill me and I had to stop him." He leaned back, looking pleased with himself. "I have a theory about cops,
Burt. They know, when they go into the racket, that
eventually they're going to find themselves in a position
to kill legally—"

Joss rose. "Rolf, come over here a minute."

"Let me finish," said Rolf with sudden peevishness.
"You see what I'm getting at, Burt?"

Burt felt sticky perspiration beneath his clothes. At
the beginning of Rolf's soliloquy he had thought, Well,
so Rolf's hobby is cop-baiting. He'd been over this
route before and, rather than anger, had felt only a
faint boredom. But now the man was dealing with the
subconscious motives of a policeman who kills, and
these were the precise questions Burt had been asking
himself.

"Rolf, joining the police doesn't get you a license for
killing—"

"How many cops have burned for it?"

"Rolf, I want to talk to you," said Joss.

Rolf sighed and stood up. "My theory is that cops are instinctive killers who've found a socially accepted way of going about it. Think it over."

Burt watched Rolf and Joss walk over to the edge and pretend to be looking through the telescope. Joss would no doubt tell him about the boy, and Burt would have preferred that she mind her own business. But of course Joss would say it was her business to see that no misunderstandings arose between guests.

Well, unfinished business, Mrs. Rolf Keener. "Could I borrow your comb?" he asked.

She looked up in surprise. "Sure."

She delved into her little handbag and came up with a sequinned comb. She wiped it with a napkin and gave it to him. He saw with dismay that it was clean of hair. Scratch one effort. . . .

He combed his hair and gave it back. "The temperature has cooled since last night," he said casually.

And just as casually she replied, "I threw you the ball and you dropped it. You want to pick it up again?"

He had only to stir the ashes.

"I just wanted to say, if you need help with anything, tell me before he gets back."

He'd been thinking about the letters, but she pointed a finger at the untouched pigeon on his plate. "You can. Slip that under the table to me, quick."

There are times when a man gets involved in a scene so bizarre that he must freeze his intellect, numb his mental process, before he can act. It was in this way that Burt passed her the pigeon and sat listening to the hidden crackle of tiny bones and the juicy sound of her mastication. She ate with her head lowered, devouring the entire pigeon in the time it took to rip off the meat and convey it to her mouth. Burt sat with a growing conviction that he was the only sane person at the table. Finished, she touched a napkin to her mouth with such incongruous delicacy that he burst out laughing.

She frowned toward Rolf, then leaned confidentially across the table. "Don't tell Rolf. He's trying to enforce my diet."

A bright light flashed in his brain. "Oh, you've put on weight recently?"

"You think I'm getting fat?"

"I see nothing wrong with your shape, if your clothes only fit—"

"Oh, that's *part* of it, don't you see? He's got this idea that people go through life trying to balance out their various urges. I've got an urge to eat, but I've also got this urge to wear nice things. He decided that the urge to dress well was strongest. So he went out and bought me a raft of lovely clothes for our trip, only they're two sizes too small. He figures I'll diet in order to be able to wear them; meanwhile I'm on the edge of a nervous breakdown because I'm afraid something's going to burst out any minute."

Burt managed a faint smile. The whole ridiculous story fitted Rolf's weird logic. Unfortunately, one of the main props in his theory was that the clothes weren't really hers. . . .

Joss and Rolf returned, and Joss said she'd see if the boys were ready to play music. Burt excused himself and followed her out to the kitchen.

"Joss, I wonder if you'd take your eyes off Rolf long enough to listen to Mrs. Keener. I want to know if her voice sounds . . . different than when she first came."

She looked at Burt with unfocused eyes. "I couldn't tell from the grunts she's given so far."

Burt frowned. "Yeah, that's funny. After you left she talked up a storm."

"Don't forget her husband left, too."

"What does that mean?"

"Oh, come now. Does a woman camp out where her old man can see? No, baby. She sits quiet and sedate and something like a stick until he gets out of earshot. Then she turns it on." Joss smiled loosely and patted his cheek. "That chick's got her net out for you, Burtie. Don't get tangled up in it."

Burt realized that Joss was half-drunk and a bad security risk, but he needed help.

"Listen, when we go back out there, I want you to get everybody to sign the guestbook. I'm particularly interested in Mrs. Keener."

She raised her brows. "What's on your mind?"

"Just a sneaky way to see her handwriting." He patted her shoulder. "Go on, play it natural. I'll explain when the party's over."

Back at the table, Joss carried it off . . . almost. She brought up the subject of a previous guest, forgot his name, then got the guest book, a massive bookkeeping ledger, to refresh her memory. She discovered that none of those present had signed the book. Burt signed first, then Rolf Keener, who asked Joss with a faint smile, "Is it okay if I sign for both of us?"

Joss shot Burt a brief glance, then said quickly, "Oh, no. Everybody sign."

Rolf, still smiling, pushed the heavy book in front of the woman. "Here, Mrs. Rolf Keener. Sergeant March would like your autograph."

Burt met the cold blue eyes and regretted his maneuver with the book. He'd revealed more than he could ever learn, and it gave him no surprise to look across the table and see the woman print in block capitals: MRS. ROLF KEENER.

The boys began playing a bouncy local mixture of calypso, cha-cha-cha, and Latin American rock-and-roll. They'd donned white shirts for the occasion, and Boris managed to look dignified even with a nose-flute in one flaring nostril. Coco sat on the floor with his legs hooked around a pair of bongo drums. His hands, pink-scarred by fish-bites, fluttered like black wings on the taut drum-skin. Godfrey's face hung vacuous over a guitar almost as large as himself.

Rolf pulled Joss up to dance on the wooden floor; he acted like someone playing a hilarious game—and winning it. Burt hesitated to trust his leg, but when Joss and Rolf began their third twist, he asked Mrs. Keener to dance.

"If I pop out of my dress," she said, getting up, "will you look the other way?"

"We'll have to wait and see," said Burt.

Burt found to his surprise that he enjoyed dancing with her. She moved with a boneless, sinuous grace which never brought her into contact with him, but nevertheless made him totally aware of her body. He glanced down at her muscular calves, saw that her feet were shod in flat-heeled, ballet-style slippers.

"Did you used to be a professional dancer?"

She dimpled in a way she must have practiced. "You say the nicest things."

Burt thought: She's certainly no junkie. She's a healthy female animal with beautiful coordination, a gargantuan appetite, and none of the addict's sexual apathy. He could feel her physical warmth surrounding him like a blanket. On their third dance he spoke softly in her ear: "On the slope behind your cabin, there's a concrete water catchment with a tile-roofed cistern at the lower end. Have you seen it?"

"Yes." She whirled away once and came back into his arms. "In an hour?"

So simple, he thought, like meeting her for coffee. "That's fine."

She came against him for an instant as though sealing the bargain with a sample. Burt found himself looking over her head into the icy blue eyes of Rolf. There was no jealousy there, only a crinkle of mild amusement.

But then, he asked himself, why should Rolf be jealous? For he had just learned, with a certainty that dispelled all doubt, that the woman in his arms was not Tracy Keener.

The woman pleaded a headache fifteen minutes later and the pair left despite Joss's protest that parties didn't end this way in the islands. Joss decided to stay and finish the wine and Burt stayed with her.

"Joss, what's the best way to get to this island without the authorities knowing?"

"In the hold of a ship, I guess."

Burt thought of Mrs. Keener's tight clothing, he'd returned to the theory that they'd belonged to a smaller woman. She couldn't have carried much luggage as a stowaway.

"Is there a quicker way?"

"Flying in at Grenada."

"She'd go through immigration."

"Not our immigration. We come under St. Vincent, the southern islands come under Grenada. People cross all the time and nobody knows unless they get in trouble."

"Then Rolf could have picked her up in the launch from Grenada. Of course."

"Who, Mrs. Keener?"

"She isn't Mrs. Keener."

Joss's mouth dropped open. "You mean he sent his girl friend down here—"

"I mean that the woman who came on O'Ryan's schooner is not the woman we had dinner with tonight. There's been a switch, and it happened sometime between last night and the night before."

She stared at him a moment, then shook her head. "I've had too much to drink, Burt. I can't figure it."

"Okay. I searched the purse while I was on the schooner. Her driver's license said she was five-feet-four, and weighed a hundred and five pounds. Now this woman was nearer one-twenty, wouldn't you say?"

"At least, but women change their weight."

"But not their height, Joss. While we were dancing I noticed that she was wearing low heels. The top of her head came to the tip of my nose. I'm six feet and a quarter inch tall. My nose is approximately five inches below the top of my head. That would put her height at about five-seven."

"But why? To change wives—"

"Divorce is a lot less trouble. It's bigger than that, and I've got a feeling there's a lot of money involved, knowing Rolf."

"What are you going to do?"

"Get more information—maybe. I've got a date with her out by the cistern."

Joss looked alarmed. "Burt, it's probably a trap."

"I know. I don't aim to throw myself at her feet without looking around. Rolf has a gun, you know."

"Burt, don't risk it. Look, let me talk to Rolf, I'll tell him I'm sick, get him to take me to St. Vincent, go to the police—".

"And tell them what?"

"Why . . . that there's a woman here—"

"And our proof?"

"My word—"

"Have you told anybody about seeing your husband on the beach wearing hip boots?"

"What does that—?" She closed her mouth, reddening. "Oh, I see what you mean. They'd think I was raving. Okay, you go."

"Suppose Rolf does have a big deal on; he'd see that I never got to St. Vincent."

Joss laughed nervously. "Oh, hell, this thing has sobered me up quicker than a gallon of black coffee. Who do you suppose the woman is?"

"It's not important, is it? I'm wondering what happened to the real Mrs. Keener."

FIVE

Burt squatted inside a clump of grass and peered at the woman who stood beside the cistern. Strange that she'd wear her white beach coat to a secret tryst; she stood out like neon beneath the thick crescent of the moon. The water catchment was a gray triangle on the slope above her. He could hear rats chittering in the grass around him; the booming surf had become an unchanging part of life, audible only when he made an effort to hear it. Beyond the cistern he saw the fumaroles geysering up like pale gleaming wraiths in the moonlight.

A match flared and went out. A cigarette glowed in the pale oval of her face, brightened and dimmed several times in rapid succession. Lover's getting impatient, he thought, but I'll bet she doesn't leave. . . .

A cloud obscured the moon and darkened the island. A darker shadow joined the white shape of the woman. When the moon came out again, the larger shadow broke away and disappeared around the corner of the cistern. Burt gripped the two-foot length of steel pipe and crept out of the grass. He angled to the right, down the slope and back up again on the side of the cistern opposite the woman. He peered around the corner and saw Rolf squatting with his back to the stone wall. Rolf was an old night fighter; Burt knew he could never sneak close enough for a solid blow. He picked up a stone and, holding his arm away from his body so there would be no swish of cloth, threw it over Rolf's head. It thumped on the ground ten feet ahead of the man; Rolf rose to his feet. Burt leaped forward and swung the pipe against his head with a delicate, calculated force. Rolf fell against the cistern and started a limp-legged slide to the ground; Burt caught him beneath the arms and lowered him gently. He withdrew a .38 snub-nosed revolver from Rolf's shoulder holster and shoved it in his hip pocket. Rolf's pulse and breathing were both surprisingly normal; Burt decided he'd have less than a quarter hour with the woman.

He retraced his steps around the cistern to where she waited. Like a passenger whose bus has just arrived, she pushed herself away from the wall and threw her cigarette to the ground. As she came toward him, Burt saw that her long legs were bare beneath the beach coat.

"I was beginning to get cold," she said, locking her hands behind his head and looking up with a teasing smile. "I wondered if you'd have the guts to come."

Burt spread his hands across her back and felt the muscle-taut flesh beneath it. She was not as calm as she appeared.

"Where'd you leave Rolf?" he asked.

"In the cabin, reading. He thinks I'm taking a walk." She rocked against him, an undulating warmth pressing him from chest to knee. "We don't have much time. Will you kiss me?"

"No biting?"

"Maybe that comes later."

He felt the surprising coolness of her lips and the curiously facile, impersonal probing of her tongue. He tasted wine and braised pigeon, and decided that this girl knew all the right moves at the right time, but that skill could never take the place of natural passion.

Then suddenly all her weight hung from his neck. She fell backward onto the ground, pulling him off-balance so that he had to put out both hands to avoid crushing her with his weight. The sandy soil scraped his elbows as he tried to break her grip around his neck, and Burt discovered that somewhere in midfall she had managed to unfasten the robe. He made three more discoveries in rapid succession: She wore nothing beneath the robe, she had a wiry masculine strength, and whatever her ulterior purpose in arranging the meeting, the seduction was in deadly earnest.

He jerked free and sat back on his haunches. "Cool it a minute. What's all the rush?"

She put her hands behind her head and began laughing softly.

"Did him want to chat? Did him want to be a big strong man and just overwhelm poor little me?"

Her mock babytalk curdled his stomach. "I think I get it. Rolf was supposed to catch me in the act and shoot me, right?"

She raised her head and frowned at him. "Huh?"

Burt rose to his feet. "Get up. I'll show you something."

"Oh, now wait—"

Burt seized her arm and jerked her up. "Come on."

Rolf was stirring when they rounded the corner. The woman tore free and ran toward him. "Rolf, what happened?" She knelt beside him an instant, then whirled and leaped at Burt, her teeth bared, her white robe flying out like the wings of a silver moth on both sides of her nude body. Her nails raked his cheek once, then again, while Burt wrestled with an untimely question: Where does a gentleman seize a naked woman he doesn't want to hurt? He felt he was being smothered in satin-firm flesh, she seemed to have a dozen arms, breasts, stomachs all heavy with an exciting smell of sweat and perfume. Her teeth were seeking a purchase somewhere in the region of his jugular vein when he found her shoulders and pushed with all his strength. She sprawled backward on the ground, but she was game; she bounced up and was about to charge again when Rolf's voice cracked like a pistol shot:

"Drop it, Bunny!"

She stopped as though on a short leash, her robe hanging open. Rolf sat up, drew his legs under him, and spoke in a tired voice:

"Wrap up the package, baby. It didn't sell."

She drew her robe together and tied it slowly, like a child putting away a doll which she'd been forbidden to play with until Christmas. Burt watched the pair, feeling like a stranger at a family dinner.

"It wasn't my fault," she said with petulance.

"Mine. Totally mine." Rolf touched the back of his head. "Sergeant March used an old trick. I was expecting something more original." He pressed his hand to the bulge of his jacket, sighed, and looked up at Burt. "Did you borrow my gun, old man?"

"I'll keep it for a while."

Rolf smiled. "With my compliments. I don't like guns. That one shoots slightly to the left, anyway." He fumbled beneath his jacket and drew out a cigarette. "Will you ask your question here, Sergeant, or—" he paused to ignite the cigarette "—shall we go to my cabin and have a drink?"

"This is fine." Burt pulled out the gun and squatted with his back against the wall. To the woman he said, "Get over beside him."

She obeyed, leaning against Rolf and delving into his jacket for a cigarette. She lit it from Rolf's and giggled softly. "Maybe he handles a gun better than he does a woman."

"Keep quiet," said Rolf absently. "Permit me to observe, March, that any restriction of an individual's freedom of movement is technically kidnapping. Since you're off-duty and outside the United States, you have no authority whatever."

"Let's all go together and complain to the authorities."

Rolf chuckled. "You win. First question."

"Where's your wife?"

"Sitting beside me."

"You called her Bunny."

"A term of endearment, just between us."

Burt decided it felt good to have the intellectual jump on Rolf. He smiled. "The island seems to have agreed with her. She's grown three-and-a-half inches since she arrived."

Rolf stiffened and looked sharply at the woman.

"Rolf, I didn't—"

"No, I understand it now." He turned back to Burt.
"I assumed you'd be too chivalrous to search the purse.
I was wrong." He pressed a shaky hand to the back of
his neck. "Do me, Bunny. I've got a headache." She
rose to her knees behind him and began kneading his
neck. Rolf looked at Burt. "She's Bunny DeVore, spe-
cialty dancer, late of Miami Beach. She starts her dance
in a cowboy suit and winds up wearing only a gun.
Clever act, particularly when she demonstrates the
symbolism of the gun—"

"You didn't bring her here to dance," said Burt.

"No, she goes with me on all my trips to South
America. Sort of a traveling secretary, except that she
can't type and can't take shorthand." He chuckled.
"Pity you struck so soon, March; you'd have learned
what makes her so valuable in my business."

"I know," said Burt, "But I can't say I dig the professional touch."

"Oh, you lousy fink—"

"Go to the cabin, Bunny," said Rolf. Your ego's
getting noisy."

"Stay there," said Burt.

"Burt's afraid you'd bring back a sawed-off shotgun,
I suppose." To Burt he said: "I'm your hostage, so why
worry? I can speak more freely when she's gone."

Burt hesitated a moment, then nodded. Bunny rose
and disappeared into the darkness, her back stiff.

"She minds well," observed Burt.

The secret," said Rolf, "is to give no commands
she's not already half-inclined to follow. She usually
enjoys the tasks I give her. This one tonight—I must
say she was particularly eager, but now—you know
what they say about a woman spurned. I'd watch my
back if I were you."

"What was the purpose of this business tonight?"

"I have a theory that people act because of pressure
on them. When I want somebody to do something, I
find out what pressures prevent them from doing it.
Then I set up a counterpressure in my favor, stronger
than the one against."

"And Bunny supplied the pressure."

"There are less pleasant pressures, March."

Burt narrowed his eyes; Rolf didn't seem to be threatening, only stating a fact. "I had a feeling last night you wanted something from me. Why not just tell me what it is?"

"Not until you put the gun away."

"All right. Then it can wait. Tell me why you pulled the switch."

"That was a challenging problem. My wife and Bunny are almost polar opposites. My wife is small, as you know, with a triangular face, brown eyes, blue-black hair and a faintly olive complexion. Bunny is a type particularly favored by South Americans, an ash blonde with green eyes—"

"*Green?* But they were brown—"

"Tinted contact lenses."

"Oh . . . is that why her eyes watered?"

"They do when she first puts them in. Later the tears stop." He ground out his cigarette in the dirt. "Of course it was easy to dye her hair, but that left the problems of weight and complexion. I put Bunny on a strict diet and told her to get tanned in a hurry. Meanwhile she wore dark glasses and stayed out of sight. Joss couldn't see well. I remembered that, and I figured that white women look basically alike to the native boys. The fact that my wife seldom makes close friends made the problem simpler. I told Bunny not to talk to Joss at the start, for fear the woman would recognize the change in her voice. Gradually Bunny would show more and more of herself, until the reality of her presence replaced the memory of my wife." Rolf sighed. "The only thing we couldn't change was Bunny's height. Now that's all I'll tell you until you put the gun away."

Burt held onto the gun; he didn't feel he needed it any more, but he couldn't put it aside without losing part of the initiative.

"I can tell you a few things," said Burt. "You pulled the switch night before last, didn't you?"

Rolf shrugged. "Think what you like."

"She flew in to Grenada and you picked her up in the launch, brought her here, and removed your wife. What did you do, kill her?"

Rolf looked up, startled. "Of course not."

"Then let me see her."

"No."

Burt paused. "Did Bunny come in as Tracy Keener?"

Rolf hesitated, then nodded. "You'd have a hard time proving which one was real. Bunny's papers are foolproof."

"Still the authorities would be interested to learn that two Tracy Keeners were on the island at the same time."

"It would be embarrassing," admitted Rolf, "should Grenada and St. Vincent ever compare notes, but hardly enough to excuse your taking me in at gunpoint. I can promise you this, Burt: should you try it, I could produce my wife within a few hours, and she would be in good health. She would swear that she left this island of her own free will, and has remained away only because she wanted to. And there you would stand with egg on your face."

Burt believed him; Rolf could produce his wife within a few hours. That meant . . . well, hell, it meant she could be anywhere, on the big islands of St. Vincent or Grenada, or on any one of a hundred smaller clods of land. It would take a month to search everywhere, even if he had a boat. And he didn't have a boat.

"If your wife is not a prisoner," said Burt, "what's to keep her from deciding to take off?"

"Pressure," said Rolf.

"What kind of pressure?"

"The most irresistible kind," said Rolf with a faint smile. "It comes from inside her."

Burt felt a chill climb his back; it seemed inconceivable that a man would turn his wife into a heroin

addict merely in order to control her. But then, with
Rolf, nothing was impossible.

Burt shoved the gun back in his hip pocket. "I suppose your wife knows Bunny took her place."

"She knows it's for her own good."

"How's that?"

"To remove her from danger."

"Danger on this island?"

Rolf nodded.

Burt frowned. "You could have left her at home."

"They'd know where to find her."

"Who's they?"

"I am . . . involved in a deal which puts me in considerable danger. My wife could be a means of getting
to me."

"Yes, but if the masquerade works, doesn't that put
Bunny in the same danger?"

"She's less sensitive to danger than my wife. And she
knows how high the stakes are."

"How high?"

"Mmmm. Say the liquid assets of a certain small
Latin American government in exile." Rolf leaned forward. "Interested?"

"What do I have to do?"

"Be my bodyguard while I'm here on the island."

Burt smiled. "You don't need a bodyguard."

"You're wrong. I'm an offensive fighter. I haven't the
patience to guard my back. Besides, if they come,
there'll be more than one."

"And I'm to capture them and take them to jail?"

Rolf laughed aloud. "Extradition papers, that sort of
thing? Don't be silly."

"Then you expect me to kill them."

"You'd find that more practical."

Burt felt his throat tighten. "I'm not a hired gun,
Rolf. I'm not even an instinctive killer, despite what
Joss may have told you. I'm a cop, and I serve the law.
I've been told that's far above any individual inter-
est—"

"No sermons, Burt." Rolf rose to his feet and rubbed

his forehead. "I'm going to get more of Bunny's treatment. We'll talk some more, of course. You haven't heard all of my terms. Maybe you'll find that you have no choice but to defend me."

"More pressure, Rolf? Bunny won't be so eager this time."

"Ah, Burt. There are outside pressures ... and inside pressures. I prefer the latter."

"What does that mean?"

"You're a cop. You've got the gun. Figure it out."

He walked away laughing to himself. A minute later the screen door slammed on cabin two. Burt walked back to the beach club and found it dark and silent except for the squeak and thump of rats fighting over discarded tidbits of food. He stood on the beach and watched Rolf's launch rock in the gentle swell of the lagoon. It would be easy to rewire the ignition and go to St. Vincent and ... what? He still wouldn't know where Tracy Keener was. No doubt she was the reason for Rolf's cruise earlier today; he'd know enough to dole out no more than a day's supply of the drug at a time. The secret of enslaving an addict was to restrict the supply.

So he'd be going again tomorrow.

Burt climbed up to the watchtower and sat on the parapet. He could hear the wind rippling the grass below with a sound like sliding silk. He rubbed his aching leg and thought of Bunny's cool fingers. He tasted her lipstick on his mouth and wondered if it had been all work and no play for her. ...

A rock clattered. He peered over the parapet into a pair of wide, white eyes. A familiar T-shirt bulged below them.

"Maudie," he whispered. "Go back home."

"*Maman* sleeping. She know nothing."

"Go back anyway."

"Yes, sir."

Burt sat back down inside the tower and leaned against the low wall. A minute later he heard a sound like marbles rattling. He peered over the edge and saw

Maudie huddled against the base of the tower with her arms hugging her stomach.

"Oh, hell. Come on up."

She crawled over the edge and sat down, stretching her warm young body beside him. "I help you watch, sir."

"Uh-huh," said Burt.

Five minutes later the tight-curled mat of her hair fell onto his shoulder. She snored softly. Burt stretched her out on the stones and pillowed her head with his jacket. He felt a wave of warm protectiveness toward the sleeping girl.

Yeah, he thought, that's what Rolf meant. I'm a cop, and I'm hung up with these people. Whether they like it or not, whether they accept it or not, I'm responsible for the safety of everyone on the island: Joss, Maudie, the boys, Jata, Tracy Keener . . . even Rolf and Bunny. Because if the danger which threatens Rolf should threaten the others, I will have to act.

SIX

Dawn came up unpleasantly, with a bleak drizzle which soaked Burt to the skin and rendered Maudie's T-shirt as transparent as onionskin. He sent the girl home and climbed down the hill through dripping grass. Coco sat on the steps of the beach club looking morosely at the rain dripping off the thatched roof.

"Nobody up yet?" asked Burt.

"No, sir." Coco rested his chin in his hands and gazed at Rolf's launch rocking in the rain-peppered lagoon. "My mind tells me he take me fishing today."

"Your mind gives you a bum steer," said Burt. "But I'll give you five bucks to go up to the *piton* and watch where he goes."

"Yes, *sir!*"

The pink soles of Coco's bare feet sent up spurts of wet sand as he ran down the beach. Burt went to his cabin and took a shower, then put on dry clothes and lay down on his bed fully dressed. The damp weather had brought throbbing pain to his leg; he seemed to be able to sleep only a half-hour when a spurt of pain would awaken him, and he would lie with cold sweat soaking his clothes while he tried to arrange his leg in a more comfortable position. He was doing this for the fifth or the tenth time when a shot blasted just outside his cabin. Burt was off his bed and on the floor when the second report came. He ran out onto the porch with Rolf's .38 in his hand and looked up to see a graceful frigate bird falter in flight, then begin a slow downward glide which ended in a splash far out to sea.

Burt lowered his eyes and saw the two men on the narrow beach just below his cabin. One carried a gun over his shoulder, holding it by the barrel in defiance of all gun safety rules. The other had broken open a double-barreled shotgun and was feeding in new shells. Burt shoved the .38 in his hip pocket and strode down to the beach. He'd forgotten the twinge in his leg; his ears burned with unreasoning rage.

"Hey!" he shouted.

The man who held the gun by the barrel turned to frown at Burt. He was a stocky, dark man who looked immensely powerful, with heavy, black-furred arms and a pelt of black hair poking through the neck of his crackling new sport shirt. The other man, also dressed in new sport shirt and trousers, was bigger but more loosely built. He raised his shotgun and scanned the sky, ignoring Burt.

"Why the hell did you shoot a frigate bird?" asked Burt.

The hairy man flashed a broad unconvincing smile and held out his hand. "I'm Ace Smith. Real-estate operator. This is one of my associates, Hoke Farnum."

Burt didn't take his hand. He'd always had a low opinion of men who killed for pleasure. These two didn't even seem to be having fun. "I asked you why you shot the frigate bird."

Ace Smith shrugged and waved at the other man. "Hoke thought it was a pigeon. We came here to shoot pigeons."

Burt glanced at Hoke. He had a thick fleshy head topped with coarse black hair. His face appeared the color and texture of pie dough with the features pressed in place by blunt fingers. The man didn't smile; he didn't look as though he knew how. He looked at Burt from eyes that could have been dried prunes floating in skimmed milk for all the emotion they showed, then turned away and drew a bead on a pelican bobbing in the swell just beyond the surf line. Burt leaped forward and knocked down the gun barrel. "Fool! Don't you know a pelican when you see one?"

The big man backed away with surprised annoyance. He gave Burt a puzzled look, then turned to Ace. "Who is this guy, the local game warden?"

"Bird lover," said the other. "Shoot what you want. They don't enforce game laws here."

For an instant the scene froze, with Burt facing the two armed men. Hoke's gun was a twelve-gauge shotgun; Ace carried an over-under model, twenty-gauge shotgun below, thirty-caliber rifle above.

Burt felt his skin draw tight; he hadn't smelled gunpowder since that night in the jewelry store.

He forced himself to relax; no use getting somebody killed over a frigate bird.

"You're the Smith who reserved two cabins?" he asked.

"Uh-yeah." Ace's smile was gone; like a rubber mask the face had snapped back into a taut, watchful pattern. There was violence in his eyes, but it was different from Rolf's, nearer to the surface, more defensive and, probably, with a quicker boiling point.

"How'd you two great white hunters get on the island?"

"Charter boat," said Ace.

As Burt turned to scan the shoreline, Ace said, "He left hours ago."

Burt looked up and saw the pale disc of the sun shining through the haze directly overhead. It was past noon. . . .

He left the two men and walked to the club. The cruiser was gone, as he'd expected. Godfrey, who was raking debris off the beach in front of the club, said the man and the woman had left right after breakfast. Boris was polishing the bar with an oiled cloth. To the left of the club, Joss lay in a hammock strung between two palm trees cuddling a rum punch on her stomach. Her eyes were closed, her mouth slightly open.

The tranquil scene gave Burt a queasy feeling, as though they were all sitting on the edge of a volcano, and he was the only one who could hear the rumble of the approaching eruption.

He walked up to her hammock and rocked it gently. She jumped, and liquid sloshed out of her glass and dampened the mound of her stomach.

"Burt, what——?"

"Why'd you let those new men in?"

"Boris put them up," she said, taking a sip from her glass. "I was asleep when they came in from Grenada."

"Asleep or passed out?"

"Well . . . rum makes me sleepy."

"Sure, when you drink a quart of it." He reached out and took the glass from her hand.

"Now Burt, listen——"

"You listen, Joss. I need help. I can't depend on you when you're juiced out of your mind." He set the glass on the sand beside her hammock. "Now, how many gorillas are there?"

She looked wistfully at the glass, then sighed. "Well, there were supposed to be four, but Boris said there were only three. That Mr. Smith is in cabin three, the other two are in cabin four——" She stopped abruptly. "What do you mean, gorillas?"

"I mean gorillas, gunmen, torpedoes, hoods. I've seen enough of them in lineups to know the type."

She turned pale. "But why . . . on this island——?"

"Tell me, did their reservations come in before or after Rolf's?"

"Neither. O'Ryan drops the mail off once a week. Both letters were in the same batch."

"So many visitors during hurricane season could hardly be an accident. Two and two adds up to four. Four against one."

"Four? You're not including Rolf?"

"Why not? They came in from Grenada, the same as the phony Mrs. Keener."

"Ah, that one." Joss's eyes narrowed. "She kept her date last night?"

Burt nodded.

"And you . . . did you enjoy yourself?"

Burt touched a finger to the faint scratches on his cheek. "I could have, if I'd wanted to perform for an audience." Briefly he related what had happened, including Rolf's hints of danger and a vast fortune at stake. Joss's reaction was surprising, but typical. She swung her legs to the ground and spoke with prim indignation:

"I'm going to the police and have the woman thrown out. That kind of promiscuity is just not allowed on my island."

Burt shook his head slowly. "We've been over this ground before, Joss. How would you go?"

"Rolf—"

"You'd never get there."

"Burt, don't be silly. Rolf wouldn't . . . I mean, he could be involved in a shady deal, like you say, but he wouldn't hurt a woman."

Burt smiled. "I envy you, Joss. Your feminine intuition would be such a help in detective work."

"Oh, it's more definite than that. We talked about the stars last night. He's a Leo, a perfect Leo. He's not bound by a lot of stifling rules, he's a leader . . ."

Burt stared as she talked, amazed that the accident of a man's birthday could outweigh all contrary evidence. True, it helped that Rolf was handsome, likable and intelligent, and that Joss was slightly sex-starved.

He decided not to argue with her. It wouldn't hurt to let her think Rolf was harmless, as long as the man didn't start using her for his own purposes. In any case, Burt wasn't eager to shatter Rolf's good-guy pose; he had a feeling that could only unleash a chain reaction of violence.

"Okay," he said finally. "I could be wrong about Rolf. But not about these other guys. Stay clear of them."

"I'll do better than that. I'll ask them to leave."

Burt sighed. "Here we are again. How will they go? Their launch left."

"Why, Rolf will take them off when he gets back."

Burt smiled slowly. "Go ahead and ask him. I'll be curious to see how he gets out of it."

Burt found Boris in the kitchen scratching his wispy goatee and grumbling about the food supply. The mountain of stores which Joss had hinted at consisted of three cases of Argentine canned beef and twenty-four tins of ship's biscuits. That would have been fine, Boris explained, if they'd had their usual fare of birds and seafood, but there could be no fishing without a boat, the surf was too high to get lobsters and sea snails from the reef, and the gunshots had driven all the pigeons to the highest crags.

"Maybe tonight I hold a manicou," said Boris. "But for now . . ."

Burt sat down to a breakfast of bully beef and biscuits. The biscuits rattled against his teeth, as hard and tasteless as C-ration crackers. The beef was stringy, blood-red, and so salty he used a quart of water to wash it down. He pushed back his plate and saw Boris watching him with an expression of deep sympathy.

"You were here when those new men came in?" Burt asked.

Boris shook his head. "I was up on the hill making charcoal, when I hear the boat. I do not move, for I think the blond man returning early. When I come down, the men are in their cabins. They do not let me in to open windows, show them how the bath works. I think they do not wish to give me a tip?"

The last sentence ended on a rising, querulous inflection. Burt didn't think the men were concerned about tipping; a passion for secrecy was exactly what he'd have expected after seeing the pair on the beach. It was sheer luck that they'd got on to the island without being seen. The puzzle was that only three men had arrived to occupy reservations made for four. What had happened to the fourth man?

"Godfrey didn't see them?" asked Burt.

"No, sir. I send him up to the rocks to look for bird's eggs."

"How about Coco—? Oh, hell!"

He jumped to his feet and left the club. The new arrivals had driven Coco completely from his mind.

Burt found Coco lying on his back with his white hat shading his face. Burt jerked it off:

"Did you see a launch leave three men on the island?"

Coco blinked and sat up, wiping his mouth with the back of his hand. "No, sir."

Burt threw the hat back with disgust. "That nap just cost you five bucks, Coco."

"But, sir! I watch where the other go, as you told me." He scrambled to his knees and pointed to the south. "I follow them with my eyes until they pass out of sight around that island, called Ram Island."

"Could they have stopped there?"

"No anchorage on that side. Only on this side."

"What's behind it?"

"Oh, many, many islands . . ." He named a dozen before Burt stopped him.

"The Tobago Cays. Isn't that a group of very small islands off to themselves?"

"Yes, sir. Petit Rameau, Petit Bateau, Jamesby, Baradal and Petit Tabac." Coco was obviously enjoying the chance to display his knowledge.

"Anybody live there?"

"No, sir. Sometimes boats come from Barbados, people stay there on holiday, swim, fish. Sometimes fishermen stop to dry fish for market, eat turtle. But they must bring food and water—"

"They don't visit during this season, do they?"

"No, sir. When the sea high, current rush through very swif'. Many rocks."

Burt thought about it: If Rolf wanted to keep his wife out of sight, he'd have to find a place where nobody would be likely to stumble onto her. She wouldn't know enough to stay out of sight when she was all hyped-up on junk, and that way he'd be damn sure she couldn't take off and try to score on her own—

Coco's shout interrupted his thoughts. He looked down to see the cruiser coming from the east. Now what the hell? Burt wondered. *That clever devil has circled around and come back a different way, and now I'm not sure of anything.* He felt frustration pinch his nostrils as he watched the cruiser approach, trailing a long wake and cleaving the water with two high bow waves. She was a powerful craft; she could probably outrun anything but a U.S. coast-guard cutter.

He watched Rolf ease up to the edge of the lagoon. The entrance was tricker than ever, but conversely less dangerous. The swells were higher, but if you were a good enough boatman to catch the top of a swell, your chances of getting snagged were that much smaller. Burt found himself holding his breath as the launch disappeared in white water; then letting it out as the boat reappeared gleaming wet, in the lagoon. He had to admire Rolf's dexterity with the wheel, and he wondered where he'd learned it.

Burt stayed on the tower and watched Joss meet Rolf at the jetty. While the two talked, Bunny disappeared in the direction of the cabins, walking as though she were very, very tired. The two pigeon hunters had paused in front of the beach club to watch the landing, now, perhaps in response to Rolf's call, they joined Rolf and Joss at the jetty. Burt climbed down from the tower and descended the hill. He reached the beach just as Joss slapped her hands against her hips and left the beach. Rolf gave Burt a mock, half-smiling salute as he approached.

"New fellows for the club, Burt. I offered them a lift to Bequia but they're afraid of the sea."

Ace hunched his shoulders and glared at Burt. "Like I told her, I'll leave. But after that last trip out here, I ain't ready to go again so soon."

"I've gone through rougher water than this," said Rolf, looking like a dashing cinema adventurer with his hair wet and drops of water clinging to his mustache. "In the Strait of Gibraltar, with gunboats chasing me."

"Well, I didn't. When the sea calms down I'll take your offer, if she's still got her mind made up . . ."

And Burt had a strange feeling that both men were playing parts for his benefit . . .

. . . When, from the nearest cabin, came what sounded like a ragged moan. Burt started forward, but Ace was standing in front of him with the gun in the crook of his arm. "Hold it, that's only Charlie. He has nightmares." His smile returned, too broad to be real, and he spoke over his shoulder. "Hoke, go turn Charlie over on his stomach."

Burt felt rage boiling inside him, but forced himself to speak in a quiet voice. "Smith, you act like a damn fool with that gun."

The hairy man raised his brows. "Yeah? You know a lot about guns, bird lover?"

"I know if you don't take it out of my stomach, I'll feed it to you."

Ace eyed Burt curiously. "What did you say your name was?"

"Burt March."

"March. Whaddaya do?"

"I sell insurance. And I'll give you five seconds to move that gun. One, two, three—"

"Smith!" Rolf's voice cracked. "You're not the only one who's armed. Do what he says."

Ace looked surprised, then shrugged and smiled at Burt. "Insurance salesman, huh? The island's full of tough nuts." He slung the gun to his shoulder. "I came here to shoot pigeons, and that's what I'll do, as long as people leave me alone."

He turned and walked up the hill, ostentatiously scanning the sky. Burt turned to Rolf. "I'd thank you, but I think you had your own reasons. You had to let him know I had a gun, didn't you?"

"I figured it would save his life. Or yours." Rolf smiled. "Why so disappointed? Did you want to kill him?"

"I wouldn't have killed him. He was standing too close; it wouldn't have been hard to disarm him."

"Yes, and when he came at you with his bare hands? He looks strong as a gorilla."

"I can defend myself."

Rolf shook his head slowly. "I'm glad I didn't decide to be a cop. You've tied your hands, haven't you? You have to let the other man make the first move."

He turned and started away, but Burt called after him. "Rolf, are those the men you think will kill you?"

Rolf paused and waved up at the peak. "Take a look. You think he's hunting pigeons?"

Burt followed his gaze and watched Ace settle himself on the lookout rock with the gun across his knees. He was looking down, his hard face impassive. Burt was reminded of the guard on a prison farm.

SEVEN

The afternoon sizzled by like a slow fuse. Rolf said something about fouled plugs and began dissecting the innards of his cruiser, managing to get romantically grease-stained in the process. Burt had the chilling thought that he was deliberately putting his boat out of action. Joss sat in a wicker armchair at the corner of the club, scanning the sea through her ancient tripod-telescope.

"O'Ryan should be here if he's coming," she told Burt.

"Does he come when it's rough?"

"Never has, but he might."

Bunny came out into the open without her dark glasses, wearing a halter and short-shorts which lacked a couple of inches of doing the job they were meant to do. She paced the beach like a caged tigress for a half-hour, went for a swim in the lagoon, then emerged to lie on her stomach in the sand. She unfastened her halter strap to leave her back bare. Burt could see two inches of milk-white flesh between the top of her shorts and the faint pinkness of her back. There was an engaging dimple on each side of her lower spine.

Burt wasn't the only one who noticed: Ace sat on the steps of the club flicking bits of coral at the sand crabs who scuttled sideways across the sand. He wasn't watching the crabs; he was watching Bunny through lowered bushy brows, like a fullback about to charge the line. Hoke had taken his place on the tower with the gun across his knees.

Joss left her telescope and walked behind the bar; she stood there glaring in Bunny's direction and sneaking quick gulps of rum. Boris stood beside her, pretending not to notice.

Burt tasted the bile of frustration in his throat. What can you do? he wondered. We're prisoners, but does Joss know it, or Boris and the boys? One of them might make a false step and trigger the violence. Well, he thought, you can't hold them all in the palm of your hand. Best you can do is quarantine them.

He went to Joss and persuaded her that she was tired and sleepy, then he walked her up to her house and left her stretched out on the bed with her glass beside her. He took Coco and Godfrey to the south shore of the island and asked if they'd noticed anything odd about the three new arrivals.

"Big men," said Godfrey.

"They don't wish to fish," said Coco.

"They're gunmen," said Burt. "Professional killers. You boys stay clear of them, hear?"

They nodded gravely.

"We may have to leave the island in a hurry. You boys go around and gather up all the dry wood you can find. Carry the little stuff up the hill in case we need a signal fire. The big stuff you can put right here. When the sea goes down, we'll build a raft."

The two deployed up the slope, scanning the ground, and Burt went to find Jata. She lived in a black shingle structure not more than eight feet square, hidden beneath a dark, brooding manchineel tree. He knocked and announced himself. A bolt slid back, a chain rattled, and Jata's glittering eye appeared at a crack in the door. "Sir, I don't come out 'til bad men leave."

"You're on the stick, Jata. Where's Maudie?"

"She sneakin' round. You see her, tell her come home. I lock her in tonight."

Burt searched the island and tried to look like a nature lover taking a casual walk. His leg ached miserably. Each time he emerged from beneath the trees, he was aware of Hoke watching him from the tower. The longer he walked the more uneasy he became. Mother hen March, he thought wryly; one of your chicks is missing.

He paused to look at cabin four. Could she be in there with Charlie? Surely not of her own free will, in which case she'd be making some noise. The cabin was silent behind the curtained windows. Burt thought of the moan, and of the missing fourth man of the party—

"Sir, you wish to go in?"

Burt whirled and glimpsed the white flash of Maudie's T-shirt inside a clump of bamboo. He looked up and saw that the palm trees which lined the path screened the cabin from the watchtower. He stepped back and watched her crawl from the bamboo.

"You hide well for a big girl," said Burt when she squatted beside him. "What have you been doing?"

"I watch the people pass in the path. You wish to enter one of the cabins? I watch for you."

"No, I was just wondering why one man stays in the cabin all the time."

"I know."

"Why?"

She was gone before he could stop her, then it was too late to call her back without warning the man inside. With frozen nerves he watched her climb the ladder outside the bathroom, her white cotton skirt riding high on her heavy brown thighs. Why had he assumed a sixteen-year-old girl would be clumsy? It was not true in Maudie's case. She moved with the silent efficiency of a burglar, lifting the cover off the water barrel, plunging her hand inside, and drawing out a dripping metal case slightly larger than a cigar box. She replaced the wooden cover on the barrel, climbed down the ladder, and ran across the path. Burt drew her behind the bamboo and took the box. It was surprisingly heavy, with only a hair-line crease revealing where the lid joined the box proper. A combination lock held it shut. It seemed to be made of hard carbon steel; he'd have trouble getting it open even with a cutting torch.

"Who hid it?" he asked.

"Big man who shoot the frigate bird. I see him up on top and ask myself, what he hiding in the water? Later I go see."

Burt shook the box, but it gave no sound. If it held money, it would take huge bills to total the fortune Rolf had mentioned. He doubted that they'd risk putting currency in water. No doubt it would be jewels, perhaps diamonds . . .

"See if you can put it back," he told Maudie. "No, wait—"

He'd heard the screen door slam on the cabin. Through the screening bamboo he watched a man walk around the corner of the cabin, yawning and hitching his suspenders over the harness of a shoulder holster. The coarse brutal cast of his features duplicated those of Hoke, except that his head was topped by a coarse curly mop of brick-red hair. He stood at the foot of the ladder and looked up. Burt held his breath, then released it slowly as the man walked on around the corner. Burt waited for the sound of the screen door. When it didn't come, he told Maudie to see what he was doing.

She left, moving with a silence possible only for one who had spent all her life on the island. She returned a moment later and whispered: "He stand in front smoking."

Burt cursed silently under his breath.

"You wish to hide the box? I know a place they never find."

Burt frowned. There'd be trouble when they found it missing, but maybe that's what he needed. Make something happen, end the suspense, sow discord among the thieves. If one group thought that another group had stolen the loot, and if Burt could keep his own people out of the way . . .

"Let's go," he told Maudie.

She led him over the low ridge between the cistern and the fumaroles, moving with a speed he found difficult to match with his leg hurting and the box under one arm. Beyond the cistern, she dropped to her hands and knees and started down a green tunnel in the tall, thick grass just barely large enough to sneak through. "Goutis make these path," she said over her shoulder. Burt crawled after the bobbing rump with the white skirt drawn tight over it. He was streaming sweat when they emerged on a steep rocky beach. A grove of stunted guava trees hid them from the man in the tower. Ahead of him Maudie moved along a low cliff, leaping from rock to rock with the agility of a mountain goat. Burt followed, planting his feet carefully on the slippery rocks. He saw her disappear through a crack in a cliff; he squeezed through behind her and found himself in a dark, narrow tunnel. Black water swished around his shoes; ahead, the tunnel disappeared into blackness.

"Now we mus' get wet," she said. She seized his hand, and in total innocence raised her dress to her waist and waded in. He felt the lukewarm water climb to his knees, then to his thighs. Her hand pulled him gently upward; his feet found holes in the rock and he climbed until her hand was withdrawn from his. Burt stood on level ground and sniffed musty air. A match flared, and a kerosene lamp sent probing yellow fingers against the gleaming walls of a tiny cave.

"I come here when *Maman* shout at me," she said. "Only you know now, and me."

Her eyes shone in the yellow light. Burt saw two garish, spangled dresses hanging from a jut of rock; below them lay a foam-rubber mattress and a thick woven blanket stenciled with the words: *S.S. Carlotta, New York City.* On a wooden box sat a ceramic ash tray labeled: *The Mermaid, Charlotte Amalie, St. Croix.* Beside the box were four pairs of women's shoes, a spunglass fishing rod, and an empty Haig-and-Haig pinch bottle. On top was a cigar box full of cheap bracelets and earrings, a half-dozen tubes of lipstick, a totally unnecessary home permanent outfit and, oddest of all, a squeeze-bottle of shaving cream. He felt like laughing; she was like a bower bird, lining her secret nest with glittering objects and understanding none of them.

"Now I understand why you learned to move so quietly," he said.

Her eyes grew round. "You don't tell Miss Joss? I take only what people leave about."

Burt picked up a platinum wedding band and read the engraving: *All my love, J.S.* "I'll bet there's been some hell raised," he said. "But I won't tell."

He tossed the ring back and turned to her. "Now listen, Maudie. I'm going to hide this box near here, but I won't say where. If anybody asks you, you can say truthfully you don't know anything about it. Okay? The men who lost it aren't like the others who come here, they'll kill you to get it. Understand?"

She nodded, her eyes wide.

"Okay, now go home. If there's trouble, shooting, you can come back here. Otherwise don't come near the place. Go."

After she'd gone, Burt gouged a loose stone from the wall of the cave, wedged the box iside, then jammed the rock back in place. It was sunset when he stepped onto the pebble beach. Nature seemed to be making a gesture of defiance after a bleak, gray day. The clouds on the horizon opened like a parting curtain and revealed the sun floating like a huge golden pumpkin on the sea. Streamers of rose-purple light arched overhead and draped the entire island in a glowing net. Burt had a brief stirring insight: all human activities were like the rustling of mice in a magnificent mansion; a man's hunger for diamonds was only a futile effort to capture and hold a fragment of the sun. He felt a brief urge to jump in the sea and swim away, leaving all these people to their own sick objectives.

The urge returned as he reached the path and saw Godfrey running toward him on his bandy legs. He felt a creeping fatigue; he knew he was about to be entangled in a net of other people's problems.

"Sir, you remember the guitar strings you give me?"

"Yes. Why'd you stop gathering wood?"

"Everybody wanting to eat, sir. Boris ask Coco and me to help."

Burt felt anger pinch his nostrils; how did you convince these people that there was danger?

"Well, what about your guitar strings?"

"I hang them behind the bar, now they are gone."

"Did you tell Joss?"

He nodded. "She say tell you. She sick in bed."

Lord, now I've become the island's labor counselor. "I'll try to find them later. Now get Coco and get back to gathering wood. Stay away from the club, you hear?"

The boy nodded and shuffled away.

Burt stopped by and looked in on Joss; she was propped up in bed, looking as though she felt every one of her years. She said she'd just been down to the club and wasn't going back. "It's the weather, Burt, my nerves are shot. That woman's down there throwing it around, and there's nothing but hard looks going back and forth. I've had enough nightclub experience to know there's trouble coming. Well, let them tear up the joint, let them kill each other off with those guns they carry. I couldn't care less."

At the club, Burt found Rolf and Bunny seated at one table. Nearby sat Ace Smith and the red-haired man, both looking totally ludicrous in neckties, starched white shirts, and business suits.

"Get your boat running?" asked Burt as he passed Rolf's table.

Rolf nodded curtly and looked down at his right hand. It lay on the table top, clenching and unclenching.

Ace called out with false joviality. "Hey, bird lover. Have a drink with us?"

"No, thanks," said Burt, stopping beside the table. "You two are a little overdressed for a tropical island."

"Habit," said Ace. "We're used to eating with chicks."

Yeah, thought Burt, noting that the suits were heavily padded and thick in the chest. They'd left their big guns in the cabin, but they wouldn't go out unarmed. Those suits undoubtedly concealed the small artillery.

Burt chose a table nearest the bar and sat down to assess the scene. Boris was carrying drinks, his massive dignity unimpaired by the red-headed man's playful belligerence. He kept shouting for drinks, making the kind of noise a man makes when he's afraid of silence. Ace drank quietly, his small dark eyes roving somewhere in the area between Bunny's collarbone and the bodice of her peasant blouse. Rolf seemed preoccupied, unaware that Bunny was meeting Ace's eyes from time to time, and that little electric messages were crackling between them.

The explosion came with the serving of dinner. The red-haired man demanded food; Boris came out and set a plate of canned beef and crackers in front of him.

"What the hell is this, horse meat?"

"No, sir. Bully beef, sir."

"Take it back and get me a steak."

"I'm sorry. There is nothing else."

"Don't tell me we're paying ten bucks a day for this!"

Boris stood like a soldier at attention, his black face frozen in stoicism.

"You hear me? Is this what we get for ten bucks?" The man was shouting, his face as red as his hair.

"Yes, sir."

"Well, take it!" He threw the plate at Boris, who moved just enough to allow the plate to sail past and land harmlessly on the sand outside. The blob of bully beef, however, struck him on the right side of the face. He stood for an instant without moving while the greasy red meat slid down his cheek and became trapped in his goatee. Then he turned and strode behind the bar. Burt heard the sound of sliding metal; he peered over the bar to see Boris draw out a curved, three-foot cutlass. Burt felt the hair prickle on the back of his neck.

"That's no good, Boris. He's got a gun."

Boris looked at Burt, his smeared face wrinkled up as though he were about to cry.

"I kill him, sir. Got to kill him."

"Wait a minute."

As Burt walked toward the redhead's table, he warned himself to keep cool. But he'd been under pressure too long. The anger boiling inside him had to find an escape. He stood beside the redhead's chair and spoke with tense contempt.

"On your feet, carrot-head. The bartender's waiting for your apology."

The man looked up in surprise. "The hell he is. Well, the day you see Charlie Tate apologize to a goddamn spade, you can—"

Burts actions went suddenly out of his control. His foot kicked out and struck the leg of the other's chair. The big man sprawled backward, his mouth wide with surprise. He landed flat on his back and started clawing at his lapel. It seemed to happen in slow motion; Burt was rocking forward on his feet, preparing to launch a kick at the other's wrist, when he heard a faint swish of air beside his head. The fallen man's features convulsed suddenly, then flowed loose like a bowl of mush. His coat fell back and Burt saw a spreading wetness on the starched white shirt. In the center of the stain, like a pin stuck in the heart of a red, red rose, was a knife buried to the hilt.

Burt turned and saw Rolf zipping up his jacket.

"I should've searched you for a knife," said Burt.

"I told you I didn't like guns." Rolf's eyes held a reptilian glitter; his lips were pulled back from his white teeth. Bunny was staring down at the man, breathing so hard that her bosom swelled above her blouse like a pair of inflated balloons. Ace sat in his chair with his eyes narrowed to slits. No expression crossed the mask of his face, but Burt felt it would take very little to make him draw his gun. Boris leaned over the bar in a hypnotic stare. A particle of dried beef flaked off his cheek and fell to the floor. For the second time that day Burt felt he was involved in a play; soon the curtain would close, the redhead would rise and go off-stage, and they would all gather in the dressing room for a drink.

"Hell." He turned to Rolf. "You didn't have to kill him."

"I know. I could have let him shoot you."

"He wouldn't have killed me. I was about to—"

"Kill him yourself?" asked Rolf with a smile.

"Don't kick a dead horse," said Burt. "We've been through that." He turned to Ace, who seemed to have slumped lower in his chair. "You plan to do anything about this?"

Ace gave a shrug which had no effect on his face. He mumbled, "Charlie was hot-tempered. He shouldn't have gone for his gun. He lost the toss and I guess he paid for it." He gazed up at Rolf with a vague appeal in his eyes. Burt thought of a gorilla caught in a trap. "But life goes on, don't it? What happens now?"

Rolf turned to Burt. "What happens, Burt?"

Here it was, on his back again.

"I'll take the body to St. Vincent, turn it over to the authorities. I'll need your boat." He glared at Rolf, challenging him to bring his game into the open. "You'll have to give them a statement."

Rolf nodded. "I know the rules, Sergeant."

"Sergeant!" Ace blinked at Rolf. "You called him Sergeant."

"He's a detective in a jerkwater Florida town," said Rolf. "No jurisdiction here, of course. But somebody has to take over in an emergency." Rolf gazed out over the lagoon, where the Coleman lantern sent its white light across black water and picked out the plunging spray on the rocks. "We can't go until tomorrow."

"Tomorrow early," said Burt, still puzzled by Rolf's cooperation. "I'll also take Joss and the boys, and Jata and Maudie."

Rolf raised his brows. "Evacuating the island, Burt? Declaring martial law?"

"Just getting them out of the line of fire, Rolf. Any objections?"

"No, it's a good idea. See you in the morning."

EIGHT

Burt didn't even consider trying to sleep. After throwing a blanket over the corpse, he sent Boris up to the tower to keep watch, then sat down at a table to guard the body. Joss tiptoed in a half-hour later to get a fresh bottle. Her eyes were bleared with sleep. She gave a small shriek when she saw the body, but calmed down as Burt told her what had happened.

"I'm surprised at myself," she said, slumping into a chair. "I actually feel relieved. I'm not scared about what's going to happen, because it's already happened."

"Maybe," said Burt.

"I just wonder what it'll do to business. Isn't that crass of me?"

"You'll be snowed under, Joss, by the same kind of people who crowd and push and sweat when you carry a corpse out of an apartment, that gape through the windows of smashed trains and tour auto graveyards to see the blood on seat cushions. Pretty slimy types. You won't like them."

She drummed the table absently with her fingers. "Maybe I'll close up. Wouldn't cost much to live if I didn't try to keep up facilities for guests. You could come whenever you want ... and your wife, if you ever stop being too finicky to give a girl a chance."

She rose suddenly and went behind the bar. She lifted out a bottle and shot him an inquiring look. "Something for your nerves, Burt?"

He shook his head, watching her fill a glass.

"That's right, you don't have any." She tipped the glass and drained it as though it were water and she'd just come off the desert. She filled another glass and carried it back to the table with the bottle. Four drinks

94

later she laid her head on her arms and began snoring. Burt sat and listened to the boom of the surf. The light dimmed; he lifted the Coleman lantern off a nail and pumped it full of air. When he finished, he saw three huge gray rats tearing at the blanket which covered the body. He routed them and saw two more peering over the edge of the platform, twitching their whiskers. He stamped his feet and they disappeared. Another approached the body from the kitchen, moving in a humped shuffle. He launched a kick which sent it scurrying, but there were more squeaks and chitters from the thatched roof overhead. He looked up and saw a half-dozen tails hanging down from the rafters. They know, he thought, the yellow-toothed little bastards know death has come to the island. He lifted down the lantern and set it beside the body. Its upward glow filled the club with weird, looming shadows, but it kept the rats away.

Boris came in, sat down on the bench, and laid the long cutlass across his knees.

"Everybody asleep?" asked Burt.

"All cabins dark, sir. But I think nobody sleep in number three."

"Oh?"

"The woman go there, meet the hairy man outside. Kiss-kiss. Go inside. Lights off. One hour ago."

Burt frowned; he couldn't imagine that Bunny would risk Rolf's displeasure by sneaking off on her own. Maybe Rolf had thrown the woman to Ace to keep him quiet. Bunny was nothing if not adaptable.

"Watch the body," said Burt, rising and stretching. "Don't let him bother you."

Boris smiled thinly and touched the cutlass. "I had no fear when he living. Now he is out of it."

Burt sat in the tower. Across the water came the distant sound of a dog barking idiotically, incessantly. Above him the stars sent down a frantic, coruscating brilliance. Below him the surf was a brilliant white snake which held the island in a triple coil, expanding and contracting. He smelled the sea and felt the rainwashed breeze on his face. He perceived tranquility, but didn't feel it. Something evil was slithering over the island; something worse than the rats, because it wore the body of a man.

"Burt, you up there?"

Burt jumped at the nearness of Rolf's voice. How had the man moved up so quietly?

"There's hardly room for two," said Burt.

"What are you doing—" a soft, breathy grunt, and Rolf was over the parapet and kneeling beside him "—watching the stars?"

Burt kept taut despite the friendly sound of Rolf's voice. Only a yard away lay a five-hundred foot drop to the rocks.

Rolf looked up at the stars and drew a deep breath.

"They *are* beautiful tonight, sort of washed by the rain. Orion, Cassiopeia, the pale disc of Andromeda. We're looking out into time, Burt, six billion years into the past. You know how that makes me feel?" He went on without pausing. "It's all a game, isn't it?"

"Sometimes," admitted Burt. "I feel that I'm also involved in the game, which means bound to follow the rules."

"You play by the rules because you don't trust your own nature."

"Does your master know you're out?"

Rolf laughed. "Satan? I wonder if you aren't right," He chuckled softly, obviously pleased. "I came up to talk, Burt. Killing does that; it enlarges me, intensifies my senses." He leaned forward. "Can't you feel the pygmies down below us? Their petty emotions boiling, their fears? Joss lying asleep in the club with her bottle beside her? Thinking of ... what? Strange whirling shapes and curtain-calls she missed and men she didn't kiss. Old Jata with her door nailed shut against Damballa and a dozen other red-eyed beasts; her daughter twitching beside her, fighting those teen-age chemicals with the brain of an eight-year-old ..."

"How about Ace and Bunny?"

Rolf darted him an oblique look. "Sleeping the sleep

of satiety, I suppose." He paused. "I shouldn't be surprised that you know. You have your own spy network, haven't you?"

Burt grunted. "I thought you had her under better control. You disappoint me."

"And you disappoint me for not understanding. Weren't you watching Ace at dinner? Of course you were. Jumpy, scared . . . wanting. There's a close correlation between fear and the sex urge. Look at wartime illegitimacy—"

"So you threw him Bunny."

"He'd have grabbed her anyway. Islands have that effect on people, Burt. You tend to think of direct solutions to your problems. Look at Joss. She wants a man, she makes a blunt physical appeal. If that doesn't work, she offers booze, free meals, a pad. She uses what she has. Ace there. He's a man of violence. Lives by the gun. He wants a woman, he'll take her. A man gets in his way, kill him. Simple and very effective . . . on an island. Who'd have defended her? You, March?"

Burt sighed; he was tired of Rolf.

"It's all hypothetical."

"Sure, because I didn't allow it to become real. Now Ace will awaken in a tranquil state, a little less afraid—"

"What's he afraid of?"

"Of you, now that he knows you're a cop. You represent society, and in his eyes that makes you bigger than you really are." He laughed softly. "It also makes him more dangerous to you, since Ace destroys what he fears."

"I suppose everyone tries—"

"I don't."

"What are you afraid of?"

"Everything." Rolf laughed without humor. "And therefore nothing. Hostility surrounds me; there is nowhere to run. And so I don't run."

"And your wife? What's she afraid of?"

Rolf looked narrowly at Burt. "You're very interested in Tracy. I wonder why." When Burt said nothing,

Rolf went on in a musing manner. "Actually, I don't know what Tracy's afraid of. Something, certainly, but I can't pin it down. I've never been able to reach her, which is why—" He broke off, then went on in an abrupt, businesslike voice: "I have to know if you're with me. Tonight."

Burt felt his stomach tighten; he'd been expecting the question. "If I say yes, how will you be sure of me?"

"'You'll be given a job to do. Kill Ace."

Burt caught his breath then let it out slowly. "Why?"

Rolf ignored the question. "You could do it your way. Get him cornered, box him in, taunt him until he makes a try at you. Then you cool him. Self-defense; I've seen other cops do it." He laughed shortly. "You can't lose, March. Neither of us can."

Burt forced down his anger; he wanted to learn more. "I want to know the rest of the deal. All of it."

Rolf was silent a moment, then sighed. "All right. Briefly. It started with a *mordida*, a bribe. A cabinet minister in a small Latin-American country—you'll excuse me if I slip the specifics—was getting rich on pay-offs from foreign firms who wanted to do business there. I paid—several times—and I got to know him. He lived austerely by *politico* standards, only one mistress, one Cadillac, one mansion. What did he do with the money? I was curious, and I told Bunny to find out. But then came the revolution, the insurgents won concessions from the government, among which was the purge of the corrupt minister. He made a run for it and got himself cut down by machine-gun fire. Bunny had learned only one thing; the country's ambassador to the U.S. was his closest friend. The ambassador also got caught in the purge, but he claimed asylum and holed up in a beach villa on Florida's east coast. Bunny and I returned to the States, where she met the ambassador and—in the direct manner of hers—quickly insinuated herself into his favor. It took her a year to learn his secret; not an easy year, either. The man was a greasy troll with the manners of a swamp rat. The minister had been converting his loot into diamonds and sending them to the ambassador in sealed diplomatic pouches. The diamonds were now in a strongbox locked in a safe in the villa. I had already begun building my organization. You may appreciate the way it was done, March. I went to a sleazy part of Miami, pretended to be rolling drunk, and flashed a few big bills. As I expected, three men followed and cornered me in a doorway. I'll never forget the surprised look on their faces when they realized that their victim had become an assailant. You see, I too had learned that one may kill legally in self-defense. I have left more than one unidentified body in alleys for the police to find. I killed one, leaving Hoke and Charlie alive. They were frightened, and since fear is the seed of loyalty—perhaps the only way to insure the loyalty of such men—I decided to use them. They led me to Ace Smith, who had just finished an eight-year sentence for armed robbery. I wanted to make the theft look like an ordinary burglary, you see, so that they'd never connect it with me. And to shorten the tale, I now have nearly a million dollars in diamonds."

"Converting ice to cash is no easy trick."

Rolf sighed. "March, this is my magnum opus, my greatest creation. Nothing is left to chance. Tomorrow night I shall meet two men from the ambassador's country. They will give me two hundred and fifty thousand dollars in U.S. currency. I return the loot to its rightful owners—it's all arranged."

Burt grunted. "Even the disappearance of Ace and Hoke."

"Of course. That's why I chose this island. They expect the split to be made here. It will be, but only between you and me."

"What about Bunny and your wife?"

Rolf made an impatient gesture with his hand. "You've asked enough questions, Burt. Are you with me—or against me?"

Burt suddenly felt the weight of two sleepless nights. He shook his head tiredly. "Rolf, you didn't read me well—"

"I read you. We could have made a natural team, if only you'd lost a few illusions." He rose to his feet. "I'd like to give you more time, but you're beginning to distract me . . ."

Burt was startled to see the glint of the gun appear suddenly in Rolf's hand. Irrelevantly, he said, "I thought you didn't like guns."

"I don't. They're too impersonal. But sometimes there's no choice."

Burt felt his stomach cringe; the gun was pointed directly at his belt buckle. He talked quickly to gain time, watching for an opening.

"You have a choice, Rolf. Killing the man in the club can be called self-defense; stealing the ambassador's jewels could probably be fixed, since they were obtained illegally in the first place. No need to add murder to your crimes."

Rolf laughed softly. "Burt, I was saving the news until you were committed to my side. Bunny killed the ambassador as she left his bed and board. There's a nationwide alarm from the FBI on down. One more murder won't matter—"

A scream split the night air. Burt lunged and jammed his shoulder into Rolf's stomach. The gun exploded and spat a yellow tongue of flame which burned Burt's cheek. Rolf fell back against the ledge; the ancient mortar crumbled. Rolf teetered a moment, then disappeared.

The scream came again and again; the senseless ululation of a woman in terror. Burt left the tower and ran downhill, falling once in a headlong dive, peeling the skin off one forearm. He reached the club as the screaming changed to a low, sobbing moan. He saw Joss staring at the bench. There sat Boris with his whispy goatee on his chest, his eyes half-closed, staring at the floor with a morose, pensive expression. But he was neither morose nor pensive; he was dead. The cutlass had been swung with tremendous force, lopping off his right arm at the elbow and penetrating three inches into his side. The redhead's body was gone.

"Burt . . . Oh, Burt. Look, I woke up and I. . . I. . ."

She was suddenly sick on the floor. Burt saw Godfrey and Coco standing white-eyed beside the bar.

"Coco, you and Godfrey run up the hill and start a signal fire. We'll need—"

"Hold it. Nobody leaves."

Burt turned to see Ace holding the over-under gun. Hoke stood beside him with the shotgun resting on the railing.

"Let's have your gun, bird lover. Lay it on the floor and step back." When Burt hesitated, Ace said: "These shotguns throw a helluva shower of lead. If we didn't get you we'd get the lady or one of the niggers."

Burt did as he was ordered; Ace came forward, picked up the gun, and shoved it in his pocket. He jerked his head toward the body of Boris. "His own fault he got it. I thought I hit him hard enough to lay him out for a hour. But he woke up and jumped me." Ace touched a purple swelling above his eye. "I had to kill him. I was told to get rid of the body without being seen."

"Rolf's orders?" asked Burt.

Ace gave a twisted smile. "Did you think Bunny was running it?" He stepped back to the railing. "All right. Everybody on the floor, flat on your backs with hands above your head."

Everyone obeyed except Burt. Ace jabbed the gun in his direction. "You too, birdman. You ain't privileged."

"How do you know I'm not?"

Ace glared at Burt, then called over his shoulder. "Hoke, go find the boss. I wanta know what he wants done with this character."

"Kill him," said a voice from the darkness.

A second later Rolf stepped into the club. His clothes were torn. Blood ran from a long cut across his forehead and dripped from dirt-crusted eyebrows. He was holding his right forearm in his left hand, and Burt saw that his wrist was impossibly twisted. His mouth was open, his lips drawn back so tightly that a white rim showed around them. Each perfect white tooth had an outline of blood, and his eyes held a remote, glassy look. It was obvious that Rolf had lost the hard glaze of self-control.

"Did you hear me? I said *kill him!*"

Ace lifted the rifle. "Sure. You mean, right here?"

"Didn't I say——? No, wait." Rolf strode to the body of Boris and jerked out the cutlass. It made a soft sucking sound. Joss moaned and closed her eyes.

Burt backed away as Rolf approached. Why didn't those idiots run, Coco and Godfrey? No, they had to lie and gape like a pair of fools and Joss was out cold—

His back struck the bar just as Rolf swung the cutlass high over his head with his left hand. Burt leaped aside and the cutlass buried itself in the mahogany rim. Rolf tugged at it frantically with one hand. He seemed crazed with pain, half-sobbing the words: "——I gave you a chance, I tried to be friends, I asked you to come in with me——"

"Rolf, listen——"

He raised the cutlass again. "——you tried to kill me, broke my arm——"

"——and hid your diamonds!"

Crash! The cutlass gouged a two-foot splinter from the bar. Ace ran up and seized Rolf's arm. "Boss, listen! Listen to what he said!"

Rolf shook free, started to swing again, then stopped and gazed around the room as though he'd just awakened from a long sleep. He blinked at Ace. "What?"

"He said something about the diamonds."

Rolf looked at Burt. He was breathing heavily, but the glaze was gone from his eyes. "You found them?"

"And stashed them again. If you kill me you'll never find them."

"Hoke, go check the barrel." The big man left, and Rolf tossed the cutlass to the floor. "Cover these people, Ace, especially him." He walked over to Godfrey and jammed a toe in his ribs. "Get me a pan of water and a cloth."

The boy scrambled toward the kitchen. Rolf slumped in a chair and passed a shaky hand across his forehead. He moved his wrist slightly and went pale.

"Broken, I think. I'll have Bunny splint it."

Godfrey brought the water and stood holding it with hands which trembled so violently that the water rippled and splashed. Burt felt dismay as he watched Rolf calmly wash the blood and dirt from his face. The others had missed their chance; now Rolf was once again in control of himself.

"I'm glad you stopped me, March. That isn't my scene, to kill in anger. I must have lost my head while I was wedged in that crevice below the tower." He rinsed out the cloth and watched the water turn a dirty brown. "I like to talk to a man, learn how his mind works, learn some of his background. Then when I kill, I am he. I am both victim and killer. Maybe I have a drive toward suicide, since I tend to identify with the victim. Fortunately my survival drive is stronger—"

Hoke clomped onto the plank floor of the club. "The box ain't there."

Rolf closed his eyes, then looked at Burt. "You're spoiling my time-table, and this makes me angry. Better tell where it is."

"I'll mail you a postcard from the States."

Rolf smiled thinly. "That earns you a few more hours of life, Burt. But you won't enjoy them." He waved at Ace. "Take him to cabin two. Then wake up Bunny. She'll enjoy this bit."

Burt walked ahead, listening to the footsteps of Ace and Rolf behind him. They were away from the club now, entering the deep velvet shadow beneath the palms. Burt took a deep breath, then took off in a low crouch. He heard Rolf shouting behind him: "Don't shoot! Don't shoot!" He veered off into the low bush between the cabins, saw a white shape loom in front of him. He tried to sheer off, but his weak leg buckled and he crashed against the figure. He heard Bunny's high squeal of surprise, then they were both on the ground and Burt was entangled in perfumed limbs, trying to fight free of her beach coat. Something struck him behind the ear, so heavy and solid that he knew, in his last moment of awareness, that he'd been clubbed by a shotgun butt.

NINE

"Take off his shirt, Bunny."

Rolf's voice dipped into the well of unconsciousness and drew Burt upward. He felt fingers clutching at his shirt like a tiny trembling animal. He caught the aroma of perfume and another heavy, musty odor. His chest was laid bare and caressed by the quick moist breath of the woman. Her fingertips left damp tingling tracks on his flesh and he could smell the high electric tang of her sweat. She was trembling, excited at this approaching opportunity to mortify a man's flesh. Her nails raked his shoulders needlessly as she pulled the shirt from beneath him; he heard the voiced exhalation from her nostrils and felt his stomach harden.

"I think," said Rolf musingly, "that I will let Ace begin."

"But he ain't awake."

"He'll wake up when you begin."

Still Burt kept his eyes closed. A spot of warmth touched his stomach, then pain gouged his nerves and ripped a blazing path to his heart. His eyes flew open; he saw Ace with sweat beading his forehead, bending over him with a lighted cigarette. Bunny knelt on the other side, her lips slightly open. She was bent forward at the waist, pressing her palms to her stomach as though in pain. Rolf sat in a chair and looked down at Burt through half-closed lids. His taped wrist hung from a sling around his neck.

"What did you do with her?" asked Burt.

Rolf raised his brows. "Typical cop. With his first breath, lying flat on his back, he begins the interrogation." He paused. "Do with whom?"

"With your wife."

"You've got a problem, haven't you, Burt? Can't you get my wife off your mind? Okay, let's trade information. I'll tell you where she is, and you tell me where the diamonds are."

Burt shook his head, and Rolf waved his hand at Ace. "Go on. Who told you to stop?"

Again came the fiery jolt of pain, and it took all Burt's energy to keep from crying out. He sent out the tendrils of his thought, gathered up a thousand red-hot needles of pain and drew them up into his brain. He compressed them into a ball and probed it, gauged it, rolled it around, felt it loosen up and flow through his mind with a syrupy sweetness. His fingertips went hot and tingling, as though they were shooting off electricity. The room rippled in the yellow lamplight, then resolved itself into a pattern of glowing lines. The lines dissolved and flowed into a redness so brilliant it hurt his brain; the redness became purple, then green, blue and yellow, as though a series of colored silk veils were being drawn across his eyes. He felt himself sinking into a sweet, warm bath. He was a mind and no more; his body was cold unfeeling clay.

Rolf's voice reached down again:

"I envy you, Burt. I don't fear death, but pain drives me insane. How can you ignore it?"

Burt fought to avoid returning, but the act of fighting defeated him. His chest felt as though a thousand burning splinters were stuck into it. The concrete floor beneath his bare back was slick and cold with his sweat.

"You don't . . . ignore it," he gasped. "You . . . change it."

"Interesting," Rolf mused. "Hold on a second, Ace. I've got an idea. Bunny, go get that overgrown adolescent, the daughter of the cleaning woman."

Burt tried to sit up, but his hands were bound above his head and anchored to something immovable. His feet were stretched wide apart and tied to the bedposts. He was trussed up like Gulliver in Lilliput. He lay back amid a fresh outpouring of sweat.

"What . . . do you want with her?"

Rolf smiled at him. "Obviously pain isn't your weakness. But you have another vulnerable point; you're emotionally hung up with other people." Rolf laughed. "That's a weakness I don't have. Go on, Bunny."

The woman sighed and rose from her knees. "You've hardly started with him."

"He won't talk, Bunny. Keeping quiet is his life insurance."

"Can't Ace go?"

"Go, dammit! You won't miss anything."

When the door closed behind her, Rolf waved to Ace. "Light another cigarette."

Ace frowned. "I don't get it. You said—"

"I said he wouldn't talk. From March I want something else."

"This is crazy," grumbled Ace as he lit a new cigarette off the old one. "What else can you get out of him?"

"He knows. Don't you, Burt?"

The pain came again, and through a mist of shifting colors, Burt thought: Sure I know. You want to hear me yell and plead. But when I do you'll lose interest in me; you'll be disappointed because another person had turned out to be weak and controllable. And you'll go on looking until you find a man who's stronger than you, and you'll say to him what you've been saying to everybody else. Kill me if you can. And you'll be relieved as hell when it finally happens. . .

The pain was gone, and Burt heard Rolf repeating his question. "You know what I want, Burt?"

Burt said, "You want to make me mad."

"Oh, very good, And why?"

"So . . . so I'll try to kill you." He tugged at the ropes. "Turn me loose and I'll give you a show."

"Not yet, March. You'd mark me, and I have to meet some people tonight. After that . . . there's nothing I enjoy more than a fight to the death."

Burt curled his lip. "You and a lot of other people.

As long as there's some guarantee it won't be your death."

"I can guarantee that myself," said Rolf.

"You ... you're disgusting, Rolf. You strip yourself of ten thousand years' civilization and call yourself a higher being. You're a throwback; your only advantage is that other people are civilized. In a primitive society the tribe would've stoned you to death."

"Or made me king," said Rolf quietly. "Let's leave off the cigarettes, Ace. The smell of burning flesh is beginning to annoy me."

Ace sat back on his haunches. "I watched him in the club while I waited to snatch Charlie's body. Rats drive him nuts."

"Do they?" Rolf eyed Burt a moment, then shook his head. "No, it would require too much apparatus; a live, starving rat and a metal box. Besides, the idea of using animals to torture men offends me somehow. Only man has earned that privilege—"

A scream of pain cut him off. Burt stiffened, then realized it was a man's voice. The scream came again; faded to a low sobbing moan. Rolf looked at Ace and jerked his head toward the door. "Get him quiet."

After Ace had gone, Burt said, "Charlie's nightmare is still around, it seems."

Rolf frowned. "Another hitch in the plan, I'm afraid. We had a young man driving the car. He caught a bullet from one of the ambassador's bodyguards."

Ace came in panting. "He's out of his head, boss. I found him outside; he didn't know he was on an island. He was gonna give himself up and get a doctor to look at him." Ace shrugged. "He pulled the bandage off and got the blood going again. I don't think he'll make it through the day."

Rolf chewed his lip a moment, then stood up. "Stay with March. I'll see if I can help the kid."

Ace sat on the bed and smoked in short, nervous puffs. Burt watched him, reflecting that Bunny had been gone a long time. He hoped Maudie had followed orders and gone to the cave.

Ace got up and walked to the window. He stared out at the blackness.

"Worried about the murder rap, Ace?"

Ace whirled. "Why should I be? Bunny—"

"Sure, she killed the ambassador. But if you're caught, she'll say it was you, and you'll burn. Nobody believes an ex-con."

"Nobody's gonna get caught. Rolf is smart."

"Smart, yes, but he's not normal, Ace. He doesn't figure profit and loss like you and me. He's got his own balance sheet, and you don't know what's on it."

"I know there's two hundred and fifty grand on it. That's enough."

"Maybe that's what Charlie thought, too. He didn't expect a knife in the chest."

"Ahh, shut up." Ace turned back to the window, showing Burt his massive back.

"Why did you think Rolf picked this island to make the split? One by one he'll cut down the percentages. First Charlie, then Hoke or the kid there—"

Ace whirled, his face twisted. "Shut up! I told you—"

Bunny opened the door and looked around. "Where's Rolf?"

"With the kid. What about the girl?"

"Couldn't find her. The old lady said she took off during the excitement. She wouldn't unbar the door, but I peeked in and saw she was alone. I'll go tell Rolf—"

"Stay with gabby. I'll go."

Bunny sat on the bed and lit a cigarette. After a minute she stood up and nudged Burt's arm with a slippered foot. "Want a drag, baby?"

Burt gazed up the twin white columns of her legs, past the short revealing beach coat, and saw the teasing half-smile on her face. "No, thanks."

"Come on, settle your nerves." She squatted down and brought the cigarette toward his mouth. At the last minute she reversed it and jammed the glowing tip between his lips. Burt felt the lash of pain and spat out the burning sparks.

"You hate all men, don't you, Bunny? Is that why you killed the ambassador?"

"Him! I killed him because he was a pig." She moved out of sight behind his head. "If you're curious, I'll tell you how it happened. Ace and the boys were coming in at ten, see? I was supposed to keep the old guy busy. At nine-fifty he was watching TV, and I came up behind him like this." Burt felt her fingers stroking his hair. "I rubbed his greasy old bald head, I kissed him like this—" moist lips touched Burt's forehead "—then I did this—" Burt shivered as she blew in his ear "—then this—" Burt stiffened at the touch of cold metal against his temple. "And I went . . . BANG!"

Burt jumped. Bunny threw herself on the bed and whooped with laughter.

"You're as crazy as Rolf," he said.

She sat up and brushed the hair from her eyes. "Sure. That's why we make a good team."

"I've seen your type before, Bunny. You hang yourself up with a destructive man knowing damn well that he'll wind up destroying you, too. What motivates you? You want to die?"

She opened her mouth to answer, but Ace came in and slumped down on the bed. His face was greenish-white. "Jesus!" He shook his head slowly. "I went over there." He swallowed. "Rolf is talking to the kid like a father. Telling him everything's gonna be all right, that he's gonna take care of him. And all the time he's got this little thin wire, running it through his fingers, and . . . you know what he's gonna do?" Apparently Ace had his limits.

Burt felt his stomach twist. When had Godfrey's guitar strings disappeared? Yesterday afternoon. Then Rolf had planned something like this. . .

Bunny jumped up and started toward the door. Ace caught her arm and threw her across the bed. "He doesn't want you."

Bunny bounced up, her eyes blazing. "Don't get any macho ideas from last night. I take orders from only one man."

Ace shrugged. "So go over. But he'll throw you out. He said he wanted to be alone."

Bunny sighed and lay back on the bed. She looked at the ceiling and sighed. "Men," she breathed in disgust.

Minutes passed. Ace jumped up and paced the room. He jammed his fist into his palm. "I don't understand the guy. Why does he drag it out?"

"I told you why," said Burt.

Ace took a step toward him. "I warned you, fuzz—"

He stopped as the door opened. Rolf walked in with a light step, his eyes bright. He pointed a finger at Ace and jerked his thumb toward the door. "Weight him down and put him in the launch with Charlie. I'll dump them both at the same time."

Ace merely stared, and Rolf added: "If you see Hoke, tell him the kid died from loss of blood. He would've anyway."

Ace nodded and went out, walking like a somnambulist. Rolf lowered himself into a chair and closed his eyes; he seemed calm and sated, like a lion who has just devoured a heavy meal.

"The girl is obviously hiding out," he mused. "She grew up on the island, she could stay hidden for hours. I could bring in one of the others, but that would take time. I've got to leave here in an hour." He stood up and walked to the window. "Those manchineel trees; I've heard that their sap does violent things to a man's eyesight."

Burt had an idea; he moaned softly. "You ... wouldn't blind a man."

Rolf looked down at him and scratched his chin. "I wonder if I've found another weakness."

"Going blind is a hard knock for a detective," said Bunny.

"Hmmm. Yes." Rolf reached inside his shirt and

pulled out a knife. He held it out to Bunny, hilt first. "You'll have to slash the bark to get it."

Bunny went out with a flash light and returned five minutes later with a medicine bottle full of milky fluid. They knelt beside Burt, one on each side.

"Hold his left eye open," said Rolf.

Cool fingers pried his twitching lids apart; Burt looked up into an emerald green eye with an iris splintered with gray. Her pupil was half-dilated, but he knew she wasn't drugged. She didn't need drugs. . .

Rolf held a medicine dropper above his eye. Burt stared at the glistening globule which appeared at its tip, saw it tremble and fall—

Ahhhh!

There was no need to pretend pain. It burned like acid. Burt thought of the old island doctor who'd told him the blindness was temporary, not much worse than poison ivy; he writhed and struggled and recalled that the old doc had been drunk when he said it.

"A last chance, Burt. You can save one eye." Rolf paused, then: "Okay, Bunny. Hold it, there. . ."

The pain was worse this time, double. Burt squeezed his eyes shut and stared into a fiery redness like the pit of a volcano. Molten rock spurted up and lashed his brain. Ah, but something else was down there, cool and black. He groped downward with all his being, entered the blackness. *Peace.* He curled up and went to sleep.

TEN

He awoke in terror. For an instant he thought he really was blind; there was nothing but blackness outside his eyes; it stopped his vision not in front of his eyes but at their surfaces, as though his eyeballs had been painted black. Then he made out the details of the window; just a paler shade of black against the total darkness of the room. He was puzzled. There should have been a sunrise. Then he heard the soft susurration on the thatched roof. It was raining; a heavy, windless rain, as though the clouds were not releasing moisture but rather leaking.

He lay still for a moment trying to sum up the situation. He was still tied. Maudie, presumably, hidden. Boris dead. Jata, locked in. Joss, Coco and Godfrey, totally harmless. He hoped Rolf realized that. Unfortunately, he was a psychopathic killer and capable of killing everybody on the island.

He heard soft breathing above him; occasionally there came a rustle of bedclothes and a soft high moan. Female. He was in the keeping of Bunny, and Bunny was a restless sleeper.

He waited until the wind rattled the palm leaves outside, then he tested his bonds. Tight. His hands were tied to some protuberance on the wall. He moved them and found a mortar seam jutting out between the stones. He rubbed the rope against it and the concrete crumbled damply. Damn Joss for using lousy cement. . . .

He settled back and breathed heavily through his open mouth. He wished he'd been left with Ace instead of Bunny. There was no way to reach the woman.

Something tickled his wrists, and he felt a shooting

pain in his hand. A rat, hell. Lie still:oh, if I only had something to put on my ropes so the rat would chew them. . . .

This is the rat that gnawed the rope.

But no, he's moving up, pitter-patter of little feet heavy weight on chest, he smells the blood from those burns . . .

No!

It was more than he could take; with a thrusting twist of his body he rolled over, spilling the rat on the floor. It scurried away, and from above him came the crackle of the coconut straw mattress. Her voice came sharp and clear without a semblance of sleepiness:

"Fuzz, you awake?"

Burt said nothing.

Patter of bare feet, scrape of a match, tinkle of lamp chimney. Yellow light filled the room. Careful not to blink, Burt stared at the ceiling. He heard the whisper of her bare feet, saw her face appear only inches from his. Her hair was a black, tousled cloud.

"You're awake, sure. You're really blind, are you? Rolf thought you might fake it."

Burt tightened his lips and kept staring upward. The strain made his eyes water.

"You crying, Burt? No, you wouldn't cry, would you? What have you been doing?"

"Counting sheep, what else?"

She laughed without humor. "Can you count what you can't see?" She tugged at his bonds with a skillful hand, then rose to her feet. "You should've talked sooner. You wouldn't have had to spend your last hours as a blind man."

She picked up the lamp and walked toward the bathroom. From the corner of his eyes, Burt saw the curved outline of her body silhouetted by the lamp she carried before her. Her black, ankle-length gown flowed around her like smoke.

The door closed, leaving the room in half-darkness. Burt closed his eyes and felt the tears course down his temples, into his ears. He heard the gurgle of the chain-flush toilet, then the sputter of the shower. Outside the day grew lighter.

The bathroom door opened. Burt turned his head back toward the ceiling. He was aware of the woman walking toward him on silent bare feet. She moved in a slow, stagy, hip-rolling fashion, shrugging the gown off her shoulders and catching it behind her. A moment later she stood over him, filling his vision with the twin hemispheres of her breasts bisected by the gentler curve of her stomach. She bent down, and he smelled the soap-washed odor of her skin. He felt her hand searching intimately.

She rose with an abrupt snort. "Man, you *are* blind. Blind as a bat."

She walked away and Burt heard her rummaging in her suitcase.

She appeared again in his field of vision, laid her clothing out on the bed, and began dressing. Without looking at her directly, Burt noted the difference in the way a woman dresses in the presence of a man, and the way she does it when she's unaware of being watched. There was no languor of movement; buttons and zippers were no longer keys which could open windows into a mysterious world, but only garment fastenings. It was a matter-of-fact operation, totally devoid of erotic ritual, like harnessing a horse or setting a table. Her voice filled the spaces between the swish and rustle of her clothing. She would accompany Rolf to meet the men in Caracas, she said. Rolf wanted her along because she knew the language better than he did. She talked to Burt with a vague condescension, as though she had already come to regard him as less than a man. Burt decided that it would be worth all the pain in his eyes, if it only made her careless. . . .

"Where is Rolf now?" he asked.

"He went to Petit—" She caught herself. "He went to give his wife her . . . uh, food for the day. He's picking me up on his way back. Then we'll . . ."

Burt barely heard the rest of it. Petit, he thought, Petit Martinque, Petit Baliceaux, Petit Mustique, Petit

Cannouan, Petit St. Vincent, Petit this and that. Even the Tobago Cays had three islands with such a prefix; Petit Rameau, Petit Bateau, and Petit Tabac. One of those remote clods, he decided, but which one?

He turned his attention to the woman. Dressed now in a white blouse, smoke-blue skirt and matching shoes, she sat on the bed and peered into a hand-mirror propped against the lamp. Her words became slurred as she applied lipstick:

". . . spend two days without me, Baby, but don't break up. I'll be back. Meantime you'll be tied up here in the dark like a little rabbit. No food, no water. Don't try to untie yourself because Hoke or Ace will be outside. They can't come in because I'm padlocking the door and taking the key. Don't bother to yell because they won't answer. Rolf calls it the black hole treatment; you're supposed to gabble like a turkey when you come out. I don't know, personally; I did two years in a reformatory because of guys like you and we went through things just about as bad. But maybe Rolf knows what he's doing . . ."

Rolf did know what he was doing, thought Burt; so had the Chinese Reds, the Japanese and the wardens of Devil's Island. They'd learned that you totally destroy a man's will when you bury him alive.

He watched her reach into her purse and take out a tiny black cylinder not more than a half-inch long. She spread a handkerchief on the table, unscrewed the cylinder, and took out an object which glistened like a drop of water on her right index finger. With her left hand she spread the lids of her right eye and touched the finger to it. Her eyelids fluttered rapidly. She clenched her fists and beat them gently against the table.

"Oh, brother, I know how you felt when Rolf dropped that sap in your eyes. These lenses are a bitch at first, like running around with a cinder in your eye." She pulled out a tissue and blew her nose, then bent to insert the other lens. "But I can take it another week."

"Oh, is that when you drop the masquerade?"

"That's when they stop hurting." She gave a laugh

which ended in a sniffle. "Man, you live in a dream world. This is no masquerade, this is for real. Bunny DeVore is dead; I'm Tracy Keener for the rest of my life."

Burt felt his lips go dry. "And the real one? She dies, I suppose."

"You've got the scene, Baby." Bunny closed her purse, got up and went into the bathroom. Her voice floated back through the open door. "It's been a drag running out to . . . to that island every day, practicing how she moves, how she walks and talks. Rolf's a real perfectionist. What if we meet some of our old friends, he says. Personally, I don't intend to give them the time of day, I'll be in and out of Capri, Monaco, Hawaii, and anyway there's my height. But Rolf says a woman's height is expected to fluctuate according to what shoes she's wearing and—"

"When?" asked Burt.

"When what? Oh, her. Just as soon as we get back. I've got her down cold."

Cold. The word echoed in his mind.

Bunny returned with the two-piece plastic shower curtain. She wrapped it repeatedly around his wrists and ankles, making a separate knot with each loop. Burt wondered where she'd become so skilled at tying a prisoner.

She stiffened at the sound of the launch. "There's Rolf. So long, Baby."

She bent over him, her hair brushing his cheek. Her lips touched his with brief, surprising tenderness. Her lipstick tasted of mint. She raised her head and he saw her eyes glistening. "That's so you'll remember me. And . . . this!"

He saw her arm move, but he forced himself not to flinch. Just before the hand struck his face, it curved into five bright red claws which tore furrows from his ear to his nose. Then she was gone.

Time became a succession of half-heard sounds: The heavy clump of Hoke's feet, Ace's softer tread, the scratch of a match and the whisper of rain on palm leaves. The rain ended; the sun came out and converted all moisture into steam. The walls of the unventilated room became beaded with moisture; breathing was like trying to inhale warm, damp cotton. A rust-colored, eight-inch centipede crawled onto Burt's right leg, nosed around his trouser cuff while Burt held his breath, then dropped off and disappeared through a crack in the wall.

Burt felt a tingle of excitement when he heard Ace and Hoke in mumbled conversation on the porch veranda; perhaps the seed had sprouted and borne fruit. He was certain when he heard the splintering crack of wood and the protesting screech of metal. The door crashed open and Ace walked in.

"You wanta tell us where the diamonds are?"

"What do I get out of it?"

"You live. We're getting out of here before Rolf comes back."

"How?"

"That's our problem." He snapped his fingers, and his voice showed the strain of his decision. "C'mon. Make up your mind."

"I'll show you," said Burt. "I can't tell you."

They untied him and led him outside. Burt forced himself not to blink, though the light was blinding after the darkness of the room.

"You'll have to lead me," he said. "It's near the fumaroles."

"What's that?"

"Where the water shoots up from the ground."

"Yeah, this way." Ace caught the protruding end of his belt and pulled him roughly through the tangle of vines around the cabin. "Okay. We're on the path now." Burt found it easier to fake blindness if he stared straight ahead with his eyes unfocused. He bumped once into a palm tree and another time sprawled forward with his feet tangled in railroad vines. Hoke guffawed behind him; this was the kind of humor he could understand.

Short, salt-crusted grass crunched beneath his feet.

He let himself be pulled along and felt the strength flow back into his aching muscles. He sensed Hoke behind him with the shotgun ready. He knew his life would be measured in minutes if he showed them the diamonds; killing him would be a reflex action not worth debating.

"Okay," said Ace. "Where is it?"

Burt stood two yards from the ten-foot cliff and felt the spray cooling his face. He tried to remember exactly where he and Coco had found a half-submerged cavern two years ago. Giant langouste liked to hole up there during the day, and they had taken out dozens.

He dropped to his hands and knees. "There's a hole here somewhere."

"Here's one!" shouted Hoke.

"Okay, stick your hand in. It's out of sight under the edge."

Hoke laid his gun on the grass beside him and plunged his arm in up to the elbow. Ace watched him, his attention off Burt for an instant. Burt took two running steps and dived off the cliff. He struck the hissing water and clawed for the bottom. The water was clouded with foam and sand particles. He groped along the cliff, fighting against the water which tried to thrust him to the surface. He found a hole and pulled himself inside. He swam into darkness, his lungs bursting, aware that he could be entering a blind pocket. Above him was solid rock. He visualized himself trapped beyond the point of no return, drowning with his head pressed against the roof of the cavern. Then his hand groped into air. He surfaced and filled his lungs with great gulps. He found a narrow shelf where he could stand with his head above water, and began the long wait. No sound reached him except the gurgle of water and the hiss of air. There was no light; no measure of time except the steady rise and fall of the waterline on his chest and the changing pressure on his eardrums. After a time even that became unconscious, like the rhythmic beat of his heart.

It could have been two hours or three when he detected a faint glow coming through the water from the entrance to the pocket. He watched, his mind suspended, until the glow faded and disappeared. Night-time now. He couldn't be sure that someone wasn't waiting at the edge of the cliff, but there was no way to make sure. He dived down and pulled himself blindly through the tunnel. He felt the force of the surf and came to the surface. The gibbous moon in the east seemed brilliant as day after the darkness. The black silhouette of the cliff was unmarred by any manlike shape. The sea seemed unusually calm, and there was no wind. He moved northward along the cliff, swimming silently without raising his arms from the water. He emerged on the pebble beach, found the crevice, and groped toward Maudie's cave. He saw the yellow glow of lamplight before he entered.

Maudie lay curled up on the foam-rubber cushion, dressed in a green silk dress with red chiffon bordering the neckline. Burt knelt down and shook her plump shoulder. Her eyelids fluttered, then opened wide. She sat up, her features swollen from sleep, then pressed her palms against her forehead and brushed the hair off her temples.

"You don't seem glad to see me." said Burt.

"Yes, but . . ." She indicated her dress and sighed. "I wish to change before you come."

He frowned. "You expected me?"

She nodded. "They say you walk blind into the sea and drown, but I know—"

"You've been out?"

"Yes, but nobody see. Godfrey meet me and give me these." She pointed at a case of bully beef and several cans of ship's biscuits. "They watch the others, but they never see me."

The sight of the food made Burt aware of the growling complaint of his stomach. He began to open a can of the bully beef but Maudie jumped up. "You sit, sir. I will serve you."

Another time Burt might have been amused to see

this young girl playing hostess in a gaudy dress too small for her burgeoning body, while yellow lamplight flickered on the walls of the cave. She apologized that he had to eat with a strip of shingle; she gave him water from the Haig-and-Haig pinch bottle, then squatted before him and stared with intense fascination while he ate. Gradually he extracted from her the details of what had been happening on the island.

Rolf and the woman had gone, a fact Burt already knew. Joss and the boys had been told only that Burt was a prisoner, and that if any of them misbehaved he would be killed. That had kept them quiet until Coco and Godfrey had been pressed into diving for his body. When they failed to find it, Ace had decided that he'd been carried out to sea. Joss had then been taken to her house and locked in, replacing Burt as a hostage. One of the men guarded her all the time.

Burt thought it over; apparently the two had given up their scheme to get the diamonds, and settled down to wait for Rolf's return. This posed a dilemma for Burt: should he try to sneak up, overpower the two men and . . . then what? He had to get Tracy Keener out of Rolf's way. (He had decided she must be on one of the Tobago Cays, ten miles away.) Her death seemed a foregone conclusion when Rolf returned; that of Joss and the boys remained problematical. If he tied Ace and Hoke, then went after the woman, they might get free and kill the others out of sheer vengeance. The best thing was to leave the island as it was, let the two men think him dead so they wouldn't get nervous, get the woman to safety and come sneaking back with reinforcements.

"Maudie," he said. "Do you know where Joss keeps the skin-diving equipment? The tanks, masks, fins, that stuff?"

She nodded. "In the room beside where the boys sleep. You wish me to bring it?"

"Can you get it without being seen?"

"Truly." She rose, seized the dress at the hem and

pulled it over her head. She stood in the bra and a pair of men's shorts knotted around the waist. "Nobody see me at night when I wear no clothing."

Burt wondered if he'd ever get used to the way women had lately disrobed in his presence as though he were a bronze Buddha. He watched her untie the shorts, drop them to the floor, then kneel with her back to him. "Will you help? I do not understand the hook."

As Burt unhooked the clasp, he asked: "Can you carry the stuff? Those tanks are heavy."

"I am more strong than Coco," she said. "He learn this one night when he catch me in the path." She shrugged off the bra and walked to the cave entrance. She turned, invisible except for her teeth and eyes. "You sleep. I bring everything."

Burt lay down on the cushion and tried to visualize a map of the Grenadines. Mayero was the nearest populated island to the Tobago Cays; he vaguely remembered a tiny, African-like cluster of thatched huts. He would leave the island at dawn, invisible beneath the water, swim to Mayero, leave his tanks there as a deposit on a rowboat. He'd row across the long stretch of open sea to the Tobago Cays, pick up Tracy Keener if she was there, and . . .

Maudie's hands shook him awake. "Sir, will you look?"

He raised his hands and saw the equipment lined up for his inspection. Tanks, carrying frame, fins, mask, belt of weights, knife—

"You forgot the regulator."

"What is that?" Her naked body was wet and glistening like an otter's pelt.

"A round thing on a black hose. Goes in your mouth."

"I get it," she said, and left.

This time he did not wake up when she returned. He dreamed that he was swimming and encountering a black-backed porpoise in the water. He was wrestling the porpoise, trying to push it beneath him, when he

woke up and looked down into the wide white eyes of
Maudie. She lay passive in his arms, using none of her
boasted strength.

He rolled onto his back. "Sleep on the other side of
the cave, Maudie. I've got a long swim tomorrow."

ELEVEN

He rowed across the silent, oily sea. Behind him lay the main cluster of the Tobago Cays, four islands so close together that men could converse from one to the other and hardly raise their voices. He had searched all four without finding any sign of her; only some immense turtle shells where fishermen had long ago stopped for a feast. Now he rowed toward one lonely island a mile or so from the others. The fisherman in Mayero had called it Petit Tabac; it looked odd with a single palm tree growing from the low bush-covered mound in the center. He decided to land on the sand spit which curved out at the western end. Gray rocks bit through the surf around it, but the sea was calm enough to land without danger. He was thankful for the calm sea, with reservations, for it was a heavy, threatening quietness. And so hot. He took one hand off the oars and touched the soft blisters on his nose. The man on Mayero had said: "Hurricane comin'." And Burt had said: "I've been hearing that since I came to the islands. When will it come?" "Today," said the man, and in that matter-of-fact way the islanders talk of death, had added: "You will die on the sea."

Now Burt could see the black cloud like a low obsidian cliff on the eastern horizon. He would have been thankful for rain—just a little. The sun was a white-hot rivet tacked to a blue-steel sheet of sky. Sweat made his palms slick on the oars and complicated the task of working the boat in through the rocks. He reached the line of low breakers and leaped out, seized the prow of the boat and dragged it up the steeply sloping beach. Damn, they made these things heavy. Not more than six feet long, and it must weigh a hundred pounds. It took all his strength to drag it ten feet above the surf-line. He reached beneath the thwart and took out an oilskin bag containing a tin of biscuits and two cans of bully beef. He tied it to his belt beside the plastic-handled fish-knife, then climbed up the slithering sand to the top of the mound.

The entire island was less than a quarter-mile long. It formed a narrow crescent which began where he stood and dwindled to a line of rocks on the eastern end. There the pelicans sat hunched over, like movie-goers waiting in the rain. He saw two structures of black rock, shaped like Navajo hogans. It was the only shelter on the island; she would be there if anywhere.

He jumped and slapped his ankle, saw the blood trickle down from the bite of a sandfly. He started down the beach. A gust of wind tore the breath from his lungs, stung his face with sand, and then was gone. He looked to the east and was appalled to see how the cloud had grown while he was beaching his boat. Now it covered the lower quarter of the eastern sky, black as approaching night. It was laced with red and yellow veinings of lightning, like mace on nutmeg. He felt a chill of foreboding and looked at his boat lying vulnerable on the sand. He ran back, uncoiled the heavy line and tied it to a jutting boulder. Then he ran back down the beach, his canvas sneakers slapping against the hard-packed sand.

She sat with her back against one of the stone shelters, her head sunk on her chest, her eyes fixed on her hands lying palm up across her thighs. Burt stared in frozen shock, his triumph at finding her wiped out by the appalling sight of her condition. The tangled mass of her hair was bleached a pale orange on top, hiding her face except for the peeling tip of her sun-blistered nose. Her long-sleeved denim shirt was open at the neck; the skin beneath it was welted by mosquito bites. Her long flannel slacks, once white, were now a stained, spotted gray. Her legs were stretched out before her, widespread, with the cuffs pulled up to her calves. Above her dirty white socks, her ankles were raw and bleeding from the bites of sandflies.

"Tracy Keener," he said.

She didn't look up. Beside her he saw the biscuit tin which he decided must contain her supplies. On the sand lay an open untouched can of beef, its contents dried and green and covered with flies. On a plastic bag lay a needle, its tip stained the color of rust. He knew why she didn't answer; she had just hit herself, and was now taking that first wild soaring ride which addicts call the flash. He knelt and raised her head.

"Tracy. I've come to take you off the island."

She gave him a glazed, unfocused look. "In a minute, baby. You're new, aren't you? Did Rolf come?"

So . . . she thought he was Rolf's man. He decided not to tell her he was taking her away from Rolf; the tie between an addict and the supplier was umbilical.

"Your husband couldn't make it. Come on. Let's go."

"In . . . in a minute."

"We can't wait. Look."

He held her chin and turned her face toward the east. The cloud was growing visible, sending blunt stubby fingers into the sky above them. Even the birds had grown strangely quiet.

"Pretty," she said. "What is it?"

"That's a storm. A bad one." He spoke as though explaining to a child. "We've got to get off before it hits. This island isn't more than twenty feet high. We're going to one of the higher islands. Understand?"

"Uh-huh." She smiled dreamily. "I like your voice."

"Oh, hell!" He seized her wrist and pulled her to her feet. Her legs were like wet spaghetti; she crumpled to the sand like an empty pair of overalls. He lifted her in his arms and carried her up the beach. She draped her arm around his neck and hummed as they went along, keeping time to his footsteps in loose sand. Her lightness surprised him; the skin slid over her ribs, and he felt the hard ridge of her spine beneath his arms.

"Haven't you been eating?" he asked.

"I bet Rolf told you to ask that. Eat, Tracy. I can't have everybody knowing my wife's a hypo. Eating is like putting a tongue depressor in my mouth." She giggled softly and laid her head on his shoulder. "I get everything I need through the skin—Oh!" She stiffened. "Put me down."

"We're halfway there."

"But I forgot my outfit! I can't leave it!"

Her back arched and her thin body twisted in his arms. Rather than hurt her, he loosened his grip and let her fall on the sand. She was halfway running when she touched ground; she was off like a rabbit, leaving him with the sleeve which had ripped from the shoulder seam. She ran with surprising speed against the wind, into the clouds which roiled up before her like black smoke from a refinery fire. Her shirt flapped straight out from beneath her armpits; each rib and each joint of her spine showed starkly white, as though the skin and flesh had been stripped away to leave her skeleton bare. His pursuit was slowed by his greater bulk; he sank deeply into the sand, and the rising blasts of wind stopped him like a brick wall, only to dissolve and leave him staggering forward until he hit another blast.

He reached the stone shelters as she was tucking in her shirt. The plastic bag formed a pregnant bulge above her belt.

"You pulled me down off the high," she said with faint sullenness. "I can walk now."

Going back was easy; the wind hammered against their backs like a giant fist. Surf boiled up around their knees until they had to climb the steep beach and walk in the prickly bush which grew at the center of the island. Above their heads the wind plucked a leaf from the palm tree and flicked it far out to sea.

Burt stopped when he saw the sand spit where he'd left his boat. The sea charged in from both sides, crushing together at the center and raising his boat high on a bubbling geyser of foam, rolling it over and over like a medicine ball on the feet of an athlete, then leaving it half-careened and filled with water. He turned and saw that Tracy had sat down in the sand and was gazing up at the flying debris.

"*Can you climb a tree?*" he shouted against the wind.

"Of course," she said serenely. "But I don't want to."

"You've got to! We can't get off the——!"

He stopped, for suddenly his voice rang out into absolute stillness. He looked around, and in the weird green light he saw a sight which made him doubt his vision. The island seemed to be slowly rising from the sea. Water poured off their little mound of land, cascading over the rocks, forming little torrents and whirlpools, twisting through acres of barnacled coral. He saw fish left gasping on the sand; he saw a manta ray as big as a barn roof stranded in six inches of water, its huge wings flapping like those of an enormous black moth dying from DDT. He saw a hundred crayfish scurrying between the rocks, frantically seeking the water which had left them; he saw a hundred mounded acres of rock veiled with dripping seaweed, studded with elkhorn and mushroom coral.

In the instant that his eyes encompassed the spectacle of the ocean floor exposed to the hostile air, he saw the reason for it. The sea was leaving the island, sucked up into the blackness which thundered toward them with a sound like a thousand horses drinking at once; coming in like a huge black whale which drank the ocean dry as it came. Burt stood for an instant frozen in a fear so great it was almost ecstasy.

Then he was picking her up and carrying her to the palm tree, ignoring the thorns which tore at his legs. He propped her against the tree, but she slid down, her body limp and boneless. He jammed his knee into her stomach and held her there while his hands tore at her belt buckle. . . .

Her hands fought him feebly. "Hey, what——?"

"I'm going to strap you to the tree with your belt."

She giggled. "But my pants will fall."

"That's not the worst thing that can happen." He jerked her belt from the loops. The slacks sagged to her hips and caught there. He removed his own belt and joined the two, then passed them around the tree and fastened them around her stomach. He pulled it so tight that her rib cage bulged out above it.

"I can't breathe!" she gasped.

He looked down and saw the bewilderment in her dark brown eyes. She didn't understand what was happening.

"Shut up," he said, his voice roughened by a sudden protective emotion. He peeled off his shirt, wrapped it around the oilskin bundle of food, and tied it to the strap which held her.

While he worked, he was aware of the light getting dimmer, like a lamp turned down, changing from yellow to green, and then to blue. Suddenly it became a deep purple twilight. He was gasping for air, pulling it into his lungs and finding it hot and with a strange electric taste. He looked toward the east, out past the tongue of naked dripping rock, and saw the heaving, oily swell of the tidal wave. It seemed to be growing larger as it came, rising higher and higher until he had to look up to see its crest. He could hear it, like an approaching locomotive, crashing over those two flimsy stone huts as though they were matchboxes . . .

He leaped for the tree and wrapped his arms around it. He pressed his face to the tree just as the water struck. His face ground into the rough palm trunk. He tried to gasp but there was no air, only water which had become a lashing monster wrapped around them. It was like being shut up in a tank with a frenzied whale. His feet left the ground and stretched out behind him. His arms popped in their sockets and he laced his fingers, willing them to grow together and never part, even though his arms might be ripped from his shoulders . . .

Then the water was gone, driven on by the wind. The wind was a demon of fury bent on his destruction; it peeled his eyelids apart and hammered his eyes into his skull; it rammed its fingers up his nostrils and jammed a fist down his throat, collapsing his lungs and bloating his stomach. Above him, the palm fronds were stripped away like dandelion fluff blown by a child. He bent his head and pressed it against the tree; he could feel the fibers straining in the wood and hoped it would hold; he wondered how Tracy was, but he couldn't see her. The darkness was total. The rain struck in smothering sheets like wet flapping canvas; the water rushed over the mound and tore at his waist. He felt the sand eroding beneath him, sinking him lower and lower, and he had a sudden fear that their tree might be gouged out by the roots after having withstood the terrible force of the tidal wave. He wrapped his legs around the tree, pried one hand free, and groped around the trunk. His heart sank as his hand touched nothing. He groped downward and touched her naked back; the shirt had been torn away and she was slumped forward hanging from the belts. He seized her hair and pulled her back against the tree. His hand touched her lips and felt them moving. He extended his embrace to include her, feeling the small softness of her breasts beneath his arms.

And then he ceased to think. Time is your enemy, he told himself; to endure you must become a creature without continuity in time, you are a May fly existing on the razor's edge of the instant. Eternity is now; the next breath and the next heartbeat will be another man's problem. Don't let the fingers slip, don't let Tracy's head sag ... don't think. The world has turned feral; all the elements are united against you, but don't think about that. There'll be no punishment if you survive or don't; all fear of the future is meaningless, for this is Hell ...

He had no idea how long it lasted, but a sudden peace descended like a cotton blanket. The blackness surrounded them; it was like standing in a huge silo with a tiny skylight far above. Burt looked around in the unearthly, yellow green twilight. They stood on an almost barren ridge of rock laced with tiny pockets of sand. The silence was broken only by the gurgle of runoff water and the slopping of fish trapped on the land. He saw why their tree had remained intact; it was rooted in a pocket of earth in the solid rock.

He felt Tracy move under his hands. "Please, you're hurting . . ."

It was slow work, for his joints had locked together and each uncoupling was agony. When she was free, she straightened and breathed deeply. All that remained of her shirt was the collar and a tattered strip of cloth on the right side. Suddenly she gasped and began to tear at the belt.

"Don't," he said. "We're not through yet."

She kept tugging, and he crawled around the tree and seized her wrists. "Stay put, Tracy! We're just in the center. There's another jolt coming just like the last one."

She looked at him in terror. "But it's gone! My kit is gone. I had it right here—" She pressed her palm to the sunken cavity of her stomach. "I've got to find it! Help me look!"

"*Look?*" He waved his arm. "Where would you look? It's five miles at sea by now."

She looked around, dazed, as though she had just realized that there had been a hurricane. Then she squeezed her eyes shut and screamed up at the tiny circle of light. "*Rolf! Rolf! Where are you?*"

He seized her and shook her until her jaw wobbled, and then she collapsed against his chest and called Rolf's name in a weak and plaintive voice. Her utter dependence on Rolf angered him.

"How heavy was your habit?"

"I'm not sure." Her voice was muffled against his chest. "I used to hold it down to one capsule a day, but then Rolf didn't seem to care, so I gradually took more and more. When you have it laid on you like that, you cabaret all the time. I used . . . maybe three, four a day. Maybe five, I don't know."

"You poor nitwit." Burt was appalled; a person with a habit that heavy could die if left suddenly without it. He'd known it to happen in small back-country jails: The addict thrown into a cell and left to kick the drug cold-turkey ... convulsions, incessant vomiting, muscle spasms so strong they can throw joints out of place. Eventually the heart bursts, the lungs rupture ...

He looked down into her eyes, saw the opaque film which, it was said, an addict never loses. Behind that, he saw fear ... and dependence.

"I'll die ... won't I?"

She wanted reassurance, and he wanted to give it. He remembered the letters and realized that the prospect of doing without the drug could start her down that same blind alley. He also remembered that he had been unable to see his boat on the sand spit, and that they might be a long time in leaving the island.

"We must get to St. Vincent tomorrow," he lied. "I know a doctor there ..."

When the next blow struck, he covered her with his body. Hours passed with the wind clawing at his back and from time to time the woman stirred against him. He felt a futile anger at the turn of events. Even if he brought her alive through this, she'd have another hell to go through tomorrow.

TWELVE

The wind died gradually from about midnight on. Burt loosened Tracy's belt and arranged her in a sitting posture with her back to the tree. She moaned but didn't awaken. Burt sat beside her and dozed.

Dawn came with a bleak gray light. The leaden sky was mottled by black clouds kicked along by blasts of wind. Rain drops stung his face like BBs. He looked at Tracy sleeping with her head back, her lips parted. His eyes followed the straight white column of her neck down to her wasted body; the small cuplike breasts were bare and rainwashed to an ivory whiteness. He could see the blue veinings beneath her skin, and he wondered what had given her such a frail, unearthly beauty. Her face seemed to glow with its own cold light; her eyes were shadowed and deep in their sockets. Camille, he thought, or St. Joan of Arc in the dying ecstasy of her martyrdom.

He took off his tattered shirt and put it around her. He stood up and surveyed the debris which had been deposited on their barren rock: Several palm leaves, dozens of coconuts, an entire guava tree stripped clean of bark and leaves, a few shattered boards and assorted specimens of dying undersea life, including a ray the size of a dining room table which was draped over a rock and beginning to swell. He saw that their island had been split in two; thirty yards west of their tree was a twenty-foot chasm of rushing white water. Where the sand spit had been, a few jagged rocks thrust up from the lashing foam. So much for the boat . . .

He draped palm leaves over the trunk of the guava tree and laid Tracy beneath the waist-high shelter. Her forehead was cold and clammy, but she was breathing.

133

He decided not to awaken her; when the withdrawal pains came there would be no rest for her anyway. He used his knife to open a can of beef and ate half of it with his fingers. He punctured a coconut, drank the sweet water, then gathered up all the coconuts he could find and piled them beside the shelter. At least they'd have no drinking problem . . .

He returned with his last load to find her struggling to sit up. "Lie down," he said.

"But I need my—oh!" She lay back and looked up at him from wide frightened eyes. "I . . . didn't really lose my kit, did I? That wasn't real."

"Yes," he said. "You lost it."

She closed her eyes and began to tremble. He touched his hand to her forehead; it was cold and moist, like the flesh of a dead chicken. Her teeth clattered.

"How do you feel?" he asked.

"Like . . . like th-th-they were squirting hot w-w-water up my n-n-nose." She started to sneeze, then rolled over on her side and retched. Burt sat helplessly until she finished.

"Maybe if you ate," he said.

He handed her the remaining half-can of beef. The beef dropped off her shaking fingers and down the front of her shirt. Her mouth was loose and drooling, and moisture ran out of her nose. He took the can from her hand. "Lean back and try to relax. I'll feed you."

It was a bizarre and intimate scene; he dipped the beef from the can and she ate it from his fingers. He remembered that some Indian marriage ceremony included a ritual of bride and groom feeding each other by hand. He wondered why he should get ideas like that. When the can was empty, he said, "I'll open a coconut. You can drink."

"I . . . I don't think—" Her face turned green. He jerked back just in time to escape the spew of bully beef. She doubled over and vomited again, then again, until all the beef was gone. Still the retching continued. He put his palm on her arched back and felt the spasm rip through her body. He lost track of time and lost count of her convulsions. He saw that there was really such a thing as black bile, and he wondered how much punishment the frail body could stand. He didn't leave her, though there was nothing he could do to ease her pain; he had a strange feeling that soon she would be nothing but empty skin, lying on the sand like a discarded laundry bag.

At last she sighed and lay back. Her face looked like a skull. Cold moisture gleamed on her pale skin. "The doctor . . ." she gasped, closing her eyes. "We've got to go . . ."

"I am afraid—" he began, but he saw the slow rise and fall of her bosom beneath the sweat-soaked shirt. She was asleep; she seemed to be resting.

He rose on aching limbs and walked to the break in the island. Peering beyond, he saw his rope tied to a rock where the sand spit had been. His heart stopped when he saw the rope go taut, then slacken. Could there be a boat on the end of that? It seemed impossible.

He started across the channel where it seemed shallowest. The current slammed against him and tore his feet from the porous rock. He made a leap, seized a jut of rock, and pulled himself to dry land. He lay for a moment panting, then rose and walked to the rope. During the ebb of a wave, he saw the boat wedged between two rocks and filled with sand. He found a broken counch shell and descended, using the shell flange to scoop out the sand. He worked in waist-deep water, scraping his hands raw. Twice he managed to empty the boat, and twice the burgeoning surf drove him to high ground while the boat filled again with sand. At last he managed to drag the boat up above the booming surf. A close inspection showed him that it was far from seaworthy. One hole he could have shoved his head through, a half-dozen others would have admitted his hand, and there were innumerable cracks and pits. He felt no grief; it was a boat, and he had despaired even of that. . . .

Suddenly he heard a shout. He turned to see Tracy standing on the other side of the break, her face twisted in terror. He caught only a few of her words.

"Don't . . . leave me!"

He tried to shout that he wouldn't, but his words were lost in the booming surf. He started running when she stepped into the water. When he reached the break she was a swirling patch of hair twenty feet out. He plunged in and swam with all his strength, caught her by the hair and started dragging her back. It took all his remaining energy, for he had to make a wide circle to avoid the rip current which now flowed through the island. He reached land, collapsed and lay panting, his body limp against the sand. When he raised his head, she was sitting beside him, regarding him with concern in her red, swollen eyes. He spoke with a tired, futile anger:

"How many times do I have to save your stupid life?"

"I thought . . . you were going to leave."

"I was just checking the damage on the boat. Did you think you could swim that channel?"

"No. I can't swim."

He stared at her, speechless. She passed a shaky hand over her face, as though brushing away cobwebs. "Can we go now? I feel as if spiders were crawling all over me."

He rose to his feet. "I've got to fix the boat first. You're on this side of the river now, so the swim wasn't all wasted."

Using the boat's rope to make a handline across the break, he transferred the food, some coconuts, and the most usable pieces of wood. He rebuilt the shelter and began whittling out repairs for the boat. Occasionally a pale sun shone between the clouds. Birds shrieked in the water and fought over dead fish. Two hundred yards out a long gray body left the water and crashed down again, leaving a memory of flashing teeth and streaming blood. Shark-fight, he thought; blood crazed scavengers divvying up some dead monster of the deep.

Better make sure the boat was good, he decided; there'd be small chance of surviving if it swamped.

He fitted a board in place and saw a new problem. The boat would make water like a sieve if he didn't calk the seams. He stood up and searched his pitiful pile of scrap lumber. One fragment of ship planking yielded scarcely enough tar to dirty his fingernails. Beneath his feet he saw a round, black globule. He picked it up and found it soft and sticky, with the sulphurous smell of crude oil. He looked around and saw the beach sprinkled with the globules. Hmm, an oil tanker must have gone down nearby. Well, their misfortune is our salvation. . . . He dropped to his hands and knees and began harvesting the globules.

"'Can I help?"

He looked up and saw her body streaked with the long red marks of her nails. Her hair was an impossible tangle. "Go back and lie down."

"I can't . . . sit still," she said, dropping down beside him. "I feel itchy where I can't scratch. It's in my bones."

He set his teeth and rose. Maybe work would help, there was nothing else he could offer her. "Okay, gather up all this tar. I'll get back to work."

Back at the boat, he started fitting boards in place and cramming in the tar. He half-forgot the woman until he heard her moan. He jumped up and found her lying on the other side of the shelter, the little pile of tar beside her. She was arched backward, her heels nearly touching the back of her head. He knelt beside her and asked her what was the matter, but she could say nothing, her lips were pulled back from her teeth, her eyes rolled back into her head. Muscle spasm, he thought. He placed his hand against her back and found the skin tight as stretched canvas. The muscles on her legs stood out like ropes; the veins on her head were like worms. Her face turned blue, then black; Burt stuck his fingers into her throat to free her tongue; he put a piece of driftwood between her teeth to keep her from biting it in two, then began kneading and probing her muscles.

Gradually the spasm ended. She straightened and lay gasping, her legs kicking fitfully like those of a dog which has just been shot. "I . . . never kicked the habit before," she gasped. "How . . . long does it last?"

Burt had no direct information, but he'd heard that it lasted anywhere from two days to a week. He couldn't tell her that. "You're over the worst part," he said. "From now on it gets easier."

He carried her to the shelter and returned to the boat. The convulsions came again a half-hour later. He massaged her until she relaxed, and by then it was dark. He ate, but she could not touch food. Her lips hung slack and moisture ran down her chin. He lay beside her all night, stroking her body when the convulsions tore her apart. He came to regard her as a piece of his own flesh, like an arm or leg. He felt her cramps as though they were his own; he agonized when the pain tore her apart. He could only relax when she did, and that was rare. Toward dawn he napped, only to awaken and find her gone. He sat up and saw her down beside the water stepping out of her slacks. Her nude body was tinged with a halo of pink from the rising sun. He ran and caught her before she got her knees wet. She gave no struggle as he carried her back to the shelter; her eyes were vacant and there seemed to be nothing behind them. She was limp and boneless as he put on her clothes; dressing her was like dressing a doll. When he finished she half-opened her eyes.

"You're all right now?" he asked.

"Yes."

"You don't really want to die, do you?"

"Yes."

"Oh, now look." He spoke as though instructing a child. "Death is something you don't ask for, Tracy. It'll come, that's in front. Maybe it's a kick, who knows, but it's the very last one you'll ever get. Making it happen is like going out at noon and praying for night. Night will come, it's all arranged. You don't have to push it . . ."

He broke off, for she had closed her eyes. He rose, vaguely disappointed, for he had wanted to ask why she'd taken off her clothes before she attempted suicide. So many women did. He'd always wondered . . .

He ate and got to work on the boat. He checked her frequently to see if she was dead. She never was, and it never stopped surprising him. She didn't sleep, just seemed to drift away for a time. He decided that she must have tremendous inner strength. Others had kicked it cold-turkey, but most of them had been nourished and cared for. This was the rawest, roughest setup. He wondered how Rolf had enslaved her.

At three that afternoon she said she was hungry. She was too weak to eat, and Burt fed her again from his fingers.

"I feel that I have died," she said. "Maybe I'll live again, I don't know. It seems like a lot of trouble."

"You don't have to make the same mistakes."

"Oh, but the hunger is in me. Every little nerve is going gabble-gabble-gabble, we want it we want it we want it." She closed her eyes. "When I go back to Rolf he'll be able to get it, and I can't put it down. . . ."

"You won't be going back to Rolf," he said, but she was asleep.

He worked until dark, then lay down beside her. Late that night she awoke trembling.

"Put your arms around me," she said. "Keep me warm."

He did, and her hair tickled his nose. He didn't move for fear of disturbing her. He thought she was asleep, but then she said:

"My blood is like ice-water. This . . . is in the way." He felt her hand between them, pulling apart the shirt. Then her cool bare flesh rested against him, pressing hard as though she were trying to curl up inside his body. He felt her relax and sigh.

"What's your name?"

"Burt."

"That's a very . . . abrupt name. Are you an abrupt man? No, you're not. You're very calm, in a deep sort of way. Rolf is calm only on the surface. I can't understand why you work for him."

"I don't."

She stiffened. "But you said——"

"A lie," he said, then he told her about finding her purse with the heroin, the discovery of the masquerade, and the entire chain of events which had led him to this island. "I've wondered about one thing," he said when he finished. "Did you know what was going on?"

"Oh, part of it. I knew there was something crooked. I knew that woman was posing as me, because she came out with Rolf and gawked at me. But then I thought, what the hell, maybe she'll make a better Tracy Keener than I did. You realize I wasn't really here. My body was just something you stuck a needle into. It was a chemical substance, I mixed it with dope and became real. When it wasn't mixed, I was nothing."

"You were something," he said. "Before you got hooked."

"A child. An unformed creature. You wouldn't be interested."

"I would, yes." He looked up and saw the purple dawn lacing the sky. "Right now I've got work to do."

The boat was nearly ready; Burt had saved the two best boards for oars. He ate and started work. She watched for a few minutes then said:

"I feel I could help."

"Okay, start cramming tar into the cracks."

While she worked she told him what she'd been before she got hooked: intelligent, only child of respectable parents, the kind of background that makes you feel smarter than you really are. She'd left home to seek the usual things: romance, independence, and a broadening of experience. Working for Rolf seemed to offer it all; he took long trips and would no doubt leave her in charge. Eventually she too might taste the glamour of foreign travel. But he told her nothing, and she became frustrated. Once she tried to open a forbidden filing cabinet. It burned, filling the office with acrid smoke. At first Rolf was furious, but then he cooled. "I should have warned you. If you try to open the cabinets incorrectly, it triggers an incendiary which destroys the contents." She asked, "But why? What part of your business has to be hidden?" He took her out to dinner that night and explained: The art objects were hidden in the ground; he was bringing them to a public which could appreciate them. Technically illegal, perhaps, but so was drinking on Sunday. Burt, having heard Rolf's warped and faultless logic, believed Tracy when she said she'd been confused. What confused her still more was that Rolf took an abrupt personal interest in her. He found her an apartment near the office at a rental she couldn't resist. He took her out to dinner and on boating trips. Gradually she lost touch with boys she dated and girls she'd known.

"I understand it now," she said. "He'd taken me into his confidence; now he had to take control of me. I remember the night I realized Rolf had taken over management of my life. We were eating at a restaurant overlooking the sea. I felt the kind of panic you get when an elevator sticks between floors. I told him I was quitting my job, and he nodded as though he had been just about to suggest it himself. You could never get ahead of Rolf. Then he said: 'I've decided to get married, Tracy. Why don't you think it over?' Well, you know the cool impersonal way he talks, as though he'd just recognized the need for a wife in the abstract, a need which had nothing to do with me. When I realized he was proposing, I looked down at my lobster and waited for the wave of joy which is supposed to hit you at this time. When it didn't come, I told myself I was a fool for not taking a rich handsome man when he was in an offering mood. Still I don't remember thinking it over or saying, yes, I'll marry you Rolf. Suddenly one day I was standing in front of a stranger with a Bible in his hand, and there was Rolf beside me. I ran." She laughed. "The minister's wife ran after me.

All girls felt that way, she said. Ten years from now I would laugh and wonder how I could have been so foolish. So I thought, well, you've got to play the rules, Tracy, marry this man and be blushing and happy. So I went back in and the ritual came off. I didn't even have to think; they told me every move to make. If it wasn't set up that way there'd be a lot fewer marriages. What they need now is some ritual to carry you through the wedding night."

She was silent, looking down at her tar-blackened fingers. "I don't even like to think about it."

"Don't."

"Why not?" She squinted at him. "How could I keep secrets from you? You've fed me, dressed me . . . I've been like a baby just being born. This is another bit of the old Tracy. So I'll tell it and get rid of it."

But she fell silent again. He put one finished oar aside and was starting another when she spoke again:

"He brought a bottle up to the room and fixed me drink after drink. He never touched it. I poured it down, my nerves stretched tight, getting sorrier every minute about what I'd done. And Rolf watched me with that faint smile, until finally I asked with a little laugh: 'Well . . . don't we go to bed or something?' He laughed too and said: 'You don't want to.' And I said, 'But I do, certainly I do,' even though he was right, as he usually is. Then we got into this unbearable discussion of whether I wanted to or not, and I began to wish I hadn't drunk anything, because he was twisting my words, making me say things I didn't want to say. And finally I shouted: 'What am I supposed to do?' And he said, 'If you wanted to, you wouldn't have to ask.' I left him and went out to a bar, and drank more liquor until I was just sober enough to fall into a taxi and give my address. Then I sort of dozed off, half-aware that we had pulled off the road, and the taxidriver was getting in the back. Suddenly the door opened and there was Rolf. I just remember his white teeth shining and his grunts of violence, then the driver was slumped down between the seats, unconscious. And then Rolf

... while the cars whizzed past on the highway and the driver gurgled through his broken mouth ... Rolf consummated our marriage." She looked down for a moment. "Before I came out of my daze, Rolf took me off to Nassau and treated me like a queen for two weeks. I'm ... susceptible to that sort of thing. When we got back, we got into another fight about a trip he was making, and taking that woman along. I knew about her. And ... it happened again. Only with a guy in a bar; Rolf came in when he was trying to buy me a drink and cut him to pieces without even mussing his hair. And then ... home again. I began to realize he couldn't make love without fighting first—"

"He is crazy, didn't you know that?"

"I thought so. But he talked so logically. You try to tell him and he winds up proving you're the one who's crazy. Arguing with him is like firing bullets against a rock; he catches all your words and throws them back at you. And the bottle was always there, for me ..."

"How'd he get you on the needle?"

"Oh, a bad hangover. He gave me some white powder to sniff. It was ... wonderful. I'd been taking it for about a week and thought it was some fantastic new headache powder—don't laugh, I was stupid, I know that. I started complaining about it burning my nose, and he brought home a needle. Then I knew it was heroin. I threw a scene, I told him no, no, no, and he just smiled and said, "Well, I'll leave this here in case you need it. I didn't want it. But then I learned for the first time that nobody wants it. You need it, like food. Somebody mentions it and your insides light up. Your mind says, take it away, and your body says *gimme, gimme, gimme*. So ... I got hooked. Rolf was finally in complete control. He kept me supplied and ignored me. I didn't care; all my troubles were soft fluffy things I could blow away like dandelion seed." She looked up in sudden fright. "I've lost the last four years, Burt. Can I ever get them back?"

He shook his head. "What's gone is gone, but there are more years to come."

"And what if I see Rolf and he says, 'Here's some stuff, baby, in case you want to get straight?' "

"We'll have to make sure you don't meet him." Burt held up the finished paddle. "Ready to go?"

"As ready as I'll ever be."

THIRTEEN

Tracy bailed with half of a coconut shell while Burt rowed. He was heading north, but the current pulled him inexorably south into the open sea. The handmade oars twisted in his palms; they were blistered and bleeding when Tracy looked up and shouted:

"Look!"

Burt turned to see a schooner bearing down on them. A moment later O'Ryan leaned out of the wheelhouse and beamed down. "Man, they tell me on Mayero you crazy. I sail over to get the body."

In the wheelhouse five minutes later, O'Ryan produced a quart of black rum. He looked at Tracy shivering beside Burt and trying not to choke on her rum. "She look nothing like when I see her first."

"She's been through a hurricane out in the open."

"Eh—eh. That was a bad one. Many people die." He told about a fishing village on St. Vincent which had been destroyed by the storm. Flooding rivers had cascaded down out of the mountains, swept the shingle huts into the sea and buried the site in twelve feet of silt. A hundred bodies had been recovered and the digging continued. O'Ryan then passed from the tragic to the commonplace without changing his tone; Joss's island seemed to have suffered little damage, he said; a few palms had blown over and half the roof of the beach club was gone. He was sure nobody was hurt, otherwise Joss would have signaled him in.

"You saw her?"

"Yes. She come out on the beach and waved me off."

Burt frowned, then he understood. No doubt Ace had watched from hiding while he held a gun on Coco or Godfrey or one of the others. Rolf's men knew how to get the most out of hostages.

"Was there a launch in the lagoon?"

"No."

Ah, thought Burt, then Rolf's return had been delayed. There might be a chance to bag the whole crew.

People stared as they walked down the cobbled waterfront street of Kingstown, St. Vincent. O'Ryan had loaned Burt a shirt which was far too big for him, and had produced a gaudy dress with red polka dots which hung from Tracy's shoulders like a laundry bag. She stumbled beside him, and Burt saw the gleam of perspiration on her pale face.

"Is it coming again?"

"A . . . little."

He watched her carefully as he said: "The doctor isn't too far from here—"

"Don't say it." She seized his hand in a painful grip. "I'm too near the edge. Stay with me, don't let me out of your sight. Please. You're my backbone."

The sergeant raised his brows as they stepped into the police station. He was a tall, thin blue-black Negro, dressed in a white jacket, black shorts, and white knee socks. Burt read in his eyes the temptation to eject such a disreputable looking pair, then the second thought that these people were white tourists, and that nothing could be lost in giving them quiet and respectful attention. He offered them chairs, introduced himself as Sergeant George, and fingered the buckle of his leather crossbelt while Burt talked. When Burt finished, he said:

"You're a detective sergeant?"

"Yes. I don't have my badge—"

Sergeant George waved his hand. "It wouldn't have any standing here anyway." He nudged some papers on his desk. "I recall reading about the ambassador's death. The papers said nothing about missing diamonds, nor about any international art dealer and his wife. Thieves broke in, shot the ambassador, presumably kidnapped his mistress, girl friend or what have you." He turned abruptly to Tracy. "He says your husband engineered the robbery. Is that true?"

"Yes."

"You would sign a deposition to that effect?"

"Of course."

"Not that it would hold up in our court, but it would give me something to take to my superiors." He turned to Burt. "You understand that nearly everybody is attending the disaster at Layou. The governor as well. All communications are out, so it will be necessary for me to drive up and get the necessary warrants. The roads are washed out, but I should probably be back late tomorrow."

Burt felt a cold fury pass through him, but he kept his voice level. "Do you know Joss, Sergeant?"

"Of course. Quite a fascinating person—"

"She's on the island with two gunmen. They've already killed one of her boys. While we're sitting here talking politely, making depositions, and going through channels to make sure we don't get any demerits against our next promotion, she could be dying."

The sergeant's face froze for an instant, his nostrils flaring in anger. Abruptly he stood up, opened a drawer, and took out a pistol in a button-down holster. He clipped it to his belt, reached in another drawer and took out a .32 automatic. He put it on the desk. "Take it. Officially I didn't give it to you." He looked at Tracy. "We'll take you by the hotel."

"I'm going."

Burt read in her eyes the fear of being alone. "Yes, she goes with us."

Sergeant George sighed. "Life was simpler before I became a sergeant anyway. Come on, you two. I'll requisition a launch at the jetty."

"What if Rolf comes in at Grenada?" asked Burt.

Sergeant George clenched his jaw muscles, then bowed to Burt in exaggerated politeness. "Thank you,

Sergeant, for your assistance. I shall radio the authorities their descriptions."

They started across the wide sweep of Kingstown harbor in a battered cabin cruiser which looked as though it had barely survived the Normandy landing. Burt, standing behind Sergeant George at the wheel, looked up through the port and saw a seaplane dropping down for a landing. "Where does it come from?"

"Trinidad, via Grenada." He looked at Burt. "You suppose they're on it?"

"Let's find out."

Their old cruiser made less than fifteen knots per hour. The floatplane had landed and a customs boat had pulled up alongside by the time they drew near. Burt peered through the window and saw Bunny step onto the customs boat. She looked chic and lovely in her smoke-blue suit.

"That's her," said Burt. "She's alone."

"I'll get her."

"She could be armed."

"Stay out of sight. I'll show you what official courtesy can do."

Burt watched through the porthole as Sergeant George stepped across to the customs boat, spoke a word to the officer, then bent his long body into a bow toward Bunny. She smiled and gave him her arm. He helped her onto the cruiser and opened the bulkhead door for her. Her eyes flew wide as she saw Burt and Tracy. She started to back out of the cabin and bumped into Sergeant George who blocked the door. She clawed open her purse, but Burt leaped forward and jerked it out of her hand. He lifted out a pearl-handled .32 and dropped it into his pocket.

"Where's Rolf?" asked Burt.

She showed her lovely white teeth in a sneer.

Burt shrugged. "Okay, you'll make me work for it." He turned to the sergeant. "Can you get us out into the harbor? I'll go on deck and have a talk with her."

When they were out in the harbor, Burt had her

standing facing the waist-high railing. She gave Burt a half-smile over her shoulder. "You won't throw me overboard, fuzz. I know you that well."

"I'll make you wish I had."

He stood for a moment thinking of how she'd tortured him, of Joss and the boys at the mercy of Ace and Hoke, and finally of her plan to take over Tracy's life after she was dead. The last thought gave him the will needed. With one swift movement he bent and seized her ankles, lifted her, and pushed her forward with his shoulder. She screamed as her head struck the rushing water. Burt held to her silk-clad ankles as she twisted and tried to raise herself. The skirt fell over her head and he noted that she'd worn the black panties decorated with kissing red lips. He counted to ten, then pulled her back halfway across the railing. "Where's Rolf?"

She coughed and sputtered. "Go to hell, you dirty—"

The water stopped her voice as he lowered her again. This time he counted to twenty. When he pulled her up, she collapsed on deck and threw up a gallon of sea water.

"He's. . . coming in at Grenada . . ." she gasped finally. "He's got the man with him . . . the man with the money. He planned to stop off for Tracy."

"Why?"

"To use her to . . . make you tell where you hid the diamonds."

Back in the cabin, she slumped on the low bench which ran across one wall. Burt told Sergeant George what he'd learned.

"That counts him out," said the sergeant. "They'll pick him up in Grenada. Now how do we get the others without getting Joss killed?"

Burt looked back along the low cabin. Tracy sat in a corner with her knees under her chin, her gaudy dress pulled down to her ankles. The faint trembling of her shoulders told him she was fighting a silent private battle. Bunny sat across from her in the damp wrinkled suit, her hair like a wet mop atop her skull. Her chic, expensive look was gone; she now looked as beaten as Tracy. Looking from one to the other, Burt was surprised to see how near Bunny had come to making herself a perfect copy of Tracy. He walked back and knelt in front of Tracy. "There's something you could do," he said. "It's risky, but it might save the lives of five other people."

She raised her head and regarded him gravely. "I'll do anything you say. You should know that."

Her complete trust nearly caused him to abandon his plan, but he had no other. "All right. Change clothes with Bunny. You're going to be a decoy."

Bunny, with her shapeless polka dot dress a forecast of less colorful but no less shapeless prison garb, was left on Bequia in the custody of a corporal and his six-by-six concrete jail. Sergeant George had exchanged his uniform for the clothes of an island seaman: white canvas trousers cut off at the knees, a sleeveless undershirt, and no shoes.

Burt watched the island draw near in the late afternoon sun. He was relieved to see nobody on the tower; Ace's vigilance must have waned during the long days of solitude. Burt directed Sergeant George to approach the island from the west; the sun would be at their backs, he explained, and a tongue of rocks screened the sea from the clubhouse. He wrapped his gun in oilskin and sat down to remove his sneakers. "I'll be behind them in ten minutes. Tracy, just show your head and shoulders above the cabin. Don't talk!"

"Yes, Burt." She knelt in the wrinkled suit, smelling faintly of wet wool. She kissed him with lips that were hot and cracked but strangely sweet. "Don't worry about me. Take care of yourself."

He crawled to the side, slipped over into the water and stroked silently along the rocks. He crawled out onto a hidden patch of sand and unwrapped the gun from its waterproof cocoon. Holding it in his right hand, he crawled through the low bush until he was twenty yards from the beach club. He could hear the low grinding of the boat's diesel engine. He peered out and saw Joss sitting on the steps of the beach club, her face like that of a robot which has been turned off. Coco lay in the sand with his hat over his eyes. Godfrey sat beside him and pulled ravelings from his frayed shorts. Hoke stood behind the bar, his shotgun resting on the polished wood and pointing at Joss's back. Ace walked down to the jetty, shading his eyes and peering toward the sound of the launch.

Burt watched the launch approach the break in the rocks; his stomach sank when he saw how vulnerable Tracy looked in Bunny's suit, like a small girl dressed up to play adult. Burt held his breath, then Ace called over his shoulder. "Okay, Hoke! It's Bunny."

The big man left the club and walked toward the beach. Burt waited until both men stood on the jetty, then he ran out in front of the club.

"You're covered, Ace! Don't move!"

As though it triggered a reflex action, Ace doubled over and swung his gun around. Before he completed the half-turn, Burt fired. Ace threw his arms wide and did a backflip off the jetty. Burt swung the gun to Hoke, who dropped the shotgun and raised his arms. Burt walked forward and looked down at Ace. A redness oozed from his chest and tinted the crystalline water a delicate pink. The gentle surf rocked his lifeless head from side to side as though he were saying, in a slow, tired manner, no . . . no . . . no . . .

"Burt!" Joss seized his neck and shouted in his ear. "They said you were dead. When you jumped in front of me, I thought . . . good God! I've *really* wigged out now."

Sergeant George nosed the launch up to the jetty; Burt helped him tie Hoke and lay him in the cabin. Joss invited everybody to the club for drinks, and Burt remembered the diamonds.

"I'll join you later," he said.

Tracy ran up and seized his hand. "You don't leave me, remember?"

They walked along the path, past cabins four, three, and two. "Where are we going?" she asked.

"To a certain cave—"

He stopped, frozen. Rolf had stepped out from behind the banyan with the gun leveled in his fist.

"Don't move, Burt. She gets the first shot. Tracy,
take that gun from his pocket and bring it to me."

She hesitated, and Burt licked his dry lips. A burst
of Joss's half-hysterical laughter came from the direction of the club.

"Do as he says," Burt told her.

She delivered the gun to Rolf, who dropped it in his
pocket. He caught her arm and pulled her in front of
him. "All right, Burt. Take me to the diamonds."

"You won't hurt her?"

"You're in a poor bargaining position, but . . ." he
shrugged. "Show me the diamonds and she goes unharmed."

Burt led the way across the crusted grass. He
remembered the last time he had made this trip, with
Ace and Hoke behind him. He had known they would
kill him; he was not certain about Rolf. The man could
kill on a momentary whim, true, but a similar whim
could stop him from killing. Rolf was logical in his own
way; perhaps the diamonds would be enough. . . .

"They were watching for you in Grenada," he said.
"What happened?"

"I saw them before they saw me. They weren't
watching for a man carrying a baby." Rolf chuckled.
"It pays to be chivalrous. My companion wasn't, and
he got caught."

Burt climbed down the low cliff and started along
the pebble beach. He heard Rolf's voice behind him:

"Something like old home week, isn't it, Tracy? I
presume he took you off the island. Has he been
treating you well?"

"Better than you ever did."

"Isn't that sweet?"

Burt heard a low grunt of pain. He turned to see
Tracy fall forward onto her hands. He clenched his fists
and took a step forward. Rolf pressed the gun against
the back of her neck.

"Come on, March. Come and get her killed."

Burt stopped, trembling with suppressed rage. "You only get one shot, Rolf. Then I'll kill you with my bare hands."

"Ah, the beast is out, is it?"

"It will be if you kill her."

"What if I kill you first?"

"You never find the diamonds."

Rolf nodded slowly. "Beautiful. Beautiful impasse. I like you for an enemy, Burt." He straightened. "Get up, Tracy."

When they were walking again, Rolf said, "You must have had an interesting time on the island, Tracy. Plans for the future and all that. Will he be your connection? It won't be hard for a cop."

"I don't use it any more."

His only answer was laughter.

Burt walked along the low cliff, thinking fast and getting nowhere. He could have escaped easily, but the fact that Rolf had Tracy made it useless. He couldn't depend on Rolf not to kill her. . . .

Burt saw the lamplight before he entered the cave, but Maudie wasn't there. She must have heard the launch coming and run up to the hills. Burt turned as Tracy came in, followed by Rolf.

"Where are they?"

"Let her walk out of here first," said Burt. "When she's out from under the gun, I'll show you."

Rolf's teeth showed like fangs in the lamplight. "You picked a poor time for an ultimatum, Burt. The diamonds are here?" His eyes flicked around the cave. "Sure. This is that girl's rathole. Over there, both of you." He shoved Tracy over beside Burt and had them both squat down with their hands clasped above their heads. Then he rummaged swiftly through Maudie's trove of treasures. Finding nothing, he started checking each crevice in the cave wall. The gun never left Tracy's heart; Burt was watching it.

"We made a deal, Rolf. I thought you always fulfilled your contracts, even with Nazis."

"Technically," said Rolf, "you have taken me to the diamonds, though I don't have them yet. And technically I am fulfilling my contract. I haven't killed Tracy—yet."

Burt's heart sank. "Why should you kill her?"

"Because I can."

"Then it's as good as done, isn't it?"

Rolf frowned, tugging at the rock Burt had jammed against the box. "You sound as though you have a point to make."

"I mean," said Burt, "you'd be getting a sitting duck. There'd be no problem in killing her, a little touch on the trigger and the machine stops. Click. She's dead, and there's no more kick than shutting off a radio."

"Maybe to you—"

"To you, too. Man, I know this score. Half the kick is anticipation, the other half is danger. Getting the other guy before he gets you. You think you're unique in this world? Rolf Keener, the incomparable killer? You and a hundred thousand Nazis, you and Caligula, you and probably a billion others since the beginning of time. You go around shutting other people off because you see yourselves in them, and you hate what you see."

"You see yourself in me?"

"Sure."

"You hate me?"

"I understand you. That cancels out the rest of it."

Rolf's lip curled. "You want to take me in and be a character witness for me?"

"I want you to take the diamonds and go."

"Suppose I were caught—"

"I'd do all I could to see you fry."

Rolf laughed. "That's better, Burt. I thought you were about to come on with violin music. Ah!" He pulled out the strongbox. Burt rocked forward on his feet, and Rolf's gun boomed like thunder in the cave. A rock fragment gouged Burt's cheek.

"Sit tight, Burt. We haven't finished our talk."

Rolf spun the combination, opened the strongbox,

and glanced at the glittering fortune nestled in velvet. With his left hand he began stuffing the diamonds in his pocket. When one pocket was full, he shifted the gun and began filling the other. To make room, he took out Burt's gun and dropped it behind him. To Burt he said: "You seemed about to suggest another deal. What was it?"

"A hand-to-hand fight. Winner take all."

Rolf laughed. "You always suggest that when you're at my mercy. I'm already the winner." He finished emptying the strongbox and stood up. "Let's put it up to Tracy. Tracy, you want to stay and die with him, or you want to live with me?"

Tracy gasped. "You mean, Burt—"

"He lives—if you come with me."

She looked at Burt, and he read the anguish in her eyes. "Decide for yourself," he said.

"I did that a week ago. I'd rather die than live with him."

"Then that's your answer."

"Look here, Tracy, before you decide." Rolf squatted on his heels and opened his palm. Inside it was a small white capsule.

She gasped. "No!"

"You could sniff it right here. Right now."

"I don't . . . want it."

Rolf moved his hand, and the capsule landed at her feet. She stared down at it, trembling, the sweat beading her brow. Rolf spoke softly:

"You just imagine you've kicked the habit. You really haven't. You'll go back to it sooner or later. Why go through a lot of pain—?"

Burt saw his chance and lunged between Rolf and Tracy. The gun boomed, and the bullet ripped through his upper arm like a lance of fire. Burt drove his knee into Rolf's face and knocked him backward. He leaped on Rolf and ground his knee into the other's throat. He seized the wrist of Rolf's gun-hand in both of his, hammering the knuckles against the rock until the fingers gave up the gun. Burt seized it just as Rolf arched his

back and threw him off. Burt rose to see Rolf lunge out
of the cave. Burt ran out behind him and saw him
wading through the black water.

"Stop!" he shouted.

"Shoot me," yelled Rolf.

Burt fired, and his bullet struck sparks from the rock
beside Rolf's head. Rolf left the crevice and turned
right. Burt followed and saw that Rolf had walked out
on a blind ledge, fifteen feet above the rocky beach. He
stood with his back to the wall, his face smeared with
blood.

"All right, Rolf," said Burt. "Come on back."

Rolf threw back his head and laughed. "You'll have
to shoot me."

"The state handles executions."

"They don't have the right! A bunch of moronic
electricians, what have they done? *They* didn't beat me.
You did. So shoot!"

Burt started edging toward him.

"Your gun isn't much good, is it?" Rolf laughed and
leaped headfirst off the ledge. Burt thought he'd decided to dash out his brains on the rocks, but the lean
body knifed the water three feet beyond the rocks and
came up swimming. Burt saw the power cruiser riding
at anchor a hundred yards out. He felt a curdling anger
in his stomach; Rolf had been sure he wouldn't shoot.
Now Rolf was getting away; the old diesel could never
catch him.

Burt dived out over the rocks, thankful that the
beach was narrower here; he struck the water, arched
his back, and came up swimming with all his strength.
He saw that he was slowly closing the gap. Thirty feet,
twenty . . .

A twinge in his arm reminded him of the wound.
Losing blood . . . He heard Tracy's distant scream. He
glanced over his shoulder to see a huge dorsal fin knif-
ing through the water. Tiger shark, he thought in panic, must have been nosing around the rocks. He saw
the fin turn sideways as the monster twisted for the
bite. Burt surfaced, dived, and clawed for depth. He

glimpsed a bulking shadow above him, then a huge body like a stucco wall slammed against him and sent him spinning down into the depths. He rose slowly, watching for the monster's second pass. It didn't come, and Burt saw why. Rolf was sinking down through the sunbeams that speared the air-clear water, turning slowly over and over. It was an oddly foreshortened Rolf, ending at his hips. Each stump gave forth a blue fountain which turned to red and drifted away like tenuous pink veils. The impossibly huge bulk of the shark returned, and the scene dissolved into churning red froth. Burt turned and stroked rapidly back to shore.

Tracy was waiting on the rocky beach. "Rolf—?"

"He's dead."

She lowered her head and looked at the capsule in her palm. "I've been holding this, fighting with myself . . ."

"Yes?" said Burt. "Who won?"

"There are no winners," she said. She tossed the capsule into a pool of water trapped by the rocks. Together they watched the ripples spread out and disappear.

THE
DEVIL'S COOK

God may send a man good meate,
but the deuyll may send
an euyll coke to dystrue it.

—ANDREW BOORDE
Dyetary of Helth (1542)

God sends meat,
but the devil sends cooks.

—JONATHAN SWIFT
Polite Conversation (1738)

Cast of Characters

1

Handclasp, which is not defined in the dictionary, connotes friendliness. If your dictionary has a gazetteer, you might find Handclasp listed as a city, population 125,407, in north-central United States.

It is reasonable to assume that the founders of Handclasp named their settlement with fair visions of an inland oasis in which the habitants would live in harmony with each other, and maybe even with the Indians. Alas for visions! Although there is no record of trouble with the Indians, there has been, from time to time, a generous dollop of it among the citizenry. Some of this trouble has been trivial, some has ben serious, but most of it, as in the wider world, has been neither one nor the other. There has been a continuity of political wars, social antagonisms, personal vendettas, and marital shenanigans. Here and there, in this haphazard chronicle of standard deviations, some of which went as far as the courts, an occasional item of gaudier aspect pops up.

Like murder.

The propaganda issued by the Chamber of Commerce to entice new industry will tell you that Handclasp has, in addition to parks, libraries, and wide streets, over one hundred churches of various denominations and almost fifty elementary and secondary schools, public, parochial, and private. The inference is clear. Although dedicated to profits and progress, the Chamber is civilization-conscious. If further proof is demanded, look at Handclasp University.

Founded as a private institution in 1869, taken over by the city in 1893 and by the state in 1924, Handclasp University has grown into a flourishing association of five fully accredited colleges boasting a total enrollment of nearly seven thousand students. On or near the campus there are almost enough dormitories and fraternity and sorority houses to accommodate the enrollment. For the overflow, including tenant faculty members, there are convenient rooms in private houses carefully screened by the university lodging service, and habitable apartment buildings. Of these, although it is not mentioned by the Chamber, The Cornish Arms is one.

The grandest thing about The Cornish Arms is its name. Otherwise, it is fair to call it ordinary. It is a buff brick building set flush with the sidewalk and rising two stories. The ground floor is bisected by a hall from street to back-alley and this design is duplicated on the floor above. There is an apartment to each side of each hall—four all told—and they are, if not posh, at least comfortable. In the basement there is a fifth apartment which is occupied, or was, by Orville Reasnor, the superintendent and maintenance man.

The Cornish Arms, in brief, is not singled out for attention because it is in any way distinguished. It is described because, at this particular time, certain people lived there.

One of these was Terry Miles. Terry cannot be casually dismissed. From metatarsus to auburn crown, she stood five feet four of scenic stuff. It was scenery, moreover, that she knew how to display to most graphic effect. Cézanne never did more with a landscape than Terry did with hers; and if he did it to more people, it was only because Terry never hung in a gallery or was constructed of materials as durable. While they lasted however, they did have the advantage of mobility. She could, for example, pick her spots and a special class of tourist. Let it be said that the lucky nature-lovers who were permitted to pause and admire Terry's scenery in detail, while differing considerably among themselves, possessed a common denominator. They were all men.

On this afternoon, which was the afternoon of a Friday in November, Terry went calling. She had not to go very far—to be exact, seven feet, which was the width of the hall outside her door. Having crossed that distance and reached another door exactly like hers, she knocked on it,

2

and it was opened after a delay by a young man in a deplorable gray sweatshirt, wheat jeans, and rather soiled sneakers. His dark hair was tousled, having a tendency to curl, and his eyes were a disconcerting pale gray in color, darkening near the pupils to a shade that seemed sometimes slatish and sometimes green. His mouth was small, but it was filled with good if small teeth, and so it appeared to be bigger than it was. He was, in sum, a young man of striking good looks; he might have been handsome enough to look dull if he had not, being shrewd, fought the effect off with deliberate sloppiness.

In his right hand he was clasping a can of beer that had been plugged in two places and was perspiring invitingly.

"Hello, Terry," he leered. "Come in and join the orgy."

"Really? A real orgy?" Terry stretched on her toes to peer over Farley's shoulder in search of the lurid details. "I don't see any signs of it."

"We've taken cover. We thought you might be the vice squad. Damn it, Terry, come on in before the super gets suspicious."

Terry stepped into a room that was, except for personal items and colors and an accumulated disorder, a mirror image of the one she had just left. Books were stacked on a straight chair. More books were tumbled carelessly onto one end of a well-worn sofa. At the other end of the sofa, slumped on his spine with a can of beer balanced precariously on his stomach, sat a young man who seemed to have one eye that was incapable of opening as wide as its mate. This produced the disconcerting effect of a squint; he was apparently peering malevolently when he was in fact only looking at you. Below the eyes jutted a crooked nose, surrounded by a face of engaging ugliness. Furthermore he was short, slight of build, and seemed at the moment overcome by a feeling of unshakable lassitude. He made no move to rise when Terry entered the room, compromising on a limp wave that caused the can of beer to tilt dangerously on his stomach.

"Hi, Terry," he said, in a surprisingly baritone voice. "I'm afraid Farley was telling you a whopper. No orgy."

"Oh, Ben, I knew he was just joking," Terry said. "I

3

mean, there would have been a lot of noise and everything. Orgies are by definition noisy. Everyone knows that."

She went over and sat down on the sofa between the young man named Ben and the books. The other young man, the one called Farley, seated himself by the simple expedient of backing against the arm of an overstuffed chair and falling across it into the seat. During this maneuver, he adroitly preserved the integrity of his beer.

"Are you disappointed?" Farley said.

"I am, rather," Terry said. "Orgies can be quite pleasant if they're conducted properly."

"That comment," said the young man with the squint and the crooked nose, "requires some excogitating. It raises an arguable point. Are orgies ever proper?"

"Moreover," said Farley, "I doubt that they are 'conducted.' In my experience, they just start somehow and grow."

"That is exactly the kind of academic quibbling I'd expect from a law student and an embryo historian," Terry said. "You're just making excuses for not providing me with interesting entertainment."

"You're right." Ben, the young man on the sofa, deftly snared his can, took a long swallow from it, and rebalanced it on his stomach. "If I had time, I'd get an orgy started. Unfortunately, I have to leave soon. I hate to walk out on any kind of entertainment, proper or otherwise."

"That's true," said Farley. "Old Ben is off on a mysterious excursion for the weekend. Even I have not been admitted to his confidence, but I suspect the complicity of my sweet little sister in the apartment upstairs. Damn it, Ben, would you actually consort with the little sister of your friend and roomie?"

"Nothing of the sort." Old Ben squinted at his friend and roomie with incredible malevolence. "Fanny has nothing to do with it."

"Where are you going?" Terry said.

"That," said Ben, "is for me to know and you to find out."

"There's no use asking him," said Farley. "He simply

4

won't tell me. For my part, I'm reconciled to his lack of faith in me, shabby though it is. We were just having a couple of parting beers."

"As I see it," Terry said, "you are still having them, and *I* would have one with *you*, if only someone had the good manners to ask me."

"Farley," said Ben, "what in hell has happened to your manners? Why don't you ask Terry to have a beer?"

"Excuse me," Farley said. "Terry, will you have a beer?"

"Yes, I will," Terry said.

Farley bailed out of his chair over the arm, as he had got in, and started for the kitchen.

"While you are in the refrigerator," said Terry, "I'd appreciate it if you would get me three fresh carrots."

Farley came to an abrupt halt. He seemed to be having difficulty with the message.

"Did you say three fresh carrots?" he said.

"Yes, medium-sized, if you please."

"Why in the devil, if I may ask, would you simply assume that you could borrow anything like three fresh carrots from a couple of bachelor students?"

"Why not? You and Ben cook most of your own meals, don't you? It's perfectly reasonable to assume that you might have carrots around the place."

"I consider it most unlikely. Ben, do we have any carrots around the place?"

"As a matter of fact, we do," Ben said. "I bought some yesterday at the market."

"Well, I'll be!" Farley turned again and got into motion. "I wouldn't be more surprised to find the damn refrigerator stocked with opium."

They could hear him rattling around in the refrigerator and cursing mildly because he couldn't remember where he had left the beer opener.

"How long have you and Farley known each other?" Terry asked Ben.

"Not long. We met on campus a week or two before we decided to move in here together."

"I've been wondering about that. Why did you? I mean, decide to move in here together?"

5

"Because it's better than a single room. Two can pay the rent on an apartment easier than one."

"I thought maybe it was so Farley could live near Fanny."

"You thought wrong, honey. It's true that Fanny put us on to the vacancy, but Farley grabbed it because there wasn't anything else available. You didn't take that brotherly indignation seriously, did you? Fanny's a complicated little devil. Declaration of independence, and all that. She knows her way around."

"Farley's very goodlooking. I wonder why he always deliberately looks as if he bought his clothes at a rummage sale? After all, he's going to be a lawyer in a year or so. Aren't lawyers supposed to wear collars and ties and coats and like that?"

"He practicing to be Clarence Darrow."

"Really? Who's that?"

"Never mind."

At that moment Farley returned bearing beer and carrots. He gave both to Terry, who laid the carrots on the sofa beside her and took a drink out of the can. Farley, employing the same technique as before, resumed his seat in the chair.

"As a matter of curiosity," he said, "would you mind telling me what you're going to do with those carrots?"

"It will be a pleasure," Terry said. "I'm going to put them in a Student's Ragout."

"What the hell is a ragout?"

"A ragout," said Ben, "is a hell of a mess cooked together."

"Roughly speaking," Terry said, "that's it."

"But what, precisely," Ben said, "is a *Student's* Ragout? As a dyspeptic bachelor, I'm always interested in recipes."

"Student's Ragout is the Crown Prince of all ragouts."

"Well, you needn't sound so damn esoteric about it. Is the recipe a jealously guarded secret or something?"

"Not in the least. Would you like me to tell it to you?"

"That's what I was hinting at."

"It's quite simple. To begin with, you take a heavy pot or a deep skillet. Myself, I use my electric skillet. Then you cut strips of bacon in half and cover the bottom of the skillet with them. Next, you cut a pound or so of lean round steak into strips about one-half inch by an inch and a half. Cover the bacon with these and salt and pepper them. Take the carrots next. Slice them paper-thin and spread the slices over the steak. Then slice three good-sized onions paper-thin and spread them over the carrots. Finally add three or four potatoes, depending on the size, also sliced paper-thin and spread over the onions. Salt and pepper the potatoes and cook covered, over low heat. In my opinion, you should add a generous amount of water to be sure that the ragout stays good and moist. There's lots of liquid in the vegetables, of course, but a little more is necessary, and quite a bit more doesn't hurt."

Farley and Ben, during this recital, stared at Terry with expressions of astonishment. When she was finished they were silent for a moment, then Farley turned to Ben.

"Did you hear how she rattled that off?" he said.

"By God," said Ben, "it was absolutely incredible."

"That's true," Farley said. "Somehow you don't think of old Terry in the kitchen. You think of her in the bedroom, surrounded by silk sheets and mirrors and oceans of lotions, painting her toe-nails and plucking her brows and doing other things."

"What do you mean by 'other things'?" demanded Terry.

"What he had in mind," Ben said, "was sex. You'll have to admit, in all fairness, Terry, that you're sexy."

"Well," said Terry, "what's wrong with sex in the kitchen?"

"Now that you ask," Ben said, "I can't think of a thing."

"Returning reluctantly to the ragout," Farley said, "I must say that I was fetched by the sound of it. Ben, you're a better cook than I am. You'll have to try it when you get back from your weekend."

"The proportions are just suggested, of course," Terry said. "You can change them to suit your taste."

"The principle, I would say," said Ben, "is the same as that of Huck Finn's garbage cans. The object is to get the flavors swapped around."

"Besides being delicious," Terry said, "it has another

7

great advantage. You don't have to stay around and watch it. That's why I decided to fix it for dinner this evening. I have an appointment after a while, and I'll just leave the ragout simmering in the skillet. When Jay gets home, screaming for his dinner, it will be ready to serve."

"Where are you going?" Ben asked.

"None of your business. If you can be a clam about your affairs, so can I."

"That's right, Ben," said Farley. "Fair's fair. If you'll tell us where you're going, Terry will tell where she's going."

"Never mind," Ben said.

"Neither will I," said Terry.

Farley sighed. "Speaking of Jay, Terry, how is he?"

"Who was speaking of him?"

"You were, damn it. You said something about him screaming for his dinner."

"That was an exaggeration, to be honest. Jay never screams. He never even yells. It wouldn't fit in with being an assistant professor of economics. If you are an assistant professor of economics, you must be dignified and stuffy. And if you are the wife of an assistant professor of economics, you are expected to be dignified and stuffy also."

"That's not reasonable," Ben protested. "How can a sexy wife be dignified and stuffy?"

"It's very difficult," said Terry. "If not impossible."

"It's worse than that—it isn't even *healthy*. As between dignity and sex, I'll take sex every time."

"Has a tone of discontent crept into this conversation," Farley said, "or do I imagine it?"

"It is no secret," Terry said, "that Jay and I are not on the most amiable of terms. He disapproves of almost everything I do."

"Is that a fact?" Ben said. "I can't imagine why."

"Are you being sarcastic?"

"Yes, Ben," said Farley, "you mustn't be sarcastic. It's hardly appropriate for a fellow who is going on a top-secret weekend. As for me, Terry, I am on your side in the matter. If old Jay walks out on you, I'm prepared to console you."

8

"If so," said Terry, "you will have to wait your turn."

Ben looked at his wristwatch, drained his can, and managed to stand up.

"I'm beginning to feel like a crowd," he said. "Fortunately, it's time for me to leave."

He carried the empty can into the kitchen, came out again, and went into the bedroom. When he reappeared he was wearing a hat and topcoat and carrying a leather bag.

"I'm off!" he said. "See you Sunday evening."

"I'm convinced that you have no intentions whatever of being good," said Farley, "so just be careful."

"Right. Old Ben Green proceeds with caution."

He went out. Terry shook her beer can, which was empty, and rose after depositing the can on the floor.

"I suppose I should leave, too," she said.

"Why?"

"I told you I have an appointment. And I have to fix the ragout before I go."

"You could stay for a little while, couldn't you?"

"It wouldn't look right."

"Damn the looks. Have another beer."

"Since you ask me, I will."

She sat down again while Farley went to the kitchen and returned with two fresh cans. He handed one to Terry and sat down beside her on the sofa.

" 'Shoulder the sky,' " he said, " 'and drink your ale.' "

"Is that original? Didn't someone else say it first?"

"Doesn't someone always?"

"Anyway, it isn't ale we're drinking. It's beer."

"A mere technicality," Farley said.

2

Soon after five o'clock Fanny Moran, Farley Moran's little sister upstairs, returned to The Cornish Arms. She did not, however, climb directly to her second-floor apartment. She spoke cheerfully to Orville Reasnor, who was on his hands and knees in the vestibule near the entrance, and paused briefly to check her mailbox, which was empty. While she was thus engaged, Orville exploited the opportunity to survey her with considerable admiration from end to end, and he concluded as usual that she was a neat little package. It was a short excursion, actually, from end to end of Fanny, for she stood only one inch over five feet, although a natural tendency of the observer to linger on the way usually prolonged the trip. Orville, who was a trained observer, took his time going from strawberry blonde hair, cut short and slightly shaggy, to a small pair of nyloned feet raised for added height on high heels.

"You ain't got any mail," Orville said.

"So I see," Fanny said. "Thank you for looking for me, Orville."

"I didn't look. You'll never catch Orville Reasnor prying into tenants' affairs. I was working in the hall when the postman came, that's all, and I saw what boxes he opened. Miles and Bowers is all."

"Oh?" Fanny turned and looked down at Orville. "What are you doing down there on your hands and knees? Saying your prayers?"

"Not hardly. I been replacing some of this asphalt tile. A couple pieces got kicked up and cracked."

"Is my brother at home?"

"Not knowing, I couldn't say. He ain't come out this way. 'Course, he might have gone out the back door."

"Yes, Farley often goes in and out of back doors. It's a kind of instinct with him."

"You want to see him about something?"

"Not particularly. I wonder if Terry Miles is home. Don't bother to answer, Orville. I'll just go back and knock on her door and find out, if you don't mind."

"I don't mind. Why should I?"

Not knowing, Fanny couldn't say. At any rate, she lingered no longer. Orville Reasnor, still in a prayerful posture above his pot of tile cement, watched her ascend four steps to the lower hall level, and offered thanks for short skirts.

Down the hall a way, Fanny knocked on Terry's door. There was no answer, and she knocked again. This time there was an immediate response, but it was not the one she was waiting for. The wrong person opened the wrong door. The wrong person was Farley, and the wrong door was his.

"Hello, Fan," Farley said. "No use banging on Terry's door. She isn't home. She said she was going out somewhere."

Fanny jumped as if she had been caught with a jimmy in her hands. When her heart had snapped back into place, she turned and glared at her brother, who was, technically, only half a brother. (They had shared a father who had been accommodated in the course of his marital fiascoes by two wives who had succeeded in becoming mothers. The third wife, fortunately, had failed.)

"Damn it, Farley," Fanny said, "I wish you would quit leaping out of doors at people. It's very disconcerting, to say the least. Went out where?"

"She didn't say. Just out. She said something about having an appointment."

"Did she say when she'd be back?"

"No, she didn't. I assume, however, that it will be before six. I'm invited at six to share the ragout with her and Jay."

"What ragout? Please don't be so cryptic about everything!"

"The ragout that Terry left cooking in her skillet. Don't you smell it?"

11

Fanny sniffed, and did, and it smelled good. She was getting hungry herself. The good smell made her mouth water.

"How do *you* rate an invitation? I should think *I'd* be the one, if anybody. After all, I'm her friend."

"So you are. She doesn't have too many of them, does she? Friends, I mean."

"Women don't like her because she's pretty and sexy. With me that's no issue, because I'm pretty and sexy, too."

"The hell you are. I hadn't noticed."

"Brothers don't. Not normal ones. Do you think I could be included in the invitation?"

"I doubt it. There probably wouldn't be enough. Besides, I was invited out of compassion. I'm a poor young bachelor with nothing to look forward to but his own cooking or a Greasy Spoon somewhere."

"Well, you're welcome to your old ragout. I'll make Ben take me over to the Student Union. I'll even pick up the check if necessary."

"You may find that a little bit difficult, little sister. Ben's gone."

"Gone? What do you mean?"

"How can I be more explicit? Taken off. Deserted his nest."

"Did he go with *Terry?*"

"Oh, no, nothing like that. With Jay confined by his duties at the university, why should they go off together? For the accomplishment of certain things, there's no place like home."

"You have a lecherous mind, Farley Moran. What makes you think I was thinking of such certain things?"

"Weren't you?"

"To be honest, I was. Ben's an enchanting little scoundrel. I may decide to marry him if he ever shows signs of being anything more than a perennial college student. The only thing is, I suspect him of being susceptible to seduction."

"What makes you suspect that?"

"Never *mind*. Did Ben say where he was going?"

"No. In fact, he was damn secretive about it. He said he'd be back Sunday evening."

"Well, blast his treacherous little heart. He's simply never around when I want him. Are you sure you don't know where he went?"

"I said I didn't. Don't you believe me?"

"No. And it may take you quite a while to convince me, so I guess I'd better come in while you try."

She walked past him into the room and sat down on the sofa, crossing her knees and thereby displaying—thanks to the short skirt—a pair of legs that were extremely ornamental as well as useful. Farley followed her as far as a chair, into which he collapsed.

"There's nothing to be gained by nagging me," he said. "I've told you all I know."

"Nevertheless, it might be interesting to speculate."

"Well, it's obvious enough, if you ask me. No speculation is necessary."

"I'm not so sure. Just because he was secretive is no sign he had some kind of assignation, or something. As a matter of fact, if that were the case, the little devil would probably have bragged all over the place about it. Men have no honor in such matters."

"Do you think so?"

"Still, one can't discount the possibility entirely. He might do something like that just to annoy me."

"Why should it annoy you if you don't know?"

"He may tell me afterward. In the meantime, I'm forced to speculate, which is even worse than knowing. What time did he leave?"

"About two. Just a little while before Terry left."

"Was Terry here?"

"I said so, didn't I? I thought I did."

"I'm sure you didn't. What did she want?"

"She wanted to borrow three fresh carrots for the ragout."

"What on earth would make her think she'd find fresh carrots in this warren?"

"Well, it just happens that we had some. Ben bought them yesterday at the market."

"If that isn't just like him! He's completely unpredictable. It shows, however, that he would be useful around a house. I wonder if I shouldn't be a little more generous and give him a fair chance."

"It might keep him home weekends. Incidentally, speaking of generosity, how about a fiver?"

"You had your monthly allowance from our wayward daddy. What the devil did you do with it?"

"My monthly allowance is hardly adequate. By the time the old man gets through paying alimony, there's not much left for his lawful progeny."

"As you know, there isn't anything at all for *this* lawful progeny. As an efficient secretary with a thorough command of shorthand, as well as attractive legs, I earn my own way. When are you going to get that law degree, anyhow? You're already two years past due."

"You know I had to lay off and work a couple of years."

"Perhaps you'd better lay off and work a couple more. Every month, what with twenty bucks here and ten there, you're costing me at least fifty bucks."

"Oh, come on, Fan. A lousy fiver won't kill you. I need some gas for my car."

"Why don't you sell that heap? What business has a pauper got with a car?"

"Are you going to let me have the fiver or not? Be a good sis, Fan. Some day you'll get it all back with interest."

"I suppose I'll have to. Here, damn it. And make it last."

She dug the five out of her purse and, after wadding it in her hand, tossed it to him. It fell short between them, and he eyed it for a moment, as if not quite sure that picking it up was worth the effort.

"Thanks, Fan, you're a doll. I'd offer you a beer, but Ben and Terry and I drank them all."

"That's all right. I prefer a martini, which I'm going up and fix for myself this instant."

"I don't suppose you'd want me to come up and have one with you?"

"You're right, I wouldn't. You have your ragout. And wash your face and hands before you go, for God's sake."

14

Fan got up and left, stepping carefully over the crumpled five-spot. Walking to the stairs, she saw that Orville Reasnor had vacated the vestibule.

Upstairs in her apartment she peeled to the buff, showered and, after a fierce struggle, got into a sweater and a pair of adhesive pants. This done, she went to the kitchen and mixed two martinis, one of which she poured and began to drink. Since she had been practically deserted by Ben, the devious little devil, she supposed she might as well eat out of the refrigerator and spend the evening at home. There was a small steak to broil, a potato to bake, and some head-lettuce for a salad. There was also this martini to finish drinking, another to follow, and more where they came from if it began to seem like a good thing. Later, for amusement, there was *Joseph Andrews* in the bedroom.

Not so amusing as Ben, Fan thought.

Where had he gone? Fan wondered.

And with whom?

If anybody?

3

At the precise time that Fanny was placing her potato in the oven, her brother Farley was crossing the hall. It was one minute to six, and Farley, following Fanny's departure from his apartment, had not only washed his hands and face, he had also put on a reputable shirt, and a pair of pants with a crease in them. His hair was brushed; his shoes, which had replaced the soiled sneakers, were shined. He had not gone so far as a coat and tie; but he had at least transformed himself into a presentable dinner guest, however casual. As such, with an air of anticipation, he knocked on Terry's door.

The door was opened by a tall young man with that particular kind of thinness which forecasts, instead of increasing corpulence, a gaunt and cadaverous middle age. His hair, still thick, was light brown and limp, brushed laterally across a long skull from a low part on the left side. He looked out upon the world, including Farley, through thick lenses set in enormous black frames. Although he was still on the nether side of thirty, he already gave a harried effect, as though he had hunted too long in economic cyles in search of a way out.

"Oh," he said, "it's you, Farley. What can I do for you?"

"Hello, Jay," Farley said. "I've been invited to dinner. Didn't Terry tell you?"

"Terry isn't home yet. Do you happen to know where she went?"

"She mentioned an appointment, but she didn't say with whom or where. I'm sure she expected to be back by six, though. No doubt she's been delayed."

16

"No doubt. Terry's always being delayed for one reason or another. Well, you may as well come in and wait."

"Thanks." Farley stepped into the room and waited while Jay, after peering down the hall, closed the door behind him. "I hope I'm not imposing."

"Not at all. Sit down, Farley, and I'll fix you a drink. Gin or Scotch?"

"Scotch."

"Soda?"

"Plain water."

"That's good. I'm not sure I've any soda left, now that I think about it."

Jay went into the kitchen and took a bottle and glasses out of a cabinet. Farley, at ease in a chair, could hear him excavating ice in the refrigerator. The simmering ragout filled the room with the most delectable odor, of bacon and steak and carrots and onions and potatoes. A happy combination, thought Farley. He regretted that he wasn't very hungry. What he wanted most was the Scotch and water that Jay was now conveying. He accepted the glass Jay offered, raised it in salute, and took a large swallow.

Jay, holding a glass of his own, sprawled in another chair. His long thin legs gave an effect of disorganization.

"I'd better warn you," Jay said, "that we may have a long wait. Promptness is not one of Terry's virtues."

"She specifically said six. She'll probably be along in a few minutes."

"I wouldn't count on it. No affront intended, old man, but she's probably forgotten all about inviting you."

"In that case, perhaps I'd better not stay."

"Oh, no. I wouldn't hear of your leaving. If she doesn't show up soon, we'll eat the damn ragout ourselves. That's what we're having, you know."

"I know, I can smell it. Besides, Terry came over earlier to borrow some carrots for it."

"Terry never has everything she needs for anything. What time was she over?"

"It must have been shortly after one. Ben hadn't left yet. He's gone for the weekend now. I think that's why Terry took pity on me and invited me to share your ragout. She and Ben and I had a beer together."

17

"You said she mentioned an appointment. Did she mention what time it was for?"

"I think she said three, but I'm not sure."

"Well, she'll be here when she gets here. That's about all you can say. It's an ulcerous job keeping up on Terry's whereabouts. I learned long ago not to try. Would you care to hear some music while we're waiting?"

"That would be fine."

"Any preference?"

"Anything you like."

Jay gathered up his scattered legs and went over to the player in a kind of slow-motion lope. Adjusting his glasses on his nose, he peered down into the machine.

"There's a Beethoven quartet already on. How about that?"

"Beethoven? Ah."

Farley would have been just as agreeable to an offering by the Beatles; he had no taste for music of any kind. But the pretense of listening would relieve him of the necessity for making conversation, which would be a relief to Jay as well. So they sat silently in the shimmer of sound and the odor of ragout, and their glasses were empty when the recording was finished. Jay got up again and refilled glasses and turned the recording over.

"We'll hear one more," he said, "then we'll eat. And to hell with it."

His voice was edged with a kind of resigned bitterness. However empty Jay's belly was of food, Farley thought, it was full to capacity of Terry. Small wonder, really. Even after maximum concessions to Terry's obvious allure, a man had to resent eventually the ease with which she kept slipping the ties that bind.

Not being able to think of anything appropriate to say, Farley said nothing. They sat and listened, or pretended to listen, and there was still, one string quartet and a Scotch highball later, no Terry.

"That's *it*," said Jay. "I won't bother to apologize, Farley. Let's eat the damn ragout before it dries out."

Farley looked at his watch. "Terry's an hour late, Jay. Aren't you concerned?"

"Why should I be? This is an old story."

18

"Just the same, I'd feel better if we at least made some effort to find out where she went. Honestly, Jay, she was so definite about the invitation and the time that I just can't believe she forgot or ignored it."

"It's decent of you to be concerned, but I assure you it's uncalled for. Anyhow, what can we do? She doesn't seem to have told anyone about her plans, *whatever* they were."

"Are Ardis and Otis Bowers home from the university yet? Perhaps they'd know."

"No chance. Ardis loathes Terry, quite justifiably, and poor Otis isn't allowed within speaking distance if Ardis can prevent it."

"It wouldn't do any harm, Jay, to ask them."

"All right. Let me turn down the heat under the ragout first."

He went into the kitchen with the empty glasses, and returned in a moment without them.

"That should hold it all right," he said. "Talking with Ardis and Otis will get us nowhere, Farley, but I suppose you're right about making some sort of effort. Let's go."

In the hall, at the foot of the staircase to the second floor, Farley, with one foot lifted to the first tread, stopped suddenly. He had been struck by an idea, apparently, and he stood pinching his lower lip while he considered it.

"I was just thinking," he said. "Orville Reasnor may have seen Terry leave. If so, he could probably tell us about when it was. It seems to me Terry mentioned an appointment at three, but if she was a lot later than that getting away it might explain why she's so long getting back."

"I doubt it." Jay was clearly impatient. "Anyway, I'm skeptical of Orville Reasnor's ability to contribute anything enlightening to anything."

Farley, with Jay abreast, took a turn and descended a short flight to the basement. He knocked on the door of Orville Reasnor's bachelor quarters. In a few seconds the door swung open to reveal Orville. His lack of shirt or shoes, his attire of long johns and heavy socks, indicated that Orville had been roused from a well-earned nap, and

19

the indication was supported by his belligerent expression. Clearly, he was anticipating a gripe.

"Evening, Doctor," he said to Jay, ignoring Farley. "What's the trouble?"

Orville invariably conferred the doctorate when speaking to a member of the University faculty. Sometimes, as in Jay's case, it was appropriate. One always had an uneasy feeling, however, that Orville used it not so much as an expression of respect as, on the other hand, of some esoteric personal insult.

"No trouble, Orville," Jay said. "Mr. Moran and I were expecting my wife home for dinner about six, and she hasn't got back yet. We thought, if you happened to see her leave, that you might remember what time it was."

"I never saw her. If she'd have left between a little before two and a little after five, I'd have seen her."

"Oh? Why so?"

"Because I was working all that time in the vestibule. She'd have had to go right past me."

"Well, she's gone. Maybe you just forgot."

"Not Orville Reasnor. I don't forget so easy. That's not to say she couldn't have gone out the back door into the alley. The hall's a lot higher than the vestibule, and I couldn't have seen nothing in the hall when I was down on my knees, which most of the time I was."

"I guess that's the way she went. Thanks, Orville."

"I wouldn't worry none if I was you, Doctor." Orville's little eyes had acquired a sly expression; his lips, surrounded by the day's growth of gray stubble, twitched on the verge of a grin. "She'll be back in her own good time, I expect."

Jay's lean face was wooden as he turned away; Farley, having caught the innuendo, understood Jay's reluctance to pursue the matter. Further inquiries about Terry were an open invitation to ribaldry, and no man enjoys the cuckold's role.

On the way upstairs Farley asked, "Does Terry often use the back door?"

"She does when our car's parked out on the apron. Today it wasn't. I had it on campus."

20

"Well, she must have gone out that way. Maybe it was a shortcut. In the same direction she was going, I mean."

"Of course. There's nothing odd about using the back door. All of us do on occasion."

Having reached the first floor, they ascended the longer flight of stairs to the second. Beyond the Bowers's door, someone moved in response to Jay's knock. It was Otis Bowers himself who opened. Behind Otis, wearing an apron and holding a dish towel, and watching curiously from the kitchen, was his wife Ardis.

Otis was approximately the same age and height at Jay. He had a weight problem, as Jay did, but in reverse. Where Jay was lean, with the prospect of growing leaner, Otis was fat, with the prospect of growing fatter. He was an assistant professor of physics. Ardis was a graduate student and instructor in the Department of English. Her claim to prettiness, which had some basis, was disputed by a hint around eyes and mouth of chronic acrimony; even her speech had a sour flavor.

"Hello, Jay," Otis said. "Farley. Come in. We've just finished our dinner."

"Sorry to intrude, Otis," Jay said, stepping into the room with Farley at his shoulder. "We won't be a minute."

"No intrusion at all. Sit down and stay a while. We have nothing planned for the evening."

"Thanks, Otis, but we just came up to ask if you've seen Terry. She invited Farley to dinner, and she seems to have gone off and forgotten all about it."

Ardis had retreated into the kitchen. She now reappeared, as if on cue, without her towel and apron.

"Otis hasn't seen her," she said. "Have you, Otis?"

"No, no, I haven't seen her. Sorry, Jay."

Otis's chubby pink face, normally benign, was a picture of misery. As they all knew, Ardis's abrupt interception of Jay's question was an oblique allusion to a painful episode involving Otis and Terry. The affair, if it could be so exaggerated, had been incited by Terry, not Otis, and he nursed no ill feelings. Ardis, however, would neither forgive nor let Otis forget.

"I meant the question to include you, Ardis." Jay's face

21

was again wooden. "She might have been on campus. If so, you might have seen her."

"Well, we didn't. Neither Otis nor I."

"That's right, Jay," said Otis. "We haven't seen her today at all. She's probably been delayed by something or other."

"Yes," said Ardis. "Something or other."

Jay turned to the door. Otis hurried forward and held it open in a gesture of courtesy. His embarrassment was still pinkly evident.

"I'm sorry, Jay. I wish I could help you."

"Forget it, Otis," Jay said.

He and Farley went out into the hall, and the door closed behind them. Ardis's voice immediately began beyond the door.

"What a bitch!" Farley said.

4

Farley's remark, as it developed, was a cue. The door across the hall swung open and Fanny Moran popped out.

"Did someone mention me?" she said.

Farley stared at his half-sister in amazement, as if he had witnessed a minor miracle when it was least expected.

"Would you mind telling me," he said, "how in hell you managed to hear me through that closed door? By God, you must have rabbit ears!"

"No such thing. The door was cracked open, as a matter of fact. I was listening."

"Spying, you mean. Has anyone ever told you that you have acquired some deplorable habits?"

"There was no spying to it. I was curious, that's all. I heard you two when you knocked on the Bowers's door, and I was waiting for you to come out. What did you want to see Ardis and Otis about?"

"I won't tell you. It would only be rewarding your eavesdropping."

"Jay will tell me. Won't you, Jay?"

But Jay and Farley had moved off down the hall. Fanny trailed after them. They paused again at the head of the stairs.

"We were inquiring about Terry," Jay told her. "We thought they might have seen her, or might know where she went."

"Hasn't she come home yet?"

"No."

"How odd. I wonder where she could be."

"It's not so odd, really. It isn't even particularly unusual. I keep telling everyone."

"Well, in my opinion, it is odd. I consider it most unlikely that Terry, after inviting Farley to dinner, would deliberately stay away."

"We've been over that point, too. There's nothing to be gained by discussing it again. Farley, you must be starving. Let's go down and eat the damn ragout, if it's still edible."

"Haven't you eaten it *yet?*" asked Fanny.

"No. We kept thinking Terry would be along any minute."

"There you are, Farley," Fanny turned to big brother with a frown. "You said I couldn't share the ragout because there wouldn't be enough. As it happens, there would have been plenty for all."

"How the hell was I to know Terry wouldn't show up? I'm no fortune-teller."

"There would probably have been enough in any event. You were determined to exclude me, that's all."

"Anyhow," said Jay, "there will be plenty now. Will you join us, Fanny?"

"It's too late," Fanny said. "I've already gone to the trouble of cooking and eating a steak and a baked potato. However, I'll come along to keep you company. Perhaps you can give me a drink or something."

"Agreed," said Jay.

"She's incorrigible," said Farley. "She has absolutely no sense of propriety whatever."

In the downstairs hall, outside Jay's apartment, Farley paused and looked down the hall toward the alley exit. Like the vestibule, it was at the bottom of a shallow flight of stairs.

"I don't suppose there is anything to be learned from checking the back door," he said.

"I don't see what," Jay said, pushing his own door open. "It has a nightlatch. Anyone can go out that way. Besides, it's left unlocked most of the time, so that anyone who parks on the apron can get in. I think Orville locks it for the night at eleven. After that, anyone who wants in has to come around to the front entrance. Damn it, don't try to make a police case out of this, Farley. You know and I know that Terry's simply on the loose. Let's leave it like that."

24

They went inside; the ragout, keeping warm, still smelled good. Fanny and Farley stopped in the living room, and Jay went into the kitchen. China and silverware, being removed from the places where they were kept, made identifiable noises.

"Are you wearing pants," Farley said, "or has your skin turned blue?"

"Don't be absurd," Fanny said. "All girls wear tight pants these days. It's the style."

"It's a wonder to me how they get in and out of them."

"You mustn't be prudish, big brother. It doesn't suit you. If I am any judge of male character, you know perfectly well how they do."

Jay appeared in the kitchen doorway holding a large serving spoon, with which he gestured like a cop directing traffic.

"Come and get it, Farley," he said. "There's no use making a production out of this. Serve yourself from the skillet and eat here in the living room if you like."

"I'll serve," said Fanny. "I can be useful as well as ornamental."

She went into the kitchen, relieving Jay of the serving spoon as she passed, and began to fill a plate from the skillet. She passed the plate to Farley, who had followed, and began to fill another.

"Just a little for me," Jay said. "I'm not very hungry."

"Neither am I," said Farley.

"The ragout looks wonderful," Fanny said, "in spite of cooking so long. I must learn how to make it."

"Won't you have some?" Jay said. "There's more than enough."

"I couldn't possibly. I'll put some coffee on to perc."

"Thanks, Fanny. As long as you're being useful, would you mind fixing your own drink? The stuff's there in the cabinet."

Fan put the coffee on and got a bottle of gin out of the cabinet. She couldn't locate any vermouth for a martini, but she found a bottle of quinine water and made a minimum gin and tonic, not bothering with lemon or lime. She carried it into the living room, where Farley and Jay were eating the good ragout with less enthusiasm than it

25

deserved. Sipping her gin and tonic, she looked at a Picasso print on the wall; she went over and stared for a moment at the record player; she examined carefully, one by one, all the items on the telephone table; finally she drifted into the bedroom. When she returned her glass was empty, and so was Farley's plate. Jay's plate, however, still held some of the ragout, pushed to one side as if it had been emphatically scorned and rejected.

"Shall I serve you some more ragout?" Fanny asked.

"No more for me," said Farley.

"No, thank you," said Jay.

"How was it?"

"Delicious," Farley said.

"Too damn many onions," Jay said. "Terry knows very well that I like her to use fewer onions than the recipe calls for. They don't agree with me—a soupçon is plenty. She did it deliberately. We haven't been exactly congenial lately."

"Oh, nonsense!" Fanny's derision was palpable. "If you ask me, Jay, you are simply being petty. There was nothing to compel her to fix your dinner at all."

Jay said something impolite. "See if the coffee's ready, will you, Fanny?"

Carrying the two plates, she went to see. The coffee was.

"Sugar or cream?" she called.

"Black," they both said.

She delivered the coffee and returned to the kitchen. She found a plastic refrigerator dish and put the leftover ragout in it. Then she washed and dried the two plates, the silverware, and the electric skillet. She considered another gin and tonic, decided against it, and went back into the living room. She sat down on a sofa, raising her knees and hugging them to her chest, thereby creating a perilous tautness over a choice section of her anatomy.

"While you guys were eating," she said, "I looked for clues."

"Clues to what?" Jay said.

"Clues to wherever Terry might have gone."

"Of all the colossal nerve!" Farley said. "I wondered

26

what the devil you thought you were doing, prowling around and prying into everything."

"Looking for clues is not prowling or prying. Obviously, Farley, you're determined to put everything I do or say in the worst possible light. If Terry had an appointment, it's reasonable to assume that she might have made a note of it somewhere."

"Now that you mention it, it is," Farley conceded.

"I couldn't find it, however. Not on the table by the telephone or on her dressing table in the bedroom. Can you think of any place else likely to look?"

Jay's voice was quietly desperate. "Terry's appointments are rarely the kind she'd make written notes of to leave lying about. I don't want to appear ungrateful, but I'd appreciate your just cutting it out. I have a notion where Terry went, if you must know, but I have no intention of proving myself right by going after her. I've become weary of painful scenes."

"Well," said Fanny, "I have no wish to intrude where I'm not wanted. But I'm compelled to point out that a lot of people seem to be jumping to a certain conclusion. It's being assumed Terry is out having a time. That is not, as I see it, necessarily so."

Jay shrugged angrily. "What do you expect me to do?"

"If I were her husband, I would at least call the hospitals and see if there have been any accidents or anything like that."

"She was carrying a purse with identification in it. If she'd been in an accident, I'd have been notified."

"Perhaps she was mugged and robbed. If so, the mugger would have run off with the purse and thrown it away somewhere."

"All right, damn it! If she isn't back by ten, I'll call the hospitals. Nothing will come of it, but I suppose I'm expected to act like a husband."

"If you ask me, you aren't even acting like a husband whose wife may be out having a good time."

"I used to act like one," said Jay, "but I got tired of it."

Farley had been pinching his lower lip, thinking hard. Now he said suddenly to Fanny, "Was there a memo pad on the table by the telephone?"

"I didn't see any. Why?"

"I was just thinking. When there isn't anything else handy, don't women often make notes of appointments on old envelopes, the margins of magazines, things like that?"

"Farley, sometimes you show faint signs of intelligence," Fanny said. "There are some magazines in that bucket at the end of the sofa. I believe I'll look at them, Jay, if you don't mind."

"Help yourself," said Jay.

The bucket was just that. Fanny removed its contents, half a dozen magazines and a newspaper. Kneeling, she began to examine the magazines, looking at the covers, riffling rapidly through the pages to check the margins. Jay leaned back in his chair and closed his eyes, bearing the futility of it all with a pretense of patience; Farley, after a moment, went over and sat down on the end of the sofa, by the bucket. He reached for the newspaper and began to examine it, holding it folded over in his hands just as he had picked it up. It was folded twice at a page of classified ads, including a column of personals.

"Wait a minute!" Farley's voice had acquired all at once an excitement qualified by incredulity. "What's this?"

"What's what?" said Fanny, looking up.

"It's damn funny, that's all I can say. Here, Jay, you'd better read this."

Jay Miles opened his eyes. Farley, rising again, walked over and handed him the newspaper, indicating with his index finger an item. Jay stared at the item for a long time. Then he sighed, twisted the paper into a tight roll, and slapped a bony knee with it. Leaning back, he closed his eyes again.

"Damn it, what is it?" Fanny said. "Am I allowed to know, or not?"

Farley took the paper from Jay's hand and read aloud: " 'T. M. Friday at three. Stacks. Level C. O.' "

Fanny jumped up, snatched the paper, and read it for herself. Then, as if to dispose of it once and for all, she dropped the paper back into the wooden bucket.

"That's that," she said. "T. M. is Terry Miles. Today is Friday. Three is when she said she had an appointment.

Stacks and level clearly refer to a library, probably the one at the university. But who in hell is O?"

"That," Farley said, "is none of your goddam business."

Jay stirred. His face was strangely untroubled. The Personal, rather than increasing his anxiety, seemed actually to have relieved it.

"It's just a coincidence," he said.

"Are you serious?" Fanny stared at him. "Some coincidence, if you ask me!"

"No." Jay rose and jammed his hands into his pockets, shaking his head with a kind of dogged stubbornness. "Think. Terry is devious and inclined to do weird things, but why not a note in the mail? Why not a telephone call? For that matter, why not direct contact at the apartment? Terry's alone here almost every day, and there wouldn't have been any problems. Then why a Personal? There's simply no sense to it."

"There may be no sense on the face of it," said Fanny, "but there may be more to it than the face."

"I don't think so." Jay removed his glasses, polished the lenses on his handkerchief, and replaced them. "Believe me, I know Terry. Anyway, no one has anything to worry about except me, and I've developed a kind of immunity. Thanks for your concern, but I'm rather tired. Do you mind?"

"He means," said Farley, "will we get the hell out."

"I know what he means," Fanny said. "I must say, however, that he is kicking us out like a perfect gentleman."

5

Farley veered off toward his own door.

"Farley," said Fanny, "get your topcoat on. I'll be down in a minute."

"Topcoat?" Judging by the astonishment in Farley's voice, he might have been ordered to remove his pants. "Why in hell should I put on my topcoat?"

"Because it's cold outside, that's why."

"It may be cold outside, little sister, but I'm inside. And inside is where I'm going to stay."

"Please don't drag your heels, Farley. You and Jay may feel inclined to leave things as they are, but I feel differently."

"Oh, butt out, Fan. Can't you see the poor guy just doesn't want to make a display of his embarrassment?"

"Yes, but it has also occurred to me that Jay's embarrassment may not be the only consideration in this matter. Or even the primary one."

"Nuts. I admit I was worried at first, but now I'm not. At this moment Terry is loitering at the first corner of the current triangle. Jay's occupying the second corner; and if you ask me, he knows the occupant of the third corner, if he cared to go there and make a fool of himself."

They had been talking in low voices outside Farley's door. Farley, after making this statement, which he meant to be conclusive, opened his door with the obvious intention of shutting it again between him and Fanny. But Fanny, with other intentions, slipped quickly past him into the room and turned to face him as he shut it in defeat on the space she had been occupying.

"The first corner is what's bothering me," Fanny said.

"There are some very suspicious circumstances here, if you ask me."

"You mean the Personal?"

"Partly that. Mostly, however, I'm thinking how Ben, the ugly little devil, just happened to go off somewhere a little while before Terry went. They could have met outside. It wouldn't surprise me a bit if they did."

"Ben and Terry? Little sister, you're getting brain-fag, or you've had too much gin."

"I'm not, and I haven't. It's easy to underestimate Ben. As I know from experience, he can be extremely fascinating when he wants to be. He appeals to the mother instinct."

"In that case, you have nothing to worry about. Terry doesn't have a mother instinct. Look, Terry and Ben were here with me this afternoon. If they had anything cooked up between them, they were the best actors that ever lived."

"I'm hardly convinced by that. To be honest, brother, you're not as smart about such things as a lawyer ought to be. Almost anyone could deceive you."

"Do you agree that the Personal was directed to Terry?"

"In spite of Jay's pretense that it was a coincidence, I agree that it probably was."

"There you are, then. Why the hell should old Ben resort to such a stratagem when all he had to do was step across the hall almost any time he chose?"

"Did I say the Personal was put in the paper by Ben? I don't recall that I did."

"You implied it. Surely the Personal was Terry's reason for going wherever she went."

"I implied no such thing. I merely said it was suspicious that Ben and Terry went off so close together. Perhaps he waited somewhere nearby and *took* her to keep the appointment. Perhaps he met her somewhere *after* the appointment."

"Well, if you don't have a mind like a scatter gun! It's impossible to tell what you'll think of next. As Jay pointed out, why should *anyone* publish the Personal?

Why not write or phone? Do you have an answer to that, little sister?"

"It could have been placed by someone who didn't *know* Terry's address or phone number. She must have talked to this person, whoever he is—she wouldn't have known otherwise to look out for the Personal. But she refused to tell him how to write or call her."

"That narrows it down a lot. We now know that we are looking for an illiterate. Someone, for example, who can't read names in a telephone directory."

"No such thing. It so happens that the Miles telephone is unlisted."

"The hell you say! How do you know?"

"Because I wanted to call Terry from the office one day, and I couldn't find the number in the telephone book. Later she told me it was unlisted and gave me the number in case I ever wanted to call again."

"I must say you have a way of finding out things."

"I am merely observant and intelligent."

"As well as sexy."

"That's true. And a little curious. My curiosity has been aroused, and I intend to satisfy it. There is something ominous, if you ask me, about that Personal. It is not at all the way to conduct a love affair. In my opinion, it involves something else entirely. And whatever it involves, I suspect that Ben is in it somehow, on Terry's side or the other."

"You're getting worse and worse. First you suspect old Ben of simple fornication, and then of mysterious involvements. Maybe he's a kind of poor man's James Bond or something. He just likes to combine business with pleasure."

"Don't be silly. I've already told you what he is. He's an idiot. I confess that I've become too damn fond of him, however, and I wouldn't want him to get into trouble."

"If you want to keep him out of trouble, why don't you keep him home? Apparently you haven't been making things interesting enough for him."

"I'm afraid you're right. Perhaps I should allow him more privileges. Anyhow, we have deduced that Terry went off to meet someone at the university library, and I'm going right over there to see if I can learn anything. Are you coming with me or not?"

"Not. And you're not going without me. Damn it, you can't be wandering around alone at this hour of the night!"

"Can't I? Try and stop me."

"Be reasonable, Fan. It's almost ten o'clock; the library will close in another hour. It's been seven hours since Terry was there, if she ever was. What can you hope to learn now?"

"That remains to be seen. It's better to be doing something than nothing, especially if circumstances have made it impossible to sleep or anything trivial like that."

"Since when has sleeping become trivial?"

"Oh, go to sleep, then! I don't care. I might have known you'd fail me the first time I asked you to help."

"All right, all *right*." Farley slapped his thigh in a gesture of disgusted concession. "I suppose I'll have to go along. If you want my opinion, though, I think it's no better than invasion of privacy."

"That's just like you, Farley. You ask if I want your opinion, which I don't, and then go right ahead and give it to me anyhow. I'll run up and get my coat."

She hurried upstairs. In her bedroom she donned a lined trench coat, which seemed appropriate to detection. Since she did not like to return to a dark apartment at night, she turned on the bed lamp before switching off the ceiling light. Then she went into the kitchen and turned on a small light above the range. While there she briefly considered the advisability of having a quick nip against the cold, but rejected it. Back in the living room she switched off the ceiling light, pausing only long enough to note with relief how light splashed into the darkness from the bedroom on one side and the kitchen on the other. Downstairs she found Farley, in his topcoat, sulkily waiting in the hall.

They went out the alley door to Farley's old Ford on the apron. It was cold outside, near freezing, but the sky was clear, with lofty stars and a slice of moon. Farley was

33

sullen at having to go, and they drove in stiff silence to the Handclasp campus, which was not far away, and across to the library, the only building on the campus left with a blaze of lights.

Parking was no problem at this hour. They parked at the curb and went up a long walk to the building, passing reference rooms to right and left, and upstairs to the charging desk. The girl at the desk was trying to sustain the illusion of efficiency, but her eyes were heavy behind her thick glasses. She answered Fan's questions dully. She had not been on duty at three o'clock, so she could not tell if Mrs. Miles had been in the library or not. She did not know Mrs. Miles, moreover, and could not have told in any event, unless Mrs. Miles had presented her stack permit.

"Say!" said Fanny, "I didn't think of that. How could Terry have met someone in the stacks if she didn't have a permit? Farley, do you happen to know if she has one?"

"I'm sure she has," Farley said, "as the wife of a faculty member. It's a courtesy."

"That's so," said the heavy-eyed girl.

"Well," Fanny said, "Farley is only a student, and I am only a sister, which is not so grand as being a wife, but I'd like to be admitted to the stacks, anyway."

"Do you have a permit?" the girl said to Farley.

"Certainly."

"Go ahead," she said.

"I guess I'll have to," Farley said. "Although I can't see any sense to it."

They passed through into the stacks, which were erected on low-ceilinged levels from basement up. Level C was below them, and so they descended narrow steel steps and turned down an aisle between shelves of books. At the far end, beyond a cross-aisle, ranged a row of carrels, each furnished with a desk and chair. All the carrels were dark, except one in which a late bookworm toiled over a tome.

"I am thinking," said Fanny, "that one of these alcoves would make a dandy place to meet somebody."

"That depends," Farley said, "on the purpose of the

34

meeting. For private conversation, yes. For private frolic, no."

"What other purpose can you think of, where Terry is concerned?"

"None at the moment. Incidentally, whoever she met had to be someone with a permit."

"Logical. It also narrows the suspects down to about ten thousand people."

"Fewer than that, I think. I'm sure we can eliminate the freshmen."

"With Terry how can you be sure of anything? But I'll concede on other grounds. Freshmen are not admitted to the stacks."

"In any event, it is clearly impossible now to tell if Terry was here at three o'clock or not. We had better leave."

"We had much better," said Farley, "never have come at all."

They left the library. At the curb beside the Ford, Fanny stopped and stared for a moment at a cast-iron VIP posed on a marble pedestal across the street.

"You're thinking again," Farley groaned. "What now?"

"I'm thinking that a library is not, after all, an ideal place for a tryst. Especially if something more than conversation is contemplated."

"If there *was* a tryst, remember? If Terry was ever here at all."

"That's understood. It isn't necessary to qualify every statement, Farley."

"It isn't necessary to prolong this foolishness, either. Let's go home."

"Well, I can't think of any place else to go, except the Student Union. We could ask there if anyone saw Terry with anyone."

"The Student Union! I've got news for you, sister. The Student Union is not an ideal place for a tryst, either, if something more than conversation is contemplated. All you can contemplate there is billiards or watching television or something like that."

"It wouldn't do any harm to ask."

"It wouldn't do any good, either. Chances are a hundred to one against finding anyone who even knows Terry, let alone who saw her there this afternoon and remembers it. I'm going home, Fan, and that's that."

"I dare say you're right." Fanny, for a wonder, was submissive. "We may as well. Perhaps Terry will return before morning, if she hasn't already."

Arriving shortly thereafter at The Cornish Arms, they drove up the alley and onto the apron, below the rear window of Farley's apartment. Moments later, at the door Fanny cursed softly.

"Damn!" she said. "Orville has locked the back door for the night. We'll have to walk around."

They walked around to the front entrance and up the steps from the vestibule into the hall.

"Come have a nightcap," Farley said.

"Beer? No, thanks."

"I'm out of beer. I told you that this afternoon. I've got a little gin."

"In that case, I accept."

They had the nightcap, which Farley fixed in the kitchen while Fanny waited in the living room, and then Fanny went upstairs and struggled out of her tight pants and climbed into the loose ones of her pajamas. It was going on midnight, and in spite of the worrisome, puzzling developments of the night she was very sleepy.

She slept through the night like a log, as the saying goes. Although as Fan often pointed out, it has never been established that a log sleeps.

6

Fan slept so soundly that she woke the next morning with a hangover. On her stomach, her face buried in her pillow, she raised her head heavily and squinted at her alarm clock. If she were seeing right, and if the clock were not telling a lie, she had exactly fifteen minutes to bathe and dress and get to work—clearly an impossibility, even if she skipped breakfast.

Her own alarm system began ringing dire warnings of an irate employer and immediate dismissal. Fan bounced out of bed and sprang wildly for the bathroom. She was standing there with her pajama pants in a limp little heap around her feet before she remembered that this was Saturday morning, no work today, and to hell with alarm clocks and employers.

Weak with relief, she hoisted her pants and retied the string and strolled back to her bed and sat down on the edge of it. She had been shocked so widely awake that it was now hopeless to try to go back to sleep.

She began to think in terms of a leisurely shower and breakfast. The soft and silken feeling of having two whole days with nothing to do was nicely developing when all at once the events of the previous evening returned to her clearing head.

Had Terry come home in the night?

And where the devil was Ben?

Fan put coffee on in the kitchen and returned to the bathroom for her shower. Dressed and brushed, she boiled an egg, toasted a slice of bread, and ate the egg and toast with two cups of black coffee and strawberry jam. She washed her breakfast things and put them away, and then she was ready to apply herself to the problems at hand. A minute later she was rapping briskly on Farley's door downstairs.

No answer—clearly, Farley was still asleep or had gone out. Of these alternatives, the former was more likely. This conclusion called for repeated and louder knocking, which Fanny was prepared to administer; but then it occurred to her that the best policy, when you wanted information, was to go to the horse's mouth. So she moved across the hall to Jay Miles's door and, stooping to plant an ear close to the panel, listened shamelessly. She was rewarded by the faint sound of movement within, and Fan knocked. After a moment the door was opened by Jay, who had been interrupted in the act of tying a knot in a black string tie.

"How do you do that without a mirror?" Fanny said. "It looks hard."

"It's easy," Jay said. "What do you want, Fanny? I'm in a hurry."

"Are you going somewhere?"

"I have a Saturday morning class."

"Oh, then Terry got home all right last night."

"Your concern is commendable, but your assumption is wrong. Terry didn't get home last night, or this morning either."

"Well, are you just going off calmly to meet a ridiculous class when your wife is missing and unaccounted for?"

"Exactly. What alternative would you suggest?"

"Did you call the hospitals last night?"

"I did. As I predicted, quite needlessly."

"If she were my wife, I'd call the police this instant."

"If you were and did, Terry would have your scalp. Believe me, the last thing Terry would want is the police messing around in this. How can I make you understand, Fanny? I don't want to appear churlish, but I'd appreciate it if you would stay out of my personal affairs."

"Oh, all right. I know when I'm not wanted."

"I'm sorry. Now, if you will excuse me, I have to finish dressing."

He shut the door quietly in Fanny's face; and Fanny, ignored at one door and rejected at the other, climbed upstairs to her own apartment and had a third cup of the coffee. She felt by no means deflated. If Terry was Jay's business, Ben was hers, and she was not prepared to relinquish her rights in the old devil so long as there was even a suggestion of his involvement. Or the least hope of rescuing him from his delinquency. On second thought, it was probably just as well, everything considered, to delay notifying the police.

The Personal was what made things so confused. If Ben was involved, the Personal made no sense. Besides being too devious for Ben's tastes, it was susceptible to detection and correct interpretation, and thereby risky. And why the 'O.' instead of 'B.', inasmuch as 'T.M.' was used instead of something deceptive? It made no sense whatever. Could it be, as Jay insisted, that the Personal was just a coincidence? It would surely be enlightening, Fanny thought, to know who had placed it in the paper.

The thought became instantly a resolution to find out. It would give her something to do while Farley snored and Jay taught his class. Something constructive *might* come of it, although Fan had reservations. It did not do to expect too much, she had learned, because it only increased your disappointment when you got too little—or nothing.

She was not sure that newspapers divulged the identity of users of their Personal columns. They might consider it confidential information like doctors and lawyers and the clergy. There was no point in speculating about it, however. She could learn by trying, and that was what she was going to do.

The Personal had appeared in *The Journal,* the only paper in town with considerable circulation. Fanny happened to know where its offices and plant were located, for she passed the building every day going to work on the bus. She put on hat and coat and gloves and went down to the bus stop on the corner and caught a bus going downtown.

At the Journal building, Fan was directed to Classified Ads. She found it without difficulty. Behind a high counter, a breasty woman asked her crisply, in a voice that defied her to do so, if she wished to place an ad.

39

"I don't wish to place one," said Fanny, "but I'd like to find out the name of someone who did."

"Wasn't the name published with the ad? Can you tell me the kind of ad it was?"

"It appeared in the Personal column of the Thursday evening edition."

The woman's expression immediately said that she had just been asked to commit treason.

"I'm *sorry*. The identity of Personal placers is *not* revealed."

"It's important."

"No, no. It's quite impossible."

"Well," said Fanny, stretching the facts to fit the occasion, "it is probable that whoever inserted that ad is some kind of criminal. Well, I suppose you're honor bound to protect him."

"There is no certainty that we *know* the identity of the party. We often don't in Personals, you know." It was now evident in the woman's face that rules and curiosity were at odds. "Do you have a copy of the newspaper with you?"

"No, I don't, but I can quote the ad."

Fanny quoted it verbatim, having a retentive memory. It was apparent at once that the woman remembered it. It was equally apparent, from the way honor rose above curiosity, that honor had won a cheap victory.

"I remember the item very well," the woman said. "It came in the mail with cash payment enclosed. I know because it came to my desk, and I arranged myself for its publication. I haven't, of course, the least idea who sent it. Sorry I can't help you."

When Fan left the Journal building, it was approaching noon and seemed a long time from her boiled egg. She decided to lunch downtown. But first she spent half an hour in a department store resisting the temptation to buy several items she did not need. Then she went to the café in a hotel where the blue-plate special was corned beef and cabbage and little boiled potatoes sprinkled with parsley. After lunching on this, with just one martini be-

40

forehand to whet her appetite, she caught another bus and returned to The Cornish Arms.

From the vestibule she walked directly back to Farley's door and began to knock on it loudly, convinced that it was high time Farley was getting up if he hadn't already done so. As it turned out he had, but only recently, for he was, although dressed, still disheveled and surly. He glared at Fanny with animosity.

"Stop that damn banging!" he said. "What the hell do you think you're doing?"

The order to stop banging was *ex post facto,* since it had necessarily stopped when he pulled the door away from her fist. So Fanny, ignoring it, slipped past into the room and turned to face him with disapproval.

"I think I'm doing things that need doing, that's what I think. While you have been sleeping and Jay has been off doing inconsequential things, I have been busy trying to discover what's become of Terry. How do you expect to accomplish anything by lying in bed?"

Farley fell into a chair and finger-combed his tousled hair with a temperate despair. His glare had diminished in animosity.

"Which means," he said, "that you have been making a pest of yourself again. Fan, why don't you have the common decency to mind your own business? What, precisely, have you been up to now?"

"I've been downtown to the newspaper office to see if I could find out who placed the Personal, but I couldn't. They have some kind of rule against telling. They didn't know, anyhow, because the Personal was sent in the mail. My efforts went for nothing."

"Serves you right. Maybe now you will butt out and stay out. Did you inquire before you left if Terry had come back or not?"

"I'm not as addle-headed as you seem to think, Farley. I asked Jay."

"What did Jay say?"

"He said Terry hadn't returned."

"Did he also suggest that you quit meddling?"

"Well, yes, he did, as a matter of fact."

"Good! I recommend that you comply."

"You're as bad as Jay, Farley, and that's the truth. Neither of you is willing to take any action whatever in this matter. If you ask me, it's not natural for a husband to be so indifferent to the unexplained absence of his wife."

"Jay's not indifferent. He's stoic. He has become inured by constant repetition."

"I don't care a hang what you call it, it's not natural. And, as I recall, you were kind of disturbed yourself in the beginning. What suddenly happened to make you change, I'd like to know?"

"Nothing happened. I merely decided to observe a period of quiet out of respect for the dead."

"Dead!" Fanny gave a startled little leap. "Are you implying that Terry is dead?"

"Hell, no. I was referring to the Terry-Jay marriage. Surely you're perceptive enough to see that it is, as the saying goes, as dead as last year's bird nest."

"Is *that* all?" Fanny relaxed. "I know you and Jay are convinced that nothing is indicated but a peccadillo, but I have been making an effort to learn the truth, and it's my opinion that it's time you did a little something to help."

"Not I. I've withdrawn from the fray."

"We'll see about that. There is something helpful you can do without setting foot from this apartment."

"Such as?"

"Such as calling the taxi companies. They must keep a record of calls, and one of them may be able to tell you if someone was picked up here, or near here, about three o'clock yesterday."

"Like hell! I don't intend to waste my time calling taxi companies."

"Why not? Your time is largely wasted, anyhow. We could find out where Terry was taken, if she *was* taken."

"If there's anything to this Personal that's got you so hot and bothered, she only went to the university library. The distance is easily walkable."

"Because she *went* there is no sign she *stayed* there. She could have gone on in the taxi to some place else with whomever she met."

"I simply won't call any taxi companies. There's no use asking me."

"Very well. And next time you want five or ten or twenty dollars, I simply won't give it to you. There'll be no use asking me."

"So that's the way it is!" Farley glared at her with a resurgence of his early animosity. "Blackmail!"

"I prefer to call it fair pay for services rendered. No services, no pay."

"All right, damn it! If you're going to be so nasty about it, I'll have to humor you. Now get out of here, Fan. Go think of something else useless to do."

He got up and, taking her firmly by an elbow, ushered Fanny to the door.

"Wait a minute," said Fanny. "Not so fast, brother. I'm sorry to say that you can't always be trusted to keep your word. When will you make the calls?"

"Just as soon as I've had some breakfast."

"Breakfast! It's past lunch time."

"Breakfast, lunch, shmunch. As soon as I've eaten. Not before."

"All right, then. But see that you do. If you don't, I'll make you sorry."

Fanny permitted herself to be pushed into the hall. And at that moment, as luck would have it, there was Jay Miles, returning from the university.

7

"Hello, Fanny," said Jay. "I was hoping to see you."

"Were you?" said Fanny skeptically. "Why?"

"Well, I was pretty rude to you this morning. I want to apologize."

"However rude you were," Farley said, "it probably wasn't rude enough. When you learn what this femme has been up to, you may want to insult her some more."

"What have you been up to, Fanny?"

"Go on, Fanny," Farley said. "Tell him what you've been up to."

"I went down to the *Journal* office and inquired about the Personal. I wanted, if possible, to know who placed it."

"Oh? Did you learn anything?"

"Nothing. The Personal was mailed in with the fee—in cash—enclosed."

"Too bad you went to so much trouble for nothing." Jay seemed surprisingly docile about the episode. "I told you last night the Personal was a coincidence, not directed to Terry at all. Didn't you remember?"

"I remembered, but I didn't believe it. And nothing's developed, so far as I can see, to make me believe it now."

"You see?" said Farley. "She simply will not mind her own business."

"To be fair, I can't say I blame her for being concerned. I'm really not so indifferent as I seem." Jay, although he spoke without urgency, was clearly appealing for Fanny's understanding. "As a matter of fact, I've been cudgeling my brain over this ever since last night, and I think I've finally come up with the answer. I owe you an

44

explanation for all your worry and trouble. If you'd care to come in——"

"I accept both your apology and your invitation," said Fanny. "Farley, go get your breakfast, or whatever you want to call it."

"Not much," Farley said. "If Jay's going to explain something, I want to hear it, too."

Jay unlocked his door and they all went in. He was carrying a briefcase, which he took into the bedroom while Fanny and Farley helped themselves to chairs.

"May I get you a drink?" Jay said, returning.

"Not for me," Farley said. "My stomach's empty."

"Nor me," said Fanny. "I had a martini with my lunch, and I can't have any more until five o'clock. Where do you think Terry has gone? I'm dying to know."

"I think she's gone back to Los Angeles."

"*Back* to Los Angeles?" said Fanny. "Is that where she came from?"

"Yes. Didn't you know? Actually, we were married in San Francisco. I had a job at the university there, and Terry had moved up from L.A. and was living alone in an apartment. Not attending the university, you understand. She just wanted to try living in San Francisco for a while. New experience. Terry was always keen for a new experience. Anyhow, we met at a party and got married. I don't quite understand why. I went head over heels for her, of course, but somehow I never felt that I was the type to make Terry reciprocate. Perhaps she just had an urge to try the academic life."

"But why would she run off to Los Angeles without a word to you or anyone else? If you ask me, it makes no sense."

"It makes Terry's kind of sense. If you knew her better, you'd understand that. She is perfectly capable of doing on impulse something that someone else would plan carefully."

"Even after inviting Farley to dinner?"

"That would be no deterrent to Terry. She was probably halfway to L.A. before she even remembered it."

"What about luggage?" Fanny pounced on the thought triumphantly. "Did she take any?"

"Apparently not. But it's no more than two hours from here to L.A. by jet, and after she was there, she could easily prevail on Feldman to supply anything she needed."

"Feldman?" Farley said. "Who's Feldman?"

"Yes, Jay," said Fanny, "please don't just throw in new characters. It's very confusing."

"Maurice Feldman, an attorney. To be exact, he's the executor of an estate left to Terry by her father, who was a minor movie executive."

"You mean Terry is an heiress? I didn't dream of such a thing!"

"Well, we didn't talk about it much. It's a pretty large estate, I think, but Terry won't get control of it until she's twenty-six, which will be about a year from now. Meanwhile Feldman doles out a limited allowance from the interest on the principal."

"Why would Terry's father want to tie things up that way?"

"Need you ask?" Jay shrugged. He fished in a pocket for cigarette and matches and, having found them, did nothing further about them. "Surely it's evident by this time that a sense of responsibility is not one of Terry's attributes. Her father didn't want to cut her off, but he hoped a delay would bring a little more maturity. Wishful thinking, I'm afraid."

Fanny rose, took the cigarette and matches from Jay's hands, lit the former with one of the latter, and sat down again.

"Since you are not going to smoke this," she said, "I may as well. I must say, Jay, I'm not completely convinced. Is there any particular reason why Terry should suddenly have decided to go back to Los Angeles?"

"She was always threatening to. She didn't want to come to Handclasp in the first place. She was never happy here. If the offer by the university hadn't been so attractive, I'd probably have stayed in Frisco."

"If she's gone back to Los Angeles, it should be easy to check. As you say, she'd certainly get in touch with this Mr. Feldman, because of the allowance and all. Why don't you call him and ask?"

"I intend to, this evening."

46

"Why don't you call him now?"

"No. I've decided to wait a little longer."

"There you are, Fanny," Farley said. "I hope you're satisfied and will stop making a nuisance of yourself."

Fanny's retort, which was on the tip of her tongue, was stymied by a knock on the door. Her first thought was that here was Terry, home from the wars. But, on second thought, it would be ridiculous for Terry to knock on her own door. On the other hand, she might consider it wise, under the circumstances, to throw in her hat before entering.

It was not Terry at all, of course, but Otis Bowers.

"Hello, Otis," Jay said. "What can I do for you?"

"I wonder," said Otis, "if I could borrow some matches. I seem to be out."

"Sure." Jay stepped back, giving Otis a clear view of Fanny and Farley, whom Otis had been trying to see around Jay's shoulder. "Come on in."

Otis came in. Jay headed for the kitchen, where the matches were.

"Hello, Fanny, Farley," Otis said. "I just knocked on your door, Fanny, but I couldn't raise you."

"Obviously," said Fanny, "since I am here and not there. What are you looking for, Otis?"

Otis's head, which had been turning this way and that, suddenly assumed a fixity, eyes front, as if he were afraid of the consequences of turning it at all.

"Nothing," he said. "Nothing at all. I just came to borrow some matches."

"I thought maybe you were looking for Terry. If you were, you can quit. She isn't here."

"Little sister," Farley said, "why don't you shut up? If Jay wants a mouthpiece, I'm sure he'll ask for one."

"Well, what's the matter with you, Farley?" Fanny said indignantly. "What's the harm, I'd like to know, in telling Otis that Terry isn't here when he can plainly see for himself that she isn't? I don't understand your attitude at all."

"Oh, I give up!" said Farley. "By God, I do!"

"What's all the fuss about?" Otis said. "Didn't Terry get home last night?"

"No," Farley said, "she didn't."

"Jay thinks she went to Los Angeles," Fanny said. "Isn't that so, Jay?"

"Yes." Jay, having completed his round trip to the kitchen, handed Otis half a dozen matchbooks.

"But why Los Angeles?" Otis said.

"We've been all over that," said Fanny. "If you want to know things, Otis, why don't you get in at the beginning?"

"Never mind," Jay said. "There's no point in dwelling on the matter. Otis, I believe there's enough matches there to last until you can get more."

"Yes. Yes, this is plenty, Jay. Thanks very much."

Jay, when he had come away from the door after admitting Otis, had left it open, possibly as a hint to his guests, but the effect, unfortunately, was only to gather another. Otis, on his way out, was suddenly face to face with his wife. Ardis had appeared on the threshold and was nosing into the room.

"Otis," she said, "what are you doing down *here?* I thought you were just going across the hall to borrow some matches from Fanny."

"Fanny isn't home," Otis said.

"As you see," said Fanny.

"Did you get some matches?"

"Yes. Jay loaned me some."

"Then we had better go back upstairs." Ardis leaned forward into the room and craned, like her husband before her, this way and that. "Where's Terry? Didn't she come back last night?"

It was evident from her tone that she considered it Jay's good luck if Terry hadn't. Jay obliged woodenly by confirming her hopes.

"Jay thinks she's in Los Angeles," said Fanny.

"Los Angeles! Whatever for?"

"There are good reasons," said Fanny, "that are too involved to relate."

"Is that so?" Ardis shifted a sweetly venomous stare from Fanny to Jay. "Even if there are, I'd look closer to home before leaping all the way to Los Angeles. As I have good reason to know. Even next door or upstairs is not too close for Terry's operations. Jay, have you asked Brian O'Hara if he knows where she is?"

Otis was pink and Jay was white and Farley was red, but Fanny was mostly interested.

"What the hell do you mean by 'next door'?" Farley said.

"What I would like to know," said Fanny, "is what she means by 'Brian O'Hara.' Jay, what does she mean?"

"Shut up, Fan!" Farley said. "For God's sake, shut up!"

"Brian O'Hara," Jay said stiffly, "is a local and lesser version of Arnold Rothstein. He is a gambler who specializes in collegiate athletic contests. He owns a couple of night spots geared for college students. He is reputed to be honest by his own liberal standards. I wouldn't know."

"Oh, I know who he is, of course," Fanny said. "What I mean is, what does he have to do with Terry?"

"Ardis is trying to tell me," Jay said, "that Terry and O'Hara have been seen together under suggestive circumstances. Thanks, Ardis, but I already knew."

"Well, you may have known, but I didn't," said Fanny. "Did you know, Farley? Why didn't you tell me?"

"I'm no damn scandal-monger, that's why," Farley said. "Besides, it's incredible that you hadn't found out. It's a miracle."

"It's evident that I've said too much," Ardis sniffed. "I was only trying to be helpful. Come along, Otis!"

She marched away, Otis trailing. Passing through the doorway, he cast a glance backward.

"Jay, thanks for the matches," Otis said miserably.

"You're welcome," Jay said.

When they were gone, Farley rose and turned immediately to Fanny with grim decision, as if he were prepared to do violence if necessary.

"You, too, Fan. *Stand up*. Let's leave Jay alone."

"Sure*ly*." Fanny stood up as ordered. "You are quite right for a change, Farley. I must say, too, that you were quite right in the hall upstairs last night. I am always inclined to see the good in a person instead of the bad, but that Ardis *is* a bitch."

8

It has been said of patients in mental hospitals that one of the therapists' most difficult problems is to get them to do anything. Although some kind of work is thought to be as important to the cure of mental disorders as aspirin to the alleviation of a headache, the patient displays a remarkably obdurate insistence on submitting to the tricks of his nervous system. Jay Miles was not a mental patient, but in this respect, at least, he felt and acted like one.

Left to his own devices, with many things to do that might have been done, he did nothing.

He merely *thought* about doing them.

He thought about getting his lectures in order for Monday's classes; but economics, ordinarily a stimulant, seemed at the moment abysmally dull. He thought about preparing himself lunch, but he couldn't think of anything available in the larder that appealed to his feeble appetite. He thought about having a drink; but drinking, if started, was something he might be tempted under the circumstances to continue, and he needed to keep a clear head with which to think of all the things to be done that he wasn't doing. He thought about listening to music, which would really have required no effort; and he would have done this, if only it hadn't been so far from his chair to the player.

It was even farther to the telephone.

What he ought to do, if anything, was to call Maurice Feldman in Los Angeles and inquire about Terry. Appearances demanded it. He was expected by his neighbors, especially that bothersome little Fanny, to make a display of anxiety he by no means felt; indeed, that he was no longer capable of feeling.

50

In the beginning he had been ardently in love with Terry. But ardor diminishes, and love dies, from chronic neglect and frequent betrayal. (Sometimes the love becomes hate, and then the ardor grows strong again.) It was too bad that things had developed with him and Terry as they had. But there it was, bad gone to worse, and it was far too late to do anything about it. It had been, in fact, too late from the first.

Jay consulted his watch and found that it lacked two minutes of being three o'clock. Allowing for the time difference, it was almost one in Los Angeles. It was, moreover, almost one of a Saturday afternoon. Barring urgent business Feldman would not be in his office; barring inclement weather, if Jay knew his man, Feldman would not be at home. A golf bug, he would almost certainly be on some course trying to break a hundred. The thing to do, Jay decided, was to place a call to Feldman's home and leave word for the attorney to call him back when he got in. But what was Feldman's home number? Jay remembered the area code, 213, but the number had slipped his mind. He thought, however, that Terry had written it in the back of the directory on the page provided for listing out-of-town numbers, and he got up with great effort to see, and there it was. He dialed the number and was given the information he expected. Feldman was not at home, but he was expected at five o'clock L.A. time. The woman who answered the phone, a maid, assured Jay that she would relay his request that Mr. Feldman return the call. Jay cradled the phone with an exorbitant sense of accomplishment. There! The thing was done, the gesture made. Now it was possible to resume doing nothing, or next to nothing, until seven o'clock.

Doing nothing, or next to nothing, for four hours is in itself a difficult job. One must, paradoxically, do something in order to accomplish it. Sleeping is as close to doing nothing as a man can get; and Jay, who had slept very little the previous night, went into the bedroom and took off his shoes and lay down on his back on the bed.

It was a precarious position, for it is peculiarly conducive to unpleasant reflections while awake, and to bad dreams when asleep. The trick, of course, was to think of

51

something or someone besides Terry, but this was impossible because she was immediately everywhere at once in the room, even creeping beneath his eyelids when he closed them. He did not resist her presence, which would have been a mistake, and so he achieved a kind of passivity that in the end induced unconsciousness. He slept fitfully until he was awakened by the strident ringing of the telephone in the living room.

The apartment had grown dark while he slept, and he groped his way toward the ringing. As he expected, his greeting brought on the gravelly voice of Maurice Feldman.

"Jay? Feldman here. What's on your mind?"

"Well, it seems that Terry has wandered off, and I was wondering if she's shown up in L.A. Have you heard from her?"

"If she's here, she hasn't got in touch with me. How long has she been gone?"

"Since yesterday afternoon. When I got home from the university, she was gone."

"Didn't she tell anyone where she was going?"

"Apparently not. No one seems to know."

"What makes you think she came out here? Did she take any clothes with her?"

"Just what she was wearing, so far as I can tell. That's why I thought she'd be in touch with you right away."

"Well, if I hear from her, I'll let you know immediately."

"I'd appreciate it."

"I rather suspect, however, that you'll be hearing from her soon, if she doesn't return. God knows what makes Terry so erratic. Keep me informed, will you, Jay?"

"Right. Sorry to have bothered you."

"No bother. I'm glad you called. It's probably too early to get excited, though, where Terry's concerned. I suppose you're accustomed to her habits by this time."

"Thoroughly. How was your golf game today?"

"Golf? I didn't play golf. I was tied up at the office."

"Oh? If I'd known that, I'd have called you there."

"I'm involved in a rather important court action at the moment. Demands my personal attention. If there's nothing else on your mind, Jay, I've got to dress for dinner. We're having guests."

"Right, Maury. Thanks for calling back."

He hung up and returned to the bedroom. After turning on the ceiling light, he sat on the edge of the bed and put on his shoes. He still wasn't hungry, but it was a long time since his last meal, and he decided that he had better eat something. On the other hand, he didn't feel like going to the trouble of preparing anything; besides, he had an urgent need to get out of the apartment. Wearing a topcoat but no hat, he left the building and walked over to a small restaurant near the campus that catered largely to students.

Consuming a bowl of soup and a cold roast-beef sandwich, Jay Miles began at last to face the issue he had heretofore avoided. He considered Brian O'Hara and what, if anything, should be done about him. He would have preferred to do nothing at all, but appearances clearly dictated a gesture in O'Hara's direction. Terry's relationship with O'Hara, however much or little it amounted to, incited no anger in Jay, only a soiled sense of shame that he could feel none. This had the effect of augmenting his bitterness toward Terry for stirring in him an emotion that was, at most, no more than incidental to the one he should have felt. Be he did not blame O'Hara for Terry's initiative. Once he would have blamed O'Hara, but no longer. There had been too many O'Haras.

His attitude was hardly understandable by those who expected him to react "normally." Ever since Ardis Bowers had made her point about Terry and O'Hara, Jay had realized that, if he wanted to keep the respect of those who were aware of the circumstances, he would have to go through certain motions. To say nothing, perhaps, of allaying dangerous speculation. At any rate, he was faced with the disagreeable necessity of seeing O'Hara, and of letting it be known afterward that he had done so.

This being so—acting on Macbeth's principle in the killing of Duncan—he decided that now was better than later; and he paid his check and left the restaurant.

It was a long walk to the residential hotel in which O'Hara kept a suite. But it was a good night for walking, which also had the effect of delaying the disagreeable encounter. Jay went all the way afoot. It was almost nine o'clock when he reached the hotel, an impressive stack of stone and steel whose marquee advertised The Rinaldo.

He had to ask at the desk for O'Hara's suite number, and he was forced to wait while the clerk rang up to see if O'Hara was there in the first place, and if he would receive a caller in the second. Jay rather hoped that he wasn't, or wouldn't. But the hope was wasted both ways. O'Hara was and would. Suite 1502, top floor.

Jay went up in the elevator, which rose too fast.

He was admitted by O'Hara himself, alone in the living room of his suite. It was anyone's guess, of course, as to who might have been in other rooms.

O'Hara, who was sometimes a ruffian in behavior, was far from one in appearance. As tall as Jay, he was wider and thicker in the shoulders, and even narrower in the waist. He held himself erect, but with an effect of being at ease, and he moved with grace. His eyes were cold pale blue. His hair, which was blond, was cropped. His voice, amiably modulated, was a lie.

"Come in, Miles," he said. "It's Doctor, isn't it?"

"I don't make a point of it. Mister's good enough."

"Let me take your coat."

"No, thanks."

"You could use a drink, couldn't you?"

Jay could have, but he said he couldn't.

"I can't stay," he said. "I'm looking for my wife."

O'Hara permitted the slightest flicker of surprise to disturb his expression, but he had the good judgment not to put his reaction into words. Clearly he had no intention of either confirming or denying a relationship of which Jay apparently was aware. He had, in fact, a genuine aversion to the kind of angry attention, both public and private, that his activities naturally invited.

"Am I to understand that she's missing?"

"That's right."

"What made you think you'd find her here?"

"Why not? If I'm not mistaken, she's been here before."

"Sorry. This is not my night for confessional. She's

54

your wife, for the present, and you can think what you like about her."

"Thanks. That's liberal of you, but why the time qualification?"

"We needn't pretend with each other. Terry is a dissatisfied wife. You know as well as I that it's only a matter of time till she leaves you. If you say she's missing, maybe she already has."

"Maybe. How do you know so much about it? Did she tell you?"

"All I'll tell you is that she isn't here. I haven't seen her for a week."

"I'd hardly expect you to say otherwise."

O'Hara's only physical reaction was a narrowing of the lids over his eyes, but Jay was suddenly aware of cold menace.

"You're wrong. If she were here, you could expect me to say so, and to hell with you. Would you like to look through the place?"

"No," said Jay Miles.

"I'll tell you this, too. We had a date for cocktails at one of my places yesterday afternoon. She didn't show up. I assumed that something had developed to prevent her coming. For her sake, I hoped so. I don't like being stood up."

"Don't you? Somehow, the idea doesn't disturb me. You'll understand my indifference, I'm sure."

"I don't give a damn how you feel about it." O'Hara occupied himself for a few seconds with finding and lighting a cigarette. "I'll tell you what I do give a damn about, though, since you've brought it to my attention. I give a damn about what's become of Terry. How long has she been missing?"

"Since yesterday afternoon."

"That long? And you have no idea where she can be?"

"I've had a couple of ideas. Both seem to have been wrong."

"Maybe you know more about it than you're admitting."

"What the devil do you mean by that?"

"You have plenty of reason to work up a hate for

Terry. It would be smart of you to kick up a fuss as a cover-up."

"Don't be a fool. It's been all over between Terry and me for some time now."

"Then what's the uproar about?"

"She's still my wife, O'Hara."

O'Hara smiled. "Are you getting tough with me?"

"Let's not underestimate each other. A mistake either way could be costly."

"Fair enough. And now, if you won't have that drink, I have an appointment at one of my clubs. I'm already late."

He went to the door and held it open. "I'll make a point of looking into this," he said. "Let's hope we hear from Terry soon."

Jay said nothing more.

He descended to the lobby in the fast elevator, from the lobby into the street. A cold wind had come up. He felt that he had survived an ordeal with as much dignity as the circumstances permitted.

Turning up his collar and lowering his head, Jay walked home against the wind.

9

Otis Bowers awoke with a sensation of rising slowly through brackish water to the surface of a stagnant pool. His teeth felt smeary and his face, with its growth of meager beard, dirty. It took him a moment, dreading the day, to remember that it was Sunday, a fact which by no means diminished his dread. He did not plan the traditional pause for worship and rest, having no conviction in the one and little hope of the other. Ardis, stirred by current events to an old animus, was hardly a restful mate. He could feel her beside him, hear her breathing. He knew without looking that her back was turned against him, a position she seemed able to maintain even in the tossing and turning of sleep.

Carefully Otis eased his legs over the side of the bed. This slight effort exhausted him, and he sat slumped for a few minutes, braced by his arms. Then he struggled to his feet and padded into the bathroom. Now, with a kind of sustained rush, he brushed his teeth, washed his face, lathered, and shaved. Returning to the bedroom, he saw with despair that Ardis was sitting up against the headboard of the bed.

"Good morning," Otis said.

"Is the coffee making?" Ardis said.

"Not yet. I just woke up."

"What time is it?"

He looked at the alarm clock, which she could have seen for herself by simply turning her head.

"Twenty minutes past nine."

"I want my coffee."

"I was just going to make it."

He went out to the kitchen and put cold water into a

Pyrex pot and leaned against the table until the water boiled. He removed the pot from the burner, measured in the instant coffee, and watched it while it steeped. This done, he poured two cupfuls and carried the cups to the bedroom. Thus far, he had been reasonably successful in not thinking about things he didn't want to think about.

"Here you are," he said.

She carried the cup immediately to her mouth, afterward closing her eyes and letting her head fall back against the headboard. Her face looked grayer and older than it was.

"I wonder if Terry's back," she said.

"I don't know. I haven't seen Jay since yesterday."

"Aren't you terribly concerned?"

"Don't start that again. Please don't."

"Oh, excuse me." Ardis raised her head and opened her eyes, disclosing the malice behind her lids. "I'd forgotten how sensitive you are on the subject of Terry. She made a fool of you with so little effort, didn't she?"

"I suppose she did. You are welcome to think so, if you like. Can't you forget it, Ardis? Can't you let me forget it?"

"That would be nice for you, wouldn't it? It's not as easy as all that for *me*."

"Can't I make you understand that there never really was anything between Terry and me? Nothing ever *happened*. She was only playing a game with me. Terry's got a cruel streak in her. She enjoys things like that. I'm not the type Terry would take seriously."

"Why not? Aside from being a fool in your personal affairs, you're a brilliant physicist. You have a wonderful career ahead of you. All you have to do is use common sense."

"Terry doesn't give a damn about physicists, brilliant or otherwise, and she didn't give a damn about me."

"Are you saying that what's good enough for me isn't good enough for your precious Terry?"

Fool or not, Otis could see the folly of going any further in *that* direction. It was futile, in fact, to go anywhere in any direction. His offense had not been infidelity, but a fatuous gullibility that in her view reflected on his legal

58

bedmate. He would have been in less trouble, actually, if he had done as well in adultery as in physics. He had not, however. He had been involved in a fiasco, not a conquest; and he admitted that he deserved Ardis's scorn, although he yearned for surcease.

"Nothing of the sort," Otis said. "I'm just saying that Terry has a beastly set of values. Look at the way she treats Jay. She really has no regard for him, although he's a very competent economist. It's a mystery to me why she ever married him. She's much more taken with animals like Brian O'Hara."

Ardis sipped her coffee, staring at him slyly over the rim of the cup.

"'O.' for O'Hara?" she said.

"Must you be so devious, Ardis?" He sat down on the side of the bed, clutching his cup and saucer in his left hand. "I simply don't know what you're talking about."

"I'm talking about the Personal ad that appeared in Thursday evening's *Journal*."

"What Personal ad?"

"It was addressed to 'T.M.', and it was signed 'O.' It arranged a meeting for a certain time and place."

"What time and place?"

"Three o'clock Friday afternoon. Apparently at the university library."

Otis stared into his cup. Then he shrugged and looked up.

"It's absurd. In Terry's case, what's more, completely unnecessary. In spite of the initials, I don't believe it was meant for her at all."

"That settles the matter very neatly, doesn't it? Case closed, eh?"

"Didn't you expect me to deny that it was 'O.' for Otis? Very well, I deny it. All right, I've been a fool, but not so big a fool as to engage in any damn foolishness like this. Why should I? I could have spoken directly to Terry whenever I chose."

"So, for that matter, could O'Hara."

"That's the point. The Personal wasn't meant for Terry at all."

59

"You can dismiss such coincidence if you care to. I'm not prepared to do so."

He stared at her with a thoughtful expression, as if his mind, having dismissed one consideration, had gone off on another tangent.

"How do you happen to know about the Personal? I can't recall anyone's mentioning it."

"I read it when it appeared."

"I didn't know you read the Personal columns."

"This time I did."

"Interesting. And you thought of me the first thing, didn't you?"

"Not without cause."

"There's nothing quite so exhilarating as a wifely faith. I'm wondering what, suspecting me of a clandestine meeting in advance, you would be capable of doing to prevent it."

"Nothing. I doubt that you're worth it."

"Wouldn't you even spy a little? Just out of curiosity?"

"Not when I had a migraine headache. Friday afternoon, you'll remember, I had one."

"I know you said so."

"And so I had. I came home early and took a sleeping pill. I was here in the apartment all afternoon."

"At the scene, so to speak." He laughed without humor and rose abruptly. "Are you actually offering explanations, Ardis? It's not like you."

They looked at each other with the closest thing to understanding that they had achieved for a long time.

"More coffee?" he said.

"Yes." She held out her cup. "Please."

10

Later that same Sunday morning—the second day after the disappearance of Terry Miles—two boys were discussing seriously a problem of importance. They were in a sparsely settled neighborhood on the eastern edge of a city that was growing westward. No new construction had gone on there for a long time. The houses, all of aging vintage, were for the most part separated by one or more vacant lots; there was plenty of open space for the antics of boys. A short distance eastward the plumbing ended and the open country began. There were no suburbs here. The planners, speculators, and builders of the city of Handclasp concentrated their interests and investments on the other side of town.

The two boys, crossing a vacant lot, had stopped to settle their problem between them, the problem being what to do. They had lately escaped the horror of Sunday school; now, after changing into appropriate clothes, they were determined to salvage what was left of the day. Being of the age that both remembers toys and has premonitions of girls, they earnestly sought an adventure that would include the excitement of the one and the apprehension of the other. As they examined and discarded a number of possibilities, their breath escaped between them in frosty clouds. They were bundled against the cold morning in heavy jackets. Whatever they were called by their peers, they were soon to enter certain official records as Charles and Vernon—names which do not have, among small boys, a greatly used sound.

"I'll tell you what," said Charles.

"What?" said Vernon.

"Let's go explore the old Skully place."

"We can't do that. People live in it."

"Not now, they don't. Nobody's lived in it for over a month."

"Somebody will, though. Some real estate company downtown rents it."

"What difference does that make? Nobody's living in it right now. That's what counts."

"What do you want to explore the old Skully place for?"

"Wait'll I tell you what I saw there the other night."

"What?"

"I saw a light in an upstairs window."

"You're just making that up."

"I am not. It was a little light, like a flashlight. It kept moving around."

"What night was it? What time did you see it? Come on, make it good."

"It was Friday night. Real late. It must've been one o'clock, maybe more."

"What were you doing at the old Skully place that late?"

"I was coming home in the car with Mother and Dad. We'd been downtown to a late movie. I just happened to look up and saw the light in the window as we went past. I told Dad about it, but he said I was imagining things."

"You were."

"I wasn't. I bet you I wasn't."

Faced with such conviction Vernon, the skeptic, began to waver.

"Who do you think it was?" he asked in an awed tone.

"How should I know? I'll bet he didn't have any business being there, though. Are you game to have a look?"

His courage challenged, Vernon agreed, beginning to share Charles's excitement. Even if they didn't actually come across anything, the old and empty house would inflame the imagination to any boy's satisfaction. As they traveled the long two blocks to the house, they convinced each other that they were performing a necessary—and dangerous—service to the community.

The Skully house, named for its orignal owner—a widower who had died there harassed by the unfounded suspicions of other imaginative youngsters like the pair now approaching through unkempt grass from the rear—was two stories tall, but so narrow in construction that it seemed taller. It had a high screened back porch; small windows in the foundation indicated the presence of a basement. Although old and ugly, it was kept in repair by the real estate agency that owned and rented it.

The two young trespassers, after crossing the back porch and finding the rear door locked, retreated and found a basement window that wasn't. Charles first and Vernon behind him, they scrambled through and dropped.

The basement reeked of mustiness and junk and dust and rats and spiders. There was a coal bin, and a storage room for home-canned fruits and vegetables, its shelves still holding a supply of dusty Mason jars and a litter of rusted lids. Near the ancient furnace stood a workbench with a vise attached; a flight of ladder-like steps ascended to the kitchen door. Charles and Vernon, still in that order, climbed the steps and tried the door. It was unlocked, and they entered and crossed the kitchen, unconsciously walking—for no reason except the cold menace of the silent house—on tiptoes.

The first floor revealed no ghastly secrets; nor did their intrusion invoke old Skully's ghost, which was said to loiter about the place. Relieved and disappointed, they went up a narrow stairway to the upper floor, now side by side for company. There were two doors on each side of a hall, and a fifth at the end. They walked straight back to the end door and found that it opened into a bathroom; the high old-fashioned tub had feet shaped like eagle claws clutching round balls. Reversing themselves, they began to open the other doors on empty rooms. Not speaking for fear of affronting the silence, they communicated with each other through a system of gestures and grimaces.

Now Charles conveyed to Vernon the information that the last room, deliberately withheld for the purpose of climax, was the one in which he had seen the mysterious moving light.

Crossing to this door, he pushed it inward. . . .

11

"Sundays," said Farley, "last forever."

"They only seem that way to you," said his sister Fanny, "because they give you an uneasy conscience."

"Are you speaking from experience?"

"My conscience *never* bothers me."

"Maybe that's because you don't have one. Let it go, however. It so happens that I am living quite comfortably with my conscience at the moment. Why shouldn't I be?"

"That's for you to say."

"Tell me, little sister, why should my conscience kick up on Sundays in particular? Rather, that is, than on Mondays or Tuesdays or any other day of the week?"

"It seems to me difficult to rest easy on a day of rest when one never does anything else, whatever the day is. As for me, I work hard earning my living, and therefore I have nothing to reproach myself with."

"Well, what the hell would you call studying law? I'd call it work, that's what I'd call it! And damn hard work, too, between you and me."

"It all depends on who's doing it, and how much is being done. You want me to be honest, don't you? I haven't seen you crack a book all weekend."

"Thanks to you, I've been compelled to do other things."

Sprawled on the sofa in Fanny's apartment, Farley eyed her sourly. If it had not been contrary to his best interests, he would have said something insulting and stalked out. His best interests could best be served, however, by hanging on, even if it mean submitting to harassment. In short, he had eaten very little for almost two days, and he was badly in need of nourishment. He had realized this about four o'clock, ten minutes ago, and he had simultaneously remembered that Fanny, if she had Sunday dinner in, usually had it around five. So Farley had come up to see if anything edible was under way, and luckily something was—a piece of beef tenderloin in the oven that was adequate for two. But Fanny had as yet extended no invitation to stay. Worse, she was looking at him in a manner that did nothing to feed his hopes.

"That reminds me," she said. "I've been wanting to ask if you called the taxi companies, as I told you to."

"I considered not doing it, but I knew you'd devil the devil out of me if I didn't. So I did."

"What did you find out?"

"Just what I expected. Nothing. There's no record of anyone's picking up a passenger here, or near here, any time close to the time Terry left."

"Are you sure you inquired, or are you just saying so?"

"Of course I'm sure. Do you think I'd lie about it?"

"Yes, I do."

"Well, I'm not going to take an oath on it. Believe me or not as you please."

She was distracted from whatever response was on her tongue by a knocking on the door, and she went over and opened it to reveal Jay Miles. He was wearing his topcoat and was obviously either just going out or just coming back from having been out. The two wedges of flesh below his eyes, behind the thick glasses, were dark smudges.

"Hello, Fanny." He peered over her shoulder at Farley. "Oh, there you are, Farley. I thought you might be up here."

"I came up to have dinner with Fanny," Farley said, "but she hasn't asked me yet."

"Fat chance," said Fanny. "Come in, Jay. Whither away, or where from?"

"I'm just going." Jay stepped inside far enough to allow Fanny to close the door. "As a matter of fact, that's why I was looking for you, Farley. I thought maybe you might go with me."

"That's a good idea!" Fanny said. "Farley, get yourself cleaned up and go with Jay. While you're out you can have dinner together somewhere."

"Not I," Farley said. "I don't want to go."

"How do you know you don't? You don't even know yet where he's going."

"Wherever it is, I don't want to go."

"Don't be contrary. Where are you going, Jay?"

"To the police. I've finally made up my mind."

Farley sat up at Jay's quiet declaration. Fanny backed her neat little stern onto the arm of a chair and studied Jay as if she were trying to make up her own mind about something. Oddly, although she had been urging action, she did not seem enthusiastic about Jay's proposed visit to the police.

"I don't know about that," she said. "Have you made certain that she didn't run off to Los Angeles?"

"Yes. I called Feldman yesterday afternoon. He hasn't seen or heard from her."

"I hate to be bitchy, but another suggestion was made."

"Brian O'Hara? I went to see O'Hara after talking with Feldman. Last night. Terry wasn't at his place and hadn't been there."

"Do you think for an instant he'd admit it if she had been?"

"I'm convinced O'Hara was telling the truth."

"Perhaps so, but it doesn't do to be impetuous in an affair of this sort. There's such a thing as going off half-cocked, you know."

"Well, I'll be damned!" Farley was staring at Fanny in amazement. "You have been running all over the place doing things and forcing others to do things, and now all of a sudden you start dragging your heels. What's the matter with you?"

"Nothing's the matter. We have delayed going to the police this long, and it will do no great harm to delay a little longer, that's all. Ben can be expected back soon, if his word can be relied upon, and he may know something that will be helpful."

"Ben?" Jay sounded confused. "Oh, I don't think so. What in the world could Ben know about it?"

"You never know," Fanny snapped. "He's a deceptive little bugger."

66

"She persists in suspecting Ben of dark, doleful deeds," Farley said. "She's absolutely irrational about it."

"That's not true! I am only trying to keep an open mind."

"It doesn't make any difference one way or the other," Jay said. "I've made up my mind, and I'm going. I'm a great deal more worried than I was at first."

"Oh, all right. I can see there's no use trying to stop you. However, I see no advantage in going immediately. You might just as well wait until tomorrow."

"I don't see why."

"Because today's Sunday, that's why."

"What does its being Sunday have to do with it?"

"Things are closed on Sunday. Everyone knows that."

"Police headquarters? Don't be absurd, Fanny."

"At least they'll be operating with a skeleton crew. It will probably be impossible—"

"Fanny," said Farley, "you've gone too far. Even you have better sense than to believe that. You're up to something, and I want to know what it is."

"What you want is of no consequence. I am the only one who has been attaching proper importance to all this, and I don't propose to be criticized now for a difference of opinion." Fanny, having disposed of Farley, turned her attention to Jay. "Jay, are you actually determined to go?"

"Yes."

"In that case, Farley will go with you."

"Who says so?" Farley said.

"I say so. I can tell you right now that you'll gain nothing by hanging around here, for you aren't getting any of my dinner. Not a bite."

"Come along with me, Farley," Jay said. "I'd appreciate it if you would."

"What for?"

"Call it moral support. We probably won't be there long. When we're through, I'll buy you dinner."

"Since you put it that way," Farley said, rising with a show of interest, "I'll come."

He went out in Jay's wake; and Fanny, still hooked on the arm of the chair, began to consider the new development. She was not opposed in principle to bringing in the

67

police, for she had been convinced for some time that it was the only sensible thing to do. But her uneasiness about Ben and his possible connection with Terry Miles's disappearance had increased with speculation; she was not, where Ben was concerned, nearly so sensible as in the case of others. It would be a great relief if only he would get back and explain things, damn him. In the meanwhile, time would pass more quickly if it were filled with events.

Fan went into the kitchen and looked into the oven. The tenderloin had acquired a nice crust and would soon be done. She mixed batter for potato pancakes, using a prepared mix and letting the batter stand for ten minutes, according to the directions on the box. This interval Fan utilized in stirring up a couple of martinis. One she drank in what was left of the ten minutes, the other she saved to drink just before eating.

Having eaten, she cleaned up and went back into the living room and turned on the table lamp. Night had come early, as nights did in November; it seemed much later than it probably was. It was actually six-thirty; and it was unlikely that Jay and Farley, who had left approximately two hours ago, had had time to go to police headquarters, stop somewhere for dinner, and return. It was even less likely, when they did return, that they would come up and report to her as, in all decency, they should. They would go to Jay's apartment, or to Farley's or each to his own; and she, Fanny, would be left in exasperating ignorance for the whole night. This was not to be borne, of course. She decided to wait in Farley's apartment, assuming that Farley had left the door unlocked. (She could hardly take the liberty of waiting in Jay's without his permission, but Farley's was something else.)

Taking cigarettes and matches with her, she went downstairs, tried Farley's door, and found it unlocked. Farley was notoriously careless about doors, one of his few habits that could sometimes be useful. His living room was dark, but the darkness was cut by a swath of light from the bedroom. Fanny crossed the room, peeped cautiously in—and there, lying on the bed, on his back, his shoes off and his arms folded under his head, was Ben Green.

68

Fan stepped into full view.

"Hello, Fan," Ben Green said in his melodious baritone. "Come in and lie down."

"Like hell," Fanny said.

His grin expanded. "I naturally assumed that you had
slipped in for a bit of sport."

"Your error."

"Which brings us to the point. What *are* you doing
here?"

"More to the point, where have *you* been?"

"That's no secret. I've been away."

"Where away?"

"Out of town."

"With whom?"

"Do you think I'd tell you? However, I was lone-wolf-
ing it."

"Where's Terry?"

"Terry? Is she gone?"

"Yes. So have you been. Doesn't that seem a coincidence?"

"You're on the wrong track, honeyball. I'm saving myself for you."

"Well, you can be as clever and secretive as you
choose. But you had better think up a convincing lie if
you don't care to tell the truth."

Impressed by her gravity, Ben sat up on the edge of the
bed, prepared as a tentative measure to take her seriously.
Now that he had assumed a position less conducive to the
free exercise of his libido, Fan ventured to come closer.
She even sat down beside him. He helped himself to her
near hand, examined it, patted it, and continued to hold
it.

"Something's up," he said. "Tell old Ben."

"I told you. Terry's gone. No one knows where she is."

"So what? Terry has always been given to a moderate
amount of moonlighting. She'll be back after a while,
breathing sighs and telling lies."

"If she's coming back, she's taking her own sweet time
about it. She disappeared shortly after you left on Friday
afternoon."

"So that's it. Old Ben wanders away, and Terry goes up

in smoke. Natural conclusion: assignation. Sweet nitwit, it won't wash. I don't even come close to fitting Terry's prescription. Wrong ingredients entirely. I'm too poor, too runty, too ugly. And incidentally, if I may say so, too smart."

"How about Otis? What kind of prescription did he fit?"

"Otis was a joke. Otis was a comedian. All he gave was laughs, and what he got was nothing. Everybody knew the score except Otis. That's the trouble with these scientific types. They leave their brains in the laboratory. They'd be better off if they were born without glands."

"Well, you mustn't call yourself unpleasant names. I won't have it. No one can deny that you are poor, but you are not runty and ugly."

"As another runt, you're prejudiced. Not that you're ugly, I hasten to add. On the contrary, you're lovely and sexy. Would you like to recline?"

"What I would like and what I would do are two different things. Behave yourself, Ben. In my opinion, you are just as brainy and glandular as Otis ever was."

"True. My brains, however, are Machiavellian."

"Damn it, Ben, you have a positive talent for leading me off the point. The point is, Terry's been gone since Friday, everyone's worried, and what are you going to do about it?"

"I?" His eyes widened, then narrowed. "Me? Nothing. Why should I? What could I?"

"You could explain where you've been, to start with. Besides, what do you mean by running off without a word to me about it? You know very well I've decided to marry you as soon as you get your doctorate and show signs of amounting to something. I won't have you running all over the place without restraint. Tell me at once where you have been."

"I respectfully decline to answer on the grounds that anything I say you'll use to incriminate me."

"You mean you won't tell me?"

"That's it."

"Very well. It's plain that I can't help you if you won't let me. You can explain to the police."

"The police!" His voice had sharpened, and his grip tightened on her hand. "What do the police have to do with it?"

"Jay and Farley have gone down to headquarters to report Terry missing, and some sort of investigation is bound to be made."

"Why did they want to do such an idiotic thing? Well, I have nothing to say to the police. They can damn well let me alone."

"They can, but it is doubtful that they will. We will all have to answer their questions."

"Don't worry, Fan. I can take care of myself."

They sat side by side on the bed. Ben's grip had relaxed, and her hand was comfortably, in his, at home. She felt alarmingly warm and susceptible, and she had a strong notion that it would be wiser and safer, if less interesting, to devise a distraction. After all, if she was beginning to think along certain lines, it was more than likely that he was already ahead of her.

"Have you had dinner?" she said. "I have some tenderloin left. Would you like some?"

"No, thanks. I'm not hungry."

They continued to sit, undistracted.

Damn it, she thought, what has become of Jay and Farley? What could be keeping them?

12

Trouble was keeping them.

Jay had had little or no experience with police stations, and he was not sure of the protocol in the present case. There was, however, a man in uniform on duty behind a high counter, and it was apparent that he was expected to appeal here if he hoped to proceed at all. He had an idea that there must be a Bureau of Missing Persons somewhere that specialized in finding folk who were lost, strayed, or stolen; the most that would be done at present, he suspected, was the recording of a few statistics, vital and otherwise, and the phony reassurance of some cynical bureaucrat who would assume at once that Terry, of the three alternatives, was a stray of the voluntary type.

"Good evening," said the uniformed man across the high counter. "May I help you?"

This was certainly a favorable beginning, courteous if not deferential, and Jay was, sure enough, reassured.

"I want to report a missing person," he said.

"Name?"

"Jay Miles. This is Farley Moran, a neighbor."

"Where do you live?"

"I live at The Cornish Arms—I'm a professor at Handclasp University. You must have misunderstood me, though. I'm not missing. It's my wife."

The policeman permitted himself a slight smile. "And what is your wife's name?"

"Terry. Miles, of course."

"How long has she been missing?"

"About forty-eight hours. Since Friday afternoon."

The policeman had been making notes on a pad. Now

he threw the pencil aside and tore the top page from the pad. "Wait here a minute. . . ."

He left the door open behind him, and Jay and Farley could see him retreating down a hall. A few minutes later he reappeared and beckoned.

"In here. Captain Bartholdi will talk to you."

Jay was surprised; he had hardly expected, on the strength of a mere report, to draw the attention of a captain. He was no less surprised by the appearance of the man who had risen from behind the desk. Captain Bartholdi was slim, gray, handsome, urbane, and Gallic. He looked as if he would have been far more at home with an épée than a police positive.

"Sit down, gentlemen." Captain Bartholdi indicated chairs. "Which one is Mr. Miles?"

"Jay Miles," said Jay.

"Farley Moran," said Farley.

Bartholdi nodded to Farley, but he directed his attention to Jay. That is, he looked at Jay, and spoke to him. But he seemed abstracted. His gray eyes had a distant expression, as if he were hearing a faint snatch of music or listening to a faraway voice.

"I understand your wife has disappeared, Professor Miles?"

"That's right."

"She has been gone for two days?"

"Yes. Since Friday afternoon."

"Have you any reason to believe that the police should be interested?"

"I don't know. That's what I want the police to find out."

"May I ask you why you've waited two days before coming to us?"

"This isn't the first time my wife has gone off unexpectedly. I kept thinking that she would be back."

Captain Bartholdi said, "I see," as if he really did. "But now you've become anxious. Is that it?"

"Yes."

"Do you have any knowledge at all of where your wife might have gone? Did she leave home with a specific destination? Did she have an appointment with someone, for example?"

"She said something about an appointment, but I don't believe she said whom it was with. Mr. Moran can tell you about that."

Farley, thus cued, opened his mouth to speak. He was prevented by an arresting gesture from Bartholdi. The captain pushed his swivel chair back.

"Later, Mr. Moran. Right now, would you mind coming with me?"

"Where?" Jay, rising, had a paradoxical sensation of sinking. "Why?"

"Just follow me, please."

He came around the desk and went out of the room. Following, followed in turn by Farley, Jay was aware of the grace of Bartholdi's movements. (His feet, like his hands, were small and slender.) They went down the hall to the elevator. Captain Bartholdi punched a button with a delicate thumb, and the car descended. They came out in a basement corridor. It was chilly here; lights burned with a tinted pallor, as if the naked electric bulbs had been blued by the chill. Jay knew with dreadful certainty where they were bound, and what, when they got there, he would have to see. Bartholdi had paused in the corridor and was watching him.

"Professor Miles," he began.

"It's Terry, isn't it? She's dead, isn't she?"

Jay's voice was washed of life and luster. Bartholdi answered as if he were dictating mortuary statistics for the record.

"It's a body. There was no identification on it. You can tell me if it's your wife."

They went into the morgue, and saw, and it was. It was Terry, or what was left of her. In spite of the anguish and terror of violent death, she seemed at peace in this bleak depository. Perhaps it was only that she was empty. Her throat was clawed by her own nails, where she had dug futilely at whatever had strangled her; it was a miracle that any loveliness had survived. She had clearly been dead for some time. Jay's mind caught and clung to an ugly thought.

Thank God, the weather has been cold.

"Yes," he said. "That's Terry."

He spoke with a brittle brusqueness, as if impatient with the unpleasant task that fate had imposed upon him and wishing to be done with it. Bartholdi, watching him closely, recognized the last thin defense against hysteria. He took Jay by the arm and steered him away, jerking his head toward the door as his glance slid across the white mask of Farley's face beyond Jay's shoulder. In the hall, the three men stopped. A long sigh, like an escape valve, came from Jay.

"Are you all right, Professor Miles?" Captain Bartholdi asked.

"Where did you find her?"

"We'd better go back to my office."

"Poor Terry. Poor Terry."

"I'm sorry this was necessary."

They took the elevator back to Bartholdi's office. Jay had a peculiar gassy sensation, as though he were in danger of violating the law of gravity with every step; he kept lifting his feet, one after the other, with exorbitant care. He felt a great relief at reaching the security of a chair. He suddenly became aware that in the chair beside him sat Farley. He had forgotten Farley. He had no such positive feeling about Bartholdi, across the desk. Although the captain seemed kind and sympathetic, he was an unpleasant factor, brimming with painful questions demanding answers.

"Would you like a glass of water?" Bartholdi asked.

"No, thanks."

"A cigarette?"

Bartholdi passed them, and Jay and Farley accepted. The business of supplying lights accomplished, Bartholdi leaned back behind a stratum of smoke. "Late this morning, shortly before noon, we received a call from a man who lives on the east edge of town, on Wildwood Road. This man has a son, a kid named Charles. It seems that Charles and a friend named Vernon decided on Sunday to investigate an empty old house in the neighborhood. Known as the Skully place. It seems this kid Charles was curious because he claims he saw a mysterious light moving in an upstairs window last Friday night. Or early Saturday morning, to be exact. The two boys got into the house through a basement window. Upstairs, in the same room where Charles claims to have seen the light, they found the body of your wife, Professor Miles. It scared the daylights out of them, of course, and they ran home to spill everything to Charles's father, who called us in, as I said. A couple of patrolmen were sent out to investigate, and there was the body, just as the kids reported."

Bartholdi's eyes had gone dreamy again. Again he seemed to be listening for something, hearing something, a distant accompaniment to his own voice.

"That's where I came in," he went on after a moment. "I was out there within half an hour. Here, subject to revision, are the conclusions I've drawn: The victim was killed some time ago. In the light of what you've told me, I'd say it was probably Friday night, not too long after she disappeared. She had not been attacked, and so rape would appear to be out. She was, moreover, fully clothed. She was strangled either with a stout cord or a length of some kind of strong material, possibly a stocking or a necktie."

"But why there?" Jay's voice had a harsh, breathless sound, as if he himself were being strangled by invisible hands. "What was she doing in an unoccupied house? Surely she didn't go to such a place to meet someone."

"Not likely." Bartholdi paused, looking beyond Jay at a point on the far wall. "She was taken there either before or after she was killed. I think it's possible this was a kidnaping that got fouled up."

"Kidnaping!"

"It's still just a theory. Kidnaping victims must be rich to be profitable. Are you a wealthy man, Mr. Miles?"

Jay shook his head. "I live on my salary. But my wife's father left her a small fortune."

"Oh?" Bartholdi leaned forward. "Did you get a ransom note?"

"No."

"It might still come in . . ." Bartholdi mused. "Yes," he said slowly, "this might be a kidnap case, at that. It's suggestive that the body was left in a place where, except for the nosiness of a couple of kids, it might have remained undiscovered for months. That would give a kidnaper plenty of time to negotiate for ransom.

"It might interest you to learn," he went on, "that just on the chance I've taken certain precautions to keep a kidnaper, if there is one, from finding out that we know his victim is dead. I've threatened the two boys and their parents into silence, and I've given orders to every officer associated with the case. The news of this murder will be suppressed, if at all possible, for at least twenty-four hours. Not that I'm very hopeful. It's likely that a kidnaper would have had the Skully house under observation. If so, he knows we've found the body."

Jay was shaking his head. "I'm not sure about this kidnaping thing. My wife wasn't in control of her money. She wouldn't have been for another year. She's been drawing a modest allowance from the interest on the estate."

"Who administers the estate?"

"A lawyer in Los Angeles. His name is Maurice Feldman."

"Wouldn't he have paid a ransom from the estate if it meant saving your wife's life?"

"Of course. There's no question about that. But the kidnaper would have had to be aware of the circumstances, which I find questionable. Terry and I never mentioned her inheritance. I'm sure that not a soul in Handclasp knew a thing about it."

"How can you be so sure? Women are not very good at keeping secrets. Did you, for instance, Mr. Moran, ever hear Mrs. Miles mention her inheritance?"

"Never," said Farley.

"You're positive?"

"Certainly. Jay told me about it yesterday, after Terry had gone. That's the first I heard of it."

"By the way, Mr. Moran, I believe you were going to tell me about an appointment Mrs. Miles may have had."

"There isn't much to tell, really. Terry dropped in to our apartment Friday afternoon, and while she was there she said she had an appointment at three o'clock. That's all."

"She didn't mention a name? A destination?"

"No. As I recall, she made quite a point of *not* mentioning any."

"So? That's interesting. You said 'our' apartment, Mr. Moran?"

"Ben's and mine. Ben Green. He's working on a doctorate at the university. I'm in law school."

"Why did Terry come to your apartment? Any particular reason?"

"She wanted to borrow three carrots."

"Carrots?" Bartholdi's eyebrows shot up. "Did you say carrots?"

"That's right. For a ragout. She was going to put the ragout on to cook while she was out. That way, it would be ready when Jay got home in the evening."

Bartholdi's eyes slanted toward Jay. "And was it ready, Mr. Miles?"

"Yes. It was simmering in the electric skillet."

"A man must find it satisfying to come home to a hot meal. I'm a bachelor who doesn't, and I know." After this irrelevant remark, Bartholdi returned his attention to Farley. "How long did Mrs. Miles stay in your apartment?"

"Not long. She left shortly after Ben did."

"Where did Ben—Green, did you say?—go?"

"I wouldn't know. Old Ben was mysterious about it. Not the first time, either. I have a notion he goes off for a little extra-curricular fun, if you know what I mean."

"I think I do. When did he get back?"

"He didn't. At least, he hadn't when Jay and I left to come here. He said he'd be back some time this evening."

"Interesting."

"Oh, if you think there was any connection between Ben and Terry, you're way off base. I'm sure there wasn't."

"Chances are, of course, that you're right," said Bartholdi easily. "A lively imagination is one of my worst faults. Just the same, we'll have to prevail upon Mr. Green to let us in on his activities this weekend."

"It would be more helpful to know who placed the Personal."

"Personal? What Personal?"

"There was one in Thursday evening's *Journal*. It was

addressed to 'T.M.' and was signed 'O.' It arranged a meeting for three. o'clock Friday afternoon. From certain terms used, we deduced that the place of meeting was the University library."

If Bartholdi's imagination was at work again, there was no evidence of it in his eyes. They were more dream-filled than ever as he turned them slowly upon Jay.

"When did you first know about this Personal?" he asked Jay.

"Friday night," Jay said. "Farley and I had just finished eating the ragout, as I recall, and Farley and Fanny were looking around to see if they could find a note of the appointment Terry had presumably gone to keep. It was you who actually found the Personal, wasn't it, Farley?"

"It was, come to think of it," said Farley. "Fanny was looking through some magazines for a marginal note or something. I just happened to pick up the *Journal,* and there was the Personal."

"Who," said Bartholdi, still watching Jay, "is Fanny?"

"Fanny Moran," Jay said. "Farley's half-sister."

"She lives upstairs," Farley said.

"And how did it happen, Mr. Moran, just for the record," said Bartholdi, "that you were with Professor Miles in his apartment at the time?"

"I had been invited by Terry to come over at six and share the ragout. Fanny just got into it somehow. Fanny's always getting into things."

"Well, the Personal is something to start with, anyhow." Bartholdi sighed and rose. "This has been an ordeal for you, I know," he said to Jay. "I wish I could send you home, but first I want to take you out where the body was found."

"Why? So you can watch my reactions?"

"Sarcasm, Professor Miles? It's not necessary."

Jay got to his feet with an effort, feeling all the while as if he could not possibly make another. "Isn't the husband always the prime suspect? I'm beginning to have the feeling that we'll be seeing a lot of each other, Captain. Why don't you start calling me Jay?"

13

The old house seemed to have withdrawn into depth and darkness to guard half a century of secrets. The long walk leading from the street was rough underfoot, the cracks between its broken bricks still sprouting the dead moss and grass left over from the summer. Captain Bartholdi, who had preceded Jay and Farley through the thin traffic from downtown, now preceded them from street to house. He went up across the high front porch and knocked on the front door, which seemed an absurdity to Jay until he realized that the place was now, of course, occupied by the police. The door swung open with a classic creak, and the three passed in, Bartholdi still in front.

"Well, Brady," he said, "how's everything?"

"Cold," said Brady, a bulky shadow barely discernible. "I'd give a leg for a quart of hot coffee."

"You'll be relieved at midnight. No one's been around, I suppose?"

"Not a soul, dead or alive. I won't say I haven't thought about ghosts."

"These gentlemen are Professor Miles and Mr. Moran. We'll just have a quick look upstairs."

"Right. Watch your step on the stairs. The carpet's worn through in a couple of places."

Bartholdi switched on a flashlight. He held it pointed at the floor. Jay followed, Farley followed Jay, and the three men climbed single file to the second floor, where Bartholdi opened the first door on his right. Jay, beside him, could have sworn that a breath of colder air issued from the room but he knew this was only the trickery of an inflamed imagination in an exhausted mind.

"This is the room," Bartholdi said, "where the kids found her."

He played the light on floor and walls. On the floor lay nothing but a thin layer of dust, tracked now and disturbed in a far corner—where Bartholdi held the light steady for a minute—by a once-recumbent body. On the walls, only paper with a design of faded roses, just slightly brighter in one small rectangular place where a picture had hung.

Bartholdi shut the door. The trio huddled in the hall, standing in the puddle of Bartholdi's light.

"You see, Jay?" Bartholdi assumed the familiarity, to which he had been invited, without effort. "No tricks. No psychology."

"Can you tell me, then, what has been gained by bringing me here?"

"Have you ever seen this house before?"

"I have no recollection of it."

"Had your wife?"

"I wouldn't know, but I should think it very unlikely."

"She never mentioned any place that might seem, now that you are here, to have been a reference to this house?"

"No, not to me."

They stood in silence, their feet unmoving in the bright puddle, a frail and tiny circumference established against the darkness. The cold numbed their flesh. Jay's voice, when he spoke at last, was intense and harsh, almost guttural.

"Who could have done it? *Who?*"

"That remains to be seen. But we'll find out."

"But why *kill* her? If she was kidnaped, wouldn't it have been better to let her live, at least until the ransom was collected?"

"It depends on the point of view. A dead victim can't identify anybody."

"Whoever did it, you've got to find him!"

"We will. The Personal is something to go on. I have another lead, too, and I'm hoping both may get us to the same person. This house has been rented."

"Who rented it?"

"It was rented two weeks ago by a man who gave the

name of Ivan Harper. He paid a month's advance rent in cash. He hasn't, so far as I can learn, been seen since. Not by the people at the agency or any of the neighbors. The gas and electricity have not been turned on, no telephone has been installed. It's a safe bet that Harper, whatever his name really is, is our man. He rented this house solely for the purpose for which he used it. I haven't been able to see the agent who personally rented the house, but I'll get him in the morning at the agency."

"He should be able to give a description. He can surely recognize this man if he sees him again."

"Oh, he'll give a description, all right, probably inaccurate. He saw the man only once, two weeks ago, and you have to assume that anyone who risked this caper would have taken the elementary precaution of disguise."

Farley suddenly made a noise that was half sigh, half groan. His feet backed out of the puddle, and his arms made slapping sounds against his sides.

"It's cold," he said. "Do we have to stand talking in this house all night?"

"Sorry." Bartholdi's feet also began to move, taking the puddle along.

They went downstairs and out to their cars. Bartholdi stopped outside his car and spoke to Jay, who had veered off with Farley toward his own.

"I'm not sure of the location of The Cornish Arms. I'll follow you."

"Oh?" Jay stopped and turned, colliding with Farley, who was at his shoulder. "Are you coming along?"

"Yes."

"I'm very tired. I don't think I can keep going much longer. Couldn't we put it off until tomorrow?"

"I want that newspaper, the one with the Personal in it. And maybe Green has got back from wherever he went—I want to talk to him. There are other things, too."

"Well, all right."

14

"Hush!" said Fanny.

She said it softly and fiercely, leaning forward in a listening attitude. Ben, who had not been making a sound, followed directions simply by continuing to do what he had been doing, which was nothing. Fanny got up and, having removed her shoes some time before for greater comfort, padded swiftly through the darkened living room to the hall door, where she laid an ear against the panel. Then, straightening with a ladylike curse, she returned to the bedroom as silently as she had come.

"Just as I suspected!" Fan said. "They have sneaked into Jay's apartment without making the least effort to let me know."

"Perhaps, on the contrary," said Ben, "they made an effort to *keep* you from knowing."

"I shouldn't be surprised. In any event, it's a dirty trick. They know very well that I have been waiting and waiting to hear what happened at police headquarters."

"What surprises me is that you even heard them come in. I was just as alert as you were, and I didn't hear a sound."

"Have you had your ears examined recently?"

"There's nothing wrong with my ears. There's nothing wrong with my nose, either. That's because I keep it out of other folks' business."

"Well, whatever the condition of your various organs, there certainly seems to be something wrong with your head. Are you incapable of understanding *anything*? I tried to tell you that this is now police business, thanks to Jay. And the police are quite likely, in my opinion, to make it the business of everyone."

"I doubt it. A mere wandering wife? Husbands who can't keep their wives at home are not taken very seriously by the fuzz."

"Maybe so, maybe not. It all depends on what happens to the wives when they are not at home."

"True. I must admit, Fan, that you have a happy knack of going straight to the heart of a matter. I'm prepared to bet, however, that what is happening to Terry is rarely prosecuted these days as a criminal offense."

"That remains to be seen. Just because you've been off wallowing in the fleshpots, you needn't suspect it of everyone else."

"Who's been wallowing in fleshpots?"

"Do you deny it?"

"I neither deny nor affirm. I maintain a gentlemanly silence."

"Just wait until the police get to you. We'll see then how long you maintain silence, gentlemanly or otherwise."

"I'll wait, and I advise you to do the same. No doubt Farley will be over soon, and you can pump him dry."

"If you think I'm going to stay here and wait for Farley to come when he gets good and ready, you can think again."

"What are you going to do?"

"I'm going over there immediately, and you're coming with me."

"Like hell!" Ben, who had been in a prone position, came quickly erect and planted his stockinged feet on the floor. "Not on your life!"

"Oh, come *on,* Ben. You deserted me for the entire weekend. The least you can do now is be accommodating."

"Damn it, I didn't desert you. I only went off for a couple of days on my own business."

"Are you sure it was strictly your business? For your sake, let us hope so."

"At any rate, I'm quite comfortable where I am, and I refuse to budge."

"Will you come if I kiss you?"

"Don't tempt me. You know I have no character."

"I'm prepared to be especially liberal on this occasion."

"I'm wavering. As a matter of fact, I'm seduced."

"Good. You will find that I am as good as my word."

Indeed, she was a great deal better. She was by all odds, Ben thought, the most talented kisser this side of heaven. Or, he amended, his pulses pounding, it would be more appropriate to look for comparisons in the opposite direction. It was neither hurried nor scrimped, and it delayed their departure for longer than Fanny had intended or Ben had hoped.

"You know," said Fanny finally, "I'm inclined to believe you after all."

"Regarding what?"

"Regarding what you haven't been doing this weekend."

"I haven't said what I haven't been doing."

"Just the same, your reactions are not those of a man who has been satiated, or even appeased."

"I'd be happy to offer further evidence."

"*No.* I have kept my word, Ben, now you keep yours."

"All right. But we're choosing the duller of two alternatives."

He found his shoes on the floor and put them on, while she put on her own and inspected her lips for damage in the mirror above the chest. Minor repairs having been made, they crossed the hall and knocked on Jay's door; and Fanny, after knocking, opened it without waiting for a response. Jay was seated with his head in his hands, and Farley was sprawled on the sofa, supported on one elbow. Aside from looking up, neither moved when Fanny and Ben entered.

"Hello, you two," Fanny said briskly. "Jay, you look absolutely like the wrath. You must go to bed immediately after telling me what happened at police headquarters."

Jay groaned and put his head back in his hands. Farley opened his mouth to answer, and then said nothing; but he neglected to close his mouth. Captain Bartholdi appeared suddenly in the kitchen doorway.

"Who are *you?*" Fanny demanded.

"I was about," said Bartholdi, "to ask you the same question."

"Captain Bartholdi, Miss Moran," Jay said.

"She's my half-sister," said Farley. "I don't remember if we warned you about her or not. If we didn't, we should have."

"How do you do, Miss Moran," Bartholdi said.

"Quite well, thank you. Why don't you just call me Fanny?"

"Am I correct in thinking that this is Mr. Green?"

"Just call me Ben," said Ben. "I can see that we're intruding, so we'll excuse ourselves. Come on, Fan."

"Don't be absurd," Fanny said. "Are we intruding, Captain Bartholdi?"

"Not at all," Bartholdi said. "As a matter of fact, I want to talk to you both."

"I was afraid of that," Ben said. He went over to seat himself gloomily on the sofa beside Farley, who had, by sitting up, made room. There was still space left for Fanny, and she took possession of it. Bartholdi remained standing, perhaps because standing reinforced his air of command. He already had the feeling, relative to Fanny, that maintaining command would present certain difficulties.

"Are you a police captain?" Fanny said.

"Yes."

"Then it's your job to look for missing people?"

"Sometimes."

"Are you going to look for Terry?"

"I intend to do whatever is indicated."

This answer struck Fanny as evasive. She studied Bartholdi's bland Gallic face for a moment, trying to decide if he was reliable and efficient. She had a strong notion that he was both, and a great deal more when more was called for.

"You must be good at your job. You have to be good, don't you, to get to be a captain?"

"Usually. Sometimes it's politics."

"I don't believe it was politics in your case. I must say I'm relieved."

"I'll try to justify your confidence."

Bartholdi had a feeling about Fanny also, and the feeling was that the interview was going the wrong way. The

86

wrong person, that is, was asking the questions. Not that he was excessively disturbed by this. He was prepared to maneuver from any position.

"Why a captain?" said Ben suddenly.

"What?"

Bartholdi turned his eyes on Ben, startled. He was aware of having been pricked by a shrewd thrust.

"Isn't it unusual for a captain to be assigned to a case like this?"

"Why so?"

"Well, for one thing, we don't even know if it amounts to anything yet, and neither do you. In my opinion it doesn't. For another thing, Terry isn't what you'd call a VIP. It seems odd that she'd draw so much rank the first thing."

"All people are important, aren't they?" This was an interesting young fellow, Bartholdi thought. Have to keep parrying him for a while.

"There you are, Ben," said Fanny. "I hope you're ashamed of yourself. How do you think it makes Jay feel when you talk like that?"

Jay was in fact feeling very little except exhaustion and a queer sense of loss that was growing worse. Hearing his name dropped in a conversation that he hadn't followed, he looked up from his hands, and he focused on the right hand of Bartholdi, which held a newspaper narrowly folded. The newspaper was slapping softly against Bartholdi's thigh.

"What's that?" Jay asked.

"This?" Bartholdi lifted the newspaper and stared at it as if he had forgotten it. "Oh, a copy of Thursday evening's *Journal*. I found it in the kitchen in a stack of papers."

"We let them accumulate for a week or so before we put them out in the hall." Behind their thick lenses, Jay's dull eyes sharpened and turned toward the telephone. "But Thursday evening's *Journal* is on the desk there, where you left it."

"This is another copy."

"We only take one. Why would we have two?"

"A good question. There's a reasonable answer to it,

however. Since it's the copy in which the Personal appeared, it's reasonable to assume that your wife was expecting and anticipating it. She would have been anxious to see it as soon as possible. Therefore, if she was out when the papers hit the streets, she probably bought an extra copy and carried it home afterward. Do you happen to remember if she was away from home Thursday afternoon?"

"I haven't the least idea." Jay seemed to have lost all interest in the matter immediately Bartholdi offered his explanation. "She was here when I arrived shortly before six. Where she may have been earlier, I couldn't say."

"Well, never mind." Bartholdi's interest also seemed to be gone. He diverted his attention to Fanny and Ben. "Can either of you two, thinking back, recall anything Mrs. Miles said that might have been a clue to where she was going on Friday afternoon?"

"Not I," said Fanny. "I've tried and tried, but I can't remember a thing."

"I haven't tried at all," Ben said, "and there's no use trying now. She said she had an appointment, as Farley can verify, but she didn't say where or with whom, and that's all there is to it."

"All right. Now I want to ask you a question that calls for an opinion. Do you think," said Bartholdi, "that kidnaping is a likely explanation?"

It was immediately apparent from their expression that, of all possible questions, this was the least expected.

"Kidnaping!" Fanny said. "Are you serious?"

"Why shouldn't I be?"

"On the contrary, why should you be?" Ben said. "Terry isn't famous, and she doesn't have any money to speak of. What could be gained by kidnaping her?"

"She does have money."

"What do you mean?"

"She is the heiress to a considerable estate. She isn't in control of it yet, but there's no doubt that it could be tapped by a kidnaper."

"It's news to me. Is it true, Jay?"

"It's true, Ben," Jay said.

"Well, why was no one ever told? I, for one, knew absolutely nothing about it. Did you know anything about it, Fanny?"

"Not before Terry disappeared. Jay mentioned it for the first time yesterday. And that, as I see it, is the point. I didn't know it, and Ben and Farley didn't know it, and according to Jay it's unlikely that *anyone* around here knew it. Don't you see? If you're going to kidnap someone for money, you have to know that the person has it, or that someone else will pay it."

"I understand that," Bartholdi said gently. "Miss Moran, I wasn't accusing anyone here of kidnaping—"

"I should hope not!"

"—but I can't simply discard the possibility. That's why I asked your opinion."

"I suppose it's possible," Ben said. "But I don't think it's probable."

"As for me," said Fanny, "my opinion is even less favorable."

"Well." Bartholdi's shrug was noncommittal. "If there is any substance to the theory, we should soon be hearing from the kidnaper. In the meanwhile, we mustn't let it blind us to other considerations. The Personal, for instance, suggests a closer relationship than kidnaper-victim, though there's a definite chance the same individual is involved in both. And I would like to know, incidentally, how Mrs. Miles left this building and vanished without, apparently, being seen by anyone."

"I can't see that there is any great problem there," Fanny said. "She just walked out when no one happened to be looking."

"But the building superintendent was working, I've been told, in the front lobby at the time she must have left. He's positive she didn't go out that way."

"Then she must have gone out the back way. Why do you insist on making a mystery of something that can be easily explained, Captain? I should think you'd be trying to find out where she went and where she is, instead of which door she walked out of to get there."

Bartholdi smiled. He was already beginning to feel an affinity for Fanny, whom he had first categorized as a charming little nut. "We'll just accept the fact that she's gone and proceed from there. And speaking of being gone, it's time, I think, that *we* were. Mr. Miles is exhausted, and I'm sure your brother has nothing more to tell me at the moment. Do you live in the building, Miss Moran?"

"I live upstairs over Farley. Why?"

"I thought we might go there to finish our discussion, if you don't mind."

"Can Ben come with us?"

"By all means."

"That's not necessary," Ben said. "I'm like Farley. I have nothing more to tell you."

"What do you mean, nothing *more?*" said Fanny. "You haven't told him *anything* yet."

"That's what I have to tell," Ben said. "Not anything."

"That remains to be seen," said Bartholdi amiably. "If we talk long enough under the right conditions, you may think of something."

The third degree may or may not have been implied, Ben thought glumly, but the polite official tone was unmistakable. Fanny had him by the hand, damn her, and was leading him toward the door while Bartholdi said good night to Jay and Farley.

15

"I have a little gin," said Fanny, "if anyone would care for a martini or something."

"I'd care for one," Ben said. "But I imagine there is a regulation against it so far as Captain Bartholdi is concerned."

"So far as I'm concerned," Captain Bartholdi said, "regulations are flexible."

"In that case," Fanny said, "we will all have one. Please make yourselves comfortable."

Bartholdi, in an easy chair, had no apparent difficulty in doing so, but for Ben it was harder. After all, when it came to feeling comfortable in the company of a police captain on official business, it was much easier said than done. Fanny was creating small musical sounds in the kitchen with glasses and ice and a long spoon. Ben stared at his extended legs, wondering if the wiser course would be to lie or simply clam up.

"You're a graduate student at the university, Mr. Green?" Bartholdi asked.

"That's right."

"Your roommate, I understand, is studying law. Is that your field?"

"No. History."

"Oh? Do you plan to teach?"

"I've had some such notion."

"I was told that you've been away over the weekend."

"Yes," Ben said.

"When did you leave?"

"Friday afternoon. Two o'clock or thereabouts. I don't know exactly."

"And you got back this afternoon?"

"Yes. Late. After Farley and Jay had left to see you."

"Do you mind telling me where you've been?"

"Yes."

"You mind?"

"Yes."

"Why?"

"I just like to keep my business to myself."

"So do I, when possible. Sometimes, unfortunately, it's not. I congratulate you, at any rate, on reaching the better of two bad decisions."

"What decision?"

"To tell me nothing instead of lies. If you had lied, it would have been the worse for you in the end. As it is, it may be bad enough."

"Cool it, man! You don't even know there's anything wrong. Or do you?"

"A woman's missing. Isn't that enough?"

"Not to rate a captain."

"One thing about captains, we're discreet, if that's any reassurance to you."

"It isn't," Ben said.

"We'll find out anyhow. You'd be better off telling me voluntarily."

"That," said Fanny, returning with a tray of martinis, "remains uncertain. He might be better off with the police, Captain, but it is by no means established that he would be better off with me."

"Oh?" Bartholdi glanced curiously from Fanny to Ben, who was looking sourly at Fanny. "Perhaps, Miss Moran, I'd better talk to Ben alone."

Ben was not deceived, by the use of his given name, into any false sense of security.

"Don't pay any attention to Fan, Captain," he said. "She wants to deprive other girls of the entertainment she persistently rejects for herself."

"Could it be that you're admitting something?" Fanny cried.

"Damn it, you can badger me all night, and that's all it will get you! You may as well let me alone."

"That's true." Fanny addressed Bartholdi, who was tasting his martini and finding it cold and dry and as good as cheap gin could make it. "I can testify that he's a hopelessly obdurate little devil when he gets his back up."

"In that event, we will save time and effort by doing as he says. We will let him alone. Temporarily, anyway." Bartholdi settled back and looked at Ben without animosity. "I can understand your reluctance to talk about your activities since leaving here Friday, but I'm sure you won't have the same reluctance concerning events prior to your leaving."

"What events? What's to tell that's worth telling?"

"Let me be the judge. I understand Terry Miles dropped in on you and Farley Moran shortly before you left— before she disappeared. I want you to tell me, as nearly as you can remember, what happened and what was said while the three of you were together."

"Nothing of any consequence. She wanted to borrow three carrots for some damn ragout. She said she had an appointment at three o'clock, and she wanted to make the ragout before she left so it would be ready for dinner when she and Jay got back in the evening. I gave her the carrots, and we had a beer together and talked nonsense. That's all there was to it."

"This appointment. Did she say what it was, or where, or with whom?"

"No. In fact, she made a point of *not* saying."

"Did this strike you as odd?"

"With Terry? Not much!"

"If I wanted to," said Fanny, "I could say something *apropos* the pot and the kettle."

"She did fix the ragout and leave it cooking," Bartholdi said. "Did you know that?"

"She said she was going to, so why wouldn't she? I'm going to fix one myself soon. It sounded damn good."

"Did she give you the recipe?"

"Yes."

"Do you remember it?"

"Sure. There's nothing complicated about it."

"I wonder if you'd pass it on to me? I'm a bachelor, and I rather fancy myself as an amateur chef."

"Happy to oblige. You start with bacon . . ."

He stopped in response to Bartholdi's gesture. The captain dug into a pocket and produced a mechanical pencil and a small notebook.

"Here, Ben, write it down."

Ben took the notebook and pencil and began to write, pausing briefly once in a while to remember the proportions. Fanny, meanwhile, divided her attention between Ben and Bartholdi with an expression of comic incredulity.

"Well," she said, "if this doesn't beat anything I've ever seen or heard! I was under the impression that we were discussing something important, and all of a sudden, without warning, you two are off on a ragout. Can't you stick to the subject?"

Bartholdi took the pencil and notebook from Ben and studied what Ben had written. "Are you sure these are the right ingredients?"

"Positive."

"And the exact proportions? Proportions are very important in good cooking."

"That's just the way Terry told it to Farley and me."

"It's quite a lot of onions," said Fanny, who had taken the liberty of reading over Bartholdi's shoulder. "No wonder Jay complained."

"Complained?" Bartholdi looked up. "Complained when?"

"Why, Friday evening, when he and Farley were eating the ragout. He said there were too many onions. You know, Captain, that could be a clue? To Terry's state of mind Friday—her three o'clock appointment and all, I mean. Or maybe she put too many onions in it purposely to annoy him. The way I'll make Ben's martini with too much vermouth. It's a woman's way sometimes."

Bartholdi shrugged. "We had better get back to the point. From remarks that have been dropped, I gather that Terry Miles was inclined to stray a bit."

"Oh well, it's an open secret," Ben said. "It's true."

"If so," said Fanny, glaring at Ben, "it is a habit she shares with certain others I could name, not necessarily females."

"What particular man or men was she involved with? It may be important."

"There was something once about Otis Bowers, but it didn't amount to anything," Ben said. "The only reason Terry gave old Otis a little exercise was for the pleasure of seeing Ardis in the saucepan. Terry is malicious as well as glandular."

"Who," demanded Bartholdi, "is Otis Bowers?"

"He teaches physics at the university. Lives across the hall."

"And Ardis," said Fanny, "is his bitch of a wife."

"Oh? Why do you call her that, Miss Moran?"

"A bitch? Because that's what Ardis is. Why else would you call someone a bitch?"

"Is that your considered opinion?"

"Very little consideration was called for. It's perfectly evident."

"You seem to be a young woman of decided views."

"She's a nut is what she is," Ben said. "She thinks it makes her look taller when she talks dirty."

Fanny greeted this commentary with all the hauteur it deserved. She took a scornful sip of her martini just to show that she was otherwise unaffected, and scratched for a moment in her strawberry patch with fingers that weren't engaged by the glass.

"If you are looking for a lover," she said, "you are absolutely wasting your time with Otis. He is not only fat, but also home. At least, he was home all weekend. What would be the point in going somewhere to meet a lover who stayed home? It's stupid on the face of it."

"I agree," Bartholdi said.

"As well as frustrating," said Ben.

"On the other hand," said Fanny, "Brian O'Hara could be considered a favorable prospect."

Bartholdi sat up. Ben drained his glass, olive and all. It was difficult to tell if his voice was impaired by amazement or if it was merely the effect of talking around the olive.

"How in hell do you come up with these things, Fan? What does Brian O'Hara have to do with it?"

"I have it on good authority, confirmed by Jay himself, that Terry and Brian O'Hara have been seen together frequently. This, of course, does not mean a great deal in itself. What means a great deal is when they were together and *not* seen."

"That," said Ben, "is neatly put."

"Do you know Brian O'Hara, Captain?" Fanny asked.

"Very well, both officially and unofficially. Officially, I'm compelled to take a dim view of O'Hara's activities. Unofficially, I have to concede him certain qualities."

"So does Terry, apparently," said Fanny, "although I doubt that they are the same qualities."

Bartholdi finished his martini. He set his glass aside and rose. "I'll run along. In some respects, you've been quite helpful. In others—" with a look at Ben "—you haven't."

When Captain Bartholdi was gone, Ben said excitedly, "He slipped! He slipped! Did you notice it?"

"Slipped how? Notice what?" asked Fanny.

"In his tense. Once or twice he used the past tense in referring to Terry!"

"Whatever do you mean? Damn it, Ben, can't you ever say right out what's in your devious little mind?"

"Never mind." Ben was still staring at the door. "Now I know why there's a captain on this case."

16

Bartholdi was abroad early. Presenting himself at the Chubitz Real Estate Agency, he asked to see the top man. It got him into a paneled office with framed photographs of houses on the walls and a pink and white man behind a desk. The desk was an unconvincing imitation of polished walnut, and the man who rose from behind it might have done so, Bartholdi thought, behind a similar desk in a similar office forty years ago in mythical Zenith. The pink and white man with the peculiarly ancient look of an infant was Chubitz himself, with whom Bartholdi had spoken by telephone at his suburban home.

"Good morning, Captain Bartholdi," Chubitz said. "Sit down, sit down! How can I help you?"

His voice had the rather desperate heartiness of a man who had just been refreshed by two days of frantic leisure. Bartholdi eased himself into a chair and hung his hat on his knee.

"As I told you yesterday," he said, "I'm interested in one of your properties. It's known as the old Skully Place."

"It's rented," said the real estate man.

"It's the renter I'm interested in. You promised to check on the agent involved and have him available this morning. I'd like to talk with him."

"It appears that the house was rented by Mr. Jenkins, one of our most reliable men. The house was rented to a—" Chubitz consulted a note—"a Mr. Harper. Ivan Harper."

"You told me all that. Is Jenkins in the office?"

"Yes," said Chubitz anxiously. "Is anything wrong?"

"We're interested in this man Harper. Where can I find Jenkins?"

"You're welcome to see him here in my office. Shall I call him in, Captain?"

It was evident that Chubitz preferred being present to getting a secondhand report from his reliable man later. Bartholdi shrugged, and Chubitz pressed a button that summoned a secretary, who was sent to summon Jenkins. Jenkins, arriving promptly, proved to be an evil-eyed young man with the deadly earnestness of one who lives by commissions.

"Jenkins," said Chubitz, "this is Captain Bartholdi of the police. He wants to ask you some questions about the Skully property."

"Right," said Jenkins. "Right-*o*."

"To begin with," said Bartholdi, "when was the house rented?"

"On a Monday. Two weeks ago today, to be exact."

The cherubic face of Mr. Chubitz beamed at this evidence of exactness on the part of his Mr. Jenkins. The beam contrived to remain anxious.

"It was rented, I understand," Bartholdi said, "to a man who gave the name of Ivan Harper."

"Right. Right-*o*."

"Did you take him out to see the house before he rented it?"

"No. He said he'd been by earlier, and he was sure it was the place he wanted." Jenkins grinned like a shark. "You meet all kinds of kooks in the realty game."

"He paid a month's rent in advance?"

"Right you are."

"Did he pay by check or by cash?"

"Cash."

"Did he ask you to see to having the gas and electricity turned on?"

"I offered to do it as part of our agency service, but he said he would attend to it himself."

"Are you aware that he didn't?"

"He didn't?"

"As a matter of fact, Harper hasn't occupied the house at all. It's still empty."

"Well, now," said Mr. Chubitz nervously. "Well, now."

"Why would a man rent a house he doesn't intend to occupy?"

"A good question, Mr. Jenkins."

"I thought at the time there was something queer about the guy. I'll bet Harper wasn't even his real name!"

"What made you think the transaction was queer?"

"A kind of feeling he gave me. The cash, for one thing. People usually pay by check—"

"Tell me what he looked like. As accurate and complete a description as possible."

"Jenkins has a retentive memory," Chubitz said unhappily. "I'm sure he'll be most helpful. You mustn't disappoint us, Jenkins." There was steel in this last admonition.

Bartholdi, watching Jenkins quail, would have enjoyed planting a shoe on the generous Chubitz bottom. Nothing worse, under the circumstances, could have been said. It was unlikely after two weeks that Jenkins would ordinarily be able to supply more than a vague description. Now, with his employer's displeasure threatening, he would be worthlessly explicit, adding superfluous gewgaws to what might have been an authentic detail or two.

Bartholdi listened sourly. Tall. Shoulders slightly stooped. Age in the upper middle bracket. Hair graying, parted in the middle and slicked down. Horn-rimmed glasses. Teeth stained badly, as from incessant smoking or chewing tobacco. Going fat about the gut. Neatly dressed in brown suit showing signs of wear. Ditto brown topcoat and brown hat. Walked with a slight limp. And, oh, yes—hands were ingrained with grime that soap no longer removed—the hands, Jenkins had thought, of a mechanic or machinist, at any rate of someone who worked in oil and grease. Jenkins clearly felt that this was his prize item. Like an expectant dog, he waited for commendation.

Bartholdi didn't give it to him. Instead: could Jenkins identify Harper if he saw him again? Oh, positively! No question about it! Bartholdi secretly doubted it. Jenkins's description was far too detailed, and there was now no way to separate the truth from the figments of the Jenkins enthusiasm. One thing, at least, could be assumed. If Harper was a kidnaper and murderer, he had not nakedly exposed himself to Jenkins's observation, however unreliable that might be.

"All right." Bartholdi shifted in his chair. "We'll call on you, Mr. Jenkins, if you're needed further."

"Right. Right-*o*." Jenkins turned to Chubitz. "I believe I'd better have the utility people turn on the gas at the Skully house and start the furnace. If the temperature drops any lower the pipes may freeze."

"Good thinking, Jenkins. See to it right away."

"Right-*o!*"

Back at headquarters, Captain Bartholdi had the switchboard operator give him an outside line. He dialed a number he had been given by Jay Miles, and after a preliminary skirmish with a secretary was talking with Maurice Feldman in Los Angeles. Feldman's voice sounded husky and hurried, as if he had to rush words through a diseased larynx before the organ wore out.

"I'm calling in reference to a woman named Terry Miles," Bartholdi said. "I understand you're the executor of an estate left to her by her father."

"That's correct. She was formerly Terry Kinkaid. What kind of scrape is Terry in now?"

"I'm afraid I have bad news, Mr. Feldman. She's dead."

There was a long silence. Then the husky, hurried voice came back with a note of genuine regret.

"Poor Terry. I was always afraid she'd come to a bad end. Was it an accident of some kind?"

"It's murder. It may also have been kidnaping."

"Murder!" The husk in the attorney's voice was harsher. "Murder? Are you sure?"

"She was strangled to death."

"When did it happen, for God's sake?"

"By the most reliable calculation, some time late last Friday or early Saturday. Her body was not found, however, until yesterday."

"Why hasn't there been any news of it?"

"We've been sitting on it for the time being. I told you kidnaping is suspected."

"This means that you don't know who the murderer is."

"I'm going to be frank with you, Miss Page. I've got to rely on your discretion—"

"I don't carry tales, if that's what you mean."

"Good. Professor Miles's wife is missing. She's been gone since Friday afternoon."

"I know." Freda Page studied her blue pencil for a moment, then laid it carefully between the stacks of marked and unmarked papers. "He told me when he phoned this morning."

"Oh? What else did he tell you?"

"Nothing. Just that Terry left home Friday and hasn't been seen since."

"Did he say that he'd been to the police?"

"He did."

"Then you must have been expecting a police officer."

"Not necessarily. I can't see what you hope to learn by coming here."

"I noticed that you called Mrs. Miles Terry. Do you know her well?"

"Well enough."

This terse remark, Bartholdi thought, although uttered without emphasis, was susceptible to analysis. Did it imply that even a little of Terry was enough? And was the color a little higher in Freda Page's cheeks? It was an interesting speculation. Loyalty was not always a virtue. Nor was love, for that matter, at least in a police investigation.

"Can you suggest any reason why she left home?" he asked.

"None whatever. No, that isn't so. I *could* suggest one, but it would be slanderous if not true, and I can't prove that it is."

"I asked for a suggestion, not proof. Do you mean that she's probably off with some man?"

"I mean that she's wanton and faithless." Freda Page's cheeks were now hot.

"How do you know? Hearsay?"

"More directly than that. Professor Miles seems to respect my judgment and discretion. He sometimes confides in me."

"Why don't you call him Jay? That's what you call him privately, isn't it?"

If he had hoped for confusion, he was disappointed. She smiled defiantly, adjusting her glasses on her nose.

"Very well, then. Jay."

"That's better. More comfortable for both of us. I take it you think a lot of Professor Miles."

"I do. Personally and professionally. He deserves a better wife."

Like Freda Page? Bartholdi wondered. Or was theirs the kind of student-teacher relationship that breeds on every campus, not to be taken seriously? Freda Page, however, must surely be a graduate student of some standing. She was not, at any rate, a child.

"Does he think so?"

"I wouldn't presume to say. Why don't you ask him?"

"Mrs. Miles apparently had an appointment Friday afternoon. Did you know that?"

"Of course not. Why should I?"

"I thought she might have come here."

"To the office? I don't think so. Not to my knowledge, anyhow."

"Not here necessarily. To the university. Did you see her on campus?"

"I didn't see her at all, on campus or anywhere else."

"Was Professor Miles in the office here that afternoon?"

"Yes, for a few minutes after lunch. He also came back for fifteen or twenty minutes after his last class of the day."

"What time was that?"

"Two-thirty."

"Does the class meet in this building?"

"Yes, on the second floor."

"Then he must have left the office before three."

"I suppose he did. Why? I don't see how Jay's time schedule will help you find his wife."

"One more question, Miss Page. Did he say where he was going when he left here?"

"No."

"He says he didn't get home until about six."

"He may have worked in the library. He often does that. I'm sorry I can't be of more help."

Bartholdi wondered if she was. He had a notion that

104

Freda Page considered the disappearance of Terry Miles to be, at the worst, good riddance. He thanked the girl, and as he turned away she was already picking up the blue pencil to resume her work on the pile of unmarked papers.

Two hundred yards further along a curving concrete walk, swarming at the moment with between-class students, he found the administration building. At the foot of the wide shallow steps leading up to the entrance, he paused and looked back along the way he had come. The swarm of hurrying students was thinning rapidly in the final moments of intermission. He wondered if there was a perpetual competition among undergraduates nowadays to see which could devise the sloppiest costume. But then his student days were thirty-odd years in the past, and his recollections were probably distorted by nostalgia.

Inside, he sought out the registrar's office. He identified himself to a female clerk behind a high counter and asked if he might see the registrar. He was invited behind the counter and into a private office, where he was greeted by a dehydrated little gray man who reminded him, for some reason, of a hungry sparrow. The registrar's name was Wister, and he offered a dry gray hand.

"Sit down, Captain Bartholdi," he said. "How can I serve you?"

"It's a routine matter," Bartholdi said, holding on to his hat and keeping his topcoat on, "which I would prefer not to explain just now."

Registrar Wister made a tent of his fingers. "If you will just tell me what you wish to know . . ."

Bartholdi extended a page, torn from his notebook, on which he had written a list of names. "I'd appreciate it if I could see the records of these people."

Wister read the names, listed one to a line in a vertical column:

Jay Miles.
Otis Bowers.
Ardis Bowers.
Farley Moran.
Benjamin Green.
Fanny Moran.

"Doctor Miles and Doctor Bowers are, of course, members of our faculty," Wister said. "So is Mrs. Bowers, in a lesser capacity. She is, I believe, a graduate instructor."

"I know that."

"You must realize that our records are limited in this office, Captain, especially with respect to the faculty. More detailed information would be available from the heads of the various departments."

"That can come later, if necessary. I'm interested at the moment only in general background information."

"Well, let's see what we have."

Wister disappeared in the outside office, taking Bartholdi's list with him. He was back shortly with five manila folders. He placed them on the desk before Bartholdi.

"There is nothing on Fanny Moran," the registrar said. "She is not a student in this institution."

"I know. I just thought she once might have been."

"There's no record of her. If you'll excuse me, there's something I must see to."

Wister went out, and Bartholdi hunched over the desk. He culled the five folders one by one. When he was finished he had acquired, besides the knowledge that Ben Green was a brilliant student and Farley Moran no better than fair, some information that, in effect, enlarged his prospects. Otis Bowers had been a student, before coming to Handclasp, at the California Institute of Technology in Pasadena. Ardis Bowers had been at C.I.T. with him, not then a student but already his wife. Ben Green, although he had done all his college work at Handclasp, was a legal resident of Glendale. Farley Moran was a transfer student from U.C.L.A. (Fanny Moran, who had no record, could be assumed tentatively to have come, before or after or with Farley, from the same area.) In brief, there seemed to be a California colony in Handclasp. More significantly, perhaps, at The Cornish Arms.

Wister returned after a while to find Bartholdi leaning back in his chair with eyes closed. He appeared to be sleeping: he was, in fact, far from it. The manila folders were stacked neatly in alphabetical order and pushed back on the registrar's desk.

106

"Are you finished, Captain?" Wister asked.

"Yes, thank you." Bartholdi opened his eyes and pushed his chair back.

"I'm sure you will respect the rights of these individuals—" Wister indicated the manila stack "—to all possible privacy."

"Of course."

Bartholdi took the registrar's dry hand, gave it up, and left. Outside he walked slowly along the curving concrete walk in the direction of the library, his topcoat flapping about his legs.

18

There is in American legend a kind of hero. The legend has variations, as has the hero. He is not so much an individual of heroic proportions as a prototype who effuses a certain character. He begins humbly; and he is compelled, by early environment and example, to take a predatory posture. He recognizes the necessity of being hard and the advantage of being merciless. He uses his wealth to acquire charm and polish, which he exploits to consolidate his position. Perhaps he climbs through precinct and ward to political power, often behind the scenes. Or he becomes mighty in business, or in organized labor. Sometimes he flouts the law directly, rather than obliquely, and rises in the rackets.

Condemned in public, he is often admired in private. His ultimate strength is not in what he has but in what he lacks, which is conscience. He is always dangerous.

Young Brian O'Hara could hardly be expected to have achieved the dimensions of such a legend. But he was on the way.

O'Hara's history did not quite conform to the specifications. His beginning was not humble; his middle-class father, although far from wealthy, was comfortably enough situated to provide his only son with a college education, for example. At college the younger O'Hara had played football and basketball. In football he was competent; in basketball he excelled; in both, by drive and luck, he prospered. For as a sophomore he began placing bets (progressively larger) on the contests in which he was engaged, never permitting a foolish loyalty to prevent his betting on his alma mater's opponents when it seemed judicious to do so. On the gridiron his successes were largely the result of chance, but on the court his skill furthered his cause. It is surprising what a good thing a clever operator can make of this sort of thing. By the time Brian O'Hara graduated, he had a secret bank account of $20,-000.

Cast loose on the world, he saw no reason for spoiling a good thing. His instinct functioned, his luck held, and his interests spread. He now had valuable contacts of a certain kind across the country; and he became a post-graduate specialist in collegiate athletic competitions, digressing only now and then, for variety, into the realms of the pros. The bank accounts grew rapidly in spite of taxes, which he was smart enough to pay in full, and spilled over into investments that proved financially lucrative. Among these were two night spots in Handclasp where college tastes were pandered to. They were expensive, as such spots go; they made no attempt to attract patronage of those who could not afford them, and so were largely patronized by those who could. Collegians were not the only patrons. They merely set the tone; and many of them were sources of profitable information.

As Captain Bartholdi had said, Brian O'Hara was not unknown to the police. His activities did not come under Bartholdi's surveillance, but the captain knew O'Hara's reputation for running a smooth operation. If he was a habitual violator of the law, he chose with care the laws he violated. He never strayed into transgressions where the chance of failure was multiplied by unnecessary risks, and the consequences were too high for the game. At least, Bartholdi reflected on his way to O'Hara's, he never had before. But then, in the precarious dodges O'Hara engaged in, there were always unpredictable forces at work. Such as the violent potential of love, or passion, or whatever it was that a particular woman generated to make the disciplined sanity of a lifetime go up in smoke.

That was the point as Bartholdi saw it. If O'Hara was involved in the death of Terry Miles, kidnaping was no factor. Passion and violence were conceivable but not, coldly calculated, the long odds against abduction and murder. And if not, what was the significance of all the folderol about the renting of an isolated house?

Well, thought Bartholdi, pushing the button beside O'Hara's door, that remained to be seen. In the meantime, one neglected no possibility and remained always open to the long chance.

Bartholdi's having rung at O'Hara's door, the door was opened by O'Hara himself. It was nearly three o'clock in the afternoon, and the fixer was shaved and brushed and impeccably dressed in a gray suit, white shirt and maroon tie, apparently open for business. If his reaction to the sight of Bartholdi was less than enthusiastic, it was at least congenial; and his time, within limits, was at Bartholdi's disposal.

"Hello, Captain," he said. "Come on in. What brings you to the camp of the enemy?"

"Enemy?" Bartholdi stepped in and even allowed himself to be divested of his hat and topcoat. "I'm here to see if you might be willing to give me a little help."

"You selling tickets? I'll take fifty."

"No tickets. Just a little information off the record."

"Sure. Anything for good relations with the fuzz. How about a drink?"

"No, thanks." Bartholdi helped himself to a chair. "I'm looking for a stray. A woman by the name of Terry Miles. I believe you know her."

"Wait a minute." O'Hara's voice had suddenly withdrawn. It reached Bartholdi, clear and cold and no longer offering to buy tickets. "Since when do you concern yourself with stray wives?"

"Captains don't come so high. And this looks as if it might lead to something interesting."

"You'll have to do better than that, Captain. If you want me to play, deal from the top of the deck."

"All right, I'll play it straight. A man's wife is missing. She's been missing for about three days, since Friday afternoon. Apparently no one saw her leave, no one knows where she went or where she is. The husband asked for police help, and he's getting it; he's a college professor who could raise a stink through channels if he chose. We also have reason to suspect that this isn't simply a case of a woman on the prowl. That's all you're going to get. Are you playing?"

110

"A hand or two, at least till I see how the game's going. I know Terry well. I intend to know her better. She's hot stuff."

"Would you care to amplify that?"

"Isn't it plain enough?"

"There would be complications, of course. She already has a husband. Or are you shooting for something less legal?"

"Her husband doesn't seem to bother her. Why should he bother me?"

"It's a good point, and I get the feeling it's particularly valid in this case. It's my impression that her husband is on the point of leaving her."

"Really?" O'Hara's laugh was hard and flat. "Don't you think he's kind of late? It seems she's already left *him*."

"It may not be so simple. Or do you happen to know where she is?"

"I don't. I told Jay Miles that when he was here Saturday night. I've tried to find her since, without any luck. I'll tell you this, though. If anything has happened to her, somebody's going to pay for it. I'm no gutless husband. I know what Terry is, and she suits me just right. I have a notion that a woman like her quits looking when she has what she needs. And as far as Terry's concerned, I've got it. For your information, Captain, *she* was planning to get a divorce."

"Thanks for the information. You haven't seen her since Friday? Haven't heard from her?"

"No."

"You say you've been looking for her. Where have you looked?"

"Various places. She wasn't there, so it doesn't matter."

"You have no idea where she may have gone?"

"If I had an idea where, I'd look there. She had a date with me for cocktails Friday afternoon. She didn't show. I assumed that something had come up, and I didn't try to find out the reason."

"Why not?"

"Climb off it, Captain. We didn't give a damn about her husband, but why rub it in his face?"

111

Bartholdi smiled. "I get the impression you don't like Jay Miles."

"I don't feel anything about him, one way or another. At least, I didn't. Now, I don't know. There was something phony about his coming here."

"It seems to me, since he knows or suspects about your affair with his wife, that it was logical."

"It could have been a cover."

Bartholdi extended his legs. His eyes seemed cloudy. "Oh? How do you mean?"

"What would you do if you'd knocked off your wife, for instance, and wanted to hide it?"

"Are you making an accusation?" Bartholdi said, blinking. He was almost yawning.

"I'm making nothing. I'm speculating."

"Speculate some more."

"It's simple enough. You'd run crying to the police, and you'd try to throw suspicion wherever it might stick."

"It would be a dangerous game."

"Murder is a dangerous game, they tell me." O'Hara's voice was mocking.

"Why would Miles kill his wife?"

"Because she was the kind of wife that a certain kind of husband might think needed killing. I'll bet it's never occurred to our professor friend that his problems with Terry are his own fault. He's deficient. He hasn't got what it takes to keep her home. Compared to Terry he's a damn dull tool. I told you I'm under no illusions about Terry. To me, she's an exciting challenge I can handle. Our professor can't and never could. She's given him one hell of a bad time. A weak man who's been made a monkey of often goes off the deep end."

"You're quite a psychologist." Bartholdi tacked suddenly. "Do you know that Terry Miles is heiress to a small fortune?"

O'Hara's expression of surprise was, Bartholdi thought, genuine.

"No kidding. She never mentioned it to me."

"She'll get it next year."

O'Hara shrugged. He said shortly, "It makes no difference to me. I'm pretty well fixed."

"The estate was left by Terry's father, a minor movie executive, I understand. It's administered by a lawyer in Los Angeles."

"I know that Terry comes from there. I go there myself two, three times a year. She's mentioned it. But nothing about coming into a bundle."

"Maybe you know the lawyer. His name is Feldman."

O'Hara shook his head. "I don't know him."

"Well, I won't keep you any longer." Bartholdi rose and picked up his hat and coat. "I appreciate your giving me the time."

"Think nothing of it."

Bartholdi looked at his watch. "I've got to check in at headquarters, then I'm going home and make my dinner."

O'Hara was astonished. "You *cook?*"

"I'm a bug on home cooking. Matter of fact, got a new recipe I'm eager to try. It's a ragout—Student's Ragout, it's called. Ever heard of it?"

"I wouldn't know a ragout from a soufflé."

Captain Bartholdi shook his head in almost genuine dismay at O'Hara's culinary ignorance. Then he put his hat and coat on and went out.

19

Fanny got back to The Cornish Arms between five and six. Outside the entrance, she met Ben Green coming from the opposite direction. Ben was cradling a brown paper sack like a baby in his right arm.

"Hello, Ben," Fanny said. "What have you got in the sack?"

"Groceries," said Ben.

"Have you been to the market?"

"No, I bought them from my banker. Where in hell would you expect me to buy groceries?"

"Well, you needn't be so nasty about it. I was only asking to be agreeable. What kind of groceries have you bought?"

"Carrots and potatoes and onions. If you must know, I'm going to make a ragout like the one Terry told me about."

"Are you sure you still remember how to do it?"

"Certainly I'm sure. It's easy enough to remember."

"I should think you'd be reluctant to cook it, what with what's happened and everything."

Ben said a four-letter word. "Do you think the damn ragout is some kind of witch's brew that makes people disappear into thin air?"

"It's just the principle of the thing."

"I see no principle involved," said Ben stiffly.

They had moved into the building while they talked, Fanny reversing the amenities in deference to his load of groceries by holding the door open for him. In the hall she did not veer off toward the stairs, but continued at Ben's side in the direction of his apartment.

"Where do you think you're going?" he said.

Fanny said, "I thought it might be nice to share the ragout with you."

"Think again. I'm going to share it with Farley."

"No problem. We can cook enough for three."

"Does it ever occur to you that you might not be welcome?"

"That is seldom the case. Please don't be difficult, Ben. I can help you prepare it and make myself useful in all sorts of ways. Besides, if I decide to marry you, we will be eating together all the time. The practice will do you good."

"There you go again! Who the hell asked you to marry me?"

"It's a natural inference. You certainly display enough interest in what goes *with* marriage."

"That," said Ben sourly, "is not the same thing."

Having reached his door, he shifted the brown paper sack from his right arm to his left and started to dig in his pants pocket for the key. Then he remembered that he had neglected to lock the door, as usual, and he pushed it open and entered impolitely ahead of Fanny. She cheerfully followed him in.

"Where's Farley?" she asked brightly.

"How would I know? Still at the university, I suppose. He'll be here pretty soon."

He went into the kitchen, put the sack containing the onions and potatoes and carrots on the cabinet, took off his hat and coat and, returning to the living room, threw them into a chair. Fanny dropped her own on top of his.

"What do you want me to do?" she said. "Shall I prepare the vegetables?"

"You might as well, as long as you're staying. Three carrots, three onions, and four large potatoes. And be damn sure you slice them thin. That's specified."

"Will that be enough for four servings?"

"*Four* servings! You and I and Farley make *three*. Or have you decided to invite someone else to share the ragout?"

"Well, it seems only fair to ask Jay. After all, he shared his with Farley when you and Terry were away, even if it was Terry who actually invited him, and it's the least you

115

can do to return the favor. How would you feel if you were in Jay's place, with no one to prepare your dinner or anything?"

"By God, I'd prepare my own, just as I'm about to do."

"Oh, don't be—such a Scrooge, Ben. Anyone would think a few vegetables mattered."

"Bacon and steak happen to be involved, too. Round steak, for your information, costs ninety-eight cents a pound."

"Well, hell's fire! I'll tell you what I'll do. I'll give you a dollar, that's what. You'll make two cents profit on the deal."

"Fan, I'm no tightwad, and you know it. It's just that you're so damn pushy, inviting people all over the place. If you want to know the truth, I was going to ask Jay anyhow. There'll be enough for everyone."

"Do you want me to ask him now?"

"No. What I want you to do is slice the onions and potatoes and carrots while I get the bacon and steak ready."

"What if Jay can't come? Don't you think I'd better go ahead and ask him?"

"If he can't come, there'll be just that much more for the rest of us."

Fanny tied a dish towel around her waist and started slicing the vegtables. Having to slice them thin was complicated by the dullness of Ben's paring knife; and Ben, who had only to halve the bacon strips and trim and cut the steak into small pieces, was finished before her and didn't offer to do anything thereafter but stand around and watch. To make matters worse, the onions made Fanny cry, and she had to stop now and then to wipe her eyes on the dish towel.

"Is it necessary to have so much onion?" she blubbered.

"Yes, it is," Ben said. "That's what Terry said the recipe called for, and that's what we're going to have. Besides, I happen to like onions."

"Well, Jay doesn't like them. I told you he complained Friday night because Terry had used too many."

"If Jay wants any of my ragout, he'll have to eat it the way I make it."

116

The vegetables were finally sliced; and Ben, lacking an electric skillet, placed them and the meat in a heavy pot in the designated order. He added a small amount of water and put the pot on the stove. While he was doing this, Fanny was opening doors and looking into cabinets.

"What are you looking for?" Ben demanded.

"I thought you might have some gin. I like to have a martini before dinner when possible."

"In this case, it isn't. I don't have any gin, and even if I did, I don't have any vermouth."

"I should think you'd keep a little gin on hand for your guests. Surely there's *something* around to drink."

"There isn't even any beer. If you want a martini, go up and get your own makings."

"I suppose I'll have to. On the way I'll invite Jay, if you don't mind. Under the circumstances, he'd probably appreciate a drink."

"Under the circumstances, he may have had a few dozen drinks already. In his place, I would."

"Well, you're weak."

Fanny went across the hall to her first stop. She knocked on the door but got no answer. She knocked again, with no better luck. Perhaps Jay wasn't in, Fan thought. On the other hand perhaps he was; it was entirely possible that he was either ignoring the knock or sleeping. There was a good chance, as Ben had said, that he had drunk himself temporarily into a trouble-free stupor. Nevertheless, it was still necessary to compel him, for his own good, to eat something. So Fanny tried the door, found it unlocked, and without hesitation opened it and went into the Miles apartment.

She stopped short, startled. Jay was in, all right. He was sitting in the living room where he must have heard her knocking on the door. At first Fan thought he had deliberately ignored her, which was annoying; but then she saw that he was sitting in a strange rigidity, staring with wide-open eyes that did not see her. Her second thought was that he was dead. But he wasn't. He was breathing slowly and deeply. He seemed to be in some sort of trance.

"Jay," she said, "you scared the daylights out of me! Why don't you answer your door?"

She walked further into the room, leaving the door open behind her. He did not answer. His eyes, when she moved, did not follow her. Approaching him from the side, she passed a hand slowly before his eyes and then shook him roughly.

"Jay! Whatever is the matter? Snap out of it!"

His stare wavered and swung slowly round to her. Then he sighed and shuddered. The sigh seemed to deflate him, for he sagged all at once in the chair.

"Fanny? Is that you, Fanny?"

"Certainly it's me. Who did you think it was?"

"I'm sorry, I didn't hear you. Did you say something?"

"I said to snap out of it. Why are you sitting here this way?"

He pressed the tips of his fingers against both temples, as if to force his thoughts into some order and coherence.

"You must forgive me," he said. "I've had a shock."

"What kind of shock? What's happened?"

"I heard about Terry."

"Where is she? Is she coming back?"

"I didn't hear from her directly. It was someone who must have got our unlisted number from Terry."

"Someone? Who?"

"I'm not sure I should tell you. Oh, I suppose it won't do any harm. . . . It was just a voice over the phone. A man's, I think. It sounded muffled, very far away. Terry is being held for ransom. I was told what to do to get her back."

"What the voice said is neither here nor there. What you must do, and at once, is notify the police."

"Yes, of course." Jay pressed his temples as he had done before; he seemed confused again. "I seem to remember that I already did. Yes, I'm sure I did. I called and asked for Captain Bartholdi, but they said he wasn't there."

"Did you leave word to have him call?"

"I don't think so. I believe I said I'd call back. I wasn't thinking very clearly. The voice warned me against calling the police—"

"Certainly. Kidnapers always warn against calling the police. How long ago did you receive the call?"

118

"How long? Yes, I remember looking. It was just four-thirty when I hung up."

"Four-thirty! And it's six now! Have you been sitting here like a stone all this time?"

"I suppose I have. I'd no idea so much time had passed."

"Well, never mind now. Call Captain Bartholdi again."

"You're right. That's what I should do."

"Do you feel up to it? Do you want me to call for you?"

"No, no, I must do it myself. Thank you very much."

He put both hands on the arms of the chair and hoisted himself to his feet. Turning, he walked with exorbitant care to the telephone. He had just lifted the instrument from its cradle and pointed a finger at the dial when Ben's voice sounded crossly from the open doorway.

"Damn it, Fanny, what's keeping you? I thought you were going upstairs to get some gin."

Fanny whirled, an index finger bisecting her lips in a gesture commanding, for God's sake, *silence*. From behind her came the ratchet-like sound of the dial, unnaturally loud.

"This is Jay Miles speaking. Captain Bartholdi, please ... Captain Bartholdi? Jay Miles. I've had news of Terry ... Yes, a telephone call ... What? ... I'm not sure. About an hour and a half ago, I think. I couldn't reach you ... Yes, everything. Complete instructions ... No, no. No mistake ... What? ... All right, I'll be here."

He hung up and returned to his chair, easing himself into it as if his bones might snap under the effort. Now that he had reached Bartholdi, he seemed relieved of a great burden. But he also seemed left in a lassitude that made it difficult to take another decisive step, about anything at all.

"Captain Bartholdi's coming out," he said drearily.

Ben said, "Why? Will somebody please tell me what's going on?"

"Surely it's obvious," Fanny said. "Terry has been kidnaped, although I never really believed she'd been. Jay has received a call from the kidnaper."

Ben's voice was all of a sudden dry and precise. "What did he want?"

"I assume he wants money. Isn't that what kidnapers generally want? Is that right, Jay? Did the kidnaper demand money?"

Jay had removed his glasses. He held them by one ear piece in his right hand, his right arm dangling limply over the arm of the chair. His eyes were shut. He answered without opening them.

"Captain Bartholdi said not to talk about it until he gets here."

"I wish he would hurry," Fanny said. "How long will he be?"

"He's on his way. I think you two had better not be here when he arrives."

"Are you telling us to leave?"

"That," said Ben, "is just what he's telling us. Do you have to have it written out for you?"

"Well, I don't see what harm it would do to have us here."

"Excuse me." Jay's eyes were still shut. "You must excuse me."

Clearly dismissed, and as clearly reluctant to accept the dismissal, Fanny nevertheless permitted herself to be impelled into the hall by Ben, who was somewhat rougher about it than she felt was necessary.

"I didn't get a chance to invite him to share the ragout," she said. "I'll go back and do it."

"To hell with the ragout," Ben said. "What I'm interested in now is the gin. Jump upstairs like a good girl and get it, will you, Fan?"

20

Had it worked? Had it, after all, really worked? He had taken a long chance against the odds and the best judgment of his superiors; he had held from the beginning very little hope for success. And that wasn't all of it. If the thing had leaked, or broken wide open, there would certainly have been some bad publicity accompanied, no doubt, by assorted nastinesses directed against the department. It might even have become necessary to lop off somebody's head, and any head that rolled should have been, in all justice, his own. At that, it had been a close call.

There had been evidence of sniffiness on the part of the press; it was blind luck that no reporter had managed to nose his way to the neighborhood of the Skully place. The families of Charles and Vernon were not practiced in the art of deception.

Well, Bartholdi reflected as he drove toward The Cornish Arms, it would break now. With a bang. Before that happened, though, perhaps a kidnaper and murderer could be trapped. He felt, thinking this, a vast uneasiness. Withholding information from the public was one thing, but withholding it from the criminal engaged in the desperate business was another. What kind of kidnaper-murderer would have left his victim's tomb unobserved for three full days and remained in ignorance of all that had happened in the meantime? What kind of egomaniac? There lay the slim chance. Delusions of grandeur so monstrous as to make the killer indifferent to ordinary caution. It took a nut, after all, to commit this type of crime.

Bartholdi drove into the alley and parked on the apron. There was room for five cars there, and two of the places were taken. Getting out, he stood for a moment in the early November darkness to survey the rear of the buff brick building. The wall was broken by the bedroom windows of the four apartments. There was light behind the blind of the bedroom window to his lower left as he faced the building. Ben Green or Farley Moran, or both; apparently in. The one above this was dark. Fanny Moran was apparently out. The window on the lower right, beyond the rear entrance, was dark; but there must be a light at the front, unless Jay Miles was waiting for him in the dark.

Bartholdi's glance darted up the wall to the window above. The blind moved, erasing a thin crack of light that had been there an instant before. Someone in the apartment of Otis and Ardis Bowers was curious, Bartholdi thought. Watching and waiting. For what?

A car turned into the alley. It was an old car, but it ran quietly. Turning onto the apron beside Bartholdi, it parked and Farley Moran got out. He peered at Bartholdi over the top of Bartholdi's car, which stood between them.

"Is that you, Captain?" he said. "What are you doing here?"

"Making a call on Jay Miles. He's got some information for me."

"What kind of information?"

"You may as well come along with me and find out."

"Don't tell me he's heard from the kidnaper!"

"He has, as a matter of fact. You sound incredulous."

"I never really believed in the kidnap theory, to tell the truth. There could have been so many other reasons for killing Terry."

"And so many others capable of doing it?"

"I didn't say that. After all, it takes a rather special kind of kook to kill, it seems to me."

"Fortunately. Come on."

Jay, opening his door in response to Bartholdi's knock, evinced no surprise at seeing Farley, too. He seemed, indeed, to be beyond surprise, or any emotion. He sat down again and removed his glasses and began to polish them with an air of industry. Bartholdi, retaining his topcoat

122

and holding his hat, sat down facing him. Farley remained standing just inside the door, feeling like an interloper.

"How do you feel?" Bartholdi asked Jay.

"All right." Jay replaced his glasses and folded the handkerchief into a neat square as if it were a task of great importance. "Don't worry. I won't fall apart on you."

"Can you remember exactly what was said to you on the telephone?"

"I think so."

"Good. Begin at the beginning."

"Well, the phone rang, and I answered it, and there was this voice. It was a man's voice, I think, but I can't be positive. It was muffled, a kind of whisper that was very penetrating. It seemed to come from a great distance. Maybe it was my imagination, I don't know. Anyhow, it told me not to talk, only to listen, and that's what I did."

Jay paused, staring at the square of handkerchief he had smoothed on one knee, which still lay there. He seemed to be listening again to the strange, faraway whisper on the telephone. Bartholdi waited patiently.

"The voice told me that Terry was alive and unharmed and would be released after payment of fifty thousand dollars. The money was to be in unmarked bills of small denominations. I broke in to say that I didn't have that kind of money. But the kidnaper, whoever he is, knows about Terry's inheritance, as you suspected. He said the money could be got from the estate; it would require only a phone call on my part and a quick transfer of funds. I kept trying to stall, to see if I could recognize the voice, and I said the executor of the estate wouldn't just take my word about the kidnaping. But that did no good, either. The kidnaper knows I reported Terry's disappearance to the police. He said corroboration by the police would convince the executor. He seems to know everything. He's been watching me all the time."

His account was broken by a long pause.

Bartholdi kept asking himself questions that he could not answer.

Everything? Not quite. He doesn't know, it seems, that we have found the body of Terry Miles. Why? Why

123

should he be ignorant of the very thing he should know above all?

Jay's voice, drained of life, picked up the thread of his account.

"I'm to have the money ready tomorrow. Tomorrow night, at midnight, it's to be delivered by a third person. He made a point of saying that I mustn't bring it. This third person is to start walking exactly at midnight along a certain road west of town. Somewhere along the road he will be contacted. There are to be no police in the area; the police are not to be notified. He warned me Terry will be killed if they are." Surprisingly, he laughed. "What kind of monster could tell me a thing like that, knowing he'd killed her three days ago?"

"What road?" Bartholdi asked.

"West End Road, he said. I've been trying to think where it is, but I can't."

"I know it. It's a narrow road, little more than a lane, about five miles long. It begins at an isolated intersection and runs eventually into another. It's poorly maintained —hardly ever used. It's lined on both sides with hedges and underbrush."

"Anyhow, that's where the money is to be delivered." Jay sank back as if the account had depleted him of his last reserve of strength. His face, turned up to the light, was gaunt and livid. "The question is, what do we do now?"

Bartholdi said, "We do as we've been told. It won't be necessary, of course, to arrange a transfer of funds. I'll have a dummy package prepared for the contact to carry. I'll have men stationed after dark near both ends of West End Road and at intervals between. We can't have them swarming all over the place, of course—we mustn't risk scaring our man off. But we'll take all possible precautions. The contact man will be from headquarters."

"No." Jay sat up suddenly. "That won't do."

"Why?"

"Because I was told whom to send. Someone the kidnaper seems to know by sight."

"Who was specified?"

124

"Apparently he didn't know the name. His exact words were, 'The fellow who went with you to headquarters.' "

Bartholdi turned to Farley, at the door. Farley was looking as if he had bitten into a sour orange.

"Oh, I don't know," Farley said. "I'm no bloody hero to go walking down a country road at midnight to meet a murderer. There may be a few cops scattered around, but how the hell do I know they'll be where I may need them? A man could get hurt on an assignment like that."

"That's right." Bartholdi nodded. "He could."

He continued to look at Farley, who was trying not to look at Jay, who kept looking at his hands. After a moment Farley struck a fist into a palm bitterly.

"All right, damn it, I suppose I'll have to do it. It's what I deserve for not minding my own business. It's Fanny's fault, that's who! She kept after me and after me—wouldn't leave me alone—"

"That's settled, then." Bartholdi rose, slapping his hat against his thigh. "Speaking of Fanny, do you happen to know if your sister's home?"

"I haven't any idea."

"She's around somewhere." Jay lifted his eyes from his hands, escaping the contemplation of his shame. "She and Ben were in here a while ago. I think they must be across the hall."

"Do they know about the telephone call?"

"Yes. I saw no harm in telling them. Anyhow, I couldn't pull my wits together."

Bartholdi's voice sharpened. "Do they also know your wife's dead?"

"I haven't told them that. I haven't told anyone."

"You, Mr. Moran?"

"Not me," said Farley glumly.

"Good. I have some unfinished business concerning Mr. Green. I believe I'll step across the hall and have a word with him."

21

Fanny, as a matter of record, had already settled the business; in the process, she had a great many more words with Ben Green than one. She had, in fact, lost no time in initiating the settlement, and she was no sooner back from upstairs with her bottle of gin than she went to the heart of the matter.

"Ben," she said, "it was all right to be close-mouthed and two-faced so long as everything was uncertain. But now things have changed, and you'd better come clean if you know what's good for you."

Ben, who had promptly relieved her of the gin and was splashing generous portions into a pair of glasses, looked at her with a ferocious scowl that was equal parts sullenness and anxiety.

"I don't see why," he muttered.

"If you don't see why, it's high time someone told you, and I'm just the baby who can do it. Terry has been kidnaped, which is a serious crime, and you're obviously under suspicion through your own foolishness, if not for other reasons."

"What the devil do you mean by that? Why should I want to kidnap Terry? Damn it, I didn't even know she had any money."

"That's what *you* say. I happen to know, however, that you come from Glendale, which is near Los Angeles. It's entirely possible that you knew *all* about it."

"How do you know I come from Glendale? Isn't anyone's private life safe from your nosiness?"

"Never mind how I know. The point is—if I know, chances are ten to one Captain Bartholdi does, too. It stands to reason that he's going to demand an accounting of where you were and what you were doing last weekend. As a matter of fact," Fan finished ominously, "I am demanding it myself."

"How do you know it won't make matters worse for me?"

"That's possible. Nevertheless, if you're capable of kidnaping, I would like to know it now rather than later. I have no serious objections to most of your faults, but I'm naturally reluctant to marry a man who may show up on the list of the FBI's ten most wanted men."

"There you go with that marriage blather again. What makes you so sure I want to marry *you?* My guts would be constantly in the saucepan. Damn it, Fan, I'm just a simple guy who wants to become a teacher of history in some quiet little college somewhere, and here you've got me in trouble with the FBI!"

"I haven't got you in trouble with anyone. You have. Come clean, Ben. If you were just off philandering somewhere, I promise to give you another chance."

"Another chance to philander?"

"Not much! Anyhow, you'll have no reason. It would be a poor substitute at best for what may be available if you'll only start facing the inevitable."

"Oh, hell! Let's have a drink and forget it."

"I'll have a drink, thanks, but *you* won't. So you might just as well leave it sitting right there on the cabinet."

"So that's the way it is! Listen, toots, if I don't get a drink, you don't get any ragout, and that's that."

"Suit yourself."

"Come on, Fan, be reasonable. I *need* this drink."

"You know how to get it."

"If you aren't the most corrupt female! Do you make it a practice to bribe people with kisses and gin? What would it take to get the big offer?"

"That wouldn't be a bribe. It would be a reward."

"Is that a promise?"

"It's an evaluation."

"All right, I give up. Hand me that drink."

"Are you agreeing to confess?"

"I'm agreeing to tell you something that's none of your

business. I'll have to have the drink first, though, to fortify me."

"How do I know you won't take the drink and then renege?"

"I'm only a philanderer and kidnaper and such minor things. I'm no liar."

"All right. You may have the drink first."

Ben threw his head back and then looked with regret at the empty glass where the drink had been.

"I went to Corinth," he said.

"Corinth? Corinth is a town in Greece!"

"It's also a small town upstate."

"Why did you go there?"

"I went to see a girl."

"Just what I suspected! Damn it, Ben, I won't have you running all over the state to see other girls!"

"You've got it wrong. I do wish you'd quit jumping to conclusions. This girl is my kid sister."

"I didn't know you had a sister. What's she doing in Corinth? Is she married or something?"

"No, she isn't married or something. She's only fifteen."

"Why didn't you ever tell me about her?"

"I never tell anyone about her. At least, I didn't until you bribed me with one lousy drink of gin. She's in an institution. A place for mentally retarded children."

"Is *that* all? Why didn't you say so? That's nothing to be ashamed of."

Ben had been staring into his glass with an air of depression. But now he looked up at her, and she was delighted to see that depression had changed to fierce pride.

"Ashamed? Who the hell's ashamed of it? I've said over and over again that it's a question of *privacy*. It's bad enough for a little girl to be retarded without being made a goddamn conversation piece by people who have nothing better to do but chew it over."

Fanny's melting point had never been very high. She was always brought perilously close to tears by a hungry dog or a sad movie, and she had learned that the best defense was to take some sort of positive action, such as feeding the dog or leaving the movie. Now she went over

128

to Ben and kissed him on the cheek and put an arm around him.

"Ben," she said, "you dear little devil, I do believe there's more to you than I suspected. Don't you feel better for having told me?"

"No, I don't. I don't feel better at all."

"Later you will. Wait and see. Did you bring your sister all the way here from California with you?"

"Certainly. I had to have her near enough to visit once in a while, didn't I?"

"Is it expensive, keeping her in the hospital?"

"Not very. The hospital is supported by the state; I only have to pay a little extra. If it were expensive, I couldn't afford it. My parents are dead, which is some more private information I've never told you, and they left barely enough to keep me here and her there for a few years if I'm careful."

"Maybe I could help."

"I don't want any help."

"Well, it's commendable to be proud and independent and all that, but you mustn't carry it too far. After we're married, we'll have to share things equally."

"We aren't going to be married, so forget it."

"Why not? Don't you want to?"

"Yes, I do, if you must know!"

"Then what's the argument about? You can move in with me as soon as it's done, and maybe for brief periods in the meantime."

"How do you expect me to get married when I come from a family where mental retardation is likely to crop up in my children?"

"Ben Green, you're just plain *ignorant*. Mental retardation isn't hereditary."

Ben glared at Fanny with mingled astonishment and hope. "It *isn't?*"

"Of course not. It can happen to anyone, any time. Your education has really been neglected."

"I . . . don't want to talk about it any more now."

"All right. We'll talk about it later."

"I wonder if the damn ragout is done." But Ben's shoulders seemed to have a new squareness about them.

Fan wisely decided it was no time to comment. "Stick the potatoes and see, will you?"

She stuck the potatoes with a fork, and they were nearly done, but not quite.

"Not quite," she said. "They need about fifteen more minutes. Mm! It smells good. I can hardly wait."

"It would be nice, while we're waiting, if we could have another drink."

"Hereafter, my gin is yours any time you want to share it."

They had another drink while they stood around in the kitchen waiting for the ragout, and after fifteen minutes Fanny stuck the potatoes again and pronounced them done. Ben got out a couple of plates, and Fanny served at the kitchen table. They had just pulled up to the steamy succulence of potatoes and onions and carrots and bits of steak and bacon when there was a sharp knocking on the hall door; and Fanny, assuming the role of woman of the house, went through the living room and admitted Bartholdi. The latter's nose, as he entered, quivered.

"Something," he said, "smells extremely good."

"It's Student's Ragout," Fanny said. "We were just sitting down to eat. Will you have some?"

"Thanks, but I just stopped in to have a word with Ben, and then I must be on my way."

"We've been expecting you." Fanny headed for the kitchen, Bartholdi following. "Ben, Captain Bartholdi would like to have a word with you."

"The trouble with this ragout," said Ben explosively, "is that it seems to be damn near impossible to eat it! Something or someone is always preventing."

"Don't let me interrupt your meal," Bartholdi said. "You two go right ahead. I'll pull up a chair and wait."

He did so, dropping his hat on the floor beside the chair. Ben picked at his ragout as if Bartholdi's appearance had killed his appetite.

"Are you sure you won't have some with us?" Fanny said.

"Quite sure."

"It's fortunate that you won't, to tell the truth. We

planned to share it with Jay and Farley, and it's doubtful that there'd be enough for five."

"It's doubtful," Ben said, "that there will even be enough for four. Not that it matters. I suddenly don't seem to want any."

"Yes, you do," Fanny said. "You are going to get a proper meal whether you want it or not. There will be plenty, anyhow. You insisted on putting in the usual amount of onions, which is too much for Jay, and so he'll probably eat very little."

"I just left Mr. Miles," said Bartholdi, "and I'm sure he's in no mood for eating anything, with onions or without."

"That leaves only Farley. By the way, where is Farley?"

"He's across the hall. I met him out back as I was coming in, and asked him to accompany me."

"Do you think that's fair? *I* wasn't allowed to stay."

"As for me," said Ben, "I had no desire to stay. The less I have to do with this thing, the better I like it."

"Which reminds me," Bartholdi smiled. "It's time we were establishing that you had *nothing* to do with it."

"That's already established," Fanny said. "Ben has finally told me where he went last weekend."

"Is that so? Suppose he tells me, too."

"He went to visit his sister."

"Is that right, Ben?"

"That's right. In Corinth. She's in the institution there."

"She's a retarded child," Fanny said.

"I'm sorry, Mr. Green," Bartholdi said. "However painful it is for you to discuss, you can surely see the necessity."

"I suppose so."

"How did you go to Corinth?"

"By bus."

"What time?"

"The bus left the station at two fifty-five."

"Can you prove you were at the institution that day?"

"I wasn't there that day. The bus got in after visiting hours. I went there the next morning."

"Oh? Where did you spend the night?"

"At the hotel. There's only one in town."

"I see. And what time next morning did you visit the institution?"

"Nine o'clock or thereabouts."

"This can be verified?"

"Sure. There's a register for visitors. I signed it."

"You see?" Fanny said triumphantly. "Ben went to visit his sister."

"Next time I go," said Ben bitterly, "I'll hire a brass band and carry a banner."

Bartholdi, rising to leave, was sympathetic in principle. In practice, however, he held his sympathy in reserve until he was certain, after investigation, that it would not be wasted.

His melting point was considerably higher than Fanny's.

22

"Oh!" Ardis Bowers's mouth made the startled shape of the vowel she had sounded. "It's Captain Bartholdi, isn't it?"

"Yes," said Bartholdi. "I don't believe we've had the pleasure of meeting."

Ardis, recovering, made it evident by her succeeding expression that the pleasure was not reciprocal. Her position in the doorway suggested an impediment. She did not bother to explain how she had learned his identity, and Bartholdi, for his part, was not sufficiently interested to ask.

"What is it you want, please?" Ardis demanded.

"I was downstairs and, since I was here, I thought I'd have a talk with you and Professor Bowers. May I come in?"

"I'm sure there is nothing Otis and I can tell you. However—"

"Thanks. I appreciate your cooperation."

Bartholdi entered, and Otis Bowers rose to meet him from a chair under a reading lamp. He was holding a thick book in his hand, the index finger inserted among the pages to mark his place.

"This is my husband," Ardis said. "Otis, Captain Bartholdi."

"Good evening, Captain." Otis shifted the book to his left hand, thereby losing his place, in order to offer Bartholdi the one that had been holding it. "Sit down, won't you?"

Bartholdi kept his coat on and his hat in his hands. "As you know, I've been investigating the disappearance of Professor Miles's wife."

"If you want my opinion," Ardis said, "you're wasting your time."

"Your opinion is welcome," Bartholdi said. "Why do you think so?"

"Terry Miles is a tramp. She's off somewhere on the usual business of a tramp, and she'll show up again when she's good and ready."

"That's an interesting opinion, but circumstances don't seem to support it."

"Well, I know nothing about circumstances, but I do know Terry, and that's enough for me."

"What circumstances?" Otis said. "Has there been a new development?"

Bartholdi stole a couple of seconds to study the male Bowers physiognomy. They gave Bartholdi all the time he needed to reach an irrelevant conclusion. In spite of its lonely hours and arid spaces, he concluded, the life of a bachelor had its negative compensations. He wondered if Otis Bowers was expressing a genuine curiosity, or was trying to create a desperate diversion.

"I was referring to the dinner Mrs. Miles left cooking, the fact that no clothes were taken, and her failure to leave any word of explanation."

"There's the Personal," Ardis said. "Isn't that the explanation?"

"I didn't know you'd learned about that, Mrs. Bowers. May I ask how you did?"

"I read it in the papers. Newspapers are published to be read, you know."

"But Personals often aren't. Except by people with particular interests."

"I'm curious about all sorts of things."

"The Personal, I thought, was on the obscure side. It's remarkable that you were able to interpret it so easily."

"Nonsense. It was transparent. Anyone who knew Terry would have suspected immediately that it was directed to her."

"Yes. And that's a curious point. In fact, this whole matter of the Personal is curious. It's curious, in the first place, that it should have been resorted to at all. It's even

134

more curious that it should have been made, as you said, so transparent."

"I don't agree. Terry is devious, but she isn't very smart."

"Maybe so. Anyway, I've made inquiries at the university library, and no one seems to remember Mrs. Miles's being there at the time the ad specified. That doesn't necessarily mean, of course, that she wasn't there. It's a busy place, and she could have gone unnoticed." Bartholdi paused again. Then he suddenly said, "Did *you* happen to see her, Professor Bowers?"

"I?" Otis's voice, reacting to the prod, was almost a yelp. "Not I! Why do you ask me?"

"Because you were on the scene. At least the girl at the charging desk said you went into the stacks about that time."

"Did I? Yes, I recall now that I did. I had to consult a certain book. I used one of the carrels for perhaps fifteen or twenty minutes, then I left."

"The girl at the desk doesn't remember your leaving."

"I didn't go out past her. I went down the stairs of the stacks to the basement and out a rear door."

"Did you leave the campus?"

"No. I went to the physics lab and worked on an experiment until rather late. I was alone in the lab, so I'm afraid you'll have to take my word for it. When I finished, I went directly home."

"Did you and Mrs. Bowers meet on the campus and come home together?"

"We did *not*," Ardis said. "I got home about noon with a migraine headache. I took some aspirin and a sleeping pill and went to bed. I slept most of the afternoon."

By the asperity of her tone, Bartholdi gathered that Otis, having placed himself under suspicion through carelessness, design, or both, was being deliberately left to save or hang himself as best he could. Ardis, judging from the set of her jaws, did not especially care which. Bartholdi was prompted to his next remark by a contrary imp impelled by a malice of its own.

"I see," he said. "You were, as we say, Mr. Bowers, at the scene of the crime at the significant time."

"Crime?" shrieked Ardis. "What crime?"

"Just a manner of speaking." Bartholdi rose. "Thank you both."

Otis went with him to the door. Half opening it, he whirled on Bartholdi and spoke in a rush—as if, having something painful to say, he meant to say it in one breath and get it over with.

"I know what's on your mind, Captain! Fanny or Farley or Ben or someone has told you about Terry and me. Whatever they said, it must have been mostly untrue. I *assure* you there was never really anything between us. Now there is nothing at all. Absolutely nothing."

"Oh?" said Bartholdi.

"It's true. I *assure* you it is. I know things look bad because of that damn Personal. Because it was signed with the initial letter of my given name. I've been thinking about that, and I'm convinced it was done *deliberately*. As a rotten trick to get me in hot water—all over again. If my wife hadn't seen the Personal, someone would have mentioned it to her. Do you know what I think? I think Terry had it put in the paper herself! She's malicious enough to enjoy making trouble for people! She thinks it's amusing!"

Bartholdi's eyes, fastened on Otis's serio-comic face, widened briefly in surprise. Otis's explanation of the Personal was one that he had not thought of. It made a certain kind of sense. It not only explained why the item had been published, but also why it had been published in such transparent terms as to be readily understood by anyone familiar with the parties involved. And Terry's real appointment, it was practically certain, had been the one with O'Hara that O'Hara had mentioned.

"You make her sound," he said, "like a very unpleasant person."

"She's more than that. She's *dangerous*."

With a final nod of his head, like an exclamation point, Otis slammed the door. Bartholdi, retreating down the hall, was forced to agree. Terry Miles had been dangerous. And, dead, she was more dangerous than she had ever been alive.

136

The danger, however, was no longer dispersed. It was pointed, like a loaded gun, directly at her murderer.

Going down the stairs at the end of the hall, Bartholdi continued his descent to the basement. His nose told him, as he approached Orville Reasnor's door, that the building superintendent had recently cooked his dinner. The smell of it hung heavily in the hall. Among other things, Bartholdi's nose said, there was onion in it.

Orville, opening his door, brought his own odor with him; and if onion was still in it, it was not smellable. Orville's perfume, Bartholdi decided, was compounded of pine-scented disinfectant and stale perspiration.

He identified himself and declined an invitation to enter. "I just want to ask you a question or two."

"What about?" Orville's tone clearly implied that he was an employee of infinite discretion. "Has Prof Miles finally got the police after that floozy wife of his? If he has, there's no use asking me anything about it. I mind my own business."

"What makes you think I'm looking for Mrs. Miles?"

"She's missing, ain't she? Dr. Miles was here Friday night with Mr. Moran looking for her, and she ain't come back. Leastwise, I ain't seen her."

"I'm trying to find out where she's gone."

"Not knowing, I couldn't say."

"She left here, I understand, about the same time as Ben Green. I'm wondering if they could have gone away together."

"I wouldn't put it past either one of them. But it so happens that they didn't."

"Oh? You're sure about that?"

"I saw Mr. Green leave—carrying a bag, he was—and there wasn't nobody with him. I was working in the vestibule upstairs, and he walked right past me. He's a snooty bastard. Talks when he takes a notion, which ain't often."

"What time was that, do you remember?"

"I couldn't say. Some time in the afternoon. I'm no clock-watcher when I'm about my work."

"Well, that seems to settle it." Bartholdi sniffed, wishing he could somehow eliminate the olfactory evidence of Or-

137

ville. "You had something good for dinner, eh? I love the smell of onions cooking."

"I had liver. Onions go good with liver."

"I thought for a minute you'd been making a Student's Ragout."

"Student's what? Never heard of it. I don't go for them fancy dishes. Plain eats is what I like."

"I'm with you. You can't go wrong on plain eats."

On the apron behind the building, Bartholdi breathed gratefully of the good cold November air. Remembering his thoughts after leaving Otis Bowers, he felt a stirring at the roots of his hair, an electric tingling in his flesh that had nothing to do with the cold.

Yes, Terry Miles was still dangerous. She was deadly dangerous to a frightened and desperate murderer; and in spite of irrelevancies and diversions and unconfirmed assumptions, Bartholdi was sure—as he had been sure for some time—who her murderer was.

23

The lane was a tunnel in darkness; the hedges hemmed in the road; the wind whispered in the hedges. Once the road had been graveled, but the gravel was gone, pressed into the clay bed or thrown aside by wheels. The clay had been softened by rains and rutted while soft; now it was frozen hard, and the ruts writhed treacherously underfoot.

Farley had approached the lane alone, after parting from Bartholdi some distance from where it began. He walked along at a measured pace, counting his steps. He had not been told to do this, but he did it for such comfort as it provided, having anticipated that what could be a five-mile walk along a lonely road on a dark night was nothing to bring home to one's dreams.

"Take your time, Mr. Moran," Bartholdi had said. "There's no telling when you'll be contacted—if you're contacted at all—but I have a hunch it will be on your return trip. This kidnaper will want to wait as long as he can before he makes his move, just to be sure there's no trap. Remember, you won't be alone. My men have got to stay back some distance, of course, but one of them will always be close enough to protect you. Here, take this police whistle. After you've been contacted by the kidnaper and he's left, give two blasts on it. The alarm will be passed along from station to station, and in a matter of seconds we'll close in.

"The chances are at least even that the kidnaper will slip through, considering the terrain. That can't be helped. So you've got to get a good look at him, if it's at all possible. And don't go being a hero, Mr. Moran."

"Don't worry," Farley had said, "I *won't*."

"Be sure you're safely away from him before you use

139

the whistle, then hide yourself in a bush and stay put till one of my officers shows up. Here's your package. It's got nothing but paper in it, of course."

The night was cold. The sky was remote, it's blackness pricked by pinpoint stars. Farley heard the wind in the hedges; he heard from somewhere, dying, the fluty boom of an owl.

His foot struck something that rolled away in the darkness, and he sprang aside, heart in his mouth. His other foot jammed into a deep rut and he staggered, almost falling. Pain shot up his leg; he had twisted his ankle.

The road felt like cement as he knelt on it. He rubbed the turned ankle, trying to massage the pain away. Finally, the pain dwindled to a throb ... He could see, nearby, faintly on the dark clayey road, the object he had tripped over. He crawled ahead and picked it up. It was an orange from an Osage hedge. He cursed and hurled it away. It struck the frozen ground with a crash, like a rock, and bounded away.

Farley got up on his feet, testing his ankle cautiously. Limping, he walked on. His hands, ungloved, were cold, and he shoved them into the big patch pockets of his thick wool jacket. In one pocket bulged the dummy package. The whistle lay in the other.

He came suddenly on a concrete culvert spanning the dry bed of a shallow ravine that ran with water when the rains fell and the snows melted. The culvert was no more than a flat slab without railings. He sat down on the slab, dangling his legs into the ravine. All at once, it seemed, the entire earth had dropped into a profound silence, in which all living things crouched mute, listening for—what? He, too, was listening, leaning forward on the slab; then, becoming aware of what he was doing, the tension left him, and he laughed.

Farley, he mocked himself, *you are about to fall under the spell of the witches and the goblins and that old black magic. Get with it, man!*

The spell was instantly broken; the night was filled at once with a thousand small, comforting sounds. Rising, Farley went on. He had developed a blister, and the ankle prevented his going too briskly; but he came soon enough to the intersection—the end of the lane.

He had met no one on the way, he had seen no one, and now nothing remained but the tiresome ordeal of walking back. He waited for a few minutes, thinking that an officer might approach him, but nothing happened. He started back the way he had come.

Walking aggravated the pain in his ankle. He stopped every two or three hundred yards to massage the ankle, trying to determine by touch if it was swelling or not. He cursed the fatuity of his mission as he limped from one stop to the next.

It was now his urgent desire to be done with it as soon as possible. But his progress was so slow because of his ankle that he had to fight a rapidly growing irritation.

Out of this mood, having paused once more to rub his ankle, he was suddenly jolted. Ahead of him somewhere, along the dark road, he heard the throb of an idling engine. A car had entered the lane and was parked, lights off, in the most dense shadow of the hedge.

He followed the sound, limping and silent, and soon came upon the car. It was so nearly absorbed by the shadows that he might have passed without seeing it. It was pulled off the road in the rough opening of a hedge that led to a field beyond, no doubt broken through by some farmer to give access to his machines. Farley leaned forward to peer into the interior of the car. Canted against the door on the right side of the front seat he made out what appeared to be the shadow of an enormous and grotesque head.

He felt about on the hard road until his fingers came in contact with some gravel. This he tossed at the car. The head, at the ping of stones on metal, flew apart as if riven by the sound. There was a frantic flurry of movement. Farley had barely time to jump aside. The headlights flashed on, the car backed with a rush from the opening in the hedge, and tore off in a shower of gravel.

Farley resumed his trek. His feet on the frozen clay bed of the road were numb with the cold. He began counting cadence again, limping along to the count; and after what seemed infinity, he reached the terminus of the road where

141

he had started. He began trudging down the crossroad as he had been directed. He had gone perhaps fifty yards when Bartholdi materialized from the night.

"Nothing?" said Bartholdi.

"Not a damn thing."

"A car entered the road a while ago. Did you see it?"

"Yes. A couple. They parked. I scared them off."

"They were stopped at the other end."

"What do suppose went wrong?"

"Who knows? Maybe the whole-thing was a rehearsal. For whatever reason, we've been stood up."

"Well, I'm tired, and I'm freezing, and I twisted an ankle. Do you need me any longer?"

"No, Mr. Moran, you did fine. There's a police car over there. The driver will take you home."

Bartholdi continued to stand there, thinking. An officer stepped out of the darkness.

"Dry run?" the officer said.

"Dry run."

"What about the car that went in?"

"A couple making out."

"In my day, we called it necking."

"In your day, that's all it was. Today ..." Bartholdi sighed.

24

Bartholdi knew that he would not sleep. Instead of going home, he went to headquarters and sat alone in his office in a darkness that was compromised by a finger of light prying through a crack in his door from the hall outside.

His brain was as jumpy as if it had been injected with a cerebral aphrodisiac. It had happened before, and he always preferred on such occasions to sit in the dark. He indulged himself at these times in a harmless fantasy. His thoughts, he would imagine, were irrepressible imps that wriggled out at his head and scampered around with an abandon that was often embarrassing. Consequently, in order to secure a decent privacy for their performance, it was only proper to release them after dark, and when he was alone.

Now his liberated imps were uneasy and angry. He was convinced that a murderer was at that moment having a grim laugh at his expense. He was certain, indeed, of a number of things. He was certain that his quarry knew the police knew Terry Miles was dead; he knew, in spite of this, why they had been put through the antics of this dreary night.

His imps figured it out this way:

The kidnaper allegedly knew that Jay Miles had gone to the police. If so, why didn't he also know that the body of Terry Miles had been found? Having Jay under such close observation, apparently following him from home to headquarters, would he have abandoned the tail just in time to remain in ignorance of their subsequent visit to the old Skully place? Is was conceivable, granting an egomaniac with delusions of grandeur and immunity, but it was not probable. No, it was not.

In the second place, the kidnaper himself was merely a theory. Evidence of his existence was hearsay. Bartholdi had only Jay Miles's word that a kidnaper had made himself known. There had been no witnesses to the telephone contact.

It had been necessary to take the whole thing on blind faith, and Bartholdi did not count himself among the faithful blind. Yet he believed in a kidnaping of a sort.

He knew who the murderer was. He would have bet his pension and his sacred soul that he knew. But he could not, knowing, prove what he knew. He needed confirmation on a critical point.

From among his antic imps he culled the three that had directed his mind to its present state. Sternly, like a drill sergeant, he brought them to attention in rank and inspected them:

One newspaper too many.

A girl who slept too soundly.

Most important of all, a ragout with too many onions.

25

Later that day, which was a Wednesday, the story of Terry Miles was issued by Captain Bartholdi to the press. Too late for the morning edition of the *Journal*, it was lavishly treated in the evening edition—illustrated with garish photographs of the old Skully house and the bleak little room where the body was found, and of Terry and Jay, which were dug up from somewhere. And it was annotated with comment from the authorities in high places, and from young Vernon and Charles, who gave free rein to imaginations loosened at last from the threat of police displeasure. Vernon in particular revealed a talent for narrative embroidery.

Bartholdi, peppered by snipers from all sides, remained committed to his task. Early in the day he telephoned Jay to warn him of coming events; Jay, on the captain's advice, arranged for the removal of Terry's remains to a private mortuary from which, as soon as arrangements could be completed, they would be transferred to the west coast. Thereafter, still following Bartholdi's advice, he locked his door and took his telephone out of its cradle. Even Fanny, who made two attempts, was unable to rouse him.

After dark, when he was at last on his way home, Bartholdi—having greater authority—was admitted. He remained with Jay behind a locked door for half an hour.

It was the following afternoon when Jay, expecting Bartholdi again, opened to find Brian O'Hara on his threshold. The gambler was meticulously dressed, from burnished black shoes to gray homburg, which he held at his side in a black-gloved hand. His face gave the impression of having been as carefully selected and donned for the occasion as his attire. Jay had the feeling that O'Hara, in rage and grief, had deliberately applied himself to the minutiae of his appearance as a sort of emotional camouflage.

"Oh," said Jay. "I was expecting someone else."

O'Hara voice had come out of the closet with his face and tie. "I tried your phone, but it was dead. May I come in?"

"If you must."

Jay stepped aside, and O'Hara walked three steps into the room and stopped. He stripped off his gloves and held them with his homburg in his right hand.

"What I have to say will only take a minute," he said. "It won't be an expression of sympathy, I assure you."

"Good. I'm relieved that you're so sensitive to the situation."

"There's nothing to be gained by our being cute with each other. We know what the situation was last week. But now it's changed, and what it is is something to be settled between us. Terry's dead. I've been telling myself that—it's hard to accept, but it's true. She's dead, and someone knocked her off. If it was you, I'll find out. And if I find out before the police do, I'll settle with you. I'm not making a threat. It's a promise."

"Is that all you came to say, O'Hara?"

"That's all."

"You might be surprised to know how little difference it makes to me. To me, Terry's been dead for a long time. She was killed piecemeal, by you and others like you; and whoever killed her in the end, for whatever reason, was only finishing what the rest of you started. Now, if you have nothing more to say, I must ask to be excused. I'm expecting someone."

O'Hara drew on his gloves and moved to the door, where he stopped. "Let's hope—for your sake—I never have to see you or speak to you again."

He opened the door and stood face to face with Bartholdi.

"How are you, O'Hara?" Bartholdi said. "I was about to knock."

"And I was about to leave."

"Don't hurry because of me. My business isn't private."

"Mine was. And it's finished, so I'll be off."

"I'd rather you wouldn't, if you don't mind. The business of all of us is substantially the same right now. We may as well settle it together."

Bartholdi walked past O'Hara, followed by a short thin man with a golfer's tan and gray hair so tightly curled on his head that it looked like raw wool. Jay, seeing Bartholdi's companion, stepped forward and extended a hand.

"Hello, Mr. Feldman," he said. "I'm glad to see you."

The Los Angeles attorney took the hand and let it go. "I'm dreadfully sorry about all this, Jay. If there's anything I can do——"

"There's nothing."

"You're wrong," Bartholdi said. "There's a killer to talk about, and now is the time to do it. Did you invite the other tenants, Mr. Miles, as I asked?"

"The whole lot. Otis and Ardis Bowers. Farley and Fanny Moran. Ben Green. Even Orville Reasnor."

"Good." Bartholdi glanced at his watch. "O'Hara here is a bonus ... We're a few minutes early. I suggest you make yourselves comfortable while we're waiting."

They had just sat down when Fanny appeared, with Ben in tow. Fanny's eyes were dime-bright with curiosity. It was apparent that, early as she was, she would have preferred being earlier, while Ben, for his part, would have preferred being later, or even absent.

"Well, here we are," Fanny said. "Ben kept dragging his heels, but I saw to it that he didn't sneak off and hide. Jay, why have you been avoiding everyone just when we wanted to help?"

"Come in and sit down, Miss Moran," Bartholdi said, stepping between Jay and the question.

"Yes," said Ben, "and, for God's sake, shut up."

"Don't pay any attention to Ben," Fanny said. "Did you know that we're going to be married?"

"Like hell!" said Ben.

"Congratulations," said Bartholdi. "Is your brother Farley coming?"

"He's coming, but he had to go somewhere first. Ben, where did Farley have to go, and when will he be back?"

"I don't know. He didn't say."

"Never mind," Bartholdi said. "I know what he's doing."

"I don't see why Farley always has to be the one who's asked to do things," Fanny said.

Bartholdi said, "Here are the others now."

And so they were: Ardis and Otis Bowers and Orville Reasnor. They came into the room, Reasnor trailing a couple of paces as became a man who knew his place.

"I want to know what this is all about," announced Ardis. "I don't like being ordered around with no reason given."

"You'll see, Mrs. Bowers," Bartholdi said. "Please sit down and be patient."

"Be patient and be quiet," Otis snapped to his wife with rare asperity. "Jay, I won't even try to tell you how terrible I feel about all this."

"Thanks," said Jay. "I'd rather you didn't."

"Perhaps you all know Mr. O'Hara by reputation if not by sight," Bartholdi said. "This other gentleman is Attorney Maurice Feldman, who has come on from Los Angeles. His time is limited—he's got to return on the five o'clock jet. I specifically asked that you all be informed of that. Were you informed, Miss Moran?"

"Oh, yes," said Fanny in a puzzled way. "So was Ben."

"I told them all, as you instructed," Jay said.

"Good. Then we'd better start."

Bartholdi, pausing, divided a long look six ways, beginning with Fanny, as brightly inquisitive as a bird, and ending with O'Hara, as still as a stone. "What I'm going to do is to tell you who killed Terry Miles and take her murderer into custody."

Even Fanny's impetuosity was for the moment stilled.

"Practically from the beginning," Bartholdi said, "I was convinced that Terry Miles was murdered by someone who knew her well—someone who saw her regularly. Three pieces of evidence—three clues, if you want—all pointed to this.

"First, there was the companion-newspaper carrying the Personal that was assumed, as was intended, to be addressed to the victim. I found it, you may remember, in the Miles's kitchen, where it had been left with other newspapers, and where it went unnoticed by the murderer. The other paper had been planted in the living room, where it could easily be found, or pointed out if necessary.

"The only reasonable purpose of the Personal ad, I figured, was to draw attention *away* from this building, and to be attributed later to a kidnaper who was still to show his hand.

"Secondly, there was the casual remark of a certain young lady. After coming back to this building late last Friday night she had a nightcap, not prepared by her; and then, in spite of all the excitement, she got suddenly very sleepy and went to bed and slept like a log. This in itself would not be remarkable except that she was impressed enough by it to mention it afterward. The incident became significant when I considered the locations of the four apartments in the building in relation to one another. *Was the sound sleep artificially induced*—by sleeping pills in her drink, say—*to insure non-interference with something that had to be done secretly and quickly nearby?*

"Finally," continued Bartholdi, "and of first importance, there was the ragout left simmering in the skillet. It's common practice for a wife to prepare her husband's dinner, even if she doesn't intend to be there to eat it with him—yes, and even though she's invited a guest to share it. *But why, if Terry Miles did prepare her husband's dinner, should she have prepared it in such a manner as to make her husband find it disagreeable, if not inedible?* The ragout contained far too much onion for Mr. Miles's well-advertised tastes—such an excess, in fact, that he was moved to complain about it openly and repeatedly during and after the meal. Did his wife put too many onions into the ragout out of malice? Hardly—not when she thought she was bound for an assignation; under such circumstances a woman would want, not to arouse her husband's anger, but to keep conditions as normal as possible.

"The way it looked to me," said Bartholdi, "*Terry Miles did not prepare that ragout. Someone else did.*" He paused, and in the pause he could see that he had them fast in his grip. "That ragout, if it had not been made by Terry Miles, must therefore have been prepared, cooked, and left simmering in the skillet by her murderer—only her murderer would want it thought that she was still alive; and the ragout, being an extension of her, so to speak, had to be left on the stove as if she had prepared it and left it there. She had announced her intention of making a ragout for dinner in the presence of a third party, who would certainly remember it later and mention it to the police. The murderer had no difficulty preparing it, because Mrs. Miles had recited the recipe. What he didn't know, of course, was that when she made Student's Ragout for her husband she modified the recipe and used far less onions than it called for.

"And that, together with all the other facts in this case, told me who the murderer was."

Bartholdi fell silent, staring about him. The face of the murderer seemed to be hanging in midair before some of them; to others, apparently, it was a mere outline, still to be filled in with flesh and blood.

"The motive for Terry Miles's murder was certainly the ransom to be collected after her supposed kidnaping," Captain Bartholdi went on, "although the murderer had no intention of letting her live—she knew him and could identify him. What I needed was confirmation that the murderer could have had the one piece of information vital to his crime—*that Terry Miles was an heiress*; in other words, that there would be plenty of money available to ransom her. (Of course, his ransom plot never got off the ground; those two boys accidentally running across the dead woman in that empty house put a crimp in everything.)

"Who knew that Mrs. Miles had a fortune in her name? Her husband here knew—but Mr. Miles is eliminated as the kidnaper-murderer because he is the only suspect in this case who would have no reason to put too many onions in the ragout; in fact, every reason not to. Mrs. Miles knew. Attorney Feldman knew. But Mr. Feldman was in Los Angeles when all this was taking place, and there was all kinds of testimony to the effect that neither of the Mileses mentioned a word to anyone of Terry's inheritance.

"Mr. Feldman has given me the link to the murderer's knowledge about that inheritance.

"Some years ago a young pre-law student worked part time in Mr. Feldman's law office in Los Angeles for experience and pocket money, Mr. Feldman tells me. Being in the office, the student had access to the information that Terry Miles was coming into her father's considerable estate by the terms of his will. What's more, this student left Los Angeles soon after Terry and Jay Miles got married, and moved east to Handclasp to enroll in the university here.

"So there was the last link. Terry Miles was murdered because she would have been able to name her kidnaper. She was murdered by the same man who planted the Personal ad as a red herring. By the same man who gave that sleeping dose to Fanny Moran—who lived directly over his apartment and might have been disturbed by what he had to do that night. Which was—after he was left alone with her early Friday afternoon and killed her—to keep her body hidden in his apartment until the night came and he could push the body out his rear window and transport it in his car to the old Skully house. Which he had rented beforehand, in disguise and under a phony name, so that he would have a place to hide the body while he tried to collect the ransom. By the same man who, Friday afternoon, prepared the ragout from the recipe Terry Miles had recited in his presence. By the same man who, made desperate by the ruin of his plans to collect ransom, because of the premature discovery of the body, had to go through the farce of playing the contactman for the ransom payment. By the only man who fits the entire picture."

Bartholdi broke off and stood still, head cocked, diverted by the sound of a familiar action in the hall outside. He took out his old-fashioned pocket watch and carefully checked the time.

"In short," Bartholdi concluded, "by the same man who has just slipped into his apartment across the hall under the illusion that his present danger is gone with the one man who can identify him as the former part-time officer clerk—the *only* suspect in this case who found it expedient not to be present with Mr. Feldman here. I'm afraid, you see, that I had Jay deliberately misinform you about Mr. Feldman's commitment. He has no plane to catch this afternoon."

No one moved or spoke until Jay Miles, his carefully disciplined tone broken by a kind of wonder, said, "But it's incredible! How could he have lived here among us without ever arousing the least suspicion that he's capable of such a thing?"

"There's no questioning the facts, Mr. Miles. I learned a long time ago that you can't always tell a killer from a psalm-singer."

"But why didn't he wait? In another year, Terry would have controlled her own money. All the complications with the estate could have been avoided."

"We can hold Mr. O'Hara responsible for that. It must have been clear to the killer that Mrs. Miles's marriage was about to end, and that O'Hara here would be next on her hitparade. Once she left here for good, the execution of the plan would have become much harder and more dangerous. Maybe impossible."

"You had better go and get him," O'Hara said suddenly, "if you don't want me to save you the trouble."

"There's no hurry." Bartholdi's eyes engaged O'Hara's, and for the first time there was in them a flicker of something like contempt. "I have men stationed outside, of course. And they can, if necessary, take you as easily as they'll take Farley Moran."

At that point, as though cued by the name, spoken at last, Fanny Moran rose.

"I believe," she said, in a small, sick voice, "that I shall go upstairs."

Ben Green climbed the stairs and entered Fanny's apartment without knocking. She was seated in a chair by a window, staring out into the thickening darkness of the coming November night. He went over and placed a hand on her shoulder and stood beside her.

"Are they gone?" she asked.

"Yes, Fan."

"I guess I've always known there was something wrong with him," Fanny said. "I never liked him much, to tell the truth. It's a hard thing to say. It was a feeling I had.

152

A kind of—I don't know—uneasiness, when I was with him."

"Is that why you followed him to Handclasp? To try to look after him?"

"I'm not sure. I never asked myself. Maybe I didn't really want to know. But I never dreamed he would come to as bad an end as this."

"It's the end, all right, and it's bad, all right."

"Yes." She turned toward Ben Green and clutched his hand, and her voice was at once fiercely possessive and a plea for comfort. "Now, darn you, maybe you'll stop being so sensitive about your family! The shoe's on the other foot. Do you want to marry the half-sister of a murderer?"

"No," said Ben Green. Fanny's lower lip trembled; she began to blubber. "Fan—Fan, sweet bunch, don't. Damn it all, that 'no' slipped out out of habit. I meant . . . yes!"

SIGNET Thrillers by Mickey Spillane

- [ ] **THE BIG KILL** (#AJ1441—$1.95)
- [ ] **BLOODY SUNRISE** (#AJ1403—$1.95)
- [ ] **THE BODY LOVERS** (#J9698—$1.95)
- [ ] **THE BY-PASS CONTROL** (#E9226—$1.75)
- [ ] **THE DAY OF THE GUNS** (#J9653—$1.95)
- [ ] **THE DEATH DEALERS** (#J9650—$1.95)
- [ ] **THE DEEP** (#AJ1402—$1.95)
- [ ] **THE DELTA FACTOR** (#AJ1041—$1.95)
- [ ] **THE ERECTION SET** (#E9944—$2.50)
- [ ] **THE GIRL HUNTERS** (#J9558—$1.95)
- [ ] **I, THE JURY** (#AE1396—$2.95)
- [ ] **KILLER MINE** (#W8788—$1.50)
- [ ] **KISS ME DEADLY** (#Q6492—95¢)
- [ ] **THE LAST COP OUT** (#J9592—$1.95)
- [ ] **THE LONG WAIT** (#J9651—$1.95)
- [ ] **ME, HOOD** (#AJ1679—$1.95)
- [ ] **MY GUN IS QUICK** (#J9791—$1.95)
- [ ] **ONE LONELY NIGHT** (#J9697—$1.95)
- [ ] **THE SNAKE** (#AJ1404—$1.95)
- [ ] **SURVIVAL . . . ZERO** (#E9281—$1.75)
- [ ] **THE TOUGH GUYS** (#E9225—$1.75)
- [ ] **THE TWISTED THING** (#Y7309—$1.25)
- [ ] **VENGEANCE IS MINE** (#J9649—$1.95)

Buy them at your local bookstore or use this convenient coupon for ordering.
THE NEW AMERICAN LIBRARY, INC.,
P.O. Box 999, Bergenfield, New Jersey 07621
Please send me the books I have checked above. I am enclosing $_____
(please add $1.00 to this order to cover postage and handling). Send check
or money order—no cash or C.O.D.'s. Prices and numbers are subject to change
without notice.
Name_____
Address_____
City _____ State ._____ Zip Code _____
Allow 4-6 weeks for delivery.
This offer is subject to withdrawal without notice.